I0819798

DIVINE FATE

A PARANORMAL REVERSE HAREM ROMANCE

CURSED LEGACIES
BOOK 4

MORGAN B LEE

Cover Design: Okay Creations

No AI was used in the creation of this book.

READ BEFORE YOU READ

If you've made it this far, you know the drill. Here is the updated series ~~menu~~ trigger warning list:

- Child abuse (brief on-page)
- Death (on page)
- Death of a main character (don't worry, it doesn't stick)
- Drugs
- Female dominant/switch
- Group sex scenes (no M/M)
- Graphic violence
- Loss of a loved one
- Masochism (light)
- Mental health struggles
- Mentions of childhood abuse
- Mention of implied past cannibalism
- Mention of implied suicidal ideation
- PTSD
- Somnophilia (prior consent given)
- Stalking (of FMC by MMC)
- Strong language

- Torture (on page)
- Violence

Warning: This last book has a different pacing from the rest of the series because it's the series finale. As in, it's fast-paced in the plot department but also a bit of a slow burn for spice (at first) before switching to a higher heat.

It's kind of like when you're cooking scrambled eggs and you get distracted by life, so they just simmer for a long time and then BAM—you suddenly have burnt eggs.

Yes, you read that right. This book is like burnt eggs.

You've been warned.

THE GODS: A REFRESHER

Arati - The Queen

Goddess of passion, love, anger, war, vengeance, fire, and more. The fraternal third of the Celestial Triplets. Pronounced "Are-uh-tee"

Galene - The Knowing

Goddess of life, healing, prophecy, the arts, and history. The oldest in the pantheon. Pronounced "Gay-lene"

Koa - The Wise

God of earth, riches, magic, truths and lies, knowledge, plants, and fertility. Arati's lover. Pronounced "Ko-uh"

Raan - The Serene

God of water, moonlight, serenity, storms, invention, discovery, and the oceans. Pronounced "Ran"

Syntyche - The Reaper

Goddess of spirits, reaping, fate, soul, time, dreams, darkness, death, and more. Eldest of the Celestial

Triplets and identical twin to Sachar. Pronounced "Sin-tick"

Pheli - The Jubilant

God of air, sky, levity, hope, wind, light, laughter, change, and second chances. Pronounced "Fee-lee"

Sachar - The Judge

One of the Celestial Triplets, but not considered part of the pantheon anymore. Eternal judge of souls sent to the Beyond by his identical triplet sister, Syntyche. Pronounced "Suh-car"

EVERETT'S PROPHECY (PARTIALLY TRANSLATED)

Favored_ _, ye walk alone
_ _ _ _ fate _
_ telum_ cursed, _ _
Vice of _ _ _ keeper dead,
_ death's _ _ _ _
_ _ to _ five _ _.

PROLOGUE

SILAS

Not right now, Maven's alarmed voice echoes through our bond.

Smoke and ash fill the air, along with so much death that I can damn near taste it. I run through the battle, an ominous desperation tugging me in this direction as I use my remaining reserves of blood magic to hurl a group of Undead out of my path.

My back still bleeds from where a wendigo shallowly clawed it, but that hardly matters. My blood blossom needs me. She was asking for me to heal Everett before she went silent for too long—and now my every instinct is screaming at me to return to my keeper as fast as I can.

Godsdamn it, where is she amidst all this violence and bloodshed?

Just as I take down a hideous, scorpion-like Nether creature that I can't put a name to, a deep, inexpressible dread sweeps through me.

Something just went wrong. I felt it in my very blood.

What's happened? Where are you, sangfluir? I demand, nearly tripping over a dead ally shifter as I scan the battlefield for any sign of my keeper.

Above this symphony of screams and turmoil, the golden dragon arcs into a circle as Baelfire also searches for Maven, thunder crackling behind him in the tempestuous sky.

Mayflower? Answer us right the fuck now, he growls telepathically, his rising temper steeped in fear.

Crypt reaches out for her, too, but the hammering of my heart turns painful when his voice grows muffled before cutting out. It's as if the bond that allows us to speak telepathically is glitching.

No—it's altogether failing.

Which must mean…

Blind panic takes over. The next moments blur together as I avoid every confrontation, rushing toward the place where I see a large bubble of thick ice. Everett must be in there with her. If I can reach them in time and use whatever necromantic abilities I now possess to help my keeper—

As if in slow motion, I see that damned formidable figure appear, cloaked in darkness itself and emanating primordial fear unlike anything I have ever experienced. None of the warring opponents near the ice shield notice her presence, but I freeze in abject terror as the goddess of reaping lifts her gleaming scythe.

No.

I can't breathe.

I can't witness this. It cannot happen.

The shadowy cloak still completely obscures the goddess's face. As always, she does not acknowledge me—but one broken breath later, I feel it.

The severing. The loss.

Pain erupts in the emptiness left behind where the bond to Maven just vanished. I choke and fall to my knees. Overhead, Baelfire's dragon lets out the ear-splitting roar of agony that every fiber of my being is making.

Maven.

I can just make out a hollow whistling above the lingering

ringing in my ears. The sound of Syntyche reaping the beautifully twisted soul I fell so hard for.

No. No, no, no, no—

I drag myself to my feet, stumbling to the icy enclosure with deathly power numbing my blackened fingertips. The ice shatters at my touch, falling to pieces around the bloodied elemental with tears freezing on his messily bandaged face.

Maven is lifeless in his arms.

Gone.

Permanently.

You'll never see her again, a faint voice titters somewhere in the corner of my mind.

I want to demand how this happened. How could we have possibly failed her? I need answers—I need *her*, but the sight of my dead keeper is so petrifyingly surreal that my surroundings seem to fall away. Vaguely, I'm aware of the temperature plummeting sharply around us. Ice crackles across the ground, shock-freezing brambles, corpses, and a ghoul on the attack as it blooms outward from the spot where Everett kneels. Thick snow begins to billow around us.

Bright royal blue flames ignite in the gray distance of this living nightmare as Baelfire's dragon unleashes hellfire on friend and foe alike, so far gone to the rage and loss that he's no longer himself.

And still, I cannot move.

You lost her just as we said you would, a voice snickers.

My father's voice sneers, *Good riddance to that worthless bitch.*

"Stop," I whisper helplessly.

The voices mock me. They cackle with one another as my world fragments. Slinking madness curdles my stomach as distant screams continue to echo in this newfound hell.

I would give my soul to bring hers back.

I would do *anything*.

Crypt materializes beside us, covered head to toe in blood. He drops a lich's decapitated skull before falling to his knees beside Everett and Maven, visibly trembling. For a moment, his expression reflects everything I feel—the horror and stark, hopeless anguish as the absence of the bond takes its toll. Our hair and clothes begin to waft as if we've collectively been plunged underwater, and a burning smell like ozone singes the air.

I see the instant the DeLune snaps for good. His face goes eerily vacant before he vanishes.

A moment later, inhuman shrieks and screams of a different nature go up like a chorus of horror itself. Madness has joined us on this hellish battlefield, and gravity continues to malfunction around us as Limbo tears into the mortal realm.

Let the end of the world begin, voices crow inside my head. *Without the scourge, you are all but broken, cursed legacies.*

For once, the voices are right.

I don't care.

The only thing I can manage to still care about as insanity encroaches is Maven's lifeless body, frosting over in Everett's arms. The surreality of her being gone still hasn't registered fully, but I know one thing. If nothing is done, she will decompose. Return to dust, as all living things do.

But no. I won't allow it. The dust can't have what's left of my keeper. She said she was mine, and she will be mine no matter where her soul wanders without me.

Necromantic power pulses through my veins, heightened by the thick atmosphere of death surrounding us. The voices in my head shriek and shout over one another as I fight through the insanity to prepare a potent preservation spell—

But the moment I take one more step closer to the only trace of my keeper left upon this earth, her body vanishes like a shadow in daylight.

Just…gone.

My ears are ringing, but I can still hear Everett's shout of rage directed at the heavens as this mad world begins to freeze and burn at once.

Because she's gone.

Yes! Gone! The bitch is gone! the voices in my head cheer, ripping my mind to bits.

My keeper has been utterly wiped from this earth thanks to her revenant purpose, taking my will to fight for sanity with her. As everything around me dissolves further into chaos, I let the madness have whatever is left of me that didn't just die with my blood blossom.

PART I

THE BROKEN

1

MAVEN

My chest burns until the familiar ambience of stale death wakes me.

I bolt upright, more disoriented than I've ever been as I blink at the cathedral-like temple surrounding me. I'm sitting haphazardly on top of a cold, ornate onyx altar that's cracked as if an impact struck it. In front of me are several rows of pews filled with withered, dismembered skeletal husks.

High above, a partially shattered stained glass dome lets in the cold light of a heavily clouded midday. Thick ice has encrusted much of this massive room, but I can still make out a mural of the reaper goddess on one wall, her face obscured by a hood. Graphic images of violent deaths, terrified mortals, and peaceful graveyards are painted around her.

This is one of Syntyche's temples.

Or, it *was*. Something cataclysmic must have happened because it's an abandoned tomb now.

I stare at the frosted mural for a moment, a strange feeling tickling the back of my brain.

Then I notice the skeletons of two purple-dressed priests on the floor near the altar. They lie entangled, looking as if they died strangling each other. Other dismembered, shriveled corpses pepper the room, dressed in black since they came to worship Syntyche by mourning the dead. They look partially preserved, as if this bone-deep cold has been around long enough to prevent them from decomposing properly.

What a disturbing scene to wake up to.

I wish I could appreciate it better, but I feel so fucking *odd*. My torso continues to burn as the rest of me feels weaker. When I press a hand over the scar on my chest, I'm still missing a heartbeat...and my quintet emblems. Not to mention, I'm dressed only in a ripped, sleeveless black slip, and—

Is that stained glass embedded in my arm?

I pick a few pieces out, grimacing at the throbbing in my head. How did I get here? Memories of my not-life are a swirling cesspit of confusing information, but it all comes to a screeching halt around the moment I cursed the gods while dying in Everett's arms.

Oh, fuck. My revenant purpose was fulfilled.

Which means that I *died*, died.

But this isn't the Beyond. If it were, Sachar would be standing over me, judging the ragged remains of my soul and sentencing me to an afterlife of eternal misery for all the shit I did to survive in the Nether.

So what the hell is going on?

And more importantly, where are my guys?

Gods, this temple is *freezing*. Whenever the whistling wind outside slows, snow dusts down from the shattered ceiling, making me shiver. I slide off the altar, avoiding shattered glass all over the icy stone ground, but I pause when I notice a gleaming scythe on the ground nearby.

The rest of this eerie space is coated in layers of dust, frost, spiderwebs, and that faint, enthralling feeling I've always sensed around death, fresh or old. But this scythe is dust-free, so it was placed here recently. And the blade—

It's etherium.

I know because I'm drawn to the wickedly sharp, glass-like curve the same way I was drawn to Amadeus's crown years ago.

Hissing at the overwhelming soreness throughout my weakened body, I lean to scoop up the scythe. But my fingers pause when I sense a ripple of magic emanating from the weapon. Deep green runes slowly appear running down the snath, glowing faintly. Just being this close to the weapon is hair-raising, as if I'm about to touch a live wire.

So, of course, I absolutely must touch it.

The moment my fingers wrap around the weapon, breathtaking power sears through my veins. A woman's voice echoes in my head.

"When you learned that memories take years longer than souls to transcend certain planes of existence, you requested that I place your memories of Paradise within this weapon to be returned to you more quickly. Consider this a favor. May fate bless your scheming, or else may your second death be equally honorable."

I recognize this solemn voice: Syntyche, the goddess of this temple.

My mother.

That abrupt recollection is jarring, but as I consider it, pieces of my past that I never lingered on start to make sense. Being so drawn to darkness and sensing death. Seeing ghosts as a kid. The fact that I could make a blood oath without a priest or priestess's holy magic sealing it, despite Felix insisting it would be impossible…

I must have tapped into my dormant nature without knowing.

I should have known you would take after her.

That's what Pia said to me after First Placement—only now, I vaguely remember that the so-called "prophetess" was in Paradise when I woke up there.

She wasn't a mortal prophetess, but Galene the Knowing in disguise.

No wonder that bitch left so many annoyingly cryptic little remarks.

I startle when a strange current runs into my hand from the scythe just before a burst of images and words sweeps through me. Dancing constellations, liquid gold dripping from my fingertips, glossy black feathers and beady eyes, an endless sea of clouds—and then another woman's powerful, angry voice.

"There is no use crying over spilled ambrosia. You are a goddess now, Maven. You belong in Paradise—you earned *your place here. Your future is final, so stop fighting it and learn to be happy. You will thank me in a few millennia when you've forgotten your mortal life and everyone you knew therein."*

More flickers of vague memories, and then Pia—no, Galene's gentle voice.

"If you had matured into your true nature, instead of being corrupted into a revenant, your inherited abilities would have manifested as you neared adulthood. However, if you pursue this path–"

"You see the future. Tell me what will happen," my own voice echoes.

"I cannot, for the future is ever-changing until it comes to pass. If you are determined to attempt reversing apotheosis, I see many possibilities…but the foremost possibility is your final demise. Is not Paradise better than facing the Beyond, my fearless one?"

She sounds sad, almost pleading, but my voice remains firm.

"For shits and giggles, let's say I do survive. Will I still be a revenant?"

"No. That dark magic corrupting you would never withstand Paradise, so it must be gone. If you survive this brutal pursuit, you will return as a half mortal, as you were born to be. The blood of a goddess will run through you, and with it, your true abilities and holy magic. But without a heart, you cannot end the suffering of…"

Her voice fades before I suddenly remember free-falling—plummeting from the heavens, careening out of control as agony pumped through my veins just before I blacked out.

I jolt back to myself, bracing against the broken altar as I try to catch my breath, my pulse pounding in my veins. No matter how hard I struggle to remember more, I can't. It's infuriating to have this glaring gap in my brain. I obviously fell from the heavens to crash here, but I don't even know where here is.

I do know where I'm going, though. I need to find my guys. It won't be easy, with our bonds broken—

Oh, fuck.

Fuck.

Our bonds broke. That means their curses would have returned worse than before.

Damn it, how long was I gone?

Straightening, I take in the temple once again, finally registering the freakish cold and the dismembered husks of worshippers who seem to have turned on each other. Reaching up, I feel the left side of my neck. Even though my emblems are gone with the bond, I can still feel the slight divots of the mating mark Baelfire left on me.

It's comforting, but it only reinforces my need to track down my quintet as soon as possible.

First things first, though. I need to find some actual fucking clothes before my fingers and toes snap off. Trying to ignore the pervasive chill and the agonizing soreness in my limbs, I again grip the scythe—which promptly morphs into a dagger.

It's almost a twin to Pierce, but the blade is etherium instead of adamantine.

I grin, tilting my new toy from side to side to admire it better. "Not bad, Mother."

At least in this size, it will be easier to stash, sort of like Crypt's enchanted lighter sword. The thought of my incubus makes my smile disappear before I turn to stalk between the pews, stepping over frozen husks. I pause as I'm stepping over someone who died wrapped in a thick, fluffy black shawl.

I mean…it's not like they're using it.

Or their shoes, which seem almost my size.

A few minutes later, dressed slightly warmer, I manage to

break through the ice and force open one of the tall double doors of Syntyche's abandoned temple to slip outside. It's difficult to make out the landscape through all this hazy snow and the wind biting through this shawl, but a low, throaty squawk pulls my attention.

A raven is perched on a broken statue of Syntyche nearby, and it's not alone. Other large black ravens have gathered outside the temple despite the freezing temperature, and they're all staring right at me.

Yet somehow, it doesn't feel malicious.

Instead, it's the best kind of unsettling. It almost feels like these glossy-feathered, beady-eyed creatures are…waiting.

On me.

Gods, I hope I'm not about to feel stupid for trying this. I wrap the shawl tighter around myself and clear my throat.

"Know if there are any living people nearby?"

All of the ravens flutter in a swarm before flocking closer to me. In synchrony, the feathers on their heads and necks fluff out before one of them squawks at me, tipping its head.

I stare at it before trying again. "Take me to the nearest warm place."

Several ravens take flight, winging their way to settle on telephone lines in the distance that I had missed before. They're in disrepair, but they'll lead me to something sooner or later.

Moving *hurts*, my chest keeps burning, and I feel weak as fuck as I trudge through the thigh-deep snow to follow the lines, ignoring the birds that flutter along nearby. After only a few minutes, the cold makes my hands and feet so cold they burn, so I pause to try casting a basic fire spell. I'm shit at fire spells, but at this point, I'll take anything.

Yet the incantation I recite does nothing. I don't even feel the strained fizzle of magic I used to get when I had nothing to fuel my death magic.

I try again in fae. Still nothing.

Maybe I need to kill something. Pausing, I study the ravens

that are still fixated on me. As if they pick up on what I'm thinking, they all croak and shriek, flying away quickly.

Whatever. I can find something to kill after I track down warmth and a map. I'm shaking too damn much to try wielding my knife, anyway.

I glance up at the sky. "How about some divine providence before I freeze my ass off?"

No response.

Nice to know that divine nepotism isn't on the table.

2

MAVEN

AFTER NEARLY FIFTEEN minutes of stumbling in the same direction as the telephone lines with cold sinking deeper into my bones, I spot a house on the lightly forested horizon. As I approach, I note that the lights inside aren't on. Maybe it's abandoned.

But then I see the car parked haphazardly in the front yard. Very little snow has accumulated on the top of it, so it must have been driven recently. On top of that, the house's front door has been left open.

A couple of ravens flutter to a tree nearby, croaking ominously at me as if to say this isn't safe.

They're right. When I silently move closer, I sense it: fresh death sitting heavily in the air. Just before I reach the front door, chills run over my skin. My nerves tighten as each sense goes on high alert.

Somewhere in this house, danger of the Nether variety lies in wait.

How...convenient.

I *did* want to find something else to kill, after all. I just hope it's something alive that will fuel my magic, instead of Undead or banshee or some shit. Lowering into a ready stance despite the screaming soreness lingering in my limbs, I slip soundlessly through the front door.

Bloodstains saturate the white entry carpet, with more red smeared along the wall and up the stair railings. The corpse of an older man lies crumpled at the foot of the stairs. My attention zeroes in on the puncture marks on his broken neck half a second before I register the slight squeak of a wooden door to my right.

I leap aside immediately, narrowly dodging a Nether vampire. Its fangs snap in the place my neck just was before it whirls on me again, black eyes gleaming with inhumane, predatorial thirst. My etherium knife is in my hand immediately as I dodge another attack.

It's almost as fast as I am, which makes this an appealing combat opportunity until another vampire appears at the top of the stairs. The second one blurs down to join the fight at the exact second I plunge my knife into the first vampire's neck.

The first vampire screeches as its throat gurgles, overflowing with blood as it collapses—and simultaneously, I shout in pain when the second vampire's teeth sink deeply into my right shoulder. I throw my elbow back hard to knock the monster away, but Vampire Number One is still not completely dead, and I hiss again as it bites down hard into my right ankle.

The pain that explodes there is far worse than the bite wound on my shoulder.

Fucking vampires.

Still, with the pain comes adrenaline pumping through me, filling me with the usual dark thrill of a fight.

I dodge another attempt by the second vampire before plunging my hand into its chest and ripping out its heart. It drops dead. The first vampire is now twitching on the ground, blood pooling around its head. Typically, I would end a monster quickly just for the fun of it, but that ankle bite will be annoying to deal with, so I let it suffer.

Tossing the heart aside, I check my bitten shoulder and try rolling my ankle.

Gods, that hurts.

The first vampire finally goes still. I pick up my knife, ready to kill whatever else may be in this house, but then I halt.

Both vampires are now dead. Their deaths are on my hands.

So…where's the buzz?

Once again, I test my magic, trying to heal my shoulder. Once again, nothing happens.

"You've got to be fucking kidding me," I grit, glowering at the sky I can't even see.

Galene was right. I'm not a revenant anymore, which means I'm a demigoddess with no idea how to use holy magic.

Years of torturous training to learn how to use death-fueled magic, wasted.

"You're all sadists," I mutter at the gods.

Ironically, that makes me being related to them make some sense.

Bending, I yank my knife from the dead vampire's neck. Embarrassingly, it takes a couple of tries to get it out—gods, I'm way too fucking weak for comfort right now.

I finally turn into another hallway. A dead woman lies face down here, deep wounds marring her back and legs, with an axe embedded in her spine.

Why would a vampire use an axe on a human? Unless…

Unless another human was influenced to use it against her.

Which means—

"The daughter of Amadeus yet lives?" a raw, wind-like voice hisses.

My body's response is visceral. Blood rushing through my veins, hair on end, fear replacing the adrenaline in my system.

It's not Gideon. It's some other wraith. Still, the instant I see movement in the shadows from the corner of my eye, my knife shifts into a scythe and is swinging before I can pause to consider that it isn't made of blessed bone.

A sharp, haunting whistle fills the air before the etherium blade rips through the center of the shadowy wraith's chest. A sound like shrieking storm winds fills the room, deafening until the intangible creature dissolves into dark liquid that sinks into the carpet alongside the blood.

Again, no buzz from a kill floods my veins, but the clear etherium of my scythe lights up softly for just a moment. The burning in my chest eases ever so slightly.

Etherium in the hands of a demigoddess bitch must be pretty effective. Good to know.

I freeze, noticing a woman watching me from the kitchen's threshold. She's dressed in winter clothes that are stained red, but the blood splatter pattern on her face tells me that it's not hers. At least, not all of it is. But then, it's well within a wraith's ability to drive someone insane enough to kill their loved ones. That skulking wraith must have caused the bloodshed that drew the vampires here.

The woman is speechless as she mouths, *Maven Oakley?*

Right. I was all over the news before my soul took an unmemorable detour to Paradise. She clearly recognizes me.

"Hi," I say awkwardly. If she's scared of me, she's not showing it. "This might be bad timing, but do you have a map or—"

She floats towards me, and that's when I realize this woman is the axe murder victim I saw lying in the hallway.

Evidently, I can see ghosts again.

Just as I noticed when I was a child, new ghosts are ever so slightly transparent and can only speak in unintelligible whispers and soft wails. Otherwise, they look as if they could be alive. Only when spirits are left unreaped for a while do they lose their color and become foggy, humanoid blurs that become difficult to identify.

As she gets closer, I stand my ground. "Look, I've been through this before. I can't help you."

The woman pauses and points at my scythe like she's

confused. I'm about to explain that the real Reaper will have to collect her soul later, but I stop and examine my new weapon again. Galene said something about inherited abilities.

Maybe…

I swing the scythe toward the dead woman.

A soft whistle fills the house as the etherium blade glows. The ghost evaporates just before a buzz fills me. It's not at all the same morbidly insatiable sensation I once got from killing—instead, this buzz is gentle. Soft. Almost…peaceful.

Ugh.

Curiously, I hold up a hand and try again to recite a common fire spell, since this house is no less cold than it is outside. When nothing happens, I try again in fae. Again, nothing except a bit of warmth tickling across my palm.

Interesting.

As cautiously as possible, I scout the rest of the house. I find what I assume was the woman's husband lying dead in the kitchen, covered in axe wounds and vampire bites. His ghost is nearby, staring out a window. He tries to say something when he sees me, but I can't read his lips through his thick beard.

He hovers closer. I raise my scythe again, but pause.

"I need to borrow your car."

He gestures at keys left on the kitchen table beside messy stacks of newspapers, extensive notes, and books filled with bookmarks.

"Do you have a map?" I check.

The ghost points at the table again, so I assume one will be buried under that chaos.

"Great. Have a nice afterlife."

Or wherever I'm sending them to. Who fucking knows?

I swing my scythe again, admiring the sinister tune of my new weapon as another quiet buzz washes over me.

Once I'm sure the house is ghost-free, I get to work raiding it for what I'll need. Upstairs, I dig around for a first aid kit and some of the women's clothes that mostly fit me—an oversized light grey sweater, a dark blue coat, pants that are more figure-hugging than I like, a thick scarf, and much better winter boots that are only a bit big for my feet.

Limping back into the kitchen, I tuck the keys in my pocket and rummage through everything on the table, searching for a map. As I'm moving newspapers out of the way, I pause when a headline catches my attention…because it's about me.

Breaking News: Maven Oakley, Assassin of Immortal Quintet, Dead at Battle of the Nether

Underneath it is a familiar grainy picture of me standing in front of Del Mar's lightly censored dead body, Pierce at the ready in my hands.

I check the date. It's from January, but that doesn't tell me enough. How long have I been gone? Rummaging through the newspapers, I skim date after date in my search until my eyes snag on a homemade calendar on lined notebook paper sitting nearby. Picking it up from the table, I stare at the last exed-out square.

The year is the same, but despite the arctic chill outside, this crumpled, frequently-used piece of paper shows that it's the beginning of July.

July.

Oh, my fucking gods. *Six months?*

My throat grows tight with apprehension. Quickly, I flip through several more newspapers, trying to piece together what else I've missed.

Millions Evacuate to Strongholds in Mass Panic Amid Severe Cold Front

Maven Oakley: Scourge or Savior? Freed Nether Dwellers Mourn Deceased Enigma

Great White North Bathed in Blue Hellfire

Legacy Council Abandons Ship as Human Cities Overrun by Never-Before-Seen Fiends

Limbo Zones Emerge Internationally: How to Identify and Avoid Them

Fiends Arrive in Europe, Ice Age Begins, and Death Tolls on the Rise

Everett Frost: From Beloved Supermodel to Reformist Warlord

I freeze on the last one, re-reading his name over and over. Before I can get to the actual article, something moves in my peripheral vision.

Gripping my scythe, I whirl to see the two ghosts of the Nether vampires. They drift toward me, faces unfeeling as they seek my help to reach whatever afterlife monsters have.

This ability is already getting annoying.

"Nope. You two assholes can wait for Mommy Dearest," I mutter, ready to get out of here and track down my quintet.

Grabbing the map marked with a big star showing I'm somewhere in West Virginia, I slip it into my borrowed coat pocket and leave the house. A conspiracy of ravens greets me with throaty croaks as I crunch through more snow, exhaustion weighing heavily on my strangely weak body.

Starting the engine of the car, I try to figure out how to back the damn thing up. After a few futile minutes, I scowl, put the car in drive, and hit the gas despite the pain flaring in my ankle. Crashing through part of a picket fence, I swerve haphazardly onto what I hope is the road.

If I'm in West Virginia, at least now I have an idea of where to go.

I just hope Halfton is still standing.

3

EVERETT

WALKING THROUGH THE WHITE, mind-numbing nothingness of the blizzard is soothing. It almost makes it easier to stop thinking. To stop remembering.

Almost.

I love you.

The echo of the worst moment of my life haunts me even here, in the middle of bumfuck nowhere on a Tuesday in what is supposed to be summertime. Behind me, Asher Douglas nearly trips over something buried in the rising snow and cusses me out for the ninth time since we started this trek ten minutes ago.

"If you could stop with this never-ending winter, that'd be great," he grits, catching up to me again.

The redheaded, burly ex-bounty hunter is taller than I am and bundled in so many winter coats that he would probably roll if I pushed him down the slight slope we're on.

I'm tempted. This mercenary is almost as much of a loud-mouth as Baelfire was.

The passing thought of that dragon makes me wince before I turn to scan our surroundings. We're on a large hill leading up to a copse of trees, which must be where we're headed. Little black shapes are scattered in the tree branches, which is fucking irritating.

I already know what those are.

"Just transport us closer next time," I mutter, annoyed when I hear a deep croak from up ahead.

Douglas adjusts his scarf to scratch at the bounty hunter tattoo on the column of his neck, shooting me a dirty look. "I've told you, transportation magic is an exact form of common magic. I'm only good with healing and wild magic spells. I've proven I'm shit at transporting, yet you have me transport you all the fucking time. It's like asking a godsdamned toddler to paint you a portrait. Next time, hire a caster whose specialties match your needs."

No point. This useful mercenary has earned my trust, which is rare nowadays.

Plus, *she* once took an inexplicable liking to him. That makes him a reminder worth keeping.

I ignore his continual griping and the exhaustion weighing on me as we approach the trees where there's less snow. Sure enough, all the black blobs turn out to be ravens. There are half a dozen of them here, watching me.

They're always watching.

I am so fucking *sick* of being stared at.

Douglas doesn't notice my growing irritation or how it makes the wind howl with more snow. He gets his bearings and quickly leads me to a crumpled skeleton at the foot of the biggest tree.

Trying to ignore the damn birds, I squat and brush aside dead leaves and snow to examine the remains. Sure enough, dark runes emblazoned on what's left of the bones tell me it belonged to a necromancer. This one has all the same markers as the others we've found.

According to the medical examiner who almost shit himself when I dragged him to a similar site months ago, all signs point to these necromancers' cause of death being strangulation by their own intestines.

Which means Crypt was definitely here.

This is his preferred way of killing necromancers who venture outside of the Entity's ever-expanding territory. In other words, anyone who may have contributed to magically experimenting on...on *her* when she was just a child.

My chest pangs. I rub the right side of my face and stand to yawn.

Another raven squawks.

Unfortunately, this thing has been decomposed for a while, even with the cold preserving it. Meaning, that damned incubus hasn't been here anytime recently.

Where the hell is he? The last "mission" I sent him on was almost three months ago. That emotionless dick was pushing himself too fucking hard on purpose, trying to burn out. If Crypt's curse finally got the best of him...

Damn it. Past me would never believe it if I told him we would miss those assholes.

The moment I lost *her,* I lost it all. Including them.

I failed her. Us. Myself.

I'm the only one left in this purgatory. All because my greatest fear came true, and I was unlucky enough to survive it. Turns out, being the last man left standing is a far different, far worse brand of loneliness than the kind my prophecy hinted at.

Squawk. Squawk.

The ravens are still staring.

I hate them. Those beady eyes just never leave me.

"Hey, Frost. *Frost.* You good?"

Realizing Douglas has repeated my name several times, I let him have my cold, vacant stare. It's become my default expression nowadays to disguise everything I can't stop feeling. Luckily, this mercenary has gotten used to me spacing out.

"I'm fine," I say flatly.

"Uh-huh. Sure." He kicks aside one of the necromancer's bones, steals a look at all the birds watching us, and grumbles something about demon chickens before changing the topic. "Three of my men came back from Pennsylvania this morning. It's completely colorless over there now. Thought you should know."

As the Nether has crept further into the mortal realm, unleashing all its horrors, the places falling under the power of the Entity have had their color slowly sapped away. And it's not just along the eastern borders where the Divide once stood. Now, anywhere inhabited by his escaped forces becomes a shadowy, twilight land.

Nether monsters, fiends, liches, necromancers, Undead, and countless creatures—including ones I've never heard of—have oozed into the world like ink dripped in water. A lot of places aren't safe for humans to live anymore. Wraiths run free along with demons, wendigos, banshees, and more.

Then there are the Limbo Zones. Inconstant, distorted areas without gravitational pull that are plagued by wisps, shades, and insanity-inducing mists. They exist thanks to the Nightmare Prince letting that plane of existence collide with this one six months ago, when we lost everything.

"Update the other Reformists," I rasp through the ache in my throat.

He grunts in agreement, squinting at the creepy birds again.

One of the ravens flutters closer. I try not to visibly flinch as frost climbs up my arms to my shoulders. When another one moves closer on a tree branch to get a better look at me, ice locks inside my chest.

My parents once told me that ravens are messengers sent by the gods. They're bad luck—symbols of dark transformation and wretched prophecy. The gods have been sending them to torment me for the last six months as some kind of sick joke.

When another raven squawks at me, I can't fucking take it anymore. Throwing my arm wide, I freeze all the stupid birds and watch in satisfaction as they thump to the ground, a couple of them shattering immediately and scrambling to fly away. I don't let them. I skewer them on ice spikes that jut violently up from the ground, and then *finally,* I don't feel any of their beady little eyes on me.

It won't last long. Never does. Somehow, more of the fucking birds always find me.

Still, it's cathartic while it lasts.

Douglas isn't surprised because he's seen this happen a few times. He just kicks one of the frozen ravens aside and grunts, "I'm ready to get back. Dev is going to be a whiney fucker about not seeing me all day."

Dev, as in Devil. That's what Douglas calls his freakishly loyal, oversized pet hellhound. This mercenary is about as creative as Baelfire when it comes to names.

Again, the thought of the once-smiley, oversized lug makes me rub my temple, trying to soothe the headache building there.

"Fine. Send us back."

The caster pops his neck and begins laying the transportation spell. One bright green flash of light later, I brush the snow off the shoulders of my trench coat and walk through more snow toward Everbound University.

I took over the massive gothic building immediately following the battle where we lost it all, during the beginning of the period of time everyone now calls the Upheaval. As the world started going to shit, I fortified this entire castle, much of the surrounding area, and even Halfton with massive walls of nevermelt.

A lot of Reformists praise me for it. They say I was brilliant to keep the depth of my elemental powers a secret. They think I was insightful and prepared this place to become one of the main strongholds holding back the Entity's forces.

The truth is? I'm just a glutton for pain.

This is where I met her. Where we trained together. Where I stole as many lingering glances as I could justify when I thought she wasn't looking, hating myself for putting my keeper in danger—or so I'd thought. Each of those fleeting memories clings to every corner of this barren, damned fortress just like the frost and shadows and emptiness.

The reminders of her are agonizing.

But I need that. It's all I've been left with.

I can't handle losing anything else, so I preserved any trace of what I lost.

4

EVERETT

DOUGLAS PUSHES through the extremely heavily warded double entry doors of Everbound Castle. We pause when we see Lillian Oakley waiting for us, bundled in a couple of colorful coats since this place is constantly freezing.

My keeper's longtime caretaker and friend looks a hell of a lot like Kenzie Baird, but shorter and somewhere in her fifties. I brought her here right after the battle because anyone who was a friend of my snowdrop is now under my protection. I thought I would be the one taking care of her, but when I was too far gone to the world to remember to eat or sleep or breathe after my world shattered, it was Lillian who took care of me.

Even on my worst days, she's kind.

Too kind. Especially when she lets people into my stronghold—and I can already tell from her small, apologetic smile that she's done that.

Again.

I rub my face wearily. "Damn it, Lillian."

"Any luck?" she asks hopefully, avoiding my accusatory tone.

She's one of the few people who know about Crypt's disappearance. Hell, she's one of the few people who gives a shit about that monster spawn.

I shake my head. Her hope wilts, but she quickly falls into step beside us as Douglas and I make our way into the castle toward the library, where I'm sure Lillian has whatever guest she let in waiting. We pass through two hallways and then out into one of my more decorated courtyards.

The sun is bright through the haze of white in the sky, putting a soft golden gleam on all of the ice sculptures out here. Well, they're not *actually* sculptures.

They're people.

Some of them are stray Legacy Council members who came here trying to manipulate me months ago, before the rest of the fallen council disappeared. Others are shadow fiends or hired hitmen I caught before dragging their frozen bodies out here to stand with the rest of them. One was a dissident acolyte messenger who claimed he came here to deliver a message from the Garnet Wizard's Sanctuary. He made the mistake of brushing my hand when he handed me a forged letter.

And then there are the ravens.

Countless frozen ravens. Even now, I hear the low croaks of those damned birds from somewhere high above, like they're watching me beside the gargoyles perched high on the castle.

Douglas grumbles as he walks behind Lillian and me. "Your collection of frozen corpses is creepy as fuck. I swear I can feel their eyes on me."

"You do. They're frozen, not dead."

"People don't usually survive being frozen," he argues, frowning over his shoulder at the ice-encased figures.

"They do when it's nevermelt."

Which is something I discovered by mistake. When my curse returned tenfold, I didn't know that meant I would lose control of how much power went into my abilities. Now there's roughly a fifty-fifty chance that I'm accidentally creating an unbreakable substance instead of regular ice.

I have no control.

Lillian tosses a sympathetic look over her shoulder at the frozen decorations. I throw open another door before finally stopping in front of Everbound's smaller library, where a legacy in a Reformist uniform dutifully stands guard outside.

I recognize him as a caster I met during my second year as a student at Everbound. When he sees us approaching, he salutes me, but his attention lingers on the left side of my face.

"Dude," Douglas prompts after too many seconds pass, exasperated.

The legacy realizes where he's staring and clears his throat uncomfortably. "Forgive me, Commander, it's just the first time I've seen you since…you know."

Yeah. I know.

Hard to forget when people keep staring like he is yet again.

"Move," I say coldly. He moves aside quickly, but I pause to look at Douglas before entering. "You have an hour to eat and visit with your pet flea ball before we head out again."

"Sure thing, hard-ass." He turns and strolls away, whistling.

I push through the doors, and Lillian follows quickly after me. When I see two purple-clad prophets and a priestess standing in the room next to the large hearth Lillian constantly keeps lit, I'm surprised.

I'm also pissed.

"Oh, look. There are liars in my stronghold." I give them my dead-eye look.

"Everett, please," Lillian chides gently, gesturing at the quacks. "This is Priestess Anna, Prophet Julius, and Galene's Second High Prophet, Vincent. They've come from the makeshift temples in Halfton."

The only temples left are makeshift ones. As far as I know, the others have all been destroyed by shadow fiends, Limbo Zones, rioting humans, and Crypt. Now, there aren't many prophets, priests, or other holy servants left. Those who survived ended up fleeing to strongholds and building shabby temples for the six gods.

"And?" I ask flatly.

I don't miss the way my flippant tone makes Julius's eye twitch.

"Well—" Lillian begins diplomatically.

"*And* we are the gods' servants," Prophet Julius admonishes me, lifting his chin. "I have heard much about you these last months, Commander Frost. I came because I received a great divination from the gods, who told me your soul desperately needs redemption. If you would only turn your substantial monetary support to the building of the temple of—"

I freeze him solid to shut him up.

Yet another greedy idiot. No fucking surprise there.

The other two temple workers startle in shock. I overhear Lillian's muttered prayer to the gods—something about mercy for hurting one of their chosen saints.

What a waste of her time.

As if a damn prayer is going to save these con artists from me. The last time I prayed was six months ago, when my first and only love died in my arms and took the better version of me with her. All that hell and suffering my keeper fought so damn hard to survive for the sake of countless innocents, only for her to be gone in the next breath?

Yeah, no. The gods can rot for all I care, right along with everything we should have had together.

I level a look at the other two. "Anyone else want to join my collection?"

The priestess wisely rushes out of the library without a single word, dipping her head respectfully as she goes. But my irritation lingers when the Second High Prophet of Galene remains in place, watching me calmly in his ceremonial purple robes.

"Everett Frost," he greets quietly. "The Knowing has blessed me with a great sense of clairvoyance. Knowing what I do of these last several hours, I am compelled to share what I have sensed of the *telum*."

The irritation quickly transforms to silent outrage, crystallizing in my blood.

Of course. Of fucking *course* I have to go through this again.

I'm not surprised another corrupt jackass is milking my keeper's posthumous infamy for attention. Her name is on everyone's lips—a whisper, a rumor, a byword, an inspiring story. They use her name like it's a godsdamned *joke*. Amid the Upheaval that some blame her for, everyone wants to pretend they knew her.

Worship her or loathe her, no one will let my keeper or her name rest in peace.

It's torture of the purest kind. I won't sit here and listen to it anymore.

"Get out," I warn him.

The prophet perseveres. "Everything is about to change. I have sensed Maven Oakley."

"From the Beyond?" I snap. "In case you haven't noticed, my keeper is *dead*, so keep her precious name out of your godsforsaken mouth before you join your friend."

When he has the gall to open his mouth again, I freeze him, too.

Lillian starts to protest, but I turn and stride out of the room. I'm too riled up and volatile right now. Being around anyone is a bad idea unless they deserve it, which she doesn't.

Lillian catches up with me as I storm back through the large courtyard.

"Everett—"

"Save it."

"It's not about what you just did. Please slow down."

I don't want to slow down. I want to get to the only place I've wanted to be for six months—at the honorary graveside of my keeper, whose body the gods didn't even leave for me to mourn.

Lillian huffs. "Wait. Everett—"

"What?" I demand, whirling to face her as snow flurries around us. "Just spit it the fuck out!"

Lillian winces, stumbling, and I realize ice just encapsulated one of her feet.

Shit.

Now shame is mixing with the bile and anger. I glare at the ice I summoned by accident. Even after it's melted, Lillian waits patiently for me to calm down, which just makes me regret losing my temper more.

I cover my ruined face and try to even out my breathing. "I wasn't trying to—"

"I know. It's all right."

It's not all right. *I'm* not all right. I will never be all right again, because the memory of my snowdrop's beautiful voice is like a dagger in my head.

I love you.

Ravens squawk nearby, fluttering to places where they can see me better.

Lillian is quiet for a moment before sighing. "You haven't eaten since Sunday. I made soup and bread. If you sit down with me for a proper meal, maybe you'll feel bet—"

"I'm not hungry," I manage, but I know I sound tired as hell.

Lillian clearly wants to protest out of concern, but she shivers because the snowfall has gotten more severe the longer I've been out here. She motions for me to follow and hurries back into the castle for its little warmth. I go indoors and start toward the isolated western wing of the castle because I haven't checked on the iron prison yet today.

She doesn't leave my side, blowing warm air into her hands as she tries to find the right words. "I think you should have listened to more of what that high prophet had to say."

"No need. It was a lie. They keep leeching off of her memory, and it's fucking disgusting."

"This time could be different," Lillian insists gently. "I've heard a lot of prophecies and listened to a lot of holy people throughout my life, Everett. I know he's truly clairvoyant. Maybe—"

We both slow to a stop when we hear the screaming.

"Foirnach ahr stad! Oculi ima mo'ceblath uraiseth!" Silas screams from inside the old classroom that he converted into a prison.

None of us know what he's saying most of the time. Not even Lillian, who speaks fluent fae. He's the one who built the damn iron enclosure, but I've kept him in there, hidden from anyone who would kill a necromancer on sight.

Which is most people these days.

Silas's frantic voice breaks before he dissolves into hysterical sobbing.

"Did he eat today?" I ask, my voice barely audible as I decide this isn't a good time for a visit.

She shakes her head.

I'll have to tell Douglas to magically force-feed him again. Keeping this deranged fae alive has been exhausting, but I refuse to give up. And it's not just because my keeper had me promise to take care of him. If I'm honest, seeing the cutthroat, annoyingly sharp prodigy I knew as a child reduced to this condition is just…harrowing.

I turn away from the iron hell comprised of stone, bare-boned iron fixtures, chains, and the iron cocoon he stays in most of the time. Heaviness weighs on my chest as I try not to think about what's left of my old quintet.

"What about the Decimuses? Any word from them?"

Lillian tries warming her hands again. "A caster transported here earlier with a message about the water elementals you sent as reinforcements to the Purcell mountain range last week. They've been helping to contain the worst of the fires, but…"

Her hesitation tells me it's bad news, so I make an educated guess. "But the dragon's been killing them again."

"Yes," she admits sadly. "And there have been more hunters than ever trying to get to him."

On autopilot, I've started wandering toward the only courtyard not filled with frozen trophies. The one that contains a large greenhouse now filled with snowdrops and a simple, honorary headstone, along with what few things she left behind. Douglas enchanted it so that only I and Lillian can enter, but I want to be completely alone right now.

Hurting alone is always better.

"Don't let the soup go cold on my account," I tell Lillian.

It's clearly a dismissal, but she stays. "Everett. Can't you sense it? Even as we speak, I feel like something has changed. Maybe my prayers are finally being answered. If you could hang on to hope for a bit longer—"

Bitterness makes my words too sharp. "Hope is useless, and praying is for idiots. I should've listened to my keeper sooner because she was right about the gods. I'm done with them."

Lillian studies me for a moment before sighing sadly. "Maybe visiting Syntyche's makeshift temple to mourn would help you rest better at night."

Damn it. Is it that obvious that I haven't been sleeping again?

"There's no shot in hell of that happening," I mutter, turning toward the exit that will take me to the greenhouse. Back to the sweet oblivion of mourning the only woman I've ever loved, before I go out to see if I've lost another piece of my broken quintet. "Enjoy the soup."

5

MAVEN

THE CAR TOOK me two and a half hours closer to Halfton before it ran out of fuel. Since all the gas stations I passed were out of service and abandoned, I got out to hike the rest of the way.

That was ten minutes ago, and I'm already freezing my ass off again.

Not to mention, everything fucking *hurts.* Especially my injured ankle.

I limp through the snow as quietly as possible, my lungs burning from the sharp cold as I try to make decent time. If I don't get to Halfton or find somewhere relatively safe before nightfall, I'll be a demigoddess Popsicle.

That first aid kit was mostly empty, with only enough bandages for my shoulder. It still stings like hell from where the vampire bit me, and I can't put weight on my bitten ankle for longer than a second before it tries to buckle with each step.

The thin road I'm following is surrounded by wintry, frost-glazed trees whose barren branches reach for the hazy white afternoon sky like millions of skeletal fingers. Wind picks up occasionally, whistling softly before it fades to a heavy, foreboding silence. The increased tension in my nerves ever since I got out of the car tells me that shadow fiends and other dangers lurk out here, even if none have ventured close to me in this beautifully haunting white wilderness.

Ravens flutter nearby, their throaty calls disrupting the silence for a moment. Now and then, my chest warms to an alarming extent before it fades again.

Walking gives me time to think.

I remember almost nothing about Paradise, but apparently, I did something drastic to return. Something Galene thought would kill me. Whatever I did, I'm not a revenant anymore, but I still have no heartbeat.

My hand slips to my pocket where my new weapon is stored, along with my memories of the last six months. Right now, figuring out how I returned isn't important. My priority is tracking down my quintet. They're suffering from their vengeful curses while the rest of the world has gone to shit thanks to me.

Now that I'm back, my first order of business is checking on everyone I left behind.

The Nether humans. Kenzie. Lillian.

My guys.

I try not to think about what six months might've done to them. By now, maybe they've come to their senses and decided to despise me for not fighting them harder and preventing all of this. I chose to be selfish with them, and now they're far worse off.

But they can hate me as much as they want as long as they're still alive.

You'd all better be alive, or I'm destroying what's left of this gods-damned world.

I pause, tipping my head when the faintest sound catches my attention. It sounded like a nearly imperceptible voice, calling someone's name in a whisper. I move away from the road as quietly as possible, limping into a thicker section of frost-encrusted trees for cover—until I hear the hissed voice even closer.

"Randy!"

Oh, my gods.

Kenzie?

Shock and relief flood me. I keep still, listening until I can make out the faintest crunching of someone walking through the snow. As soon as I can tell she's still moving in my direction, I step out of the cluster of trees, ready to greet her.

But Kenzie's bright blue gaze flashes to me for barely a second before a vicious snarl rips from her. Before I can react, she launches toward me, shifting midair.

Winter clothes rip as golden fur sprouts all over, her bones snapping and reshaping in the blink of an eye. All at once, the air is crushed from my lungs as I'm pinned to the snowy ground by a lithe, majestic lioness, her sharp teeth bared in my face and animalistic, feline glare fixed on me.

Holy shit.

She can shift, which must mean that she's fully bonded now. Her curse is broken. It's the happily ever after she's wanted since the moment I met her.

I immediately have questions, but my innate reflexes kick in when her teeth go straight for my jugular. Magic explodes outward from me—only, this isn't what I'm used to. It's not fueled by death.

Instead, it's the same burning, powerful sensation I felt when I fought Gideon in Alaska.

Holy magic. The kind I have no fucking idea how to fuel or control.

The lioness yelps in pain and jolts away from me, writhing in the snow. I sit up, alarmed when her animal cry transforms into Kenzie's voice. Her shift back is obviously forced and painful, but finally, she's left naked and shaking in the snow, glaring murderously at me.

This isn't how I pictured our reunion.

"I didn't mean to—" I start.

"Shut the fuck up!" she snaps with impressive vitriol.

I've never seen her so pissed off as she gets back to her feet, wiping sweat off her brow and baring her teeth as a shifter warning. My attention slips down to one of her bare arms, which is marked with all four quintet emblems running down her tricep. There's also a faint bite mark on one side of her neck.

I open my mouth to congratulate her, but she cuts me off. "It's bad enough that you look like her, but I swear on the fucking gods, if you even *dare* use her voice–"

Kenzie's own voice breaks before she's on me again, pinning my arms to the snow, pure hatred on her face as her wild blonde curls curtain around my head. If looks could kill, I'd be dead again.

"Haven't you monsters taken enough from me already?" Kenzie growls. "Stop fucking mimicking her or I'm going to—"

Mimicking?

Oh. That explains her fury.

"Changelings have square pupils," I remind her.

She freezes mid-threat, staring at my eyes. I stare back. I can see the wind leaving her sails as confusion floods her chill-pinkened face.

"Y—you're not…who the hell are you, then?" she manages. "Because I know you're not my best friend. She died."

"Often," I nod. "Probably will again once this hypothermia sets in."

Kenzie's breath catches, and she stops clenching my arms so tightly. To my extreme horror, her eyes fill with moisture.

"M…May?"

Yikes. "If you're going to cry, do hypothermia a favor and just kill me now."

Kenzie's watery eyes get wide. "Oh, my gods. *Ohmygods, ohmygods, ohmygods,* it's actually you!"

I'm abruptly wrapped in a tight hug. Kenzie squeals and cries at once, a feat I've never witnessed before, but quickly decide is completely horrifying.

I'm elated to see my bubbly lion shifter alive and well, but when she sobs into my neck, cold panic sweeps throughout my body as I realize her touch is *all over* me. My nerves pinch as bile rises up my throat, all the old repulsion flooding my system until I can't breathe.

Unable to muster words, I gently push Kenzie off me and scoot away.

Kenzie wipes tears from her eyes with a half-laugh, half-sob. "Right. Not touchy-feely. Fuck, you really *are* my moody monk, aren't you? Oh, my gods! How the hell—what—where in the world have you—"

She's struggling to get out a single question, so I speak instead, ignoring the way my veins are still pumping with lingering panic.

"You have claws now. Congratulations."

"Y—yeah, my quintet was bound at a temple in Hastings after you…" Kenzie sniffles and shakes her head, waving off that noticeable topic change to arrest me with a serious look. "May, how in the world is this possible? You were absolutely *gone* this time. Your guys' curses came back, and everyone's been mourning you, so how in the world did—"

Somewhere in the distance, an inhuman shriek rises before it falls too quiet. The tension clinging to my muscles starts to creep into my spine, a subtle warning that danger could strike at any moment.

I stand with my weight on my left foot, brush snow off myself, remove my outermost coat, and hand it to Kenzie. "Let's talk somewhere we won't be sitting snacks for shadow fiends."

She sniffles and nods, getting to her feet and blowing a blond corkscrew away from her face. "Right. Yes. Sorry, it's just—gods, I can't believe you're actually standing here like this. I can't even tell you how many times I've wished I could talk to you again, just to chat or tease you or tell you about all the wild shit that's happened and…" Her voice breaks and she clears it before fanning her eyes. "Oof, I seriously can't stop crying. Sorry, I'm just really fucking overwhelmed."

As elated as I am to see Kenzie again, it's strange that I don't remember the time I spent missing her. I know I did, but there's just a big blank when I try to remember thinking about her in Paradise.

I'm shit at fake empathizing, so I offer a smile. "Your lioness is a badass."

"Right? I *love* shifting," she half-gushes, half-sobs before wiping her face and taking a deep breath. "Okay. I'm good. Back to being just plain hot instead of a hot mess."

A thought crosses my mind as I survey our surroundings again. "Who's Randy?"

"Oh, right! I almost forgot what we came out here for. Randy is Jackie's husband. He went out with a scouting group earlier, but he's the only one who didn't return. He either got lost or... well, eaten by something," she grimaces.

"Jackie from the Witch's Brew?" I frown, thinking of the heavily pregnant woman I met in Halfton what feels like forever ago.

Kenzie nods, picking through the snow for her winter boots, which are somewhat salvageable compared to her other clothes. "Halfton is kind of close to some high danger zones, but Randy is one of our best scouts. It just kills Jackie every time he goes outside the walls, but this time it's way worse than usual because—did you know it's common practice for humans to bring their six-month-old babies in for a divination at Koa's temple, just in case they're picked as saints or the gods want to bless them or whatever? I had no idea, but anyway, Jackie is taking their triplets to Koa's makeshift temple soon and she's freaking out that Randy hasn't returned yet."

"Makeshift," I repeat, distracted when a couple of ravens flutter to settle in trees nearby, watching me.

"Well, yeah, all temples are makeshift because—oh, shit." She straightens to look me in the eye, a boot in each of her hands. "Yeesh, you don't know about that, do you? Okay, how do I phrase this in the least bitchy way possible? Um...May, your matches went off the deep end. I mean, don't get me wrong, I feel *awful* for all of them because losing you royally fucked them up and I can't imagine losing my quintet or us having our curses come back, but like…your guys have *not* had a good six months. Everything I hear about them is all murdery and terrifying. They're actually the reason that there aren't many temples left, on account of..."

"Crypt," I guess, recalling the ripped-apart husks in Syntyche's temple.

No wonder I thought it looked like my Nightmare Prince's handiwork.

"Honestly, I'm not sure who's worse: him or Everett." Kenzie visibly shudders. I can't tell if she's being serious because I can't imagine my upright, sweet elemental doing anything shudder-worthy. "Also, Baelfire, since he's pretty much burning down Canada. Those three turned into totally unhinged, brutal, violent psychopaths. We're talking monster-level crazy."

And I thought I couldn't wait to see them before.

"Although it's been a while since I've heard about any more horrors left behind by Crypt," she grumbles, slipping into her boots before setting off in the easterly direction Halfton should be. "Come on. Gods, I hope Randy is still alive."

"He is."

"Wait, really? How do you know?"

If he died in these woods recently, his ghost probably would have gravitated to me by now.

But before I can say that, a bright light flashes in my peripheral vision—a transportation spell. Old training kicks in hard, and I tackle Kenzie out of the way before rolling to my feet despite the pain that zips up my right leg.

A microsecond later, my new knife is in my hands, the etherium blade at the throat of the caster who just appeared beside us.

"Wait!" Kenzie yelps, scrambling up from the snow. "Don't hurt him!"

I blink when I realize that this guy has his only arm raised in surrender, his eyes wide as he holds perfectly still. He looks different enough that I almost didn't recognize him, but the way that he carefully avoids showing too much of a reaction tips me off.

"Felix?" I frown.

Kenzie's alarm suddenly makes sense, and I narrow my eyes at the caster.

As in, *her* caster.

I fucking knew it.

I pull the knife away, but he's still watching me in stunned silence. For the years I knew Felix in the Nether, he was always malnourished, painfully thin, and nearly devoid of color, just like everything else there. Now, although his skin still has a slight gray quality to it, his hair is darker, and his eyes are a vibrant hazel. His face is no longer gaunt, which makes him surprisingly good-looking. He's filled out, still lean but much healthier.

Life in the mortal realm looks good on him.

Felix is still staring without giving away much expression. "You died."

I shrug, because I'm not sure about the technicalities.

"But you're back," he says slowly, processing.

"So far."

"How?"

I shrug again.

Felix scoffs, reaching up to rub the spot I almost cut into his neck. "Good to know you still really suck at conversing." He turns his attention to Kenzie, spotting her torn clothes and immediately moving to her side. "Dirk found Randy, and they're headed back to the stronghold. You look like you've been crying—are you all right? Did Maven scare you? Is that why you shifted?"

His careful composure has dropped away, and now he's practically oozing worry and pure adoration, stroking his keeper's cheek with stars in his eyes.

It's so sappy that I gag, which earns a glare from the atypical caster.

Kenzie beams at him lovingly. "I thought she was another changeling, but it turns out she just has a *lot* of explaining to do—but she's back and I'm so fucking excited to see her take charge and make heads roll! I mean that metaphorically, but knowing her, it's probably also kind of literally."

She turns back to me, suddenly extra emotional again as her shifter emotions swing hard and fast."Whatever absolutely wild, unhinged explanation there is for this, I'm just so happy you're back. Gods, I really, *really* missed you, monk."

Emotion tries to cling to my throat, so I clear it and brush off more snow to avoid eye contact. "Missed you too, slut."

Not that I have a recollection of it. But still. Six months without her? That would be awful.

"Don't call my keeper a slut," Felix huffs, putting his scarf on Kenzie.

"Aww," Kenzie boops his nose when he falls into step beside us on the way to wherever we're going. "Don't worry, it's our thing. Okay, May. I'm ready. Hit me with it. What's the plan?"

"Get warm as soon as fucking possible."

She laughs. "I meant after that. If there's one thing I know about my badass bestie, it's that she always had—*has* a plan," she corrects, her voice catching like she's still adjusting to the idea of having me back.

I consider her words. Before I was taken to Paradise, I had a lot of shit to do. Freeing the Nether humans to fulfill my blood oath, taking out the Immortal Quintet for my revenant purpose, keeping my quintet out of harm's way, trying not to die permanently…basics like that.

Now? Aside from tracking down my quintet, no supernatural promise or purpose is driving me. It all comes down to what I want to do, and it's true that I have a few things in mind.

Vengeance. Sex. A bit of torture, if I have time.

But first…

"Outside of your quintet and mine, no one can know I'm back yet," I decide out loud.

"Probably wise," Felix says, striding through the snow beside us as he scans for threats.

As he's warily watching the ravens that have started to join us in these woods, he reaches up to scratch the side of his neck. I notice a bite scar there—Kenzie's mating mark.

"Your infamy didn't exactly die with you," he goes on. "If anything, you've become an icon of change—but also of death and carnage. There's already a bizarre number of claims that your death was a hoax. If the *telum* were to show up out of the blue...gods above, that'd be too much. People have enough on their plates trying to survive in this hellish winter, no thanks to your match. Not to mention the Limbo Zones, fires, growing Nether, and fiends running rampant, since the Divide is history."

"Hey," Kenzie chides, shooting him a look. "Don't you dare make my bestie feel guilty. Let's not forget that she saved your sexy ass along with thousands of helpless people."

"I'm being candid," he clarifies. "She always hated people beating around the bush."

True.

"I need to get to my quintet," I add, trying to disguise my limp.

"Your elemental runs the stronghold we're headed back to, so you could try to start there. Not that I recommend being around him in general," Felix grumbles. Apparently, I'm not hiding my pain as well as I thought, because his attention drops to my ankle as he pauses our trek in the snow. "Hey, if you're hurt, you should heal yourself."

"Lacking common sense isn't the issue here," I sigh, still annoyed about how helpless I feel without my revenant abilities.

"What do you mean? Is there something wrong with your morally-repugnant magic?"

"It's complicated."

Felix sighs. "It always is with you. Stay still."

I don't protest as he crouches down to hold his hands near my damaged leg, concentrating as he recites a fae healing spell. I'm no longer a revenant, so I wonder if common magic will work on me.

But no. The stinging remains until he finally scowls.

"I forgot. You'll need a necromancer for that, right?" he checks, distaste in his voice.

I'm honestly not sure, but he's always been so hilariously disgusted by darker forms of magic that I smirk. "You volunteering?"

"Anyone who voluntarily transitions into a necromancer is certifiably insane," he retorts, turning to start our trek again as more ravens flock to the surrounding trees.

He has no idea how aptly he just described my gorgeous blood fae, but it makes my chest ache again. Gods, I just really need to track down my guys.

Kenzie tuts over my bloodied ankle and slips one arm under my right shoulder to help me limp less, careful to only touch me through my clothes. "Come on, May—let's sneak you into the Everbound stronghold, get you thawed out, and then figure out how to sneak you into the castle without anyone seeing."

6

MAVEN

As soon as I hobble into the giant tent that belongs to Kenzie's quintet, Luka looks up from studying a map on a desk. The vampire's attention immediately skips to my shoulder, where my bloodied bandage is starting to seep through, before he squints to check my pupils.

His own eyes get comically wide. "You have got to be shitting me."

"I shit you not," I reply, examining this space as I distractedly rub the aching, overheated center of my chest.

It's big enough to comfortably house a quintet-sized bed, the desk where Luka sits, a small cooking area, a wardrobe, and a few pieces of Kenzie's erotic art. Mage lights keep it well-lit and cozy.

It's also warm in here, thank the fucking universe.

After taking an unfrequented path out of the woods, we approached a massive nevermelt wall patrolled by Reformist guards, both legacy and human. Before I could be spotted, Felix used an admittedly impressive cloaking spell to get me into this tent city on the outskirts of Halfton unseen. Felix then went to check on what he called Everbound stronghold's "shielding measures," promising he'd rejoin us soon to cloak me and take me to the castle.

Kenzie steps into the tent beside me and gestures at everything with dramatic flair.

"Behold, *mi casa!* For now, anyway. Even with *thousands* of legacies and humans flocking to this area to build it up and make it a safe haven for months, it's slow going. Resources are limited, winter is harsh, and casters are spread thin, so they can't use their magic to whip up houses left and right. Anyway, Everett provided these tents for a lot of people, and they're actually pretty damn nice in the meantime. Felix has been perfecting heating spells to keep everyone as warm as possible—not to mention sound-proofing charms, since *hello*, we get extra loud at night. And in the morning. And let's be real, during the day, too."

She's still happily oversharing, and Luka is still staring at me like I'm a gruesome specter when Dirk pokes his head into the tent. He breaks into a huge smile when he sees Kenzie.

"Whoa, are you wearing nothing but a coat? Message received. Let me just slip in here and..." He spots me and startles so hard his voice goes up an octave. "Gah! Oh, my fucking gods, there's a changeling in our—"

Kenzie quickly covers his mouth, hissing, "Shh! Not so loud!"

She ushers him inside and zips the tent shut before turning to the vampire and shifter, who both also bear her mating mark on their necks.

"There. Now no one will hear us. Guys, this isn't a changeling. Go ahead and welcome Maven back."

They're quiet for several long beats as I pretend my right leg isn't throbbing like hell.

"Welcome back," Luka finally echoes warily.

Dirk looks incredibly disturbed. "Yeah, hi. Um…so is she, like…Undead?"

Kenzie starts to say no and then pauses, glancing at me to make sure.

"At this point, who fucking knows?" I joke.

I nearly laugh at the strained sound Dirk makes before he hastily excuses himself from the tent. Kenzie sighs, turning to me.

"He had an ugly run-in with Undead a couple of months ago, and he's kind of paranoid about them now. And we're already all on edge since the world is kind of in tatters thanks to, you know…"

"Me," I supply.

To my surprise, Luka snorts. "Like you can take all the credit. It wasn't your fault."

"Actually, it was."

He stands from the desk, tossing down the pen he was holding. "Whatever else happened, you were just trying to free Felix and a ton of other people from that shithole. Give yourself a break, Muriel."

Kenzie puts a hand on her hip. "Hey. Come on. You know her name is Maven."

"Yeah, I know."

He must think that messing up my name is an inside joke now, but I'm more focused on the fact that he's attempting to be…*nice* to me. What the fuck?

He shuffles uncomfortably when I analyze him, trying to pick up on what I'm missing here.

"Uh, yeah. I don't have a curse anymore. Mine made me a real dick—more than usual, anyway. Kind of a self-sabotaging, hereditary thing. My birth mom called it the Mean Streak Curse, and it was impossible not to say or do stupid things, and…anyway. Sorry for whatever shit I said back then."

Huh. I'd never really stopped to wonder what Luka's curse was.

But so long as we're clearing the air…

"There's something you should know before you help me anymore," I confess.

This is about to get awkward, but I clear my throat and glance from Kenzie to him. I hope she forgives me for this.

"I killed your brother."

Kenzie covers her mouth, eyes wide as she pieces that day together, but Luka just stares at me. I can't tell if he's angry, dubious, or disgusted until he finally speaks again.

"In self-defense. Right?"

"You knew?"

The vampire shakes his head, shoulders slumping as he looks away. "I didn't know it was *you*. Levi and I survived a lot together, but as we got older, I heard rumors about some things he started doing. I could never condone the shit he chose to do—made me fucking sick. He was digging his own grave. You were just the one to finally push him into it."

Well, then. This isn't how I expected this to go, but I'm not complaining.

I worried Kenzie would be hurt and pissed that I harmed her match's family, but when I look at her, she nods in melancholic understanding. It's quiet momentarily until Luka's attention moves back to my stained shoulder.

He wrinkles his nose. "Your blood smells weird. It's not exactly human, not monster, not fiend or legacy or…okay, what the fuck *is* that scent? It's way too strong. You should cover that before other vampires catch it."

I sniff my bloody shoulder curiously, but I don't smell anything out of place.

Safe to say a heightened sense of smell isn't a demigoddess thing.

Kenzie reaches out to touch Luka's jaw, smiling gently. "Could you go check on Vivienne for me? She's still helping take food to some of the newest refugees. And remember, we're not breathing a word about Maven to anyone outside our quintet."

Luka nods, kisses his keeper's forehead, and leaves. It's odd to realize that Kenzie and her quintet don't have the ability to telepathically communicate, like mine did. I know it isn't common, and it most often happens with powerful legacies that have been bound for a while, but it still makes my chest ache.

I miss talking to them in my head. If our bond was still intact...

It will be. I'm going to get it back. Whatever it takes.

Kenzie fills up a cup of water in the small kitchen sink, grabs a wrapped package from a tote, and offers both to me.

"That's a protein bar," she clarifies when I squint at the packaged food. "No meat in it."

I thank her, sipping the water and unwrapping the protein bar to take a bite. My fingers and toes slowly warm up as she changes into regular clothes and sets the coat I loaned her on the desk in front of me.

And then the lioness shifter stares at me expectantly.

"This is the part where you tell me what the hell happened, May."

"I don't—"

She holds up a hand. "This has been really, really hard, and not just because of the Upheaval. When you died, I was a fucking *wreck*. I spent months mourning you."

"Thanks, but I don't—"

"I know you hate talking about anything more than necessary, but I deserve answers—and you already know I'll take your secrets to the grave. So, please, please, *please* just talk to me. Where did you go? How are you back? What the hell is going on?"

I wait a moment to make sure she's done this time before trying again. "I don't remember."

"Oh. Shit."

I glance down at the cup in my hands, recalling the liquid gold dripping from my fingertips in my flashback. Something niggles in the back of my mind, like a memory trying to rise from the depths of a tar pit. I know Kenzie is serious about taking my secrets to the grave, so I decide to tell her what little I do know.

"I woke up in Paradise."

She blinks. "Paradise?"

I nod.

"Like...where the gods are? The plane of existence that mortals can't see or go to that floats way up in the heavens filled with a bunch of divine beings like angels and nature spirits and *gods? That* Paradise?"

I nod again. "You can't tell your quintet this next part."

Kenzie pantomimes...I'm not sure. Putting on lipstick, maybe? When she sees my confusion, she repeats the gesture.

"Locking up my lips and tossing the key," she explains, as patient as ever with the glaring gaps in my knowledge of the mortal world.

I take a deep breath to brace myself. "I learned that my father was a man named Pietro Amato."

Her mouth drops open. "Whoa. Hang on, you're *the* Pietro Amato's daughter? My parents told me about him! They knew him way back in the day. So many Reformists still totally love that guy, and he's only gotten more revered since the Reformist movement is so huge now, and—hang on, if he was your dad, who was your mom?"

"Syntyche."

For a moment, I think I broke her. Then Kenzie coughs. "Come again?"

"Syntyche. You know, the goddess of reaping, memories, fear, dreams, death, darkness, souls..."

I could go on, since each of the six gods holds dominion over so many things, but Kenzie is extremely pale as she holds up a hand. She's uncharacteristically silent for so long as she stares blankly at me that I get concerned.

"Kenzie?"

She breathes out finally. "Oh my holy fucking gods. Shit—sorry, I probably shouldn't say stuff like that around you—"

I snort. "Blaspheme all you want."

"But aren't you, like...one of them now?" Her voice is thin, and her wide blue eyes are almost frightened.

She's nervous. Unsure of me, now that she knows the truth.

Damn it.

"Don't look at me like that," I insist vehemently. "Whatever I am, I'm still myself."

I describe it all to her. How my purpose was unexpectedly fulfilled during the battle, how I found myself in Paradise, and then waking up in Syntyche's desecrated temple with only blips of memories returning through the scythe I now wield.

"I did something to return to the mortal realm," I finish. "I just don't remember what I did, or why it took me six months to return. Having no memories is absolutely fucking infuriating."

Kenzie looks down at her hands, picking at her chipped nail polish. "Yeah. It is."

Right. That was insensitive of me—she would know better than anyone else.

I study her. "Have you been able to rediscover much about your past?"

She nods. "Turns out, I was a shady bitch back in the day. But even though I can piece things together and even though my quintet has been incredibly supportive as I rediscover myself, it still sucks that I'll never get those memories back, you know? Gods, I wish I had a magic memory-returning scythe," Kenzie sighs. Then she wrinkles her nose. "Or, not a scythe. Something I'd actually use, like a badass paintbrush or something."

The lioness shifter stares at me again, like I'm something new she's never seen before. At first, I worry she's going to treat me differently now that she knows my pedigree, but then she grins.

"So...you look almost exactly like Syntyche, huh? No wonder I always thought you were so pretty—you literally look like a fucking goddess!"

"Thanks for the sentiment, but you're the only person who thinks that."

"Oh, girl, no—I *promise* all of your guys would agree with me, plus anyone else with the capacity to appreciate actual beauty."

Her mention of my guys makes me notice the burning in my emblem-less chest again. Being back even this long without seeing them feels empty. If Felix doesn't return soon, I'll find a way to sneak myself into Everbound Castle.

Needing a topic change, I make a face. "Speaking of guys... Felix. That's weird."

Kenzie grins, back to normal, even though she keeps eyeing me more than necessary. I'm pretty sure she's trying to picture me two feet taller and deathly pale with a cloak and scythe. But as long as she doesn't treat me differently because of my mother, she can picture me naked for all I care.

"It's not weird," she disagrees. "Felix is so fucking perfect for me, just like the rest of my quintet. I mean, it might be a bit weird for you since Felix once told me he thought of you as a little sister, so it could seem like I'm banging your big brother—"

"Ew. No. Like I said, he was just an accomplice."

Kenzie snickers. "Well, your *accomplice* had never even kissed a girl before he met me, let alone seen one naked. Who knew it would be so hard to seduce someone who gets turned on so easily? Getting that gorgeous caster into bed for our first time was—"

"Stop."

"—like trying to crack a *really* shy, really tough nut, but once I finally got *him* to nut, that man got super kinky super fast. Seriously, the first time Felix whipped out magic in the bedroom, he—"

Oh, my fucking gods.

"Shut up before I find a way to smite you," I warn.

She bursts into laughter. I shake my head, stubbornly fighting a smile. Finally, she stops cackling and wraps me in a surprise hug, still careful not to touch any of my skin.

"Gods, I am *so* happy you're back. You have no idea."

I blow at one of her wild curls so it will stop tickling my cheek. "The gods themselves couldn't keep me from coming back to watch the next season of your favorite sappy forbidden romance show with you."

"Actually, that show is super canceled," she sighs. "I think every single TV show is. Now it's all just news and livestreams of the shit going on. A lot of places don't get electricity or wifi anymore, anyway. What's left of the internet is so terrified and dismal that all I do with my cell phone right now is take filthy pictures of my quintet. They've gotten the hang of posing naked so I'll have all these hot pictures to use as inspiration for painting. Felix in particular—"

"*Kenzie,*" I warn.

She laughs and then gets solemn quickly. "Seriously, though, the world has been going through a lot."

She recaps some things, like the fact that some of the Garnet Wizard's former acolytes, a prophet, and Felix figured out how to harness the Immortal Quintet's life forces using the etherium pieces I contained them in. They created three shielding spells that require regular magical upkeep, but otherwise function like an invisible dome that keeps most shadow fiends out. One is stationed here at the Everbound stronghold, one is used for a safe haven in Europe where children and older people were sent from all over to be safeguarded, and the third went missing months ago.

Humans and legacies are fighting at the front lines of the expanding Nether, trying to stave off the worst of Amadeus's forces. They're led mainly by the Reformists now, since the Legacy Council fled like cowards as soon as the Divide fell and the anti-legacy Remitters have all but fizzled out. Some wealthy humans and legacies have created their own safe places, hiring others to protect them from the fiends on the loose.

"Things aren't great, but they would be less dire if it weren't so damn cold all the time," Kenzie adds, grimacing. "Even with magic, growing plants or sustaining animals for food is harder during a never-ending winter. I don't think Everett is making people suffer on purpose, but then again...gods, May. With how much he's changed, I'm not actually sure. He's a Reformist commander now, but he's fucking brutal."

So far, she's mentioned Everett, Baelfire, and Crypt. But...

"Where is Silas?" I manage to ask through the sudden panic trying to climb out of my stomach.

She grimaces like that's exactly the question she didn't want me to ask. "The last time I saw him was on that battlefield six months ago, when he went kind of...well, *super* crazy. Crazy enough to try raising a bunch of people from the dead. I saw Everett freeze him so he couldn't do that, but I haven't seen or heard anything about him since then. Sorry, May."

He's fine. He has to be fine.

When repeatedly reassuring myself doesn't help, I reach up to run my fingers over Baelfire's mating mark, shifting aside the scarf. Feeling his trace on me is a small form of comfort.

Kenzie notices. "Oh my gods, that poor dragon. That must have been recent when everything happened, right? No wonder he went feral."

My throat constricts as I remember Baelfire's bright smile and his intense pride in the mark I left on his neck. He was over the moon about being bound together, but we were still in the fresh, newlybound stage when the bond was ripped away.

If his curse returned with a vengeance, and his dragon took over...

Nausea churns in my gut as that strange burning returns to my chest.

I'm going after my feral dragon soon. I'm going after all of them with everything I've got. Cursed or not, they're always going to be *mine.*

"You were right," I murmur, looking at Kenzie. "I shouldn't have held back telling my quintet how I felt about them. They deserved to hear at least that much from me before everything went wrong."

Kenzie smiles softly. "Well…now you have a second chance."

Someone unzips the tent. I tense, but it's just Felix, who steps inside with a solemn expression.

"What's wrong?" Kenzie asks, brow furrowed.

He peers at me. "You did want to see Everett Frost, right?"

I grab the coat Kenzie borrowed, slipping it back on to cover my stained sweater. "Sooner, not later."

"Well, things just got a bit more complicated than strolling up to Everbound Castle." He holds up his arm until the thick coat slides back to show off a scrying brand. "Because I just received word on Commander Frost's whereabouts. He's in the middle of a massacre on the front lines about seventy miles east. Intel marked him as still alive an hour ago, but that's a rough area known to be plagued by wraiths. We'll go once we track down blessed bone—"

"No," I cut him off, storming toward the door as dread and adrenaline make me push through the injuries still staining me. "We'll go now."

And when I get there, my beautiful elemental had better be unscathed.

7

EVERETT

Ice blooms from each step I take, spreading over fallen Reformists and monster corpses as I pass them. Wind howls, so thick with snow that I can't see three feet in front of me.

Underneath my ripped trench coat, blood drips heavily despite my body trying to freeze over the wound that I clutch from where an ally bear shifter clawed me earlier. Exhaustion helps me ignore the sparks of physical pain as I wander down Main Street through this abandoned town.

I've been awake for over three days straight, ordering Reformists around and fighting and killing fiends the same as I've done every day since Brigid Decimus appointed me to this station. She insisted I was someone people look up to. An influential figure to give others hope in a dark time like this.

What a fucking joke I turned out to be.

I love you.

I cough, pain ricocheting up my torso. Going through the motions for six months has left me psychologically, physically, and mentally depleted. Now, I'm just…empty. Injured. Unmoored.

Hopeless.

How long am I supposed to just fucking *exist* like this? I may as well be one of the Undead. Besides, no matter how hard I've tried to keep them safe, what's left of my quintet is gone in every way that counts.

Squawk.

I nearly trip over a day-old corpse when I hear a raven caw somewhere nearby. Changing direction, I skirt around an abandoned car with busted windows. Now and then, shrieks and other inhuman sounds of fiends are carried to me on the wind. Beyond this blizzard, twilight is falling over what's left of this razed town, which, ironically, used to be called Snowfall Ridge. Now, it's an active combat zone. I've been sending Reformists here weekly to maintain our hold.

The most recent troop was just massacred before my eyes—by each other, mostly. The wraith who got to them is still here, trying to find a way to get inside my head and feed on my fear.

But the wraith doesn't stand a chance, because all my biggest fears have already come true, yet here I fucking am. Utterly alone as I walk without purpose, the nevermelt saber in my hand dragging loudly across the frozen road.

Gods, I'm so tired of this. Of everything.

A sudden wave of dizziness from blood loss sends me stumbling, the saber clattering out of my hands as I hit the asphalt. I cough again, grimacing as I roll over. My body isn't able to keep the pain in my side numb anymore.

Killed by a wraith-crazed bear shifter. What an anticlimactic way to go.

But if I'm moments from the Beyond…

"Just let me find her there," I whisper at the sky I can't see, pretending like someone is listening to distract me from the doom closing around me.

And if Crypt beat me to her, Sachar had better assign that asshole some kind of punishment for leaving me alone like this, after all the shit we went through together.

As if the cruel gods decided this really is my time to go, I hear grunting and heavy footfalls before a massive figure appears standing above me. A ghoul. They linger in areas like this to feast on the fresh dead. This one is covered in gore like it was doing just that.

When the shadow fiend's attention drifts down to me and it makes a hideous sound, I decide this is it. I'm too damn tired and tapped out to defend myself—and so what if a ghoul does me in? It's all the same at this point.

I close my eyes and speak under my breath, willing these words to carry me to her quicker.

"I love you, too."

So much that it's killing me.

It's what I should have said when she was in my arms. It's what I'll say to her over and over again in the Beyond as I beg for forgiveness for failing her in every way possible.

Just as the beast lifts a foot to crush me, a gleaming *something* arcs through the air.

The ghoul's head rolls off its shoulders before the body collapses, thudding heavily onto the icy road right next to me. It twitches and goes still as a smaller figure emerges from the dimming whiteout. Black hair billowing in the wind. The perfect height. Probably beautiful, if I could see more clearly through the blizzard.

Look at that. The gods are allowing me to dream about her in my last moments.

The figure rounds the fallen ghoul to crouch beside me, and as soon as I get a better look at her face—

No.

This isn't real.

She's not real.

But this face is too fucking perfect to be drummed up by my memory.

Dark, beautiful eyes filled with the fury of hell itself. Olive skin. That perfect curve in her lower lip. A slight redness to her nose and cheeks from the cold. Ghoul blood dripping from the scythe in her hand. Even Baelfire's bite scar on the side of her neck when the wind blows her hair aside again.

"Were you going to defend yourself?" my hallucination demands.

And I *know* she has to be a hallucination. There's no other explanation, but I can't stop staring. I'm too stunned by the sound of the voice that's been haunting me for months. It's dripping with protective warning like she's livid that I was ready to give up.

"Everett," I vaguely hear her prompt.

I trace every feature with my gaze. This delicate, understated beauty, contrasted with her powerful presence, is a drug I can't give up.

My hallucination's attention settles on the left side of my face, and she reaches out to brush the haggard scar with her fingertips.

Her very real, very *warm* fingertips.

My heart skips several beats, my entire body reacting like I was just struck by lightning. She touched me. I know that touch. I've ached for it so long that I can't breathe through a sudden wave of confusion and sharp fear.

This can't be real. It can't be. Because if it's real and she's touching me—

"Maven?" I whisper, my reality twisting in on itself as I realize hallucinations don't have warm fingers.

Fingers that are quickly turning pink and purple from frostbite.

Oh, gods.

Fuck. She's real. She's real, and she touched me, and now she's going to pay the price.

Pure horror floods my system, choking me. Darkness has coagulated around us, chilling whispers and laughter dancing in the howling wind as I watch my keeper begin to freeze, ice crackling up her arm and neck. Her eyes widen, a scream lodges in her frozen throat, and—

An inhuman screech cuts through the air beside us so violently that it startles me. As soon as it cuts off, the scene in front of me ripples and changes. Maven is crouching beside me exactly how she was, only now her attention is on the wraith beside us…which was just cut in half by her scythe. Both pieces of the shadow fiend drop to the ground, shrieking and hissing before evaporating.

I'm left trembling, shaken to my damn core as I realize the wraith just made its move, using my newfound fear against me —and she killed it.

Because she's here. Real.

Maven looks back at me. The scythe in her hand shrinks instantly, now a clear knife that she tucks away without an explanation. She's just crouching here, all…*alive*.

When my breathing turns quick and labored, her gaze slips down to my bloodied side. She moves the torn trench coat aside and immediately moves to put pressure on the wound, but I panic.

"Don't," I warn hoarsely, propping up on one arm to scoot away as my head spins.

She can't touch me again. It's not safe for her.

Maven's dark eyes lock onto mine. "I understand if you hate me."

Wait…*what?*

Hate her? What the hell is she talking about?

"It doesn't change the fact that you're mine," my keeper clarifies firmly, reaching up to brush snowflakes out of my hair before I can protest.

She removes her coat, tears a strip out of it, and takes advantage of the fact that I'm propped up to start wrapping my bleeding midsection.

"I did try to prevent this," she goes on, not even flinching at the cold emanating from me. "If you four had just accepted my rejection at the beginning, you would have had a different keeper, and none of this would have happened. Unfortunately for you, that was your one chance out. Now, I'd sooner raise myself from the dead than let you go."

I still can't move, but a sound somewhere between agony and relief escapes me by accident when her fingertips glide gently over the scar on my face again.

An unbearably tender sensation follows everywhere she touches. It's like being infused with pure peace.

And gods, this *warmth*. I haven't felt anything like it since she stopped breathing in my arms.

Just the reminder of that moment when everything shattered has my reality again rearranging itself. Between the exhaustion, pain, and shock, I can't get a grip.

"Prove this is real," I demand raggedly, closing my eyes when her fingers trace the scar down my neck to where it dips below my clothes. "Say it again."

If she's real, I need her to ruin me again.

Maven knows exactly what I'm talking about. She considers for a moment before her free hand slips into my hair. She tugs my head back gently to make me look at her again, but it's just enough that my heart skips another beat.

"I love you," she admits quietly, still endearingly reticent about those words. Then her eyes narrow in steely warning. "Which is why you're about to promise me that you will never again sit on your ass doing nothing when you're in danger."

It's her. She's back.

"I promise," I manage.

And finally her lips are on mine, so heated and perfect that two things happen. My long-neglected cock twitches, and my fragmented heart starts to pound. This moment is beyond surreal. I think I'll wake up any second, but when she continues to kiss me, something savagely dark and incurable cements itself deep inside my bones.

Maven thinks I regret being bound to her? How fucking asinine. She should be a million times more worried about who exactly she just confessed to loving, because I am not the same match she knew.

I thought I wasn't worthy of her before, but now…

Gods. Would she still want me if she knew how much I've changed?

I should warn her about it, but I'm too damn selfish. Too desperate to never miss her warmth again.

When she finally breaks the kiss, more emotions bombard me as it finally starts to sink in. She's here, but she's not dressed warm enough. She's in single layers of ill-fitting clothes and must be fucking *freezing*.

And then I spot the dried blood on her clothes.

Absolutely. Fucking. Not.

"How did you get here?" I demand, suddenly unable to think about anything except getting her out of this active zone.

She tips her head in a western direction. "Felix transported me here. He and Kenzie took cover in an abandoned store half a mile that way." She pauses, rising to her feet—no, foot. Something is wrong with the other one. "I sense shadow fiends headed in this direction. Stay here on the defense while I take care of the fiends and fetch Felix."

Yeah, right. Her, leaving me?

Not an option ever again.

The residual adrenaline racing through me in the face of my keeper's impossible return is pushing me into full-blown crisis mode, and it only gets worse with every second I stare at her injured shoulder and ankle.

She needs to be healed. *Now*.

Shakily, I get to my feet, slipping out of my ripped, snow-dusted trench coat and cursing the fact that this filth is the most I can offer her. Maven protests me giving it to her, but she gets even more annoyed when I scoop her into my arms despite the screaming agony lacerating my side.

"You're hurt," she snaps. "Put me down."

So my injured, combat-hungry keeper can dive headfirst into

danger? So she can be taken away from me again while I'm just as helpless as I was last time?

"No," I seethe vehemently.

And knowing that my keeper isn't about to accept that answer, since she's the most determined person in the entire five planes of existence, I turn and storm in the direction she indicated.

"Put me down," she warns again.

I can tell she's about to start struggling, so I freeze her wrists and ankles together with nevermelt without looking down.

The second she's restrained, Maven goes perfectly still in my arms. When her unbreakable poker face slips into place, I'm pretty sure that means she's royally pissed.

Which is fair, since I'm a world-class dick for doing this. But there's no fucking way I'm about to set her down in this dangerous area, injury be damned.

For the next ten minutes, I cradle Maven close to my chest and do my best not to stagger too much as I walk through the raging blizzard. Any shadow fiends or other creatures that try to approach are frozen instantaneously before they can get too close.

I freeze more ravens, too.

Meanwhile, the shards of my heart continue to thump painfully inside me. I'm on the verge of a breakdown at just the thought of setting my keeper down. The sooner I get her out of here, the sooner I'll be able to breathe again.

She's alive.

She's back.

She's mine.

I have questions, but they'll wait until she's safe and warm. I need time to hold her until the alarms blaring in my head pass, and then she can tear me a new asshole all she wants.

Soon, I shoulder through a broken door and into the remains of what was once a small grocery store. Like most other stores, it's in shambles and looks like it was heavily raided before it was left to rot with the rest of Snowfall Ridge.

Once we're out of the blizzard, I let the nevermelt around Maven's wrists and ankles melt, but I keep her in my arms.

"I'm sorry," I finally whisper. "I just needed to get you out of there."

She stays silent, refusing to show any emotion. That kills me a little.

Kenzie Baird and her caster are huddled together for warmth nearby, but the shifter startles at the sight of us. "Thank gods you guys made it! I kept hearing shadow fiends out there and was starting to get really worried–oh, shit. Uh, Profess–I mean, Everett? You're kind of dripping blood everywhere, so I really don't think you should be holding Maven like that."

I ignore her just like I ignore the blood saturating my side.

"Transport us. Now," I tell Felix.

The atypical caster glances at Maven for her input. To my chagrin, her expression remains ironclad, the same way it used to whenever something was deeply bothering her.

I'll apologize again later over and over, if she lets me.

Felix begins laying the spell to transport us out of here. Moments later, the bright light of stomach-flipping transportation magic deposits us abruptly into the dark, cold, blizzarding night just outside of Everbound's massive front double doors. I barge through them immediately, ignoring Felix and Kenzie having to wait for magical clearance.

Their unfamiliar presence at the wards will tip off someone in my security detail, so they'll get let in eventually, even if they're pissy about waiting in the cold for a bit. Or maybe they'll simply go home to Halfton. I don't care.

The fact that Maven says nothing at all about that is…mildly alarming. I glance down, but it's impossible to tell what she's thinking.

Is she indifferent? Upset? Hurt that I refused to let her fight back there?

Finally, I can't take it anymore. As I stride toward my old staff office, I blurt out the obvious. "I took over Everbound."

She says nothing.

"You'll be safe here," I try again.

The barest nod.

"I'm sorry. I know I'm an ass. I swear I'll get a fire started for you and warm food and—"

"You kept the scar the lich gave you on purpose," she says quietly.

That was the last thing I expected her to say, and it makes me slow to a stop. My injury is on fire. Between that intense pain and the need to hold her close, breathing is torture.

Maven reaches up to gently trace the scar on my face again, sending shivers down my spine.

"I'm curious. Why didn't you have Silas heal you?" she asks.

"He couldn't." He was too far gone.

"Someone else could have."

"There was too much going on."

That's an excuse, and she must know it because she raises a brow expectantly. I swallow hard, turning my chin so she won't have to look directly at my new face.

"I know it's hideous. But I…I deserved it."

For many reasons, but mostly because I failed her and deserved every reminder of it. Besides, it's not like my so-called pretty face ever did my keeper any favors.

But if my keeper hates how I look now—

"Hideous, my ass. It's annoyingly sexy."

I'm so surprised that I blink down at her, warmth rising into my cheeks. There's no way I didn't just mishear her.

"W—what?"

"And I thought you couldn't get any more gorgeous. So fucking unfair," she mutters almost under her breath before fixing me with a glare deathly enough to actually make me flinch. "Put me down before you bleed out."

I steel myself, the crisis alarms still going off in my skull. "Not happening."

"Fine, then I'll—"

"You're back, Commander?" a surprised voice interrupts.

It's a vampire approaching down the hall—one of the mercenaries working under Douglas's command. Protective panic washes over me, and I angle my body so it will block his view of Maven. With how infamous she's become, she'll be too easily recognized, and the last thing I need is more idiots spewing my keeper's name every chance they can.

"Send Douglas to my old office. *Now,*" I order. "He needs to heal someone, and he needs to come alone."

He agrees, salutes, and darts away with vampire speed to fulfill orders. I'm about to march Maven to safety, but another sudden wave of empty dizziness hits me so hard that all at once, darkness swallows me whole.

8

MAVEN

When I set out to reunite with my elemental, I didn't envision having to drag his stubborn, beautiful, unconscious ass down a ridiculously long hallway with an audience of ghosts watching the entire damn thing.

I pause outside his old office and blow hair out of my face. Even with the grueling soreness plaguing my limbs, I must still be physically stronger than average, because I've dragged Everett this far without too much difficulty despite my injured ankle. I'm not sure if that's due to my godly side or thanks to all the irreversible experiments my body was put through over the years.

I'm just glad I'm not doing this while still wearing those fucking ice cuffs. I loathe restraints. They bring back too many memories of the Nether. Just feeling them around my wrists was enough to make me start disassociating.

I wipe my brow and glance at the specters that have been slowly accumulating around me ever since we entered Everbound.

"Good thing you guys are already dead, or I'd have to kill you for seeing shit this embarrassing," I grumble.

Some ghosts look fresh, while others look faceless and foggy, like they've been here for a while. It makes me wonder if Syntyche has fallen behind in reaping souls. High death rates around the mortal realm must mean she's busy as fuck.

Shoving the door open with my good foot, I drag Everett inside the cold office, which brightens slightly thanks to dim mage lights. As I try to catch my breath, I again find myself staring at the scar etched into the left side of his gorgeous face.

The shiny scar tissue is jagged, a darker shade than his pale skin, and runs nearly vertical. It crawls up his neck and over his jaw, passing the left corner of his lips on the way up his cheek and over his eye until it thins out and stops above his temple, bisecting his eyebrow on the way.

It's not the most severe facial scar I've ever seen, but it completely changes his appearance. Where my elemental was once perfectly flawless, there is now an unmistakably savage harshness to his scarred beauty. His already stunning face now has a vicious edge that makes my pulse pound.

He looks like a scarred angel.

It's fucking sexy.

I'm still ogling him when a ghost impatiently waves its hand in front of my face. I glance at the veritable crowd of dead people hovering around me and realize most of them are also checking out Everett.

Or maybe they're just waiting to see if his ghost joins them, since his breathing has grown alarmingly shallow and he's still bleeding.

Damn him for insisting on carrying me in that state.

Annoyed, I withdraw my new etherium knife. By the time I face the whispering ghosts, I'm holding my scythe again. Just as I finish reaping the last of them, a strange current once again ripples from the glowing scythe, directly into my system.

Abruptly, I'm jerked into a memory.

• • •

I find myself standing on a floating balcony, overlooking a crowd of richly dressed beings. I can make out glowing fairies, animals chatting excitedly in a language I somehow understand, and men and women who appear almost human, except for their angelic, feathery white wings. They stand beside nature spirits made of leaves, trees, pure water, earth, starlight, and more elements.

They're all looking up at me and smiling. Cheering. Clapping.

Their applause is overwhelming, but a powerful woman's voice beside me rings out effortlessly over the thousands below.

"For the first time in nearly three thousand years, it is my great pleasure to introduce another member into our beloved pantheon: the daughter of my dear sister Syntyche and our new goddess, Maven!"

"I'm not a goddess," I say in this recollection, quiet enough that only the woman speaking should hear me.

Something is bothering me in this memory. I'm annoyed.

No—I'm *livid*, but I can't remember why.

I catch the barest glimpse of the goddess beside me. She is built like a true warrior and fiercely beautiful, with fiery red hair, golden eyes, and faint scars along her arms, chin, and one of her cheeks. She's dressed in gleaming golden armor and a crown made of fire.

This must be Arati, the queen of the gods, introducing me to the Paridisians. She brushes off my irritation, beaming at the crowd below.

"As you know, my niece lived no ordinary mortal life. Though we gods have no power in the Nether and therefore could not see where she was raised, we eagerly observed once she emerged—and lo and behold, she earned her divinity by rescuing thousands of souls and their future posterity from the very hell she once endured. Because her mortal life and death exceeded nobility, fate has decreed her future here in Paradise. One and all, welcome our newest goddess—"

"I am not a motherfucking goddess," I snap.

Yikes. My voice carries much more than expected.

The Paridisians fall into a shocked hush, and Arati turns to glare at me just as the memory cuts off and another swirls into place. This time, I'm walking with Galene through a bizarrely idyllic forest dappled with otherworldly sunlight.

"What was the point of matching me to them if they were just going to be left behind like this? What game were you playing, binding us together like that?" Paradise Maven asks.

Galene smiles softly, her all-seeing kaleidoscope eyes shifting between all the colors of the rainbow. "There was no game, my fearless one. That was all you."

"I think I'd know if I was—"

I cut off, recalling the intimate moments with my quintet. During sex or not, as I grew closer to each of them in irreversible ways…

Galene nods. "It's true. You bound them to yourself, albeit unconsciously. You see, we gods derive our power from worship. As you grew closer to your quintet, who worshipped you in their own way, you naturally became more powerful. As a revenant, you could not access many abilities that were your birthright. However, you gained access to your holy magic—the very same magic that binds legacies together. Thus, your bound quintet and their broken curses."

I'm quiet for a moment. "But if you knew I would end up here, why bother matching us together like that at all? Why put them through this?"

"Despite what is believed in the mortal world, we gods have no real control over soul matches. Whether those matches are platonic or epic loves, they are the design of fate itself, and fate is a force that even we gods must bow to," Galene explains gently. "Whomever quintets belong with is out of our hands. I only foresaw that you would need your soul matches, though I admit that I *did* have to meddle in order to get all of your quintet to Everbound at the same time. An anonymous tip to the Frost family, falsifying correspondence with the Garnet Wizard, circulating rumors about an escaped wicked man for a certain steward of Limbo to follow…"

Her gentle voice fades away, and abruptly, I once again find myself beside Everett's unconscious body. It's jarring, having memories shoved back into my head like lost puzzle pieces.

I slump onto the floor with a grimace at the soreness lingering in my limbs. My scythe once again turns back into a knife that I tuck away.

If I unconsciously bound my matches to my shadow heart before, does that mean I can use the same holy magic to bind them to me now?

I snap to attention when Asher Douglas knocks loudly on Everett's ajar office door, striding through it bundled in a ridiculous number of jackets.

"Damn it, Frost, I know you don't sleep anymore, but I need some fucking shuteye if I'm going to keep putting up with—"

He cuts off, halting in place when he sees me. His hand drops to a small gun at his hip.

I scoff. "If you're going to attack me, at least use something fun. Like a knife. Or a mace."

Gods, it's been too long since I got in a good fight with someone wielding a mace.

Douglas makes a face, pulls out a flashlight, blinds me with it for a second as he checks my pupils more thoroughly, and finally grunts as he clicks it off again.

"Okay, you're officially the freakiest thing I've ever encountered. How did you even—"

"Heal him now, ask me questions never," I advise, testy thanks to the pain flaring up in my shoulder and ankle.

The bounty hunter shakes his head, muttering something under his breath about me being a "cosmic cockroach" as he kneels beside Everett. He removes the tattered trench coat and blood-soaked shirt underneath to take a look at the deep claw marks.

Seeing such a nasty injury on my elemental makes my throat tighten painfully. I can't stop remembering how defeated he looked as he lay there on that damn street staring up at the ghoul that was about to end him.

If I'd been a moment too late…

No. I can't think about that.

Douglas is focused as his hands light up with soft green magic over the injury. His eyes glow slightly, too, reminding me that he has a gift for sensing magical signatures, even his own.

It's the first time I've seen him use healing magic up close, and I catch the microexpression of pain that flashes over his features when he starts healing the worst of Everett's wound. It's so subtle that someone raised in a normal world of expression would've missed it.

But like everyone from the Nether, I grew up deciphering the tiniest changes in expressions. It's not hard to figure out why a legacy would have that reaction.

When he sees me analyzing him, he shoos me away. "Give me room to work, you fucking zombie."

"Feeling the pain of those you heal. What a poetic curse," I muse, admiring the sadism.

Douglas startles before pinning me with a glowing glare. "Look, however you figured that out, you keep your fucking mouth shut about it."

I glance down at the impressive progress he's already made on Everett. He seems extremely skilled at healing, despite his curse.

"I'll heal you next. Pretty sure that's why Frost summoned me at all." He flicks a glance at my bloodstained shoulder. "Vampire bite, right? Should be fast enough."

"Don't bother."

"Look, *telum*. I'm beat and I don't really give a rat's ass about your little ouchies, but Frost pays better than anyone, so if he says to heal his creepy Undead girlfriend—"

"It won't work, so drop it."

Asher Douglas completely ignores my words as he finishes with Everett and moves on to me. His hands light up with green magic and hover over my shoulder, but as I expected, nothing happens.

He makes another face. "You're just too fucked up for normal treatments, huh?"

Guilty as charged.

Douglas sighs long and loud, like this is beyond annoying. He glances at the doorway to make sure no one is passing by, checks that Everett is still unconscious, and then fixes me with a serious stare.

"I can still heal you if you swear by the gods to keep your mouth shut about it."

I arch a brow, curious. "Fine. I swear by myself."

The caster scoffs, missing my inside joke, before focusing on my shoulder again. This time, his hands light up with a soft white light, but his eyes don't glow. Tingling power washes over my shoulder as liquid warmth, vanquishing the pain at once. I can sense the magic spreading further, soothing the lingering aches and soreness I've felt since waking up. If Douglas feels the pain this time, he doesn't show it.

I glance at his glowing hands. "This is holy magic."

The same untraceable power that Pia—no, Galene—used to heal me even when I was a revenant. The same kind of magic I can supposedly wield, once I finally figure out how.

Maybe this is the only kind of magic that can heal me now that I'm a demigoddess and not a revenant.

He moves on to my bitten ankle without having to ask where the pain is. "Yep."

"You're a saint?"

"None of your damn business. But no."

Aside from Silas, this is my first time meeting another hybrid caster. I guess holy magic plays nice with all other types of magic.

Douglas finishes and touches my shoulder. It's clinical, but my stomach still lurches. I jerk away from the contact, leveling him with my most withering look.

"Whoa. Relax. Message received." He shifts to a crouch, wisely putting distance between us while squinting at me. "Hey. You could've killed me while I was hunting you months ago. Why didn't you?"

I roll my shoulder, relieved that I no longer have to tune out the pain.

"Your death would have been less fun than fighting you again in the future. Also, I don't take lives without good reason. You haven't given me a reason. Yet," I tack on so that he knows we're not about to get chummy.

"Huh. Fair enough."

Not one to linger, Douglas grunts as he picks Everett's unconscious body off the floor before stepping into the attached professor's quarters. Aside from the frosted windows and ice everywhere, it's clear this is where Everett has been living since everything happened.

The towering bounty hunter deposits Everett on the bed, stretches, and turns to leave, but I cut him off.

"If you tell anyone I'm back, you won't have time to regret it before you're dead."

"You're not much of a people person, are you?"

"Pot, kettle."

He barks a laugh. "Believe me, I'm not interested in complicating my life by getting mixed up in whatever shitstorm you're about to create. As long as Frost keeps paying the big bucks, I'm the best ally you'll ever have, so your secret's safe with me. Now move, because I've got a lumpy pillow and five shitty hours of sleep calling my name."

I lock the doors once he's gone, sensing fresh protective magic wards laid over them. Then I sit beside Everett on the bed.

Either I spent the last six months getting lazy in Paradise, or resurrecting just takes a lot out of a bitch, because just sitting on a comfy bed like this makes my exhaustion ten times more noticeable.

Everett shifts slightly beside me, immediately taking my full attention. Relief sweeps over me when his glacier-colored eyes blink open in tired confusion. Then he bolts upright, the temperature plummeting even more around us—until his frantic gaze settles on me.

"Oh, fucking gods on high," he rasps, pulling me into his arms immediately. "It was real."

His slight mint scent surrounds me as he buries his face in my neck. His breathing picks up into the same erratic pattern he was trapped in when he whisked me back to Everbound. He's shaking as it grows even colder in here.

I hold him back just as tightly, but when I shiver, he inhales sharply and practically launches off the bed to get away.

"Damn it. You're too cold. You're too cold and it's all my fault and you can't get close to me again or you might—"

"Everett," I say, trying to calm him down.

It's too late. He's panicking again, dragging bloodstained hands through his white hair as he stumbles slightly, his chest rising and falling rapidly.

As someone who's had more than my fair share of trauma-induced breakdowns in the past, I find it's best to be snapped out of it. I move to his side. Ignoring his protest, I take his hand and pull him into the attached bathroom. I slip out of my boots, set my etherium knife on the counter, and reach for him.

"No. Stop. You can't keep touching me," he chokes out even as I start removing his ripped clothing. "I'm too volatile right now. If I make the wrong move, I might freeze you or hurt you or—"

"Does the plumbing still work?" I check, stepping behind the glass shower wall.

Whatever his answer is, I don't catch it as I turn on the

shower, turning the dial to hot. I sense the slight ripple of a common magic warming charm before the shower head begins spraying me with hot water.

Thank the fucking universe. *Warmth.*

"Come here," I tell Everett, not caring that my clothes are now sopping wet.

He's still breathing too fast. He readjusts his ripped shirt several times before stripping it off entirely, taking a tentative step closer, then away again. In the dim light and through the fog of glass, I can barely make out the big scar traveling down and across his torso until it stops over his right hip.

Finally, Everett demands, "Are you still hurt? Did Asher heal you?"

"Only one way to find out."

Right now, my elemental is in a state of shock. I need to get him to focus on something until he can breathe fully and think straight. I'll just have to be the *something* this gorgeous legacy focuses on.

Oh, woe is me.

Through the glass, he holds my daring stare for a moment before swallowing and removing the rest of his clothes. I didn't turn on the light in here, so the only light comes from the lamp's glow through the bathroom doorway. It's still enough light that I can make out each of Everett's small, anxious ticks as he steps behind the glass with me.

As soon as the hot spray hits his cold skin, extra steam clouds this space—but it doesn't freeze, thanks to the magic that I suspect my meticulous elemental hired someone to put on the plumbing.

I take one of his hands, guiding it to my wet coat. Everett hesitates for only a moment before gently stripping me out of the wet clothing. I don't miss his shaky exhale of relief when he doesn't see an injury on my shoulder or ankle, but he immediately grabs the nearest soap and loofah to clean the dried blood off of me.

My attempt to calm him down is working. With each second that ticks by, his breathing stabilizes until he's wholly focused. He doesn't argue when I reach for shampoo to use on his hair. When my fingers tangle in the silvery wet strands, Everett moans softly, letting his forehead drop to mine.

His voice is ragged. "Even if it's not hurting you, you shouldn't touch me. You have no idea how much I'm not worthy of you. Now more than ever."

"Shh. You'll get soap in your mouth."

"I failed you. I failed all of us. And I know I'll never deserve your forgiveness, but I need you to know that I'm so fucking sorry and—"

While his mouth is still open, I slip two shampooed fingers inside. Everett recoils, gagging and spitting out the taste of soap. He sputters at me in indignant confusion, successfully ripped out of that spiral of self-hatred that I plan on never hearing again.

"Your mouth was spewing shit, so I cleaned it out for you," I inform him, reaching for the body wash next.

"Maven," he whispers. "I'm serious. I…changed. I did things I'm not proud of."

I pause, finally considering what unpleasantnesses that might encompass. "Women?"

"What?"

"Did you fuck other women?" I clarify, trying to keep my tone conversational even though I just broke the cap of this body wash bottle as electric jealousy sears through me.

It's a reasonable question. Everett is an incredibly sexy legacy with needs. He's not a shy virgin anymore, so maybe he decided to speed up the mourning process by getting with other women. It's not like he'd have a problem finding willing partners, end of the world or not.

I don't blame other women for hopping into bed with my gorgeous elemental, but if he mentions anyone by name, I'll have to kill them for touching what's mine.

Everett has been staring at me for long enough that I'm about to repeat the question—but all at once, I'm hanging upside down, thrown over one of his shoulders. I gasp, scrambling to grip onto his wet frame as he storms out of the quickly icing-over shower. I'm abruptly pinned to his bed with him above me, water droplets falling from his wet hair onto me as cold air prickles all over my wet, bare body.

In this light, I can finally see the pure, savage fury etched into his beautifully scarred face. It takes my breath away.

"Tell me you did not just fucking ask me if I was *sleeping with other women* while I spent months in agony trying to remember how to fucking *breathe* without you," he warns darkly.

"Everett—"

My pulse jumps when one of his hands suddenly circles my neck, the gentle pressure making my lips part. His ice eyes bore into mine.

"Ask me again. Ask me if I cheated on you."

"Technically, it's not cheating since I was kind of dead," I point out.

Yikes. That was the wrong thing to say. He's even more pissed off now.

"I got one good thing in life. *You*. And just like that, you were gone. Dead in my arms. Do you have any fucking idea what that did to me?"

The raw brokenness in his voice hurts me.

My poor snow angel. I reach up to cradle his perfect face, drawing it closer until I can kiss his scarred jaw.

"I'm beginning to," I whisper.

And then I kiss him.

9

MAVEN

As soon as I'm kissing him, Everett melts against me, groaning hoarsely. His hand slips from my throat to the back of my neck before he's suddenly consuming me.

This isn't my gentle elemental, trying to take things sweet and slow.

Instead, he's rough. Angry. He's kissing me like he wants to punish the time that kept us apart. For several long moments, I can't focus on anything but the way he claims my lips—until I remember how much he likes a dose of pain.

I bite his lower lip.

Frost blooms all over the back of my neck, making me gasp.

Everett swears and pulls away from me, yanking his hands away like he thinks he hurt me. "Godsdamn it. Gods*damn* it, Maven—I can't do this. I'm barely in control all the time, but when you're touching me? There's absolutely no fucking chance I won't freeze you to death if I—if we—"

He's dangerously close to getting stuck in his own head about this, so I take charge.

Pushing against his beautifully scarred torso, I flip so that Everett is now on his back as I straddle him. I trace the scar stretching across his body, admiring how his skin healed over his sculpted chest.

"You don't have to touch it," he grimaces.

I give him a pointed look. "Nothing will change how I feel about you, so don't pretend it's any harder for me to love you with your scars."

The breath whooshes out of him before he rasps, "I love you, too. I'm so fucking in love with you. It's killed me that I didn't get to say it back to you, when—when you were—"

I'm suddenly dragged back down for another fierce kiss. Everett's fingers are cold as ice as they trail over my body and press in firmly near my hips. The added chill is another burst of sensation on the backdrop of our exchange.

When I scoot back just enough to tease his erection with my ass, he makes a choking sound and ends the kiss. His cheeks are flushed as he struggles to get words out.

"I'm—fuck. It's been six months."

"Way too fucking long," I agree, scooting back further and lifting slightly until his thick, warm erection is nestled between my legs. I grind against it, shivering at the delicious sensation as it drags against that perfect spot next to my clit.

Gods, I need him so fucking bad. I can feel my wetness dragging along his cock, preparing it for me.

Everett swears raggedly, his fingers tightening almost painfully on my hips as he squeezes his eyes shut briefly. "I mean, it's been *six months*. I'm—shit, you're so fucking beautiful, I'm…"

Oh. He means he's struggling not to finish quickly from sheer excitement.

Just like he did the first time we made out.

I *love* knowing my ice elemental is this helplessly attracted to me. At least I know it's mutual as I grind against him again, relishing his soft groan.

Reaching up to tease my tits, I enjoy the way his attention drops to them and his breathing gets choppy. I rock forward again, and that heady drag of his cock against me sends more exhilarating tingles up my spine as my lips part.

"Gods," he breathes.

"Goddess," I correct, grinning.

Everett groans. "Yes. *My* goddess. Give me what I need. Hurt me."

Wanting to see him lose control again, I rake my nails lightly down his chest, just enough to give that tease of pain he wants more of.

Everett swears viciously—and suddenly, I'm beneath him. His gorgeous, scarred body presses me into the mattress, his swollen cock sliding through my slick entrance to tease it over and over as he whispers in my ear, voice rough with restraint.

"My pleasure. My pain. Whatever shattered pieces are left of me, they're all yours. *I'm yours.*"

Gods, yes.

Grinding against his hard cock, I swear at how good it feels. "All mine. Fuck me, Everett. I need you. I need—"

He lines himself up and thrusts into me so roughly that my voice cuts out. My head falls back, and before I can think better of it, the fucking *amazing* feeling of being stretched and filled like this makes me drag my fingernails down his back—and with another broken swear, Everett pulls out before slamming into me again.

"Yes," I gasp, my legs wrapping around his hips. It's been six months since I've been fucked, and apparently, my body needs a second to adjust.

Everett's glacial eyes devour me like I'm a feast he's been starved of as he waits for me. When I squirm against him restlessly, needing more, he thrusts again—hard.

Fuck, it just feels so amazing.

Everett groans again, but it's sharp this time as it turns into a chant. "Gentle. Gentle. Be gentle."

"Me, gentle? Now? Impossible," I laugh breathlessly, kissing his jaw.

He presses his forehead to mine, panting. "I was talking to myself."

He's trying to be gentle with me? Fuck that.

Lifting my head, I trap his lower lip between my teeth, biting it far harder than I did earlier while I clench around his cock, desperate for more.

That does it. My beautiful, scarred elemental rewards me with another punishing thrust, followed by another and another, his hips slamming against mine. The slap of skin against skin echoes through his cold room as pleasure careens through my system. My pulse pounds as I moan.

"Godsdamn it," Everett groans, pumping harder into me. "Gods fucking *damn* it, you feel too fucking good. So warm and wet. Your perfect pussy is *strangling* me. *Fuck.*"

When I tighten myself around him again, he loses another inch of control. He fucks me with abandon, moaning and swearing so fucking deliciously. I'm vaguely aware of frost covering the sheets below us. It's on my skin, too, an extra bite to add to the rest of the buildup coursing through my body.

But when my legs start to shake, I forget all about the frost and clutch my elemental even closer.

"More," I whisper, enjoying every one of his uncontrolled, savage drives into me. "Fuck, I need more. *Gods*, Everett, please just—"

He bites my neck really fucking hard.

I jolt as the extra dose of violent, possessive stimulation sends a shockwave straight to my lower stomach, and just like that, I'm coming hard and fast. Everett feels my pussy flexing around him and his rhythm stutters, turning wild. Desperate. The room dips several degrees as he fucks me hard, wringing every last ounce out of my lingering orgasm until finally, he shatters.

With a hoarse cry, he buries himself deep, and everything around us is suddenly bathed in ice. In a split second, frozen crystals have formed across his headboard, the sheets, all over the ceiling, across his shoulders, and down my thighs.

The shock of the cold makes me lose my breath, but I'm safe. The burning starts up in my chest again. I try to catch my breath, my head spinning as Everett collapses against me.

I wonder if I'll ever get enough of seeing him come undone. It's fucking beautiful.

"Shit," he slowly starts to realize, lifting his head when he sees the ice everywhere. "I lost control."

I grin, softly stroking his back where I clawed it earlier to soothe the sting.

"I noticed. I loved it."

He briefly focuses on the ice around us until it all melts, dissolving into harmless, cool water before he rolls off of me. But although my pulse is thrumming and the pleasant tingling hasn't gone away, I feel the tiniest twinge of disappointment because…my chest doesn't sting.

Meaning, Everett's emblem isn't there.

I have no clue how to use my holy magic or what's keeping me from bonding with—

Oh.

Of course.

Quintets are bound to hearts, and as far as I know, I don't have a heart to bind my quintet *to* at the moment. Not even a shadow heart like they were bound to last time, since that disappeared when my revenant purpose was fulfilled.

I have no fucking idea how I'm even alive without a heart, but the *how* isn't what matters. What matters is breaking my quintet's curses again, because the absence of our bonds is really starting to grate on my nerves.

I need that connection to him. To all of them.

So I'll get a fucking heart, somehow. Right after I get them back.

I glance over to see that Everett is gazing at me adoringly. The chillingly possessive undertone in his arctic eyes makes me smile. He pulls me against his side, moving and adjusting the blankets until he can tuck the dry sheets around me to ward off the chill in the room.

"Gods, I've missed your warmth," he whispers against my shoulder.

"I've missed you," I murmur back, still coming down from fucking amazing sex.

Everett's arms tighten around me. When he takes a bracing breath, I know exactly what he's about to ask.

"Maven. How is it possible that you're back? Where the hell were you for the last six months?"

I haven't considered the best way to break the news about my identity. Should I hold off telling him until I can explain to my entire quintet at once? What if he's like Kenzie and isn't sure how to react to me at first?

"You know it kills me when you don't tell me things," Everett reminds me quietly. "You once said you'd be better about it. Don't make the mistake of thinking I've gotten more patient."

Is he threatening me? I grin, twisting in his arms to examine his face.

"Maybe I want to see you lose your temper. Angry Everett must be a sight to behold."

His gaze sparks with cold warning, and *gods,* he looks good when he's annoyed. "So help me gods, I will cuff your beautiful ass to this bed with nevermelt until you quit stalling. I need to know where you were and how you came back, because I'm still struggling to believe you're actually here. It feels like you just dropped out of the godsdamned sky—"

A laugh escapes before I clear my throat, composing myself. "I did."

Everett stares. "What?"

I have to get this over with. He'll need time to adjust to being matched to a demigoddess, whether he likes it or not, since there's no shot in hell I'll ever let any of my matches go.

I decide not to mince words. "I fell from Paradise."

He stops breathing, eyes widening as he puts together the fact that mortals can't go to Paradise.

"My mother took me there after my revenant purpose was fulfilled," I add.

For several long moments, silence hangs heavily in this room. Finally, Everett exhales slowly.

"If you went to Paradise, it means you became divine. As in, you were..."

"A goddess. Temporarily," I add, making a face. "Don't worry, I fixed it. I'm back to being a demigoddess."

I think.

"Holy shit. It explains so much, and yet..." He trails off, is frozen in thought for a moment, and then groans. "Oh. Oh, gods. *Please* tell me your mother isn't who I think she is."

"Syntyche," I confirm, then notice his cheeks have turned bright red. "What is it?"

"Nothing. Just seriously regretting some of my past prayers to your *mother*," he grumbles, burying his face in my shoulder again like he wants to hide.

He's so fucking adorable. I can feel his heart pounding against my side, but at least he's not having a full-blown panic attack like he did earlier. I'll take that as a good sign.

Then Everett tenses, sitting up to frown at me. "Hang on. In the legends that elementals pass down, it's said that when beings ascend to Paradise, it's permanent. Divine beings belong in Paradise and can't live in the mortal realm. So how did you...?"

I reach up to trace his scar absentmindedly. "I don't know. My memories of the last six months haven't returned yet. What matters is that I found a way, and I'm back. For you. For all of us. I'm piecing our quintet back together, no matter what it takes."

His expression goes from soft to agonized at that thought. "At this point, I don't know if you can piece us back together. I wanted to take care of them like you asked. I tried, but...gods, I failed. Our quintet barely exists because of me. I'm sorry—"

"Everett." I prop up on my elbow, determined to get this gorgeous man to stop fucking apologizing to me for no damn reason. "I'm the one who should be apologizing. It wasn't fair of me to ask that of you. It's not your fault I dropped dead like an idiot—and you couldn't help what your own curse did, let alone theirs."

The reminder that my quintet has been left at the mercy of their curses makes my stomach feel hollow.

"Where are they?" I whisper. "I only heard that Baelfire is somewhere in the north."

Chill nips at my bare upper half as Everett's voice turns bleak and rough.

"Honestly…I'm not sure if Baelfire technically exists inside that dragon anymore. It's just feral. Brigid updates me now and then. I send resources and aid to the Decimuses to help protect the dragon from anyone who wants to hunt it for its scales."

Anger flickers through me. They can't hunt my mate, and I refuse to believe his dragon completely took over.

Everett goes on, rubbing his face. The longer we talk about this, the more I can practically feel stress and exhaustion wafting from him.

"Silas is here physically. Mentally, it's rare. He has good and bad days, but it's been mostly bad for months. As soon as we returned here after the battle, he imprisoned himself in iron and just kind of…gave up. Let the voices have him."

Gods, I hate his curse. Determination to get them back is steeling itself even more firmly in me by the second.

I take a deep breath. "And Crypt?"

He's quiet.

"Everett. Where's Crypt?"

"For a long time, he was on a killing spree. I would dig up any information I could on the best targets for his abilities, send him off, and then he would come back for the next one. I kept finding missions for him, because if I didn't…" Everett shakes his head. "That fucking incubus was pushing himself too hard on purpose to make his curse take a heavier toll. He wanted to burn out."

What? Why would he—

Oh, my fucking gods.

He was trying to join me in the Beyond.

I sit up, disengaging from Everett's arms to breathe in and out more evenly. Angry doesn't even begin to describe how I'm feeling. I knew they would be suffering from their curses, but now I'm so fucking mad that it took me this long to return from Paradise.

One of Everett's cool hands brushes soothingly down my spine, curling around my waist to pull me closer again like he can't help himself.

"All I had were traces of you, including them. Even hellishly miserable and broken, I wanted to keep my word to you. But it's no excuse. I could have done things differently. I'm sorry—"

"That's the last time you apologize," I insist as gently as possible. "None of this is your fault."

It's mine. I failed six months ago, and my quintet paid the price. If I had only planned better, fought harder, done so many things differently…

Just like when I was a teenager, silently berating myself over my shortcomings, Lillian's voice drifts back to me.

You're too hard on yourself, little raven. Failures are not failures, they're lessons—and you've always been a fast learner. When you set your mind on something, nothing stands in your way. You were born with such strength and glorious potential, I only wish you knew.

Lillian.

More of her careful words from the past slowly come back to me, sending a new awareness through me. I straighten, glancing at Everett.

"Lillian. Is she…?"

"She's alive, here at Everbound," he says, tightening his arm around my waist and tugging.

Suddenly, I'm sideways in his lap so he can hold me close, bundling the blankets closer around me. The slightest hint of wariness pulls at my gut, reminding me that he's had his skin all over mine for a while now, but it's easy to ignore.

In fact, it's nice to be held like this, my face now pressed into his neck as he places tender kisses on the top of my head. He insists that he's changed, but he's still being so fucking gentle with me.

"I need to see her," I tell him.

"Tomorrow."

He twists, taking me with him until I'm lying with him curled protectively around me. We're both still naked. When he stretches out an arm to turn off the light beside the bed, his bedroom is plunged into peaceful, pleasantly chilly darkness—but I'm comfortable tucked against him like this, as if he's been absorbing my warmth through the blanket so he can give it back.

It's soothing, but I shouldn't rest yet. "Where in the castle is Lillian? I need to talk to her—"

"*Tomorrow,*" he repeats, a warning note in his words. "You're exhausted. I need you to rest so I don't go fucking insane along with the others."

"I can't sleep right now," I protest quietly, trying to muffle a yawn.

"You can and you will so that you'll be well-rested enough to see Lillian for breakfast tomorrow."

Breakfast with Lillian? Gods, I can't wait to see her.

She was the only person I trusted growing up in the Nether, and I've missed her ever since I left. I want to insist that we go now, but it's been one long fucking day. I still haven't had time to process everything properly, but exhaustion is weighing heavily on my eyelids.

"Maven," Everett murmurs against the top of my head.

"Hmm?"

"I need you to do something for me."

Those words send a pang of remembered pain through me.

"Anything," I parrot through a yawn.

"Don't ever fucking leave me again."

I close my eyes. "I'm not going anywhere."

10

CRYPT

It starts as it always does.

I walk unseen through a crowd of motley, nondescript auras. They're bland compared to the aura surrounding the riveting girl on the stage, the one I'm drawn to. Her aura is the very same enticingly rich, shimmering dark mauve that brought me back to Everbound in the first place.

When I step into the mortal realm and see her face to face for the first time, I'm changed.

I'm hers.

She's mine.

Those breathtakingly intelligent eyes carry haunting secrets that tantalize me from the start. Without a word spoken between us, I feel it—that there is something in the fabric of her being that is precisely what my own soul is comprised of.

That's not all I feel. I've removed the walls I put up so long ago, and now every emotion I experience in her presence is fresh. Exhilarating. Even when she attempts to reject us, it's thrillingly unexpected.

Observing her becomes an addiction. I watch her micro-expressions day by day, enjoying the smallest of insights into my dark darling's beautiful mind. I become obsession personified, relishing every moment I have with my keeper before my curse catches up with me.

There's no escape.

Discovering what happiness feels like is incomparable.

That's how it always starts.

But then, the agony begins. Every night, I witness the nightmares that plague her as permanent psychological scars. The screaming. The experiments. The *conditioning.*

The time she trusted a boy who took what he wanted from her before trying to take her life.

I never tell her what I've seen of her past in the memories that torment her nights. How could I? My keeper survived things I wish I could make her forget. I'll never remind her of them by breathing a word about it ever again.

There's no escape.

In this purgatory, numbing myself is my only defense. Yet even that is becoming useless.

Our quintet grows closer. We learn about her blood oath and her purpose. She says she knows how to survive it all in the end.

It's a lie. I know that just as she knows that my minutes are ticking away with my curse, bringing me closer to the Beyond.

But I don't fear my curse, or death.

I fear being without her. I fear existing as that numb *nothingness* that I was before finding a soul as broken as mine. I fear losing what precious time I have left with her.

And that's precisely what happens in this cycle I live on repeat.

Every breath between us in this endless cycle is something I would die to have back. Every smile and argument and whisper and kiss—

Until the moment I see her lifeless on a barren battlefield. Gone.

I was going to ask her to be my muse.

Dulling every emotion isn't working anymore, because even the numbness hurts. The cycle starts over as I'm forced to relive it all, along with my bitter past.

Again. And again. And again.

11

MAVEN

I CAN BARELY SEE through the excessive amount of winter gear Everett bundled me in as we leave his old professor's apartment at dawn. Waking up was surprisingly difficult for me since I slept like the dead after resurrecting, but I get the sneaking feeling my nerve-wracked elemental didn't sleep at all.

"We have to catch her early, before she goes to the makeshift temples in Halfton. She goes almost every day," Everett explains, holding my hand through the fuzzy gloves I'm wearing.

Every time we approach another hallway, he pauses to peek around corners to ensure no Reformists under his command are hanging around these hallways. I only got the barest glimpse of Everbound in the darkness of the night, but in the cold morning light, I can really appreciate how much more desolate this castle has become.

Everett's uncontrolled power has transformed Everbound Castle. It was always a gothic behemoth, but now its windows are frosted over, hallways are glazed with shimmering displays of ice, and even the shadows of this eerie stone maze seem chilled.

As we descend a staircase and turn down another hall, I

realize we'll pass Everbound's eastern library. An idea strikes me.

"Are there books on holy magic in Everbound's library?" I ask, encouraged by the prospect of finally knowing how the hell to use my magic.

According to Galene, holy magic is fueled by worship. But reaping souls seems to help, too. Maybe there's something I can study to learn about my annoyingly dormant new abilities.

Everett's brow furrows. "I doubt it. Records like that would be kept in temples for anyone who can use holy magic. You know, saints and prophets and..." He trails off before understanding crosses his face. "Oh, shit. You can use holy magic, can't you?"

"Barely," I grumble, petulant.

I trained for years to use the destructive magic of revenants with ease. Being out of my depth with holy magic, to the point that I can't even heal myself, let alone rebond with my matches, is really fucking annoying.

We turn another corner into what used to be the administration hallway, where Lillian has been staying. I'm dying to see her, but if there's a chance that I could start learning how to use my magic...

When Everett pauses outside one of the doors, I tug on his hand. "We may need to steal records about holy magic from a temple."

To my surprise, he agrees without a single protest. "While you talk with Lillian, I'll send some Reformists to take anything and everything you need from the makeshift temples in Halfton. A lot of refugee priests and prophets salvaged any records they could when they went on the run from shadow fiends and Crypt destroying their temples."

Crypt.

Every time I think of my missing Nightmare Prince, it hurts. I need to find a way to track him down or find out if he's even still—

No. He's alive. He has to be.

I arch a brow, intrigued by my previously upright match's apparent indifference. "You're not afraid the gods will smite you?"

"As if they could come up with a worse punishment than the last six months. If they were going to smite me, they would have done it a hundred times over by now, those fucking—" He cuts off, pinching the bridge of his nose and sighing. "Damn it. I can't badmouth them now."

"Why not?"

"Because even though it's still insane to think about, some of them are your family, Snowdrop."

Family? Yikes. I don't remember if the last six months made me consider any of the gods as *family*, but I doubt it.

Deciding to shelf that unpleasant thought for later, I get back to the matter at hand. "I need records about how divine magic works. Casting, theories, spells, rituals. Anything like that."

"Done," Everett agrees before knocking on the door.

I swallow hard as we wait, feeling oddly…nervous.

If what I believe about Lillian's past words is true, she might not be surprised to see me, but I still hope she'll be glad. If she's even missed me half as much as I've missed her—

The door opens with a soft creak.

Emotions immediately crash over me when Lillian's bright blue eyes widen. They're quickly filled with that tender, maternal look I remember so well from when I was a kid.

"Maven," she breathes, clutching her hands in front of her chest.

She doesn't throw her arms around me. She doesn't start bawling.

She knows me too well for any of that.

Gods, I've missed her so much that *I'm* the one who impulsively steps forward and wraps her in a quick hug. She startles, but I pull away just as quickly, pretending my tear ducts aren't traitors and there is absolutely no extra moisture in my eyes.

The smile that breaks over Lillian's face is sunshine itself. I've never seen her in the mortal world, but her irises are bluer than I remember. Her wildly curly blonde-and-gray hair is currently in a braid over one shoulder. She's dressed in several layers of colorful, warm winter clothes right down to fuzzy green and purple striped socks on her feet.

"I've missed you *so* much, little raven," she finally says on an emotional laugh. "All my prayers have finally been answered. Here, both of you come inside. I have a fire going, and I can make some hot chocolate and oatmeal and—"

"Make it all for Maven. I need to go give an order, but I'll be right back," Everett says, squeezing my hand one more time.

We both wait for him to leave, but then I realize his other hand has gone to fidget repeatedly with his coat buttons. His teeth are clenched as a muscle jumps in his jaw.

He's clearly freaking out internally.

A big part of me understands his anxiety about being parted, even for a second. The world has changed since my demise, and not knowing all the potential threats means anything could happen to my elemental, no matter how briefly he's gone.

But Everett has clearly gotten far stronger and more brutal than I ever would've guessed. He can handle himself, and I need to talk to Lillian alone, so I lift onto my tiptoes to kiss his cool cheek.

"You'll be back quickly."

It's more of a command than a reassurance. Once I've finally stepped through the threshold and I'm safely inside Lillian's warm chambers, he lets out a slow breath before striding away like a man on a time-sensitive mission.

Lillian shuts the door and ushers me closer to the crackling fireplace. As I glance over this room, I begin stripping out of multiple outer coats and scarves.

Lillian has turned this from an administrator's office into a cozy one-room living area. Happy, bright yellow drapes curtain the window that lets in fresh dawn light. Various herbs hang drying on one brightly painted wall. There's also a wardrobe, a colorful bookshelf, a bed overflowing with pillows tucked in one corner, and books stacked ridiculously high on a light blue nightstand.

My eye catches on a frame beside the stack of books. It's a grainy photograph of a little girl dressed in some kind of uniform, with a big cheese grin that shows off several missing teeth. Between her softly pointed ears, bright blue eyes, short curly hair, and button nose, I realize the girl is Lillian's... daughter.

She never told me she had a daughter.

This revelation is stunning enough that my attention lingers on the picture even after I sit on a stool by the fireplace.

Lillian follows where I'm looking. A soft, far-off expression crosses her face. "Her name was Annabel. I was so relieved to find that picture in the rubble of my old apartment after returning to the mortal world."

I look at her questioningly.

"It wasn't that I wanted to keep secrets from you. It's just that it's so difficult to think about her, never mind talking about her," Lillian explains.

Using a woven mitt, she grabs a pot boiling over the crackling fire before moving to a small table. She quickly dishes up oatmeal and pours hot chocolate for each of us. I accept a steaming mug and bowl from her as she sits on the other stool. We sit in comfortable yet teeming silence as we eat for a moment.

But it's time to get everything out in the open. Setting the dishes down, I face my oldest friend and caretaker.

"You knew all along."

Lillian sips her hot chocolate before meeting my gaze with a sigh. "Yes. I knew who you were even before I was sent to watch over you in the Nether."

Sent?

I study her in the glow of the fire. "Syntyche sent you?"

"Galene did, actually." Lillian takes a deep breath and sets her mug aside to give this conversation her full attention. "Do you remember what I told you about my life before the Nether?"

"You were married to a fae, but it didn't work out." That's mostly all she ever said about it, but I look at the photograph on the bedside table again. "You had a daughter with him before you divorced."

"It wasn't his fault, or mine. See, Annabel was our entire world. It didn't matter to us that many people, including our families, disapproved of a legacy and a human getting married. We were just a happy family until..." Lillian's eyes water. She smooths her jacket, clearing her throat. "There was an accident. We were on the way home one night from Annabel's first bridging ceremony. Edgar was driving carefully, but a semi-truck T-boned the back of our car at an intersection and—"

Lillian cuts off and looks away, exhaling shakily and tucking a wild curl back into her braid. "She didn't survive the impact, and neither did our marriage. I was just too lost and heartbroken to function after losing her. I can't even describe how dark that time was for me. So, naturally, I wound up in the high temple of..."

"My mother," I guess.

The goddess of darkness and mourning.

"Yes. I found peace there and decided to stay, working as an attendant to the priests and priestesses. That's where I met your father."

Wait. "You knew Pietro Amato?"

Lillian nods, wiping away a stray tear. "The other attendants didn't know him by name, but they told me that on the same day each year for three years in a row, that man came to Syntyche's high temple to spend the entire day grieving. We were under strict rules to give mourners their space and never interrupt them, but...I saw myself in him. I recognized the kind of loss that can only come from losing a child, so I approached him."

She shakes her head at the memory. "I wanted to comfort

him, but your father comforted me instead. We talked about Annabel for a long time, and then we talked about you. Only after the other mourners had left and the temple workers were long gone did he confide in me who your mother was. He was clearly a man in pain, so I didn't tell him how crazy I thought he was. But after he left the temple, Galene appeared to me."

I narrow my eyes at the fire. "Let me guess. She was dressed head to toe in white, read your mind, and made a lot of obscure remarks to annoy the fuck out of you."

Lillian laughs softly. "She was disguising her face, yes. But there was nothing obscure about her instructions when she told me it was time for me to go watch over you."

I frown. "But if Syntyche is my mother and you worked at her temple, why was Galene the one who sent you to me?"

"I don't know all her reasons," she shrugs. "But she had me swear not to reveal your true nature to anyone, including you. She could see all the possible outcomes, including many futures where you figured out what you were too soon and died fighting Amadeus before you could fulfill..."

Lillian trails off, squirming uncomfortably.

And suddenly, I can't help recalling Del Mar's dying claim that my existence was orchestrated.

"Before I could fulfill the reason I was made," I finish out loud.

It rings true in the quiet. I wasn't just born—I was made with a purpose in mind.

As in...I was always going to be a means to an end. Before the Nether. Before Amadeus picked me to be his *telum.* Before I even existed.

It's a tough pill to swallow, realizing Syntyche must have had me with Amato out of necessity, thanks to Galene's visions. I'm just a result of the machinations of the gods.

A fucking cosmic Band-Aid.

"Maven," Lillian says softly, drawing my attention back to

her earnest expression. She clearly guesses where my head went. "Remember. You're a person, not a thing."

It sounds like an obvious statement, but it's the same thing she used to tell me after a hard day of conditioning in the Nether —whenever I'd spent hours in the necromancy lab, or dripping with sweat and blood in the arena, or even after I'd lost control, berserked, and woke up feeling like a stranger in this body.

I felt like an instrument of death. I felt like Dagon's masterpiece and Amadeus's scourge, just an object with one single purpose.

I feel that way again now, but I push that unhelpful emotion deep down to ask, "What was in it for you?"

Lillian pauses. "What?"

"Galene asked you to voluntarily go into the Nether, where you could have been killed while watching over me. Surely she offered you something in return if you agreed."

Her attention flits to the photograph on the small table, and she finally nods. "She told me I needed to redeem myself if I wanted to see Annabel again, in the Beyond."

"Redeem yourself? You're one of the kindest people I've ever known."

Sometimes to an obnoxious degree, but I won't hold her better qualities against her.

"The truth is, I made a lot of extremely poor decisions before I met Edgar. I was every kind of sinner you can think of, through and through. Lying, cheating, stealing, always putting myself first, running from the law, blaspheming against the gods—"

"*You* have a checkered past? I'm impressed. And honestly, a little proud."

She laughs, shaking her head. "I was a mess and didn't care to get better. I knew I would be in trouble once I got to the Beyond, and years later, after losing my innocent little Annabel, that thought haunted me constantly. So yes. Galene did promise me that in exchange for watching over you, my past would be dismissed, and I would immediately find peace in the Beyond with Annabel again."

Lillian looks at me very seriously, tearing up.

"But even if I didn't atone for my past, and even if I never get to see my daughter again…I regret nothing, Maven. I would have gone through every single day in the Nether with you all over again, because you became another daughter to me. The truth is, I needed you more than you needed me."

Damn it. Now *I'm* tearing up.

To stop the emotions threatening to get out of control, I quickly down the rest of my hot chocolate before grumbling, "Everyone keeps eulogizing me in the past tense. It's weird."

"We thought you were dead," she shrugs sadly, staring at the fire. "I knew you might have ascended to Paradise, but I couldn't give false hope to your quintet—and thanks to my agreement with Galene, I couldn't tell them the truth about you. I considered going to other strongholds to help other Nether humans adjust, but…I just couldn't leave your quintet. Dear gods on high, Maven, these poor boys have been breaking my heart."

I look at the door, hoping Everett returns quickly. Once again, I feel the bizarre heat in my chest where a heart should be.

"Do you have any idea where Crypt could be?" I ask quietly.

Lillian's face falls. "I'm sorry to say I don't. But…I also can't say I really met Crypt in any way that counts. He was completely checked out and rarely came out of Limbo in front of anyone except Everett. I also never met Baelfire. I've tried talking to Silas in fae sometimes, but he's not usually himself, and it's not always safe to visit."

Silas.

I need to see him. I want to see those ruby irises and that beautiful intensity that's all him—and I need to see for myself just how mad my blood fae necromancer has become. But I don't doubt that Everett will vehemently refuse to let me see my fae if he poses even the slightest risk. My elemental is exhausted enough as it is, so…

Tonight, I decide. I'll find a way to help Everett sleep tonight and track down Silas's prison.

Other gears begin to spin in my mind as Lillian and I sit quietly in front of the crackling fire, until finally I ask, "Do you have a paper and pencil I can borrow?"

Lillian smiles and gets up to rummage through one of her wardrobe drawers before bringing me a box of crayons and a writing pad.

When I make a face at the crayons, she laughs. "I missed the colors here almost as much as I missed you making your lists. You started making them when you were seven years old, you know. I've never met another seven-year-old who was so serious about setting priorities."

That's thanks to Amadeus's obsession with making sure his *telum* was educated enough for his liking. I made lists to keep track of the aggressive learning marks I was held to. I doubt most other seven-year-olds spent all their time focused on acing examinations with the threat of being fed to the Undead if they didn't pass.

Moving to the floor, I pull out the red crayon so that it will at least resemble blood as I write my list.

1. *Tame my dragon.*
2. *Hunt down Crypt.*
3. *Get a heart. (Create my own shadow heart again?)*
4. *Learn holy magic ~~even though it's probably useless, like everything else pertaining to the gods.~~*
5. *Find out what became of Bertram. If he's alive, change that slowly and painfully.*
6. *Rebond to my matches and break their stupid*

fucking curses once and for all so we can live happily ever—

I pause, my hand going to the spot where the haggard scar mars the center of my chest under my thick black sweater. What I want more than anything is a future with my quintet, but if Amadeus finds out I'm back—and I don't doubt that he will—there's no way we'll be left in peace.

But I fell from Paradise for a second chance with my men. No matter what I was initially created for, they're mine now, and I refuse to have anything less than a fulfilling, normal lifetime spent with them.

With that in mind, I add a final step to the bones of my master plan.

7. Kill Amadeus and anyone else who tries to harm us so we can finally rest in peace.

12

MAVEN

TWO THINGS ARE clear after scouring all but one of the handful of texts and scrolls that Everett's men brought from the makeshift temple.

The first thing is that I can apparently read the holy tongue of Paradise now. It's annoyingly rhymed, like the poem I'm currently trying to make sense of.

Wild spirits compiled in thee,
Nature's warrior mighty,
Sealed in slumber yet to bide,
'Til this putrid blight's defied.

Gibberish.

It goes on like that for nearly a thousand ancient pages.

The second thing that's become clear is that there is nothing remotely useful about learning holy magic in these books.

I shut this tome, glowering at the small pile on the bed beside me as the fading light of the setting sun finishes sinking outside the frosted-over floor-to-ceiling windows.

Everett chooses that moment to walk back into the bedroom

from his office. His attention remains briefly on a Reformist war map before he glances up. His pale blue gaze immediately softens, as it keeps doing whenever he focuses on me.

Which is sweet and everything, but this is the first time I've officially seen him wearing his reading glasses and *holy fuck,* that's so cute. He pulls off the adorably studious look just as well as the savage battle commander look.

At this point, I'm pretty damn sure Everett can pull off any look. It's not fair.

"Another miss?" he asks.

I look at the useless pile of holy books again. "These historians spent an inordinate amount of time spewing poetry, listing qualities desirable keepers should have, outlining thousands of ancient, nonsensical personal prophesies, and penning more gods-ass-kissing poetry. I would rather rinse my eyes with chimera venom than read another page."

My ornery rant makes Everett crack a smile for the first time since my return. It shows me he has just one dimple on his unscarred cheek.

Gods, that's adorable. In combination with the glasses? Fucking lethal.

He sets aside his map to join me on his bed, pulling me close. "If it didn't have your name under the descriptions of desirable keepers, that proves it's all bullshit anyway. Are you hungry? Cold?"

He's constantly worried about me being cold. I'm pretty sure the ten magically-fueled space heaters that have appeared in his professor's apartment over the last twelve hours came from him making extra requests to Reformist casters under his command.

After I visited Lillian, she went to the makeshift temples, so Everett and I have spent most of the day inside this room. He mentioned that Kenzie and Felix returned safely to Halfton last night. Since Asher Douglas has apparently kept his mouth shut about my return, we've been left entirely to ourselves as I spent the day studying.

Everett also described the Reformist movement and shielding spells more to me, explaining that they utilized the etherium pieces in which I trapped the Immortal Quintets' life forces. He also mentioned that one of those shielding spells went missing around the time the remainder of the Legacy Council vanished.

Hearing all about the dangers and violence plaguing the world and having Everett to myself has been nice.

Plus, it's endlessly fun to tease him.

Which is why I quickly straddle him on the bed before he sees it coming and lick his cheek where his scar is. He jolts, hands gripping my waist tightly as his breathing picks up. I begin trailing kisses down his neck, enjoying the cool feel of his skin against mine.

When I bite his earlobe, he groans, letting his hands slide up under the loose black sweater he loaned me this morning. His fingers brush ever so slightly over my nipples, and a shiver of delight rolls over me when that touch leaves frost behind.

Rolling my hips, I feel the erection quickly growing in his pants and grin wickedly.

"You're such a fucking tease," he whispers. "Bite me again."

"For someone raised in high society, it's a marvel that you don't have better manners," I hint, letting my fingers slip into his white-blond hair.

He roughly cups my tits. "Godsdamn it. Please."

I bite his neck this time, grinding against him as I do. My poor snow angel didn't sleep last night, and I've noticed his exhaustion and stress all day. I'll have to tire him out if I want him to sleep deeply tonight, and also so I can sneak out and find my blood fae.

Gods, I love my elemental's soft groans and how gentle he's trying to be, even while getting worked up. I'm still waiting on more memories from Paradise, but I'm positive that I ached for intimate moments like this in the months I spent missing my quintet.

My match swears and flings his reading glasses aside. He

begins to slip the sweater off me, but we both pause when someone knocks on the front door of his office.

Everett is deliciously flushed as he meets my eye with a dark look. "From this exact moment on, if anyone interrupts me while I'm trying to adore you, I'll put an icicle through their eyeball."

I kiss him.

It's not like I can help it when this scarred angel says such romantic things.

The person outside knocks again, and I pull back with a sigh. I'm about to tell Everett that we should get rid of whoever it is so we can get back to business uninterrupted, but he's already sliding between my thighs, peppering kisses along my stomach on the way down my body. As soon as he moves my panties aside and his mouth is on me, I forget how to protest.

Several minutes later, while I'm panting and flushed from Everett's talented tongue, the person knocks again, far more urgently. When I startle, drawn out of my pleasured haze, my still-clothed elemental swears with impressive creativity and storms out of the room to see who keeps trying to interrupt.

Wrapping myself in a thick blanket to ward off the chill that still clings to this place despite the many space heaters, I stand beside the door leading into the bedroom, listening in as Everett throws the front door open and snarls, "*What?*"

I don't recognize the voice, but they sound terrified. "C—commander! Forgive me, it seems like you were just…um, I'm s—so sorry. It's only that this message was urgent, so I thought it would be better to tell you right now instead of—"

"Spit it out before I put you in a courtyard," Everett warns.

I don't understand that threat, but the Reformist makes an embarrassing squeaking sound before clearing his throat.

"Yes, sir. W—We've received an urgent scrying brand message from Commander Decimus indicating that the feral dragon may not be in the north anymore. They tried to contain him, but—well, sir, they've lost him again."

Lost him?

If Baelfire's dragon isn't corralled and protected, he'll be a target. His uncle, the last feral dragon on the loose, was hunted and killed for his scales. What if that happens to Baelfire?

All the nauseating possibilities make me move forward, stepping out into Everett's office without thinking. I'm about to demand where he was seen last so I can hunt down my dragon, but the legacy in the doorway jolts when he spots me. His eyes widen to a ridiculous degree, and something uncomfortably close to idolization crosses his face.

"H—holy...great gods above! You're Maven Oak—"

Ice erupts around him, freezing him solid in less than a second with his mouth still hanging open. Everett shuts the office door without a second thought.

"No one can see you yet. This is the easiest way to keep mouths shut," he mutters as an explanation.

He's not wrong.

Still, that Reformist may have had more information about where Baelfire could have gone.

"Send someone to track him," I blurt, trying not to picture people hunting my mate.

Everett notices my stress and smooths his cool hands over my arms, kissing my forehead.

"This has happened before, a few times. The dragon sometimes disappears into caves and goes missing for a day or two as it sleeps, but it inevitably pops up again to burn something down and be a giant scaly pain in my ass, as usual. The Decimuses are very good at tracking down their feral youngest. Give it a day or two, and we'll know where he is again. I promise."

He's being reasonable, but something deep inside me is still unsettled.

I'm seeing Silas tonight, and tomorrow, Everett will just have to accept that we're going out searching for Baelfire. Then I'll find Crypt, whether fate likes it or not, no matter what plane of existence he's in.

But in the meantime, I need to make sure my poor elemental gets the rest he obviously hasn't been getting. So I nod, take his hand, and lead him back into his bedroom.

13

SILAS

EVERY DAY and night is a new hell as confusing as the last, but at least I'm coherent right now.

As coherent as I ever am, anyway.

So shamefully weak, my father's voice growls. *This cage is your own making. You should just leave.*

He's too weak to leave now! another voice echoes. *He needs blood.*

He needs death, another argues.

Yes! more voices giggle. *Death for the weakling.*

The voices have only multiplied—but as always, the worst voice is like an iron needle through the center of my forehead.

My handsome lunatic, my keeper's voice whispers. *They're right. You're too weak. You were an idiot to think you ever could have saved me.*

"I tried," I mutter to the absence around me.

Not enough. Even with trying to sacrifice your magic for me, you were never going to be enough. I deserved better than you. You should have accepted my rejection, but now look what became of our quintet. Our fates are your fault.

My head rolls from side to side as I lie trapped in the iron chamber, confusion pounding through my skull. I try to blink away the blurriness to observe the dark room around me, but it's no use. The iron shackles have weakened me for months, just as I intended. When I am more myself, I can get out of this coffin-like chamber and move about the barren, rune-etched room—but physically and metaphorically, the shackles stay on.

Something clangs nearby. It's the same sound I hear whenever the blond, curly-haired human arrives to check on me. Or when that oversized, tattooed leprechaun comes here with orders to force-feed me through magic.

I wish the big oaf would stop that. It's merely prolonging the misery.

Yes! Let the misery end! a voice screams at full volume inside my head, making me wince.

"Shh," I tell it.

Darkness tinges the edges of my blurry vision as the voices grow louder. As usual, I black out for an indeterminable period of time, but when I open my eyes, I notice someone has lit a few candles inside my prison to ward off the darkness.

And then I hear *her* again, somewhere off to the side.

"If I didn't know better, I would think you're a masochist for doing this to yourself."

I love and loathe that voice. It's been nothing but cruel to me for as long as I've been in this hell, but it would be far crueler if it ever left my mind.

Even now, you can't let me go, her voice hisses in my head. *I reject you, Silas Crane. Leave my memory alone.*

"Is there room for me in that…whatever that is?" she asks.

"Leave me alone to rot," I slur in half-English, half-fae as the ringing in my ears increases in volume.

"Riamh sa'vita so, no gach ni vivit leanas," that voice replies smoothly.

Meaning, *Never in this life, nor any lives that follow.*

It's such beautifully spoken fae, but I know it's coming from my head just like everything else. I'm momentarily distracted by a madness that seems to submerge the world around me. Everything is warped and false, twisting inside my brain to torment me.

This is all your imagination, voices say. *We can help you, weakling.*

You only deserve one kind of escape, my handsome lunatic, my keeper's voice agrees. *The permanent kind.*

The only thing I know to be true in this hell is that none of it is. Then again, sometimes I forget to remember that truth, just like I forget myself and all I've ever been.

Letting myself forget would be easier. Fading like my sanity would be a simple thing.

Let go, my father's voice agrees. *All you've ever been good at is failing, after all.*

"As if you know. You only knew me as a child," I defend myself in garbled fae.

That irresistible voice says something nearby me, but it's drowned out as someone in my head snarls, *Who cares about your past? This is the time to escape. Break free while you still can, before this one hurts you.*

This invader is here to kill you! another hisses. *Use her to fuel your death magic, and you can end this.*

"If only I could threaten the voices in your head," her voice sighs nearby.

My breathing grows labored as horrifying paranoia skitters across my chest like a large arachnid, its needle-like legs leaving body-wracking shivers in their wake. My head continues to throb, so I try to bang it against the iron frame I lie upon, but remember the blond human put a pillow behind my head to stop me from doing just that.

"I think I know how to snap you out of it."

Death, the same voice agrees as an echo in my skull.

Snap out of it! She's about to kill you! Fight!

"Fighting is pointless," I drawl before realizing I used all the wrong words.

But then a familiarly breathtaking scent implodes the space around me.

My lungs constrict violently through the vicious burn of thirst in my throat. The voices in my head break into choruses of screams, the ringing in my ears intensifying as I instinctively struggle against my rattling iron chains. My fangs have descended on their own as blind need takes over.

That blood.

I know the scent of that blood.

I can't fucking think clearly enough to figure out where I've tasted it before, but I need it. Crave it. Desperately.

This scent is a lie, like everything else. I've had fits of insanity with daydreams exactly like this—but never has it felt so real. Never has my body reacted so viscerally.

When the scent of blood draws closer and something warm drips on my cheek just beside my mouth, I struggle against my chains once again, trying to lick at it.

"Closer," I rasp in fae as anguished thirst consumes me.

And finally, glorious blood drips into my mouth.

Holy gods above.

This flavor—the sheer power of the intoxicatingly singular magic gracing my tongue—sends my entire system into frenzied need unlike anything I've experienced.

I need more. Now.

Use your magic! my father shouts in my head.

Use this power and free yourself! other voices chant, drowning out my every thought until—

Magic explodes from my bound hands, breaking the shackles on my wrists and ankles. The fact that everything is blurred around me doesn't stop me from rolling out of what's left of the iron enclosure to tackle the source of this searing need.

My fangs puncture through a warm neck, immediately finding the carotid artery as the shrieking inside my head increases. I ignore the voices and drink heavily, squeezing my eyes shut and moaning at the flavor.

It's fucking *divine*. So much stronger than I remember, though I still can't pinpoint where I've had this delicacy before.

I want more. All of it.

I release this artery and drag my lips to a new place, biting down hard to get more of what I want. Again and again.

There's a sharp inhale.

"So greedy," a voice whispers in fae, laughing breathlessly.

How strange. It's *her* laugh. But her voice hasn't laughed in my head in this hell, not even once.

And now she's...humming a song. A very off-tune fae lullaby. It tugs at a memory, drawing me out of the damnable haze of madness that's trying to suffocate me as I draw deeply again from this perfect neck.

It's a lie! the voices in my head shriek defiantly. *The* telum *is dead! Kill her before she kills you!*

All the voices are panicking. But why are they so afraid of this daydream?

I'm too far gone to reason out the answer as I move to bite somewhere else, reveling in the flavor that renders me incapable of thought.

A hand brushes through my curls, and I realize I can make out softly labored breathing beneath me. I would know the rhythm of that breathing anywhere, mad or not.

"Silas. I doubt I'll revive from expiring anymore, and Everett would never forgive my stupidity if I die like this. That's enough. Let me go."

As the fog of insanity inside my brain begins to thin slightly, a sudden realization sets in, hard and fast. I'm drinking blood. Her blood.

I could never imagine a taste this all-consuming and potent, so it must be real. This isn't another one of my mad daydreams.

Gods above.

I immediately release her and scramble away, licking residual heaven from my lips as I blink through the frantic confusion and see her face in the dim light of the candles.

Maven.

She's covered in blood and my bite marks.

Somehow, she's *alive.*

And I hurt her. Again.

No, no, no, no—

Kill her! the voices scream. *End your pain! Free yourself once and for all!*

"Shut up!" I snap at them, my head reeling.

Dark insanity rises from somewhere deep inside me, trying to drag me away from this moment and back to the oblivion of my broken mind. For the first time in months, I fight it for all I'm worth, ripping at my hair as I stare in shock at my impossibly alive keeper.

"Thanafluir?" I whisper.

Maven's gaze turns to amusement as she cups a hand around her bleeding neck.

"Death blossom?" she translates. "For once, a nickname I don't mind."

I didn't mean to call her that. I can't speak clearly, much less detangle the mad thoughts feeding off one another inside my head. She's here in front of me, the taste of her blood igniting every cell within my body, yet…I don't understand.

She died. Her soul was reaped. I saw it all.

She's meant to be dead, someone snarls inside my skull. *She is worthless to us. Get rid of her.*

The demons in my head have always despised Maven, knowing she would end them along with my curse. That should have been my first clue that she is truly here with me, but I missed it, and now she's bleeding everywhere. I scramble back until I encounter the stone wall of this enclosure as dangerous hunger continues to hum through my system.

I'm out of control. Treacherous. My keeper shouldn't be in here alone with me.

Let her be alone with you. You have the power to destroy her now, my father's voice insists. *End her before she uses the scythe!*

My attention drops to the ground beside her and I realize that surely enough, to feed me her blood, she cut her hand with a fucking scythe.

And I've seen this scythe before. The tip is clear etherium, the snath decorated in runes. It belongs to the goddess of reaping, who used it to collect souls right before my eyes months ago. Just the memory of Syntyche is enough to have fear curdling my gut, but–

Wait.

I look back at Maven, who brought that scythe into this prison and has mysteriously returned. Though living again, she emanates a tantalizing aura of death as she approaches me with determination in her hauntingly beautiful eyes.

Despite the ravaged terrain of my mind, things begin to click together. The overwhelming flavor of sheer power in Maven's blood that is unlike any other magic I've tasted. Her ability to survive things that the other mortal children taken into the Nether could not. And when my old mentor saw her for the first time—

I didn't believe that eccentric wizard when long ago, he told me that he sees the face of Death herself almost nightly as she comes to observe his possible demise during the worst hours of his curse.

The fact that he so easily recognized my keeper can only mean…

Maven must understand what I'm trying to puzzle out, because she quirks an adorably uncomfortable smile.

"Do me a favor and don't treat me any differently."

My gods.

I'm face to face with Syntyche's daughter.

No! What chance have we against a demigoddess? This is too cruel, too cruel! the voices in my head hiss and swear, livid about this realization as my surroundings spin.

Throughout known history, demigods and demigoddesses have rarely appeared thanks to the nature of the gods and their inability to conceive easily with mortals. My keeper's origin is miraculous, but I'm far too fractured for this life-changing realization to sink in fully.

"You shouldn't be alone in here with me," I rasp, unable to stop my gaze from slipping back to the delicious red color dripping down her throat. "Keep your distance, *sangfluir*. My mind can't be trusted with you."

She ignores me. Of course, she does. My stubborn keeper's very existence seems formulated to aggravate me, yet I can't stop the exhale of relief that escapes me when she comes close enough to touch the scarred place on my wrist caused by my shackles.

Her attention is clinical as she examines me. I can only imagine what she sees. I know Everett makes that bounty hunter magically feed and clean me now and then, and Lillian tries to help me on my better days, but whenever I'm not simmering in lunacy, I black out.

Sometimes I wake up covered in my own blood. Other times, I find I've etched dark runes into the floor or walls of this room. The entire place is proof of my disjointed mania, so I'm sure I must look only more wretched.

But if Maven is bothered by my unhinged appearance, it doesn't stop her from kissing me.

It's quick. Soft. More a reminder of her affection than a true kiss.

And still, it melts something inside me. I pull her against me, desperate to have her close. The scent of her blood all around us makes mine boil, and suddenly, I realize how much she's lost.

She needs healing.

No. Let her bleed out. It is the swiftest way of dealing with this bitch, a voice in my head growls.

I'm about to snap at the voices, but metal creaks sharply just before the entire door into my self-imposed prison is broken down. Blood magic flares to life in my fingertips as I prepare to protect Maven, but ice crackles across the ground at lightning speed, encapsulating much of this prison in thick ice as Everett steps into the room.

The utterly furious brutality on his face is surprising.

So is his scar. I thought I was imagining that, the few times I've been able to make out his face when he came to visit me in my isolated hell.

"A scarred Frost. Now I've seen everything," I manage.

Judging by the ice covering the door, he dropped the temperature of the metal to make it brittle enough to kick it down himself. That's an impressive level of power to display on a whim. Was he always this strong, or am I just imagining this, too?

"What the hell are you waiting for?" Everett seethes, storming into the room with frost swirling behind his every step. "You're the one who nearly ripped her neck open—*heal her.*"

Yes! Use magic. We know just the spell she deserves, the voices in my head titter as darkness seeps into the edges of my vision.

Realizing my internal tormentors are just under the surface of my mind, I quickly disengage from Maven despite her protest. Stumbling to my feet, I put distance between us as my heart pounds painfully. She gets up, too, but I don't miss the slight sway in her legs.

I took too much.

"I can't," I rasp, swallowing down the shameful bile trying to crawl up my throat. "My casting can't be trusted right now."

In my current condition, if I try to heal Maven, I'll end up killing her instead.

Think of the suffering you've gone through because of her. Do you really want more of that? Killing her now would grant you peace, a voice in my head tries to reason.

Everett moves to our keeper's side, gently removing her hand from her neck to see the damage before he shoots me a surprisingly intimidating glare. Maven lets him fuss over her, but her dark eyes are fixed firmly on me.

"Ground artemesian blossoms and a blood amulet."

I can't tell if her words don't make sense or if it's just my insanity keeping me from understanding again, but one glance at Everett tells me he's just as confused.

"Snowdrop, what are you—"

"Is this the most present he's been in months?" she checks.

We both nod, but I immediately prop myself up against a wall as the world spins. I could swear that dark, snake-like vines are slithering across the stone floor toward me, but since Maven and Everett aren't reacting to the ominous tendrils, I decide it's another trick of my frayed mind.

I can't tell reality from the demons in my head.

"My blood helps him." Maven looks back at me, and *gods above,* I've missed her face. She's so viciously determined, it puts my stomach in delirious knots. "An amulet can be made with my blood and blessed with holy magic for extra strength. Artemisian blossoms can be spelled to help ward off evil spirits. It might help soothe the voices until I can figure out how to fix things."

Fix things?

I want to ask what she means by that, but Maven speaks again, cold and angry.

"You're too weak right now. If I can't strengthen you, you're useless to me. You'll end up getting me killed, or hurting me yourself. *Again.*"

Pain cuts through me at the reminder of my shortcomings, making my voice a violent rasp as I lean against the wall.

"I swear I won't hurt you," I insist miserably. "I'll make myself useful this time."

My keeper frowns at me in confusion before sad understanding crosses her face. "Silas, I didn't say anything about you hurting me. Whatever you just heard, it was in your head."

Damn it.

I was certain it was her truly speaking, but before I can apologize, I'm deafened by the shrieking and wailing of voices inside my head. Their cacophony of fury sends me to my knees before I black out, swept back under the inky asphyxiation of my curse.

What feels like moments later, I blink my eyes open and find myself lying on the bed in the corner of my prison, which is lit dimly by candles to ward off the freezing night. The absence of the iron shackles around my wrists and ankles is bizarre until I catch the enticing scent of Maven's blood still lingering in the room.

It wasn't in my head. She's back—no longer in this room, but I'll find her.

To end her, my father's voice suggests excitedly.

"No," I snarl. "To protect her. I don't care if I have to crack open my fucking skull to rip you out—if she's back, she deserves every godsdamned effort I can make for her safety. So long as she allows me in her presence, I will find a way."

"There's no one else in here, man," someone grunts.

It's the giant leprechaun, voices in my head inform me.

I realize the giant leprechaun—no, the redheaded bounty hunter is in here, magically repairing the door Everett broke. It takes me a moment of blurry confusion before I can pick his name out of the veritable alphabet soup that is my brain.

"Douglas."

He stops repairing the door long enough to appraise me. "You're actually in your own head for once. Not bad."

The fact that recognizing someone I was once hunted by warrants that reaction is just proof of how pathetically far I've fallen. I sit up, focusing on him and pretending there isn't a monstrously large blob of psychedelic goo dripping from the ceiling overhead.

Once again, if he isn't reacting to it, it's obviously all in my mind.

"I need spell supplies," I tell him, managing to pick out the correct English words in the correct order this time.

He nods his chin at a brown-paper-wrapped parcel near the new door, which I didn't see because of the dim lighting.

"Already brought it. Also, your freaky-ass keeper handed me a bowl of blood before Frost hauled her out of here. Turns out I'm supposed to make it into a couple of strong blood amulets for you, but did she explain that *before* handing me her zombie blood? Nope. I swear, it's like she enjoys being disturbing."

For the first time in gods know how long, my lips twitch. "She does."

I've bitterly missed her streak of sadistic amusement. I've missed all of her so much I can't put it into words, but knowing that I didn't imagine her return or her delectable blood has my heart pounding.

Six months and still so smitten? That she-monster will be the death of you, a voice in my head huffs.

Free yourself! Run from her! That fucking Undead bitch—

"Don't call her that ever again," I snap in fae, swatting at what I'm certain is a winged imp beside me, but it turns out to be another figment of my mad mind.

Douglas stares at me, mutters something about needing a raise, and picks up the spell ingredients. But just as he's handing me the wrapped parcel, some unpleasant sound begins blaring outside this cell.

I realize it's not in my head when Douglas swears, his eyes glowing slightly green. He pulls back one coat sleeve to reveal a scrying brand on his forearm. The focused frown on his face is evidence that he's magically communicating with someone.

They're colluding against you, my father's voice warns in my head. *He's receiving an order to kill you. And why shouldn't he? As a necromancer, you're no longer allowed in the mortal realm.*

That's true. All this time, my prison has helped to protect me whilst protecting others from me. But now that Maven wants me to get out of here, perhaps other people have decided my death would be better.

Perhaps Douglas is about to carry out an assassination order.

I have no bleeding crystal, but magic still begins to hum at my fingertips, eager to unleash my strongest defenses as the strange alarms get louder.

Instead of attacking me, the bounty hunter lets loose a string of curses, scrubbing his face before pointing a finger at me.

"Sit here, play with your spell ingredients, and don't walk out that door until I have time to come back and fix it. It's the only thing protecting everyone from your crazy ass."

I narrow my eyes, still suspicious. "What's going on?"

"I don't speak whatever the fuck that was," he mutters, walking to the door.

Damn it. I spoke in befuddled fae again. I try for English once more. This time, Douglas understands, pausing with one foot out the door to look back at me.

"Urgent message from one of my men. We're under attack. Looks like I get to deal with another one of you Oakley quintet assholes tonight. Lucky me."

Leprechauns are *particularly lucky,* the voices in my head agree as he slams the door on his way out.

14

MAVEN

EVERETT CARRIES me down the cold corridor while verbally tearing me a new asshole for sneaking out on him and being so reckless. It's such a severe degree of scolding that I'm actually starting to feel almost chastened until a magical alarm begins to wail somewhere outside the castle.

Everett halts. "Shit."

That must mean this stronghold is under attack. I'm already itching to grab the etherium knife from its concealed pocket at my side to make sure no one comes close to hurting my elemental.

"Put me down. If there's a fight, I can—"

"If you think I'm letting you anywhere *near* a fight after the shit you just pulled, you're more psychotic than Silas," he snaps. "You're staying in my apartment until this attack blows over."

I want to remind him that he has approximately zero control over my autonomy and I'll fight whenever I fucking feel like it.

But for once, I don't feel like it, because Silas took a *lot* of my blood.

I've been trying to hide how weak and woozy I am, but I'd honestly be screwed if I entered combat in this state. Between the lightheadedness, my untrained holy magic, and the fact that I don't want anyone else to know I'm back yet…

"Fine," I huff.

Everett is still seething under his breath about my actions until we reach his professor's apartment. As soon as I'm safely inside the office, he sets me on my feet, kisses me deeply, and then spins me to face opposite him before delivering a firm smack to my ass.

My mouth pops open at the unexpected impact. I can't tell if I liked it or if I should pin him to the floor until he apologizes.

Before I can decide, my livid, scarred elemental snaps, "If you step a single fucking toe outside this apartment's protective wards while I'm gone, I swear I will hunt you down, freeze you up to your neck, and lock you away to keep you from getting yourself killed—*again.*"

At that, he slams the office door behind him on the way to deal with whatever shit is going on.

I can't help the grin that spreads over my face.

Gods, my snow angel is sexy when he's so worked up.

I still hear the muffled alarms as I fight through waves of dizziness to search the apartment. Luckily, some standard bandages and ointment are stashed in one of Everett's semi-frozen desk drawers next to other random odds and ends.

I'm just finishing bandaging the last bite mark near my clavicle when I hear the roar. It's somewhere just outside the castle and completely unmistakable. I heard that very same beast's distinctive, spine-tingling roar on my first day at Everbound.

Baelfire.

No wonder the alarms are going off. My dragon really did leave the north. Why did he fly here, though? Was he running from more hunters, or…

I touch the grooves his teeth left on my neck once again as my pulse starts to pound. Feral or not, my intuition is screaming that my mate knows I'm back.

He came here for me.

But I'm in no shape to deal with a massive, flying, fire-breathing beast. Especially because I've heard the stories about shifters going feral and accidentally slaughtering their mates out of some twisted form of mindlessly violent, animalistic obsession.

If I could just get him to shift back to his human form—

Before I can even think about the best way of forcing him to shift back, the stone castle shudders slightly around me. The ceiling creaks as dust falls in small plumes from above me. This time, when the dragon roars, it's deafening…and directly above Everett's apartment.

Fuck.

Claws scrape against stone. My attention snaps to the floor-to-ceiling windows in the bedroom just in time to see a golden, slitted draconic eye appear. My pulse misfires when the dragon spots me, its pupil dilating.

But I can sense that this isn't Baelfire looking at me. This is a feral animal that's found its prey.

Another roar shakes this apartment as a fresh slew of blood-less dizziness makes me sway on my feet. Maybe the protective wards will be enough to keep this glorious beast from—

The dragon swivels its head and opens its mouth, baring long, razor-sharp teeth as a glow lights up below the scales of its throat. I barely have time to dive toward the office's front door before dragon fire blasts through the glass in the bedroom like molten royal blue death. Stone explodes, and wards shatter behind me as I throw open the office door. I take off down the corridor, chased by blazing heat and the ferocious snarl of my feral mate.

Magical sirens and shouts echo into this hall from elsewhere in the castle. A group of armed Reformists rounds the corner up ahead of me, led by Everett, who shouts in alarm when he sees me.

My ears are still ringing from the last roar as this hallway trembles under the weight of the beast crawling atop it. I hear the deafening boom of more castle collapsing as the dragon finally breaks into this stronghold, falling into the hallway behind me and sending me stumbling. Stone dust and soot cloud the air as I race toward the troop of terrified Reformists.

Before I can tell them to get down or run, I slam into a scaly, clawed, reptilian hand that knocks the oxygen from my lungs. I'm being dragged backward. Everett's cry of horror is drowned out by another eardrum-bursting draconic roar just before my entire world flips upside down.

I'm suddenly caged tightly inside the dragon's warm, clawed hand. The moment I'm in its clutches, Baelfire's dragon snarls and launches away from Everbound Castle, propelling us into the sky with brutal beats of its massive, magnificent wings.

My stomach is left behind, along with an echo of Everett screaming my name.

Shit, shit, shit, shit—

I can barely move in this tight, scaly grip as the dragon picks up speed, climbing higher into the freezing night sky at a breathtaking rate before flattening its wings into a steep, downward glide. Cold wind bites through my skin, sending my blood-lacking, weakened body into further shock until my vision threatens to cave.

But I can't lose consciousness now. There's no way I'm leaving my survival odds up to this feral beast, which is already practically crushing me in its hand. I can barely see through the scales encompassing me, but I realize it's dipping low over the top of Everbound Forest, close enough that its back legs skim the tops of dead trees.

If I die this way, I'll find a way back to Paradise to haunt you assholes, I mentally warn the gods before struggling to get the etherium knife out of my pocket. Gripping it tightly, I jam it between two scales of the dragon's hand.

Hot blood gushes from the wound when I rip the knife away. A snarl of pain rips through the night air, but it does what I want.

It lets go of me.

I immediately crash through treetops that barely help break the fall, and then the air is knocked out of me again when I land at exactly the wrong angle.

Crack.

Shit.

Covering my mouth, I try to muffle the sound that tries to escape as angry warmth flares down my left arm. If I had to take a wild guess, that was my humerus snapping, and it fucking *hurts*.

Weakness and unconsciousness pool at the edges of my vision as I struggle to breathe in despite the brutal cold burning my throat. Snow is clustered all around me in this dark, foreboding forest, but after a long, grueling moment, I finally manage to sit up and use my good arm to pack some of the snow around my broken bone to help numb the pain and slow the swelling.

The dragon roars somewhere above the forest. I go still when I hear trees breaking and a loud thump in the distance. The shrieks of harpies echo through the woods before cutting off with a flash of blue fire that I can just barely make out from here.

But the universe must be showing me mercy, because I'm downwind from Baelfire's dragon and its heightened sense of smell and hearing.

As silently as I can, I cradle my broken arm against my chest, grab my knife from where it fell, and shuffle backward until I'm supported by the trunk of a twisted, barren tree. I listen carefully for other threats here besides the beast hunting me. Tuning out the pain in my arm and the weakness weighing down my limbs, I try to devise a plan.

But I can't get around the hope welling in my chest. My dragon knew where to find me. It knew to come to Everbound.

It wouldn't know any of that if it didn't have access to Baelfire's memories, right?

He has to still be in there.

I need to find a way to get through to Baelfire and pull him to the surface. I refuse to believe this beast has replaced him completely. When I defended myself against Kenzie, my holy magic forced her to shift. Could I do that with him?

Maybe. If I don't get roasted first.

And if my body doesn't shut down from the cold.

And if some other monster in these woods doesn't chow down on me.

And if—

The healthy stream of pessimism in my head is interrupted by the low croak of a raven. I realize several have gathered around me in the dimness of these frigid woods lit only by a quarter-waned moon. The largest of them hops up to perch directly on the shoulder of my unbroken arm.

I'm about to shoo the chicken of death away, irked that these things have been following me. Then I pause, recalling something I read while studying fae scrolls in the Nether years ago, before a particularly brutal examination meant to prepare me to enter the mortal realm one day.

Of all fowls of the mortal sky, most fateful are ravens, those dark heralds of prophecy. Ill omens they are, carrying upon their midnight wings the souls of those to be harvested by she who reaps.

She who reaps.

Syntyche.

If any of that was true, and if I inherited abilities, then these birds are following me for a reason. Holding my breath for one moment, I listen to the cracking and groaning of trees in the distance as the giant golden dragon prowls through the woods in the wrong direction. It hisses and rumbles, clicking now and then in a strange reptilian way.

I whisper to the big raven on my shoulder, low enough that the dragon won't catch it. "Lead my elemental to me."

The raven immediately takes flight, winging toward the castle.

If Everett shows up, I'll know I'm on to something with my

demigoddess abilities. Until then, it's just me and my shifter in these haunting woods surrounded by deadly dangers.

Normally, that would make for a fantastic date, but the throbbing in my head and arm remind me that he's feral and a hundred percent capable of killing me right now. When a roar cuts through the woods again, I take advantage of the sound and rise slowly, slinking from tree to tree as I baby my broken arm.

I trained for years to have the light-footed stealth of a seasoned assassin, but I'm struggling. Sweat beads on my brow, and tuning out my broken bone is getting difficult. Shivers wrack my body as my hands and feet burn from the cold.

And then the wind changes, carrying my scent in exactly the wrong direction. Baelfire's dragon roars immediately, and I hear trees breaking as it charges after me.

"Fuck you, too, Pheli," I mutter at the god of the wind.

Thunder rumbles in the wintry night sky. I can only assume it's laughter, so I flip it off.

Turning to face the oncoming beast, I brace myself. The knife in my good hand elongates into scythe form just as the dragon crashes through the last cluster of twisted trees, all gleaming scales and golden magnificence.

The dragon's snarl is muffled thanks to the dead manticore clamped between its jaws. Flinging the limp creature aside, the dragon stalks forward slowly, golden eyes trained on me. Smoke rises from its nostrils, its tail slithers from side to side, and its teeth are bared in warning.

"Such a deadly beast. I've missed my dragon," I tell it.

And I mean it. I'll confess to loving Baelfire and his dragon—but not this feral version of it. This isn't him. It isn't even reacting to my words as its mad, slitted gaze follows my every move.

When I take one step back, the beast growls and snorts a burst of royal blue fire into the air in warning.

Everything is swaying around me, but I stare up at the dragon. "I want Baelfire."

It makes that strange clicking sound in its throat again, its wings unfolding as if to look more intimidating as it stalks me.

"I know he's still in there."

It's a bluff. I don't know for sure—not when this monster is hunting me like I'm its next dinner, and there isn't even the tiniest spark of understanding in its eyes. But if Baelfire still exists anywhere in that draconic head, I'll find a way to get through to him. I need him to fight for me the way I'm fighting for him.

"Baelfire," I whisper. "I need my mate."

There's nothing. The dragon's head lowers as it gets closer, its tail curling around to trap me. The second it gets close, I swing my scythe with my good arm and quickly find that the etherium easily cuts through the dragon's scales.

That tiny nick angers the beast. Its long neck and head snakes forward until it roars right in my face, so loud and brutal that my vision wavers and my ears ring in protest.

Ugh. Dragon breath is a real thing, and it's fucking horrible. Like slow-roasted rotting decay, smoke, and sulfur.

But its show of inhuman, animalistic anger pisses me off, bringing fury to the surface so quickly I almost choke on it. If this beast really took over completely and destroyed anything left of my mate—

No.

No.

Standing my ground, I meet the dragon's ferocious display with my own, shouting at full volume with all the desperate anger boiling inside my scarred chest.

"Give him back!"

The beast snarls and tries to snap at me, but I move quicker, slashing my scythe across its snout. It roars furiously, tail whipping harshly—and effectively tripping me.

I slam into the cold, hard ground, the scythe falling out of my hands. More pain ricochets up my broken arm beneath me, making me cry out. The dragon snarls as the glow of fire rises beneath the scales of its long throat, preparing to turn me into a charred skeleton.

On blind instinct, I reach out with my good arm. Adrenaline and desperation mix in my blood as I touch the scaly tail beside me, and then a surge of blazing power courses through me. It's the same sensation I experienced with Kenzie, uncontrollable and fierce as strange magic flows freely from my fingertips.

The fire dies in the dragon's throat. It roars in pain instead, spasming from just my touch before falling to the ground to writhe. Unfortunately, all the thrashing sends its tail flicking into me one last time, knocking me back into a snowdrift.

I'm buried momentarily in sheer cold, unable to breathe as exhaustion from whatever the fuck I just did with holy magic kicks in. Finally, I work my way partially out of the snow drift to cough and grimace in pain, brushing snow out of my face with my good arm to blink blearily at the dim, sinister forest in front of me.

Already, the dragon has shrunk down into—

Baelfire.

I would recognize that naked, golden-tan, muscular body anywhere, but right now it's collapsed on the forest floor, unmoving.

Distantly, I hear ravens cawing loudly as they approach. Ice crackles up the trunks of the nearest trees as snow starts to swirl through the air despite no clouds overhead.

I ignore all of that as I drag myself out of the snow to Baelfire's side, dropping beside him. He's in horrible condition. I'm trembling with the urge to touch his warm, smooth skin, check him for harm, and see his contagious smile.

"Bael?" I whisper, hope clogging my throat.

But when his head turns, that hope hardens and sinks into my stomach.

His eyes are still the slitted, amber eyes of a dragon. There's no recognition there as he hisses and snaps at my fingers, barely missing them.

This isn't my mate. It's still the feral thing that's replaced him.

"Maven!" Everett shouts somewhere nearby.

A second later, he comes to a sharp stop at my side. For a moment, he stares in shock at Baelfire in human form. It's not hard to gather that this is a first since I "died" six months ago.

The large raven I gave the order to flutters over and settles on my shoulder, pecking almost playfully at my torn sweatshirt. In the cold moonlight, I catch a flash of loathing on Everett's scarred face before he lifts his hand toward the raven to freeze it.

"Don't," I tell him. "I sent it to get you."

He goes still. "You..." Then he looks at the raven again, looking unexpectedly sick to his stomach. "You mean...you're the reason for all the ravens? And the whole time, I—gods, I've been..."

I'll talk to him later about my apparent connection to ravens. I barely have time to swerve away when Not-Baelfire tries to bite me again. That snaps Everett out of his miniature existential crisis, and he promptly freezes the shifter from the neck down.

Not-Baelfire snarls and hisses, saliva dripping from his mouth as he gnashes his teeth and struggles uselessly against the ice. When it's clear he's not making progress, he makes a strange coughing sound deep in his throat before breathing pure blue fire into the air, nearly singeing Everett's soot-streaked coat.

"Fucking asshole," the elemental mutters.

But he can't fool me. There's more sadness than malice in his voice.

Seeing my mate like this is making me doubt. Maybe I'm too late. Maybe he really has been replaced by this beast. I needed to return sooner to rescue Baelfire from becoming this, and I don't even know why I was held up in Paradise for *six fucking months.* If I had just—

"Stop," Everett says gently, crouching and cradling my face so I'll look at him. He appears as exhausted as I feel, but his pale gaze is earnest. "We'll get him back, Snowdrop. We'll get all of them back."

I breathe out shakily, straightening my shoulders. He's right. Panicking is a waste of time, and I'm too fucking exhausted to spiral further.

"How is the stronghold after the attack?" I ask.

"They're still putting out the fires, but the worst of the damage happened when he took you. Obviously, we won't be staying in my old professor's apartment anymore. We'll stay in our quintet's apartment."

I hesitate. "People saw me."

"Anyone who saw you was frozen when the dragon took you. By accident," he tacks on, but it's clearly an afterthought.

"Did Douglas survive?" I grimace as I shift my broken arm slightly.

Everett's attention zips to my injury. He swears and glares murderously down at Not-Baelfire. "Yeah, he's alive. I'm taking you back to be healed as soon as fucking possible. Then I'll come back for Baelfire."

"We're not leaving him like this."

"The hell we aren't. This feral asshole just tried to kill you."

I gesture with my good arm at the ice encapsulating him. "Might as well leave a sign on him that says *Free Shifter Popsicle* for the monsters craving a midnight snack."

My ice elemental groans and rubs the unscarred half of his gorgeous face. "Okay. I'll unfreeze his legs and freeze his mouth. You'll need to help me drag him through these creepy woods. But so fucking help me, if something attacks us and you get any more injured, I'll—"

"Freeze me from the neck down and lock me up," I repeat his earlier threat as I get to my feet. "Fair enough. But we need to figure out how to keep him from shifting back. I don't know what I did to him, but it may not last."

Everett glances at Not-Baelfire with a sigh. "I know how we'll keep him from shifting, but you won't like it."

15

CRYPT

There's no escape.

Only, caught in this moonlit, lust-drenched memory once again, escape is the last thing on my mind.

My tongue traces up the side of Maven's neck as she rolls her hips again, mercilessly riding me toward that brink of perfect pleasure as her divinely wet cunt squeezes my pierced cock. Her breathless sounds compounded with the groans of the others as they watch make for a sinful symphony.

We're all frenzied with need for her, thanks to the show Frost put on, preparing her. He'd spared no effort eating her out, toying and teasing until, for the first time, I got to see my keeper drench the sheets of this Sanctuary abode.

Frost hadn't lasted through that sensual performance, which was lucky because now Decimus and I get to worship my dark darling together.

On cue, just before I can reach that tantalizing peak, Decimus pulls Maven from my arms and into his lap. Thrusting up into her, he captures her mouth with his so he gets to taste the beautiful moan that elicits.

I will never tire of the sight of my keeper like this. Flushed and overwhelmed, her dark hair tossed over her back as her sinuous, smooth, olive-toned body moves like pure poetry. Her euphoric expression leaves me breathless as I watch her chase her release, clinging to Decimus as we all adore the view.

They fall together over that brink of pleasure, but I'm not done with her.

Maven gasps when I immediately pull her away, rolling and pinning her to the bed before plunging my aching cock back into her wet warmth. Somewhere nearby, Frost swears brokenly and Crane mutters something under his breath, but I'm too far gone to take note of it.

I'm so fucking desperate for her.

Desperate to have my emblem on her—to be bound.

This powerful, beautiful, *stunning* woman is going to be my muse if it's the last godsdamned thing I do. She swears, her fingertips dragging down my back as I fuck her like I'm dying.

But then again, I am.

Yet these moments of unadulterated obsession embed themselves inside me so deeply that no matter what becomes of me, there is no going back. And as her pleasure rises again, I bite down on my own tongue to try to fend off my release, tasting blood but needing to give her everything I can.

I wanted to give her everything I could of myself, right until the end.

The fact that my obsession drew her last breath before I did is an agonizing realization that seeps into this memory, pounding at my skull.

In this cycle, even the beautiful moments have become brutal.

Finally, Maven's gasp of pleasure graces my ears before I feel her clench around me—and I'm lost. I shout, burying my face into her neck as the pleasure crests, and at long last, I'm left holding her close.

"Gods," Maven laughs breathlessly, kissing my jaw.

I kiss her before rolling off, watching with lingering desire as Frost moves on the bed to kiss her next, brushing hair out of her face.

"I'll help you shower," he offers, voice thick.

Our keeper peeks over to where Crane is watching with lust-filled eyes. "Silas will. He's thirsty," she adds with a grin.

That's the blood fae's final straw before he scoops Maven up from the bed and marches her into the bathroom. Water starts, but we all hear another one of her delicious gasps as Crane does something wicked to her.

"Dear gods, those sounds she makes are going to kill me," Frost groans, dropping onto the bed.

He never bothered undressing fully, but Decimus is naked as the day he was born as he sighs happily, folding his arms behind his head. "Don't get my hopes up, Professor Popsicle."

"Fuck you, lizard."

"Hell yeah, she did," Decimus grins. "And now the sweet scent of her pussy will send me off to the best sleep of my fucking life."

Frost begins to protest that the shifter will be sleeping on the floor because he's far too large to fit on this bed with everyone else, but all my attention moves to the pain that blossoms throughout my body. My markings light up as a pull in my gut tells me there's trouble in Limbo.

I can't tend to it. I can only endure it.

There's no escape.

The memories change again, taunting and tormenting me as I relive everything over again. My desolate childhood. The empty years leading up to the moment I saw her on that stage. And finally, the darkness that consumed me after Maven took her final breath.

When she was gone, I craved even the barest shadow of her.

But I loathed reminders.

And so, when I came across one of Syntyche's temples while hunting a fleeing necromancer, bitterness made its way through the walls I'd put up.

She was going to be my muse.

Now that she was gone, the temple where we would have gone for the ritual mocked me.

Weeks of mayhem followed as I infused temples with mania, watched the holy workers turn on each other, and observed worshippers melt into madness. I ended anyone who tried to go to the now-desecrated temples until finally, everyone stopped trying.

Punishing the gods for taking my darling keeper away became my highest priority—

Until *she* found me.

Death herself.

Obscured in darkness and wielding a scythe while unspeakable fear emanated from her very being, Syntyche found me in Arati's temple. There was no escaping the goddess of dreams by slipping into the dream realm, nor was there escape from her wrath to be found anywhere else.

The agony of another memory begins again, my own subconsciousness suffocating me as this unending punishment goes on.

There will never be an escape.

But in this torture, my keeper exists. Even numbed and buried in the weight of my own broken existence, I cannot resist even the cruelest memories of her.

16

MAVEN

IT TURNS out the collar Del Mar put on Baelfire to prevent him from shifting wasn't the only one he brought to Everbound months ago.

Asher Douglas heals my broken arm and bite marks, but Everett doesn't notice the caster is using holy magic, since he's busy trying to throw a blanket over Baelfire's nakedness. He has to re-freeze the dragon shifter when Not-Baelfire immediately tries to burn his face off.

"His ass is still out," Asher points out.

Everett mutters something about shifters being naked idiots before he glances at the mercenary. "Get a message to Commander Decimus. Let her know the feral dragon has been found and contained here. Tell her I'll update her if necessary if she has follow-up questions."

Once Douglas leaves Hearst's old headmaster's office, Everett shows me the other enchanted collars in one of the desk drawers. All I can think about is how humiliating it was for Baelfire to wear one in public like a common animal.

He's sexy as fuck wearing a collar for me in the bedroom, but the idea of putting it on him right now, when he's not himself and he is *actually* like a mindless animal makes my stomach churn.

"It's either this or keeping him frozen. Unless you have a better idea," Everett says quietly, slumping into the chair beside the headmaster's desk.

We're both exhausted. The entire castle smells like smoke. It was difficult to sneak into the frozen-over headmaster's office without any Reformists seeing me while they were cleaning up the aftermath of the dragon attack.

Baelfire is now frozen from the neck down, ice sealing his mouth shut to keep him from spewing more fire. His eyes are still draconic slits gleaming with primitive insanity.

If he shifts back, he'll be a bigger target again. Hunters may still be looking for him.

Keeping him in this form gives me a better chance to get through to him.

I grab one of the leather collars and study it. I don't see runes, but since we couldn't remove it the last time he wore one until I used revenant magic to destroy it, I suspect it has the age-old *monomei* locking charm on it. That charm is simple but ironclad and makes it so that only the one who locks an inanimate object can unlock it.

Meaning, unless we find another revenant wielding unlimited destructive magic, only I will be able to remove this collar once it's on him.

"Unfreeze his neck," I mutter.

Once it's clasped firmly but not too tightly around Baelfire's throat, Everett and I lead my feral shifter to a spare apartment in the western wing. It's tedious to drag the resisting mass of muscle there, and even more tedious to fireproof the stone room. Everett finally melts the ice encapsulating my mate after we lock him in for the night.

After several more minutes of sneaking through the castle to avoid anyone else seeing me, we make it to our old quintet apartment, since Everett's rooms were ruined.

As we step inside, I stare at the quarters I shared with my quintet. Gods, it feels like forever since I was here. The last time I saw it was just before my quintet and I went on the run.

Before we were all bonded together and then promptly ripped apart.

Knowing my immaculately tidy match, I should probably step into the shower before touching anything. But when I step toward the bathroom in one of the hallways, Everett scowls, scoops me up, and takes me into the bedroom with the quintet-sized bed. He lays me gently on the sheets, adjusting the pillow under my head.

I only have time to remove my etherium knife from my hidden pocket, so it's clutched in my hand instead of digging into my side before I drop into merciful unconsciousness.

Nightmares tease at the peripheries of my deeply exhausted rest until a sudden current washes over me, dragging me back into another Paradisiacal memory.

Syntyche stands before me. Or…maybe she hovers. Her movements are so fluid that I'm not sure if she walks underneath the shadowy cloak obscuring much of her, which makes me question her considerable height.

The goddess wears no expression, but her scythe is propped up on her shoulder as she observes me with pitch black irises. It's still odd to realize I'm nearly a copy of her, minus her unnaturally pale skin and other minor differences.

Apparently, she's just as atrocious at small talk as I am, because it's a long time before either of us says anything.

"No matter what Arati says, I'm not staying in Paradise," Memory Me finally blurts.

"So you've mentioned."

"I have a plan."

Observing this memory once again, I realize that my plan is to annoy the hell out of the gods until they tell me the way to return to the mortal world for good. They're set on me staying, which is a big no. I'm currently compiling a long list of ideas to irritate them in my head.

Syntyche says nothing. A few more moments tick by.

It's official. We're the worst at conversing.

"My sister is inordinately proud of her golden armor," the goddess muses suddenly. "It was a gift from our brother before he left the pantheon and took up permanent residence in the Beyond."

I stare at her, confused.

"If something were to happen to that armor, it would invite Arati's considerable temper. Finding where she keeps it should be an easy task for you."

She's clearly guessed that I plan to annoy the gods, but…

"You're helping me?" I ask.

"You're surprised."

"More like skeptical. Let's not pretend like you've done me any favors in the past."

Syntyche considers that, twisting her scythe to examine the etherium blade. "Gods cannot see into the Nether, so I did not observe you grow up. You needed no coddling by the time you emerged into the mortal world, but perhaps my aid could benefit you now. Beginning with inciting the wrath of my sister to learn the one way to expunge your soul from this plane of existence so that you may fall from Paradise and reunite with the clingy male mortals you are so partial to."

She summed that up nicely.

I squint at her. "Is this what they call…mother-daughter bonding?"

"Let us call it anything but that."

"Then we're on the same page." I pause. "Can't you just tell me how to return?"

"Only one immortal being has ever successfully become mortal to live in the mortal realm, eons ago. Arati helped him learn a way to mortality, but she guards that secret carefully. Convincing her will be difficult."

Difficult has never stopped me before, and it means nothing to me now that my quintet is on the line. I look out over a seemingly endless sea of clouds, my scarred, emblem-less chest aching.

"Galene hinted that there may be a way I can watch over the mortal realm from here. A way to see my quintet."

"It is possible, depending on what gifts you inherited from me."

I look at her, determined. "Tell me."

The memory shifts and changes, and for a moment, I can't understand what I'm looking at. It's a view of gliding over a grayscale landscape high above. Wintry wind batters me on one side.

After several moments, I realize I'm seeing the world through the point of view of a bird.

Not just any bird. A raven.

The raven finally perches on a ruined temple in an abandoned, sprawling city. The massive temple is overwhelmingly ornate and magnificent, with fire symbols worked elegantly into the architecture now encrusted with ice.

This is unmistakably one of Arati's temples, but like the rest of the city, it's sapped of color and abandoned.

At first, I can't tell why the raven is showing me this. Then it slips through a broken window near flying buttresses and hops forward to peek down into the temple. It's dark and empty—except for a leather-jacket-clad figure lying motionless at the foot of the altar.

Crypt.

With the raven's sharp vision, I can make out concentric circles of intricate dark runes circling my Nightmare Prince. Layers and layers of magic have entangled him in a brutal malediction as he lies still, his eyes shut as his chest rises and falls slightly.

It's almost like he's sleeping.

But he can't sleep.

The memory is fading along with this precious glimpse of my incubus. Before it disappears completely, the echo of my own furious voice returns to me.

"What did you do to him?"

"Far less than he deserved," Syntyche's cold tone replies in a multifaceted echo. *"We gods have laws by which we must abide. Destroying holy things must breed consequences. Would you rather I let my sister, the goddess of vengeance, dole out the steward's punishments? She would have done far worse. If his mind survives and if he doesn't starve, consider this another favor."*

My eyes flash open. I bolt upright, my empty chest burning again. Everett is right behind me, jolting out of sleep and immediately dropping the temperature of this room several degrees as he pulls me close.

"What is it? Are you hurt? Is it a wraith?" he asks, eyes flicking to every dark place in the room despite the morning light trickling through the quintet bedroom windows.

I shake my head, releasing the handle of my etherium dagger when I realize I'm squeezing it so tightly my knuckles are white.

"I know where Crypt is," I breathe.

Everett bundles blankets around me as he frowns. At least it looks like he slept a little last night. "How?"

I explain that portion of my returned memories to him—how I could somehow watch them through ravens while I was in Paradise, and how Crypt is under a malediction in one of Arati's temples in a colorless city.

He listens to all of it before nodding slowly. "Give me an hour."

"I don't want to leave Silas and Baelfire behind," I add.

Everett nods again. "That's why I'll need an hour, to sort out a few things before we all go. With the recent attack, I want more

Reformists watching the stronghold while we're gone, since Asher Douglas will have to transport us. Give me an hour and we'll go."

Gods, I love this elemental.

Nearly twenty minutes later, Lillian hands me a bag packed with random supplies and food as I wait with Everett and Not-Baelfire in the western library, which is lit warmly by a raging hearth.

Lillian glances at the frenzied animal occupying Baelfire's body. He's in his collar, and I added a leash in case he tries to get away. He's currently perched on top of the big front desk, dressed only in a pair of shorts that Everett and I managed to wrangle him into, although we both ended up with a couple of bites and scratches.

He growls at her, but she turns back to me with a smile. "All your matches are so handsome."

"Ridiculously so," I agree. "He's actually a charismatic social butterfly whenever he's not feral. You'll love him once…"

Once it's him again. If he's still in there at all.

Lillian can see my doubt and offers a reassuring smile. "I can't wait to meet all of your matches officially. It will happen, little raven."

I never realized how fitting her nickname for me was until now. But then, she's known my true identity all along. With everything going on, I haven't had the chance to spend much time with her—which is frustrating, because I've missed her for what feels like forever.

"A chess game," I blurt. "We should find time for a chess game, once we're back."

We used to play so much chess together. She's the only person I've ever played the game with.

Lillian lights up. "I would love that. I look forward to winning once you have your quintet back and things have settled down."

I grin at her subtle trash talk before the door into the western library opens. Asher Douglas joins us, adjusting his excessive amount of winter clothes.

"Nothing like strolling through your collection of frozen people right before breakfast, Frost. Ruins my appetite every time."

What's this now?

I look at Everett, who won't meet my eye as he repeatedly adjusts one of his sleeves. "You have a collection?"

"Haven't seen them?" Douglas grunts. "It's like dozens of upright tombs of ice. Fucking creepy."

"I want to see," I declare, morbid fascination leading me out the door Douglas just walked through and into the nearest courtyard.

Everett keeps up with me, looking around quickly to make sure no Reformists are in this area of the castle. "It was just a few people who annoyed me."

A few? I stare at the rows of immaculately frozen people, monsters, and ravens gleaming in the cold sunlight. Small piles of powdery snow have gathered atop the unmoving displays.

My gaze lands on a frozen winged, tailed incubus nearby. When a shiver of familiar apprehension rolls over my spine, I raise my eyebrows.

"Are they all…alive?"

Everett nods, looking like he doesn't want to talk about this. "Most of them deserved it. Some of them will be kept like this until they can stand trial, once a judicial government of some kind is formed again. Others are just…decorations. Until I decide otherwise."

How cruel.

When he sees me smirking at him, he sighs. "I know, it's really fucking creepy."

He says that like it's a bad thing. I stroll through some statues before noticing a corner of this courtyard is filled with misshapen frozen spheres.

"What's over there?"

Everett adjusts his coat sleeve a few times, grimacing. "Crypt's contributions from before he went missing."

I walk closer and pause when I realize they're all…heads. Disembodied heads, dropped carelessly to the cobblestones and left to freeze, including the skull of the lich who scarred Everett during battle.

As in, the one I told Crypt to bring to me. He didn't let that go.

Aww.

"Of course, you're smiling," Everett sighs.

"From where I'm standing—namely, in the living frozen collection of anyone who even mildly pissed you off while I was gone—you have no room to judge."

"She has a fair point," Silas's voice agrees from behind us.

My pulse spikes. I turn, a smile breaking across my face when I see my blood fae necromancer dressed in a sharp winter coat and an amulet made from my blood peeking out from under a red scarf.

He's been cleaned up, but he's still not okay. I don't miss that his red eyes flick between all the frozen figures before he takes a step back. He flinches and swats at something that doesn't exist before trying to focus on me again. The dark circles under his eyes and his more prominent cheekbones and thinner build remind me that he's been slightly emaciated thanks to his self-imprisonment.

Still, he's finally outside. Progress is fucking progress. I'll take it.

"Is the amulet helping?" I check.

"I would not have chance threat left wrong you." Silas's words slur at the end. He flinches before trying again, except fae creeps in. When I still can't figure out what he's trying to say, he takes a centering breath and finally manages, "If I felt I was a significant threat to you, I would have stayed away longer."

"Third time's the charm," Everett grumbles.

Here we go.

These legacies love being assholes to each other, as if they haven't gone to extra lengths to help each other in secret in the past. They annoy the hell out of each other to disguise how much they care.

Silas gives the elemental a withering once-over. "Is it safe for you to stand so close to Maven, or will you freeze her like you have everything else?"

"It's safe," I cut in decisively, getting ahead of more bickering.

Luckily, Asher Douglas picks that moment to join us in the courtyard. He says something quietly to Everett, who is testy about leaving my side, but goes off to ensure everything will run smoothly when we leave the stronghold.

I've been aching to see Silas again. I step toward my fae, wanting to be closer and smell the spiced bourbon scent always lingering on him.

But he takes a step back, swatting at nothing again as his blood red irises remain trained on me. "Only trust me as far as you can throw me, *thanafluir.*"

Again, he's calling me Death Blossom. I don't think he realizes he's doing it.

Not that I mind that nickname.

"Considering the permanent alterations my body went through to become stronger and faster, that's still pretty far," I remind him, trying to lighten the mood.

He's not amused as he studies me. "I know your parentage, but where were y—I said *stop fucking calling her that,*" he suddenly snaps, gripping the side of his head and clenching his teeth.

Godsdamn it. I hate seeing him so…

Insane.

Checking to make sure we're still alone, I move closer so he can lean on me slightly.

"This is my fault," I murmur.

He shakes his head like he's trying to clear it. "No. It was not your fault. *Tha fios anima aih'leat, thanafluir."*

Meaning, *My soul knows yours, Death Blossom.*

Then he reaches down to tip my head back until I can see the feral, murderous gleam in his blood-red gaze. "I know you did not leave willingly, so tell me who took you from us."

Right.

Bertram.

Considering that he was working for Amadeus, I haven't spared that vampire much thought. My so-called "father" has the brutal but efficient habit of permanently killing off anyone he no longer finds useful, unless he decides to make them Undead instead. I'm a prime example of both those preferences.

Still, I should see if I can learn what happened to Bertram. If he's dead, I'll spit on his grave. If he's alive, I'll have the honor of spitting on him *before* I bury him for being the one to put the final nail in my coffin six months ago.

I focus on Silas again. "That's not our priority. Right now, our priority is getting Crypt back."

He pauses, eyes growing glassy as he tries to think through whatever riot is chipping away inside his head. "Crypt…Crypt. He appeared in my prison. While I was mad. He was asking whether I could *dèanamh alta facere sum…"*

'Make extra high?' I can't understand his fae.

"Try again," I suggest gently.

Silas groans. "I hate fucking."

I barely manage to keep a straight face. I'm pretty sure that's the only lie he's accidentally ever told. "You mean, you fucking hate this?"

"Yes. That one." He sighs and concentrates harder. "Crypt brought me a strand of your hair and asked for a tracking spell on…something. It was…"

He cuts off to snap at the voices in his head again, tearing at his hair as his breathing picks up.

I consider what he said. Many tracking spells call for DNA,

so that doesn't help much. But why was he trying to track me when I was already dead?

"*Pìos ostentaoth,*" Silas blurts.

I don't translate quickly enough. "What?"

"Something on display. A part of you."

On display like—

Oh, gods. My heart sits on Amadeus's mantle in his chambers within the citadel. Fuck, I forgot I told Crypt about that. If he was trying to track that down…

I need a heart, but going to Amadeus's citadel to get that one back for any reason would be insane.

"Where were you, *ima sangfluir?*" Silas murmurs, and I realize he's been studying me while I've been thinking. He reaches up to touch the blood amulet around his neck, as if that helps him maintain coherency. "Your body vanished as revenants do when their purpose is fulfilled and they pass to the Beyond. No one returns from the Beyond, yet you're here. Aren't you?" he checks with a genuine frown.

"I went to Paradise," I explain simply. "And then I came back. I'm here, and I'm staying."

Silas absorbs that before suddenly flinching to one side as if avoiding a blow. He swears and rubs his face. "Forgive me. I see things. No, I wasn't talking to *you*. Shut up."

He's talking to the voices in his head again as Everett strides back into the courtyard. My elemental slows his approach, taking in Silas's obvious bout of insanity before he sighs and looks at me.

"Are you sure you want to bring them? It might be dangerous where we're going."

He's right. I know that. Silas and Baelfire's conditions are rough to see, but gods, I *just* got them back. The thought of going somewhere where I won't be able to check in on them easily is an immediate no. I just can't.

"Good thing we're all dangerous, then," I reply.

Everett accepts my answer with a simple nod before he

turns to face the courtyard, rolling his shoulders back. He concentrates, lifting his hands before the ice surrounding the couple hundred frozen ravens in the courtyard cracks or melts away.

Some of the ravens begin crowing and freaking out as they wing quickly away. Others slump dead out of the ice, and a few flutter over to me, tipping their heads as they check in on me with their beady black eyes.

"There. You have your spies back," Everett mutters, shooing one of them away from him before fixing me with a serious look. "But if any of them shit on me, they're dead."

When one of the braver ravens flutters to land on my shoulder, Silas squints at it. "Is there a raven on your shoulder, or is that in my head?"

"It's real."

"How do I know if you're you?"

I can see that he's starting to slip again, but his question is fair. Reaching up, I brush his jaw with my fingertips and hold his blood-red gaze.

"You'll know I'm me because nothing will stop me from keeping you. Not even the tricks in your head. Whenever you're not sure, just ask and I'll remind you that...*tha galeath."*

I love you.

I expect saying it to be awkward, but it's surprisingly *right.*

Silas's pupils dilate as he lets out a breath. "You, saying that...this is in my head."

"Nach," I shake my head. *"Tha galeath."*

"Which means?" Everett prompts with a frown, looking between us.

Silas ignores him completely as his voice drops to the barest whisper. *"Tha ba'galeath thu semprah."*

I have and will always love you.

Despite the madness plaguing him, this moment feels pure as we stare at each other. It's a lifeline for him—a way that he can know this is real. And for me, it's what I wish I had told him before I fell on that battlefield months ago and left my ruthless necromancer to the hellscape of his own mind.

"Okay, that's it," Everett grumbles finally. "I'm learning fae."

"By all means, *scútráche,*" Silas replies without taking his eyes off me.

"Hey!" Douglas calls from the archway leading back into the castle, tapping a nonexistent watch on his massive, puffy green coat. "How about you gaze into each other's soulless eyes later? Your pet dragon is wrecking the library and we don't have all day, so let's get a fucking move on."

Silas frowns past me at the bounty hunter before looking at Everett. "You hired him? Why?"

"He's loud but useful. He's also right, this time. Come on, let's go get Maven's unhinged freak."

Gods, I can't wait.

Whatever Syntyche did to him, I'm getting my Nightmare Prince back.

17

SILAS

THE VOICES ARE INCREDIBLY unhelpful as we navigate this cold, barren, grayscale city.

Watch out! Over there! they shriek.

I quickly check over my shoulder for the hundredth time. For the hundredth time, there is nothing but empty streets flurrying with snow and steeped in shadows, thanks to the thick clouds suspended over Manhattan. Ghosts drift past now and then, wandering as they search helplessly for their afterlives.

Aside from us, the only other living things here are the ravens watching us from various perches.

Something is coming for you, other voices whisper in my head. *We're just trying to help.*

We're here for you. We'll always *be here for you.*

They took you out here to kill you, you know, another giggles.

They never fucking shut up. Now they're chanting, laughing, singing, whispering—

"Weird," Maven muses, and I could weep with gratitude that her voice finally cuts through the menaces living in my head. "We're well behind enemy lines, but I don't sense fiends nearby."

"You can *sense* fiends?" Douglas asks from where he walks

behind me. "You know what—no, of course, you can. Why the hell am I even surprised anymore?"

Everett, Maven, and whatever remains of Baelfire are walking in front of me. Even smeared in dirt and grime with his dark blond hair far more unkempt than usual, Baelfire *looks* like the dragon shifter I've known all my life. He's even wearing only shorts despite the freezing temperatures, which is something Bael would do.

But instead of flirting with Maven or being annoyingly optimistic or anything else our dragon shifter would typically do, he's just taking in our surroundings. His lips pull back from his teeth on occasion, and his eyes remain the telling slits of the dragon that lurks beneath his skin. Now and then, he tries racing off like a stray mutt that's scented a cat, only to get yanked back by Everett so he won't get himself killed by the fiends lurking in this abandoned city.

The shifter is gone. Only the beast remains! the demons in my head cheer.

Baelfire and I didn't always agree, but the idea of him being utterly gone to his curse is...tragic. Aside from him being a necessary member of my quintet, I once started to trust the shifter. And other than Maven and myself, I've trusted so little in my lifetime that losing that possible future is unexpectedly depressing.

Trust is for fools, my father hisses in my head.

Trusting you is what led to my death, Maven agrees.

But no. That's not Maven. My true blood blossom walks in front of me, scanning this area carefully as we get closer to Arati's high temple.

She told me she loved me.

That was real.

This is real. I try to focus, carefully stepping over a multicolored snake before realizing it's not there. Still, the blood amulet and ground artemesian blossoms I carry in my pockets seem to be helping marginally.

Feeling even the slightest bit more sane is a relief. I want to be useful to my keeper. I can't be a psychotic burden to the woman I love.

Speaking of psychotic, we all stop in front of the abandoned temple wherein Maven has insisted Crypt will be found. The stairs leading up to the front doors are just as ornate as the rest of the exquisite temple of the queen of the gods.

I notice a few more skeletons nearby. There have been quite a few littering these streets.

"You'll be a skeleton soon," something hisses nearby. I almost stop to search for the source before realizing that, too, came from my broken mind.

We ascend the grand stairs leading up to Arati's even grander temple. When Everett steps forward and tries opening the massive front double-doors, they don't budge. No ice prevents their movement, so he finally steps back and glares at the entrance.

"I've always hated this fucking building," he mutters.

Ah, right. Thanks to his horrid parents, he once received a false translation of a personal prophecy in this place.

But it's interesting. He was always so mindful of the gods, yet here he is declaring his hatred on the Queen of Paradise's doorstep. That haggard scar marring half his face must not be only physical.

"Let me try," Maven says, stepping up to the doors and handing Everett Baelfire's leash.

We all watch as she places her hands against the doors and frowns. Moments pass with nothing, until she curses and looks over her shoulder at Douglas.

"Help me get these open."

"If it's spelled shut, I may be stable enough to offer a hand," I suggest, quietly desperate to serve a purpose for my beautiful keeper.

Her dark eyes connect with mine, and she shakes her head.

"I'll need your magic inside to get rid of the malediction. This door is different. Douglas knows what I mean."

The ex-bounty hunter huffs as he moves to her side. "Yeah, yeah. Keep your mouth shut."

I bristle with irritation at him speaking to her like that. Everett scowls, too, but steps aside as they focus on whatever magic is sealing this temple shut.

While we wait for them to figure out how to unseal the temple, I glance at Everett and then away. *"Tha'me a bhith air mo frirthadh."*

"I have no idea what you're trying to say," he reminds me.

Right. I pull the correct words from my messy mind. "You could have frozen me."

"I still can."

"I meant that it would have made the last *mohsan sia*—six months," I correct, "easier for you."

Everett brushes snow off his shoulder, fixes his coat, and again pulls on the feral Baelfire's leash to keep him from trying to wander off again.

"I considered it. Thing is, I don't know what being frozen long-term does to someone's brain."

I almost laugh at the absurdity of him trying to preserve a brain as senseless as mine has become. Still, with Maven miraculously reunited with us, I have a newfound appreciation for the lengths Everett went to keep me alive, fed, and comfortable despite my self-imposed imprisonment.

It takes work, especially since the voices in my head are counting backward in fae at different intervals to confuse me for fun, but I finally get it out.

"I owe you."

"Yeah, right," he scoffs. "I don't want a favor from a fae. Your kind are too crafty with shit like that. Just shut up and help break whatever spell Crypt is under."

Only a moment more passes before Maven and Douglas finish, and the great double doors swing open. With the concentration they both seemed to be displaying, I expect to feel a tingle or awareness of their lingering magic as we all walk into the dusty, abandoned temple—but I sense absolutely nothing.

Odd.

Of course, it's odd. This is a trap. This is where they take necromancers to be slaughtered.

They're all conspiring against you.

Look! Behind you!

I whirl again, trying to see any threat, but there is none. There is only the mindless, feral creature occupying Baelfire who snaps his teeth at me when he catches me looking before sneezing blue fire.

Cold morning light illuminates this space from massive windows high above, highlighting the fact that we are utterly alone here, except for Crypt DeLune. He's just as Maven described on the way here, trapped in various layers of a heinous-looking malediction.

I've never seen this incubus unconscious before.

Incubi need to feed far less than any other creature—they can survive for months, sometimes years, before they finally begin to starve. But the longer they go without consuming dreams, the weaker they become. If he's been trapped like this for months, this monster-spawn's strength has been wasting away. Weakening. Growing more vulnerable by the day.

Now would be the perfect time to end him, voices whisper in my head as we approach.

I stop outside the hostile runes encompassing the Nightmare Prince, studying the powerful, sinuous malediction he's trapped inside as the others stay back a few steps. This is truly a terrifying spell to behold, so strong that my hair is standing on end and I can practically taste the acridity of the death magic woven into it.

There's another magic in this, though. One I can't identify.

"Yuck. Have fun, Crane. That's one nasty malediction," Douglas says.

I hesitate, looking at Maven as thousands of glowing frogs appear and hop about this space. Since no one else sees or reacts to them, I pretend I don't see them, either.

"Your magic would be superior to mine here, given my condition. The destructive force of revenant magic could shatter this easily."

My keeper pulls an adorable face. "Too bad we're short a revenant."

I'm surprised. If she's no longer a revenant, what magic did she use at the doors to get in here?

Then it clicks in my murky mind. As a demigoddess, she has holy magic.

My attention slips to the bounty hunter, who's glaring at me. He can tell I'm guessing why he was helping her with the door.

Intriguing. Perhaps Asher Douglas is a saint. That might explain why he has no quintet despite being four years older than I am. I doubt saints typically become soldiers of fortune, but what do I know?

Turning back to Crypt, I again touch Maven's blood amulet around my neck for an additional dose of clear-mindedness. Whatever the state of her magic, she wants me to retrieve the incubus I once loathed from this wretched snare of masterly death magic, so I will.

Or I'll die trying.

Yes. Die here saving this scum like the fool you are, my father growls in my head. *This one was the death of me, so it is only right that he should bring your end, too.*

Ignoring the voices and bracing myself for what I might discover, I call blood magic to my fingertips and reach into the malediction swirling around the Nightmare Prince. At first touch, a flurry of familiar spells tingles across my skin, but foremost is a spell I studied at length many years ago, in the Sanctuary.

Dormiens mortem—the sleeping death.

As a cross between a suspension spell, prolonged death, and

the deepest stage of sleep, the sleeping death is a brutally potent spell that the rest of this malediction was crafted around. Undoing it will require entering the spell itself by stepping into the victim's dreams or memories to reach the heart of the spell.

The fortunate thing about *dormiens mortem* is that undoing the dozen other interwoven hexes will be less complicated than I expected.

The unfortunate thing is that less than half of the victims of the sleeping death wake from it without dying.

If I tell Maven exactly what malediction this is, she'll likely know that and worry more.

So I don't tell her. Instead, I shut my eyes and let my newly-revived blood magic take the lead, flooding into the sleeping death and taking my mad awareness with it—into the subconscious mind of Crypt DeLune.

18

SILAS

I IMMEDIATELY LEARN that Crypt's mind is not a pleasant place to be.

Whatever memory I just stumbled into, it's stained with blood, cigarette smoke, and a putrid stench I cannot even put a name to. I'm in a crumby apartment strewn with the bodies of several dead men. Some of them are gathered around a table, wads of cash still in hand as their lifeless eyes are left wide open wherever they appear to have been stabbed or slashed wide open.

This is not a memory. It is your future if you do not flee this twisted mind, a voice in my head hisses.

Run! Run! Run! the other demons chant.

Following another trail of bodies that appear to have ripped each other to pieces, I find myself leaving out a rear door and into a back parking lot area. Three teenage women are here, hugging one another as they sit on the asphalt and await police sirens quickly approaching.

Something compels me to look up. When I do, I spot DeLune.

He appears to be fourteen or fifteen in this memory as he sits covered in the blood of those vile men, smoking *reverium* on the rooftop of the building without a care in the world as he waits to see the rescued victims safely off. He seems unaware of the imps dancing on his head, but they may be only in my mind.

From all my readings, the trickiest part of dismantling *dormiens mortem* is locating the central memory on which the spell was placed. If I interact with versions of Crypt that are not from that central memory, I'll easily get turned around inside his mind and lose myself in the spell altogether.

My head starts to ring, and hissing whispers skitter up my spine as I walk away, venturing outside this memory and into the next. Trying to shake off the paranoia, I realize I'm now standing in front of a stately, well-maintained manor in what appears to be the English countryside. It's beautiful on the outside, but even from out here, I can hear Natalya Genovese shrieking.

Cautiously, I follow the horrible sound into the grand manor. When I come across a formal sitting room, I freeze.

What a sight, what a sight! mad voices in my head sing in an overlayed chorus.

A young version of Crypt is curled into the fetal position on the lush carpet, covering his head as the immortal vampyr throws a fit of epic proportions. She breaks furniture and screams and swears until Somnus DeLune enters the room beside Melvolin Hearst.

The Immortal Quintet monsters look precisely the same as ever, but I can't stop staring at this frightened version of Crypt. I didn't know him at this age. He can't be older than six. Although it's difficult to see the bruises through the swirling light and dark markings on his skin, I notice them gradually healing.

"What is it this time?" Hearst demands, checking his watch as if bored.

"This filthy little *mongrel!*" the hysterical vampyr wails. "Just look at him! More and more, elite legacies are growing curious and keep asking to meet this little bastard. Do you have any idea how humiliating it is that he even exists? What did I do to deserve this? Me, raising this pathetic mistake, all because you are a filthy fucking *degenerate!"*

She hurls a vase at Somnus with vampyr speed. He doesn't dodge it in time and curses when it breaks against his forehead, sending him stumbling. I find it odd that he doesn't trip over the glowing rabbits hopping around on the floor behind him, but again, that's likely something my mind is adding to this dark memory.

"Look what we're stuck with, all because of your wandering manhood!" Natalya scowls and paces before whirling, baring her fangs as her blue eyes glow. "We should have killed off the entire Crane bloodline for not taking up with our idea to pretend he was simply a surprise child of theirs. He looked like them enough—it would have worked. How dare those ingrates refuse to take this knave in!"

In her fit of temper, the vampyr turns and kicks Crypt in the side. I flinch, nausea curling up my throat when I hear a crack, but the young incubus barely reacts. He remains curled up as if he's been through this enough times to know this is the safest course of action.

But Natalya's words stick in my mad head, revolving over and over. The Immortal Quintet wanted my family to take in Crypt to cover Somnus's scandal? I never heard of this.

It would have changed everything. His childhood. Mine.

In this bizarre other scenario, perhaps we would have even become something like brothers.

I would never have allowed that inferior little scoundrel to corrupt you, my father's voice snarls inside my head.

Ringing floods my ears, and darkness threatens the edges of my vision. I quickly grasp Maven's blood amulet around my throat. It helps stave off the wave of lunacy until I can hear again.

"Of course, they wouldn't take him!" Somnus spits as his bleeding head begins to heal. His tail whips back and forth angrily as he gestures at Crypt. "Take another look at him, you blathering bitch. He's the *steward*. He's half monster and will grow to look more like me. Everyone would figure out the bastard sooner or later, so of course no one wants anything to do with him!"

Natalya hisses and picks up a picture frame, ready to throw that next, but Melvolin uses magic to flick it out of her hands, glowering at everyone in the room. "We'll be late for our meeting with the Legacy Council. Quit your whinging, Natalya, and let us leave."

The vampyr is still livid about whatever set her off, but she finally storms from the room. Somnus and Hearst are right behind her, leaving me to watch this young Crypt as he waits for several long moments before uncurling and sitting up.

His purple gaze moves to me, but he says nothing.

Look at that pathetic waste of life, someone snickers inside my head.

"Shut up," I mutter in fae at the nasty voice.

This isn't the version of Crypt I'm supposed to speak with. I know that, but gods above, this little boy looks hollow. Surely *someone* in his past was there for him in cruel moments like this?

I move on, but the more of Crypt's memories I pass through, the more my disgust with his upbringing grows. My own childhood was no luxury, but at least my paranoid parents were proud of me. At least the Garnet Wizard took a liking to me later on, in his own eccentric way.

Crypt had no one, until he had our quintet.

But then I stumble into a scene even darker than the last. It's not one of his own memories—this is a dream he's observed in the past. I can see Crypt as he is now, standing off to the side with a stricken expression as bloodcurdling screams cut through his subconscious.

Maven's screams.

My heart pounds as I realize this is one of her nightmares. My keeper is a teenager here, her wrists and ankles bound tightly to a rudimentary laboratory table as gray-draped necromancers surround her. They're chanting, performing some dark ritual on her as they jam dozens of glowing needles deeply into her skin.

What a lovely sound, demons in my head snicker.

My young keeper can't stop screaming from the agony of whatever they're putting her through. They pay her suffering no mind as they continue the experiment, as if she's just a *thing*.

Repulsion and encroaching insanity choke me as I quickly leave the scene, unable to bear the sound of Maven's pain anymore. More and more of Crypt's memories are becoming like this—torturous scenes of Maven's past, blips of his time hunting predators, hundreds of vague nightmares he's fed on over the years.

Finally, I come to a stop inside our quintet's old apartment at Everbound University. There is something more viscous about this memory. I must be getting closer to the version of Crypt I'm looking for.

He and Maven are sitting on the bed in her room as she tends to severe wounds on the incubus. This appears to be a private moment shared between them that I have no interest in eavesdropping on. I turn to walk to the next part of Crypt's subconscious, but halt when I catch Maven's words.

"I heard you also killed Silas's parents' keeper. And his uncle."

"Technically, they killed themselves. I only planted the seed in their minds. Constantly."

The same sharp, red-hot anger I've always felt when Crypt has made light of destroying my family twists in my gut. Voices titter in my head.

He killed us all out of vengeance. He was bitter because we wouldn't take him in.

You should leave him in this torture.

Selfish incubus! another snarls.

"You must have had a reason," Maven prompts in Crypt's memory.

The prick has the nerve to fucking *smile.* "Must I have?"

Of course, he is so cavalier about ravaging my childhood in one blow. How could I ever have felt sympathy for this sociopathic murderer? Madness seeps deeper into my skull, darkening my paranoid, irritated thoughts until I sway, ears ringing.

When the ringing fades, Crypt is already speaking again.

"—keeper of Silas's parents' quintet was a wolf shifter with a sickness. The kind of perverted sickness of the mind that I hunt down at every chance. He enjoyed taking advantage of children, especially the children of powerful legacy families."

...what?

He's lying, a voice snaps in my head. *You know how non-fae are, lying whenever they please. He knows nothing.*

You would have known this if it were true, another voice assures me.

I want to interrupt Maven and Crypt and insist that can't be true, but...the voices are wrong this time. Crypt can get inside people's heads through their dreams and psyches. He would have seen more inside the subconscious of my parents' keeper than I ever could have witnessed or guessed.

And what reason would he have to lie, in a private moment like this?

"...and when I was in his dreams, exploring his psyche to find the best ways to unravel him, I realized that he had his eye set on..." Crypt trails off, clearly reluctant.

Maven is undeterred. "Set on?"

"Decimus."

My keeper's shocked expression mirrors my own as, at long last, I finally hear Crypt explain *why* he killed my relatives. How he did it. How he has no regrets and only targeted the ones involved in revolting practices before the rest destroyed each other or themselves as a result.

The voices in my head are screeching in fervent denial, refusing his every candid word and making it difficult to focus.

But one thought floats out of reach of the tempestuous muck inside my brain: for once in my life, I understand Crypt.

Because had I known what he knew then, and had I been capable of protecting the others from something so wretched when we were all so young…

I understand.

I would have done what he did.

You're just as hopelessly wretched, a plate-sized spider whispers in agreement as it crawls past in this memory. Either that's a figment of my mind, or…no. I'm almost certain this one was real, this time.

"Crane would never believe me if I told him that," the Nightmare Prince finishes, drawing my attention again. "He's much more comfortable hating me for it, so I've never bothered explaining."

"If Baelfire was eight, you would have been…thirteen?" Maven checks.

"Something like that."

And I was nine.

Nine years old and completely unaware. After my parents' keeper killed himself, my parents' quintet kept a united front in public even as they splintered in private. My world inverted. Gone were the proud parents so focused on our family name and my potential future as a favorite of the Immortal Quintet. Instead, their curses slowly returned to center stage. My father went mad, my mother grew uncontrollably violent, and it escalated day by day until they slaughtered each other in front of me.

I blamed Crypt for all of it. I *loathed* him.

It was your right, voices in my head insist.

He killed us.

He deserves to suffer here. Don't you dare set the bastard free. He should rot in—

"You decided ignorance would be easier for me to bear," I finally say aloud, cutting off the voices in my head as I take a chance on this version of Crypt.

It pays off.

The rest of this memory fades like mist on a warm day, but the Nightmare Prince remains, becoming more solid. He's the version I'm here for.

But when his attention moves to me, I see the same inhuman emptiness on his face that I remember so well from our childhood.

I asked my parents about it once. My mother, a vampire, quietly explained that while it's not common with modern legacies whose more monstrous instincts are much more evolved, siphons can occasionally completely numb all "non-essential" emotions. She said it would be second nature for a half-monster like the DeLune bastard to choose his monster side, silencing whatever human sentiments he could otherwise be capable of.

At the time, I took it as further proof of his horrid qualities.

Now, it couldn't be more obvious that he's simply trying to dull the same agony I have felt for six seemingly endless months. We've all mourned Maven differently—but once again, I understand him.

Crypt considers me without care. "Here to kill me, Crane?"

Do it! Kill him! He's never been weaker! the voices screech in my head, so loudly that I cover one of my ears to see if that will help.

"*Nach*. No," I amend in English.

"Pity."

The memory-like landscape around us shifts until we're abruptly standing in the headmaster's office at Everbound. This is that godsforsaken image of Maven motionless on the ground with Pierce plunged through her heart.

When Crypt sees me flinch at the raw, cruel memory, he smirks in the most inhuman show of amusement.

"It gets worse each time. You'll know that soon enough since you're stuck here now. There's no escape."

I meet his eye. "On the contrary, I'm here to get you out."

Except I've lost focus, so it comes out jumbled and half Nether-tongue.

"Such articulate company to entertain me for an eternity in purgatory," he drawls, staring numbly down at our motionless keeper.

Maven.

Perhaps thinking of her will make him shake off his numbed siphon state.

"She's back," I say, picking the correct words as carefully as possible. "Maven. She's alive."

The incubus has no reaction as he continues to watch the horrible scene before us.

"I can't lie," I remind him.

"What use are lies when you're mad enough to believe anything?"

Determined to force him to feel *something*, I push harder.

"Maven is out there right now, waiting in Arati's temple for me to get you out. See this amulet around my neck? It's her blood keeping me this sane." He's still not reacting, so I throw in the revelation that I'm still trying to adjust to. "Our keeper is a demigoddess, Crypt. She's the daughter of Syntyche."

The name of that foreboding goddess finally makes him look at me. For a moment, I wonder if he's absorbing that truth as our surroundings shift again until we're watching Maven get swallowed by a harbinger during First Placement.

"Then you can thank our mother-in-law for what you're about to endure," he finally mutters.

I pause as I again consider the malediction I'm trying to unweave. Such succinct, dark, deathly power, interwoven with so many elements. Then there was the other, unidentifiable magic worked into this impressive beast of a spell.

Holy magic is untraceable, another large spider hisses in reminder before crawling up and over Crypt's chest before skittering away. The incubus doesn't notice it.

Calling blood magic to my fingertips, I try to interact with the indomitable spell around us. My magic reverberates back immediately, sending me stumbling. I try again. And again. Each time, my counter-spells skip off the malediction as we're kept locked within these horrid recollections.

My death magic is equally useless.

Godsdamn it.

Syntyche truly did weave this labyrinth specifically to torment Crypt. I'm not surprised that he managed to incur the wrath of the gods like this.

You'll die in here! the demons occupying my headspace cheer. *This is it.*

Some begin clapping and singing excitedly while I swat at another nonexistent imp.

"Curse it all. We *are* trapped," I grit, tugging my hands through my hair when the ringing in my ears intensifies.

"If only someone warned you. Oh, wait," he deadpans without any apparent concern.

"What the hell did you do to earn a punishment like this?" I demand, correcting one or two words that come out garbled.

"Just a small bit of harmless vandalism."

The scene changes again, and we're again in one of Crypt's childhood memories. I watch as he wanders through what must be Limbo as a teenager, cutting through glowing white creatures I've read about—wisps.

The wisps converge on him quickly like luminescent piranhas, tearing into his skin at an alarming rate until he's crying out in pain as he fights through the dream world he's beholden to.

The ringing in my ears magnifies as I take a deep breath. "You should have told me."

"About?"

"Everything."

Crypt looks at me with no expression as his past self starts to scream in earnest.

"Whatever you've seen in my head, Crane, ignore it. I'd tell you to forget it, but neither of us has that luxury here."

19

MAVEN

SENDING one insane match to rescue my other insane match wasn't my best idea.

"Another hour, gone," Douglas announces from his spot guarding the temple's closed and magically sealed double doors. "That makes two."

"Congratulations on your new ability to count," Everett snarks. "Next, learn how to read a room and shut your mouth."

He's standing with his arms wrapped around me as we watch Silas stuck in a dark trance where he sits beside Crypt's spellbound body. Baelfire is hunched over on a nearby pew, gnashing his teeth at everything and snarling like a feral animal. The fact that I haven't seen even a hint of the real Baelfire yet sets my teeth on edge.

It's getting harder to believe my charming, smiley mate is anywhere in there.

Meanwhile, every moment that passes while waiting for Silas is another moment I decide I can't wait.

I needed a caster to get Crypt out, but my options were so fucking limited. My brilliant blood fae is powerful, but his curse is eating his mind right now. That's probably why he's struggling with this malediction.

Asher Douglas might possess holy magic, but he's not nearly as strong a caster as Silas—not to mention if this spell is what I suspect it is, there's no way in hell I'm letting him near Crypt's vulnerable subconscious. He was set on killing my incubus six months ago. Even if he's earned Everett's trust, I'm not overlooking that anytime soon.

As far as other casters who can step up, that only leaves me. The bitch who has no idea how to use her magic anymore.

Still, I have to try. And to try, I need to fuel my abilities in the only way I've learned how.

"I'll be right back," I mutter, stepping out of Everett's arms.

He gently grasps my hand to stop me. "Where the hell do you think you're going? Out there, where the danger is?"

"Where the ghosts are," I correct.

On the short trek to the temple after Asher transported us to this colorless city, I saw several ghosts, though they haven't entered the temple's hallowed ground. If I collect enough of them, maybe I can make a dent in that malediction.

Everett blinks down at me, surprise written all over his gorgeous, scarred face. "You can see ghosts again?"

"Yes. I need to go reaping."

"Reaping?" Asher Douglas pipes from the doors where I forgot he was standing. He frowns over his shoulder at me. "There's only one reaper, so stop blaspheming. How the hell would you—oh, holy shit. Unless..."

The mercenary is starting to put things together. Everett gives him an impressively chilling death glare as a warning to stay quiet. I take advantage of his distraction to slip away again.

Striding through the incredibly ornate temple, I pull my etherium knife out of my boot. It immediately knows what's needed, transforming into my new favorite weapon as I push open the big double doors.

Wow.

I clearly won't have trouble finding enough ghosts.

Restless spirits have flocked to my presence, and now two or three hundred blurry, translucent figures hover at the foot of Arati's high temple, staring up at me. Everett moves beside me, perplexed as he looks out, seeing nothing. Meanwhile, Asher Douglas looks more disturbed by my existence than ever.

That's a nice thought before I descend the stairs, my elemental sticking closely to my side.

Ghosts converge on me immediately, pressing silently against each other in a rush to get to their respective afterlives. I step a safe distance away from Everett and swing my glowing scythe in a wide arc, sending that haunting whistling tune echoing through this dead concrete jungle as I reap several souls at a time.

The wash of peaceful power that flows steadily over my bones is strange.

But it's also *right,* somehow. Over and over, I reap, turning and twisting as I wield the scythe. This otherworldly dance is intrinsic to something in my very being.

Before long, my veins are buzzing with an exhilarating rush of this strange magic—and with that rush comes another current of memories that pass from my scythe to me.

I blink when I find myself once again standing with Syntyche, but the scenery is different. This time, we're standing on the shore of a stretch of water glittering like millions of liquid stars, watching as winged angels sitting in ornate boats fish for who fucking knows what with golden fishing lines.

"If I stayed, which I won't," Memory Me begins, studying the shimmering lake. "What would I even be the goddess of? Baggy clothes? Trauma? Social ineptitude?"

"As my spawn—"

"Ew. Please pick another word."

"—your dominion would relate to the things over which I reign," she goes on as if I never spoke. "You've made your choice, so we will never know the future you have forsaken in

Paradise. Yet I will tell you this: I have observed death for millennia, and it always brings those who remain two things: pain and peace. As my—"

"Don't say spawn," I grimace.

Syntyche's lips twitch ever so slightly. "As she who succeeds Death, perhaps you deliver both."

The memory blurs and ripples until I'm standing inside a seemingly endless vaulted library interspersed with rolling ladders, cozy reading nooks, thriving potted plants, and glowing crystals etched with intricate runes. Every tome, book, and scroll is organized impeccably, softly lit in their never-ending displays. In this memory, I'm already holding a Paradisian tome—

And suddenly, I can recall precisely what I learned from it. It was full of useful spells for holy magic, but especially one in particular: the incubi muse ritual meant to be performed in Syntyche's temples. I was memorizing it here.

"A bit of light pleasure reading?" Koa's voice asks as he approaches, but his tone is nervous. He doesn't like finding me here. "I do hope you're not planning on doing something inadvisable to my library as you did to my love's golden armor."

In my memory, I close the tome and smile darkly. "Speaking of your love, you and Arati have been together for thousands of years. In all that time, she must have mentioned how she helped that immortal permanently return to the mortal realm eons ago."

Koa fidgets before sighing. "What need would I have of that information when I'm quite happy to exist here with her for all eternity? I swear upon the heavens that I know nothing about it, so leave my poor library in peace."

There's nothing but honesty written all over his light sage green face. That frustrates me in this memory, but this scene is again interrupted when another recollection comes barrelling in, full of raised voices and wrath.

Arati is glaring down at me as I scowl up at her. We're alone in a grandiose golden room. Her crown of fire is taller than before, her golden eyes blazing with fury.

"You dare try your hand at tormenting us with the same irritating tactics you used on your mortal matches? It won't work. We're *gods*, Maven. You cannot reject this fate."

"I can and I have."

"You will cease this nonsense. I told you, your future here is final."

"Not to be a bitch, but..." Memory Me pauses and hums. "Oh, wait. That's exactly the fucking point. I won't stop ruining your Paradise until you tell me how to return to my quintet."

Arati's powerful gaze grows more wrathful before she straightens, considering me with a slowly cooling temper as though an idea is forming in her head. "Very well."

Surprise rocks me in this memory, but I try not to show how taken aback I am to have won this contest of wills.

Instead, I lift my chin. "Great. Then tell me."

"I will, on one condition. If you want to return to your fate-given matches so desperately, it will come at a price you already know well. You must first..."

Her voice slurs, fading and distorting as I slowly rise out of these memories.

"Snowdrop?" Everett checks softly.

Coming back to the present, I realize I'm still standing in a barren, grayscale city street as those memories settle into place in my head. More ghosts are drifting into this area, but I've cleared enough that I'm ready to get back inside and figure out how the fuck I can use this power to get my matches out of Syntyche's spell.

"I'm fine," I assure my concerned elemental. "Come on."

I turn back toward the temple just in time to see four people emerge from an alleyway several yards away. Everett immediately steps in front of me, blocking their view of me and my view of them. Frost spreads out from where my elemental stands, a visible warning as he stares down the newcomers.

The tense silence implodes with the deep, gruff laughter of a man. "Well, well! What are the odds of this? If it isn't the pretty boy. But you're not so pretty anymore now, are ya, Little Frost?"

I notice Everett's fists clench at his sides, prickling with ice fractals.

"*Everett* Frost?" a young woman's voice realizes, glowing with awe.

"Must be a lucky day for us," a second male voice agrees. "Clearly, you didn't realize that Arati's sealed high temple is within the safe haven owned and operated by—" His voice cuts off. "Holy shit. Look, the temple door is open!"

"What? How?" the girl demands.

Footsteps sound as she moves toward the temple. I tense, not wanting her anywhere near my two vulnerable matches. Before I can step around Everett, a gunshot cracks through the air, leaving my ears ringing as the girl screams—but only in alarm, not pain.

Douglas only fired a warning shot.

Not much fun, but it did the job.

Everett's voice is simultaneously lethal and diplomatic. "I'm not here for trouble. We'll be gone soon, so turn around and forget you ever saw me."

"Ah, come on, Little Frost. You know that's not how this is gonna go," the first man laughs. "You know they've been wanting to see you—probably'll want to see your new face, too. Tell your friend in the temple to come out, and we'll take you to safety, nice and easy."

I wonder why Everett hasn't frozen them all solid already. When he shifts slightly, obviously agitated as he adjusts his coat sleeve repeatedly, I can see around him and barely glimpse a shielding spell in place around the legacies, thanks to the female caster.

The one reasoning with Everett is a bald, burly elemental with fire dancing on his fingertips. The fourth legacy with them is a fae woman with pointed ears and long luminescent purple hair. Her attention drops to me in this fleeting second, and her eyes grow huge.

She points. "T—that's the *telum!* That's Maven Oakley!"

"What?" the second man barks, trying to see past Everett. "Impossible. Everyone knows that bitch is dead!"

The fact that everyone knows my name is still fucking weird. I grip my knife more firmly. Since I've already been spotted, it's better to get this over with quickly so I can get back inside to help my matches.

I step out from behind Everett. He swears under his breath as I pin the hostile legacies with the same look that used to make challengers in Amadeus's arena forfeit before the fight began.

"That bitch is giving you three seconds to walk away before your disemboweled guts become snacks for the ravens."

If this situation weren't so tense, I'd enjoy how blanched and horrified they look. The purple-haired fae woman calls a transportation spell in the blink of an eye, vanishing and leaving the others behind. Meanwhile, the other three legacies are so aghast that they don't move despite my warning.

I arch a brow. "One. Two. Th—"

"Wait!" the bald fire elemental cuts me off, raising his hands as he sputters. "Please, just wait. I don't know what's happening here, but if you're really back, they'll want to see you immediately. They've got the power to pardon you. Come with me, and—"

Before he can finish speaking, the other male turns out to also be a caster when he panics and sends a magical attack hurtling straight toward me. I tackle Everett, rolling us both out of the way just before the attack chars the place where we just stood.

Shards of ice explode around us as Everett's temper slips, but he's not the only one they just pissed off. I'm on edge enough with three of my matches out for the count without having to deal with idiots who don't take my threats seriously.

Time for them to learn how seriously they should take

"Maven Oakley," because I didn't come back just to let people fuck with us.

I roll back to my feet, bolting toward the three hostile legacies. The girl caster launches an attack that I dodge before rolling under a burst of flames that the elemental directs at me. Grabbing the fire elemental's still-extended arm, I twist it sharply to maneuver him in front of me—just in time for him to become a living shield for a cutting spell the male caster flings in his blind scramble to escape.

The bald elemental screams as deep cuts rip through his stomach, spilling his innards. I drop him and realize the panicked male caster has already been frozen solid by Everett, since he stupidly fled outside of the protective spell.

The remaining caster launches a stupor spell that slams into Everett before he can reach us. He collapses. That only stokes my fury as I run toward her, hurling my etherium knife at her protective shield. It bounces off, but spells like this can only absorb so much impact before collapsing.

From the direction of the temple, I hear Douglas shout in pain before a snarl rips through the air. I don't have time to focus on it as I crash through the fleeing caster's spell—but an electrocution hex flies from her fingertips, burrowing into my skin. Tingling numbness tears through my limbs, forcing my knees to give out as I nearly bite my tongue off.

I grimace, trying to shake off the daze of painful electrocution that is still sending miniature spasms through my nervous system. I manage to roll over and look up just as the girl extends her hand over me to cast a fatal spell.

But something blurs behind her before her head is yanked back roughly, exposing her neck for Not-Baelfire to rip her throat out with his teeth.

She drops dead. The shifter flings her jugular aside before his eyes connect with mine, and—

His pupils are round.

Oh, my gods.

This isn't the beast at all. It's him.

"Baelfire," I breathe as relief crashes over me like cold water.

He's trembling with rage and shock, covered in a sheen of sweat, and wildly disoriented as he drops to his knees beside me on the cold asphalt. He pulls me tightly to his incredibly warm chest.

"Boo," he rasps, burying his blood-smeared face in the side of my neck to inhale deeply. "Fuck, are—are you really—"

"I'm here. I'm alive." I hug him back even tighter, desperate for these next words to stay with him even when his dragon takes over again. "I love you."

"Y—you…" he starts to echo in bewildered disbelief.

"I love you," I repeat firmly. "I should have told you sooner."

A sob tries to work its way up his throat, and I know I'm not imagining the moisture on my neck. It's fucking brutal to see him this broken as he clings to me, agony in his voice.

"I love you, too. So fucking much. Please don't leave me again. Ever, Maven. *Please*."

"I won't," I whisper. "I promise."

After a moment, Baelfire makes a hoarse sound. When I pull back to see what's wrong, his face is a mask of torture as he grips his head. His pained, miserable golden gaze meets mine again.

"I'm trying to stay," he chokes. "But I—I just can't get a fucking grip. I can't—"

All at once, his words cut off as his pupils elongate into slits. He's gone as the dragon takes over to bare its teeth at me, inhuman feral madness eclipsing my match's face.

But thank the fucking universe. Baelfire is still in there.

He knows I'm back.

I cradle his face. "I'm going to fix this."

In response, the feral dragon nips at my hand, managing to draw blood. I break away from him, stumbling to where Everett still lies in a stupor.

Crouching, I try to get his attention, but his confused, pale blue gaze won't latch onto me.

"You're okay," I assure him anyway, glancing around at the aftermath of the fight.

The male caster remains frozen. Both the female caster and the fire elemental now lie dead in puddles of blood with their ghosts hovering above them, wide-eyed as they stare at me. With fiends on the loose, it's only a matter of time before the wind changes and carries the scent of their blood to monsters that will be drawn here.

Walking to the spot where my blade fell, I scoop to pick it up. It's already in scythe form when I face the ghosts of the two legacies.

"May your afterlives suck ass," I tell them before reaping their souls.

Moving back to Not-Baelfire, I take his leash and lead him into the temple, where I find Asher Dougas trying to heal his own arm, his forehead beaded with sweat and blood splattered all over the marble temple floor around him.

He sees Baelfire beside me and swears. "Keep that fucker away from me. Is Frost still alive?"

I nod.

"Good. I'd hate to lose a good paycheck after all this shit," he grunts, grimacing.

Rolling my eyes, I drop Baelfire's leash to go back out for Everett. "Watch my dragon."

"Hey. No. That freak nearly ripped my arm off. Don't fucking leave me alone with—"

Ignoring his protests, I return to Everett and help the discombobulated elemental stumble back into the temple, where he collapses into one of the pews. Once we're all safely in here, I turn toward the doors, take a deep breath, and try to use magic to seal them once again.

I don't know holy magic spells, but casting in fae seemed to work a bit.

"Ima guth sigillum," I recite.

Heat pulses in my veins, and the doors glow white briefly.

When I try pulling them open, they remain locked, movable only by holy magic.

I don't realize I'm beaming at the proof that I can figure this shit out until Douglas grunts, "Your pet dragon just pissed in the corner. Pretty sure your aunt's gonna smite him for that."

My aunt?

Oh, right. As one of the three celestial triplets, Arati would be Syntyche's younger triplet, alongside Sachar.

The thought of the queen of the gods being my auntie is too fucking weird, so I once again ignore the bounty hunter and hurry to Silas and Crypt.

Silas still sits as if he's fallen into a dark meditation, eyes shut as magic slithers over his skin. Meanwhile, Crypt remains in a bizarrely restful state as the malediction ravages his mind.

Taking another deep breath, I will my holy magic to work as I step into the spell.

20

CRYPT

CRANE GETS sick all over my subconscious as one of our keeper's worst memories-turned-nightmares plays before us. Wretched hands squeeze her throat as she lies naked and vulnerable in a barren bed, thrashing as tears leak over her temples.

"Anything else," Crane demands raggedly, wiping his mouth and swatting at something that exists in his head, as he keeps doing. "Remember anything else but *this.*"

"One fluffy unicorn-filled prance through Paradise, coming right up," I reply blankly, trying to numb myself further when the Entity himself arrives as a faceless shadow in this dream of a memory.

But it's futile. My keeper's past sobs seep through the emotional barricade, cutting me.

At this point, I'm too dream-starved and weak to numb myself properly. I've not bothered to ask Crane how he waltzed in here, nor how long I've been in this twisted abyss of unrelenting memories, since none of that matters. However he came to be here, there's no escape for either of us.

Death, I would've embraced, for it would have brought me to her.

The goddess of reaping must have known that, because this

punishment for harming the temples of the gods and their servants is far worse.

"*Anh hoc uair tempore,* shut up!" Crane shouts, ripping at his dark curls and staggering slightly. The blood-red aura around him flickers like a candle on the brink of going out.

Mad as a fucking hatter.

I might've found his meltdown hilarious if I felt anything at all right now. Instead, I watch him and feel nothing as the scene around us changes to the first time I slaughtered predators disguised as foster parents, before Hearst tracked me down and put me through hell for it.

I merely exist in this void of emptiness with a madman at my side until I see it.

That heart-stopping aura.

Only now, it's ever so slightly different. It's more of a dark, vibrant violet than shadowy mauve—but still shimmering and so magnetic that the metaphorical barricade guarding me from this web of misery trembles, weakening further.

Was Crane spewing truths earlier despite his madness, then?

Deep down, I've craved that aura.

Craved *her*.

But no. It doesn't matter. There's no godsdamned escape.

I begin to resent that aura more by the second as it permeates this space, tainting these abominable dreams and tempting me to let my walls down. Obsession teases the peripheries of my mind, a small reminder of how much I yearned to share this subliminal space with her from the moment I first saw her on that stage.

I need to get closer.

I need to run so I'll continue to feel nothing.

The nearer she draws, the more my past addiction tries to drag me back. I fight it, looking away and clinging to the nothingness that's protected me throughout this cycle of hell.

"*Thanafluir?*" Crane says from beside me, and promptly sets out to look for her in this maze composed of my mind. "Come on, she's this way."

"No."

"Crypt. Maven is looking for you."

No.

It will hurt.

It will crush me, finally feeling everything I've tuned out since that cursed moment on the battlefield. I didn't numb myself to survive losing her—what use would survival be without her, anyway? No, I did it to pause the inevitable agony.

I'm still not ready to face that.

Right now, when I wish to feel nothing, I cannot face the woman who so effortlessly makes me feel everything acutely.

Crane is irritated with my unresponsiveness and leaves to find her, his presence fading until I no longer sense him. I'm left to watch as the cycle starts again, a crowd of bland legacies surrounding me as that potent aura beckons me from the stage of the Seeking.

But this time, as I approach, I sense the difference. This isn't a watered-down memory of my keeper.

It's her.

Here. Alive.

The moment my gaze falls on Maven, standing in my subconscious with those bewitching dark eyes trained steadily on me, I force myself to stop walking.

I can't survive this. I can't get closer—can't even fucking *breathe*.

Syntyche's scythe, she's mesmerizing.

Terrifying.

It's taking all my willpower to keep my walls up.

Maven can see I'm fighting this. Curse and bless her, she doesn't miss a beat as she descends the stairs. When she's directly in front of me, one of my hands lifts toward her of its own accord. I force it back down. Between the desperation to get closer and my innate monster instincts fighting for self-preservation, I'm being ripped apart.

My obsession doesn't speak as she offers me her ungloved hand.

I stare at it, still not breathing.

Maven's gaze turns piercing. "You promised to haunt me for the rest of our lives and into the Beyond. I refuse anything less, so take my fucking hand."

Adoration crashes into the barricade protecting me from my emotions, weakening it until it barely stands. Swallowing, I finally place my hand in hers.

"There's no escape," I rasp.

"Tell that to Silas."

I realize I can no longer sense the fae necromancer in my subconscious. He went to her, and now he is gone, so he must be outside this dark labyrinth. If she was able to get him out, perhaps—

But no. Maven's face tenses in concentration for several long moments as glowing light ripples around us like a colorless aurora borealis.

Nothing happens.

"Motherfucking mother," she finally swears, glowering at the heavens in my subconscious as if they are real. "Some favor this is. By the way, if he doesn't wake up, I'm destroying all the makeshift temples, too."

Amusement trickles through my tattered guard, infusing me with warmth I can't bear.

"Leave me," I mutter. "You're not confined if you—"

"Never mind. We'll do this the permanent way," my keeper interrupts, pulling my hand until I follow her through more torturous memories.

She doesn't bat an eye at the nightmares I witnessed from her. There is no anger that I never told her what I've seen in her dreams—the dreams that were so torturous for me to witness, despite how I craved the flavor of her subconscious.

She only pauses in whatever she is searching for when she glimpses me as a child, climbing through an orphanage window at night with a backpack full of stolen gifts for the children.

Maven continues, traveling quietly with me into the vague, colorless memories leading right up to my current psychological incarceration. At long last, we emerge into a vaulted, ornate hall of stone and stained glass.

When I see the onyx altar and the remains of mania-induced people who ripped each other to shreds, I'm confounded.

"This is your mother's temple. The one I destroyed."

"I'm familiar." She leads me to the flawless onyx altar before turning to face me, arching a brow. "Silas told you about my mother?"

"He's stark-raving mad. I didn't fully believe him until just now."

The shock that I would typically feel at the full realization of my darling's origin is dulled so significantly, it's like I've just overheard that it's about to rain.

Maven leaves the altar, searching for something in the dead priests' pulpit off to one side of this temple that I desecrated. When she returns, she moves to the other side of the onyx altar, facing me.

The breathtaking determination on her face makes my pulse begin to pound, despite how hard I'm fighting to feel nothing.

But it only gets more severe when I see the bronze dust that she begins to use on the top of the altar to draw a symbol I recognize immediately.

It's the holy symbol all incubi know means *muse*.

Gods above.

She's trying to do the ritual *now?*

The shock of this surreal moment is the final straw, crashing through the walls I can no longer keep up. I never had the chance to formally ask her. I wanted this melding of our souls so desperately—and incubi can only experience it once in a lifetime.

My own lifetime may now be laughably short on account of how fervently I was leaning into my curse before Syntyche sentenced me to this punishment, but I'll be damned before I miss what it feels like to be subconsciously joined with Maven.

But in order to experience this intimate moment fully, I have to feel every fucking thing.

So I do.

As the barricade finally falls, emotions flood back so quickly that I'm suddenly drowning. The shock and horror and denial and bitter fucking *agony.* The soul-crushing grief. The unspeakable emptiness day after day, existing in a world she no longer occupied.

I choke on it all.

21

CRYPT

When Maven sees me fall to my knees, she pauses the ritual and moves to my side. Her perfect fingers gently trace the markings on my neck.

"Crypt?"

Gods above, her voice.

When I was numbed, it was just another noise—but now I shudder as rivulets of feelings continue to bathe my monstrous soul. It's a baptism of previously detained human emotions that quickly suffocates me.

The lifelessness on Maven's beautiful face as Frost wept over her. The psyches I demolished to drown out the loss. The terrified victims who ripped each other apart as I watched. Feeling dead inside while I took vengeance on the gods who dared allow my darling to be separated from me.

I try to inhale, but it's too much. I'm asphyxiating on emotions.

"Breathe," my keeper murmurs, holding one of my hands as I finally start to catch my breath.

"Promise me," I begin raggedly once I can look her in the eye as myself. "Promise that you will never again go where I can't follow."

Maven's gaze is unexpectedly soft compared to her words. "Fuck promises. I'll make you a godsdamned vow. From here on out, I'll be your muse. No matter what fate has in store, you won't be able to escape me this time."

Yes.

Despite the emotions still stifling my every thought, I rise to my feet to stand across from the stunning demigoddess I ache to belong to. She picks up where she left off, using bronze dust to finish the complex runes surrounding the holy symbol on the altar.

She holds her hands out for mine.

I have no clue if this ritual will work within a memory, but I'd gladly sell my soul to find out.

Taking Maven's hands, I watch, transfixed, as she utters words I don't understand. She's hell-bent on getting this right as she recites from her memory. Towards the end, she switches to English.

"This I vow in all dreams pure
Muse-marked soul forevermore
Bind to me his consciousness
Life or death, this union bless."

Glowing light surrounds us, soft and warm as ardor burns in my chest. For a moment, it becomes painless heat until my subconscious ripples around us.

I feel the unseen change. It's a sudden completion of my soul, a connection to something so powerful, dark, and lovely that for a moment, I can only gaze at Maven with profound obsession closing up my throat.

My love.

We're not bound again—not yet—but I don't need to hear her thoughts to see everything I'm feeling reflected on her face.

My muse smiles at me.

That's it. I can't stand not touching her for another second, so I vault over the bronze-dusted altar to dip Maven, kissing her deeply as her fingers tangle eagerly in my hair.

The moment her hands are on me, a new, strange feeling buzzes pleasantly through me.

Peace, I believe they call it.

Her tongue teases mine as my heart pounds. I nip her lower lip before straightening to rest my forehead against hers.

"Do you have any idea the things you did to me without even a pulse in your pretty neck?" I demand breathlessly, cradling her face.

"If it's any consolation, I loved you just as obsessively from Paradise."

I freeze, trapped in her eyes as a dangerous dose of obsession spikes my blood pressure. "Repeat that for me, love."

"When my purpose was fulfilled, I went to Para—"

"Not that. The other thing."

The far more important thing.

Maven knows what I want. She has the same slightly uncomfortable expression she used to get whenever people became too emotional around her, but she meets my gaze, understanding how important this is to me.

"I love you," she whispers. "In life or death or in between, you're all mine."

"Oh, my dark, twisted, darling," I laugh darkly, nearly swaying from the elation of those pretty words. "Brace yourself. You've no idea the monster you just created."

She grins as if that's the best news she's had all day, kisses my chin, and takes a deep breath as if to brace herself.

"Time to get out of here. I'm shit at holy magic so far, so hold on."

Holding on to her will never be an issue again.

A moment later, glowing light floods my mind, I can sense something shatter, and we're both suddenly yanked out of the nightmarish spell I've been tangled in for what feels like years.

I wake up.

The only times I've woken up in the past happened after getting knocked unconscious. I'll certainly be waking up this peacefully more often now that I have the option to sleep whenever Maven is resting. Shaking off slumber is a foreign feeling, and it takes me a moment to find that I'm flat on my back on a marble floor, staring up at the ceiling of the high temple of Arati.

"She better be right behind you," Frost's voice warns crisply nearby.

Sitting upright despite the weakness in my limbs, I frown at the way my head feels. Is waking up always this…cloudy?

Taking in my surroundings, I see that Maven is unmoving beside me. Limbo is weighted down so heavily around her that I tense, checking her pulse.

My muse is breathing, but she's in one of the deepest sleeps I've ever seen. Exhaustion from whatever she just did to free me has her practically anesthetized.

Crane sits in the closest pew, head down between his hands as he mutters at the voices he hears. Still, he's far more coherent than the last time I saw him in his iron enclosure.

Frost moves from leaning against the temple wall to adjusting the collar of his coat six times as he watches Maven with growing concern. I grew accustomed to his notable scar in the months following the Upheaval, but I was extremely numbed then. It certainly makes for an impression now.

I'm distracted from his face by nearby growling. Leaning back and squinting, I get a better view of Decimus chewing on the arm of a wooden pew. He's not himself, but seeing him here and shifted out of dragon form is a relief.

Hang on. A relief?

How worrisome. Since when did I get so invested in the welfare of these pricks?

"*Fuck.* She's bleeding. Why is she bleeding, and why the hell isn't she waking up?" Frost demands as ice spreads across the floor toward Maven and me on the marble ground.

Damn it all, he's right. Blood drips steadily from our keeper's nose, rolling over her cheek to drip onto the temple floor. I've seen that strain before in other casters who pushed themselves too far—Crane in particular.

Looking pointedly at the encroaching cold, I pull Maven's siren-like unconscious body into my arms and off the cold ground.

"Keep that away from our goddess. She's overdone it and desperately needs rest, not frostbite."

Frost's attention flicks from Maven to me briefly, scrutinizing. "Look who finally checked back in. Good timing, because I need at least one semi-functional psychopath to help me get us out of here. Those two deadweights don't qualify at the moment," he tips his head toward Crane and Decimus.

Decimus is prowling toward a statue of Arati as if about to attack it, wholly animalistic in his blissful ignorance of this conversation.

Crane, however, grips the blood amulet around his neck and glares at us. "I heard that."

"Good," Frost and I say at the same time.

"A few more just arrived," a voice calls down from one of the vaulted windows high in the temple. "Two Voids are with them."

I realize the redheaded mercenary who Frost hired months ago has climbed up to sit in the stone sill of one of the ornate windows, using a gun to scope through a crack in the stained glass. Whatever he's seeing out there, it makes Frost swear and drag his hands over his scarred face.

"What mess are we in now?" I demand, gently adjusting Maven's oversized dark clothing in hopes that she'll be less cold.

Agony flares through my limbs as my markings light up several times, but I ignore it. That's been happening long before Syntyche got to me. With Limbo in tatters, my body is paying the price.

"Hostiles are outside waiting to capture us," Frost replies. "Meaning, my family knows we're here."

I narrow my gaze at him. "It was here in New York all along?"

"Apparently," he grumbles, cranky. "Wouldn't be surprised if they've been moving the damn thing now and then."

I wasn't paying much attention to anything beyond the urge to kill in the months before I wound up trapped in my dark memories. However, Frost made me aware that one of the etherium stones Maven used to trap the life forces of the Immortal Quintet went missing just after they figured out how to use them for powerful shielding spells.

Since his entire elite family of pompous pricks also vanished during the Upheaval, along with much of the former Legacy Council and a few dozen other "high society" legacy families, he theorized that they were all together in a secret safe haven for the cowardliest of cowards, so to speak.

Finding it months ago would have been a treat. Even now, the thought of slipping into the minds of those spineless prats and flooding their pampered safe haven with mania is tempting. I've no doubt they've been sipping champagne while the rest of the world has gone to shit.

But if we've accidentally drawn their attention…

I look at my muse, resting deeply in my arms. Her bloody nose has slowed, so I use the corner of my ripped T-shirt to carefully wipe her face as well as I can.

She never minded blood, but I can't stop touching her even for a moment.

"Tell me who knows," I mutter.

"Us, the Baird quintet, Douglas…and the fae who got away and informed my family that she's back and she's here." Frost begins to pace, glowering at the double doors at the end of this temple. "The muscle they sent can't get in, so they're just waiting. Maven sealed this damn place with holy magic, and transportation magic doesn't work on hallowed ground, which means we can't get out."

"Douglas can help with that," Crane slurs, having to correct a couple of words mid-sentence.

"Shut up," the redhead snaps from up above.

"That *scútráche* is either a saint or highly *fabhar–blessed,*" Crane corrects. "Whatever rare circumstance, he uses holy *maghikae.*"

Frost pauses, figuring out the last word before calling up, "Wait. You can use holy magic, and didn't tell me? What the fuck have I been paying you for this whole time?"

"You've gotta be kidding me. Your quintet is a fucking pain in the ass, you know that?" the mercenary gripes as he climbs back down from his perch. Once he's down, he casts me the quintessential look of disgust before squinting accusingly at Maven. "Your weirdo-ass girlfriend ratted on me, didn't she?"

A muscle nearly pops in my jaw as I remind myself we might need him alive, for now.

"Mind how you speak about her or I'll feed your dismembered prick to your hellhound while the other tidbits of you rot here."

The redhead has the good sense to step back as he realizes I'm no longer the passive, numb phantom drifting in and out of Limbo that he previously witnessed.

"She said nothing," Crane mutters, flinching away from something in his mind before focusing on us again. "I'm the one saying it. If you can unseal the doors, perhaps we can unleash Bael on those waiting outside."

"No dice," Frost shakes his head. "Only Maven can remove his collar. Besides, there's no way in hell I'm about to watch that asshole dragon snatch her away again. He's staying exactly like that until we snap him out of it."

He snatched her away as a fucking *dragon?*

Gods above, it's a good thing they have me back. That would never have happened on my watch.

Douglas stretches one of his arms. "Fine. I'll open the fucking door, but it's up to you three to have a game plan once they're open. Last I saw, there were thirty, maybe forty seasoned legacies ready for a fight."

We're all quiet in the chilled silence for a moment, considering our options for getting our keeper far away from Frost's family.

"I heard that, too," Crane suddenly snaps, glaring at the nearby pulpit.

I fight back an unexpected laugh, egging him on. "You tell them, Crane."

"Scratch that. It's up to us *two,* since he's not playing with a full deck," Frost mutters, brushing frost off his hands.

The fae rubs his forehead. "*Quid a tha tem'ah chehn?*"

None of us knows what that means, but I finally get to my feet, still cradling Maven. It's mortifying to realize just how weak I am right now when I stumble slightly on the way to get her to Frost's arms.

"Your one and *only* job is to make sure she doesn't come to harm when we step outside. Don't dare fuck it up like you did last time."

The elemental flinches, grief crossing his scarred face, and for the first time in my entire life, I decide I should have tempered my tongue.

Whatever or whomever caused Maven's purpose to be fulfilled—*that* carries the blame. Not him. Considering that Frost kicked me out on my ass the one time I came to him asking for him to put me out of my misery, and the fact that he kept the rest of us alive against all odds over the last six months…

In a bizarre twist of fate, I owe him my thanks.

Later. I'll thank him later, when our miraculous keeper is safely out of harm's way.

"I'll unleash as much mania as I can. That should eliminate most of them, and then we'll pick off the stragglers. Have a transportation spell ready, bounty hunter," I say, looking at the double doors.

But I can't seem to make myself move. I look back at Maven.

Leaving my darling muse's side after just barely getting her back feels impossible.

When Frost catches my eye, there's an understanding on his scarred face. He nods, appearing *sympathetic.*

How utterly unaccountable.

"I won't fuck it up this time," he promises quietly. "I've got her."

I believe him.

Taking one step away is laborious, but I force myself to keep moving until I stand at the double doors, rolling my shoulders back and preparing for the pain that will come from slipping into Limbo, which is something I can't do inside the walls of a temple. The mercenary stops beside me, resting his hands on the door and concentrating.

"Damn it. This was a hell of a lot easier with Oakley helping," he grits.

"Amato."

Glowing light washes over the now-unsealed doors before he drops his hands, puzzled. "What did you just say?"

"My keeper's real surname is Amato."

The bulky caster looks far more stunned than I feel is warranted before I push the doors open enough to slip outside, simultaneously slipping into the dream plane of existence.

What's left of it, anyway.

Limbo fragmented six months ago, the turbulence becoming lethal as pieces of it fell out of place, drifting about the mortal realm. Wisps and shades have accumulated at a staggering rate, using Limbo Zones to escape and feast on anything that wanders into those areas. The rest of them still roam Limbo, ready to kill.

There are a few nearby—but far more worrying are the ten or so incubi who are already here, waiting with bronze weapons in hand. These wankers came prepared for me.

We're too cursed and weak for a fight like this, and they know it.

Fucking Frosts.

22

MAVEN

My exhausted brain wants to dream about things I've experienced, but since the pieces are missing, it makes do with shadow puppets instead. I sink deeper into this heavy darkness, more exhausted than I've ever been as tendrils of nothingness try to take up my mind's stage.

The only dream I can make sense of is me sitting at the edge of a sea of clouds, golden liquid dripping from my arm and fingertips as I concentrate on…something.

Finally, the darkness ebbs until I claw my way groggily to the surface. Heat sears inside my chest in place of a heart. When it passes, a wave of weakness almost drags me back into unconsciousness.

"There's our girl," Crypt's voice rasps, but it's strained.

Blinking my eyes open, I frown at the colorless, icicle-covered chandelier above me in this freezing space. Why can't I move my arms? They're crossed in front of me, banded so tightly they've gone numb.

Then there's whatever the fuck is covering my mouth. My breathing stutters as alarm sets in.

Something is very wrong.

We're not in Arati's temple anymore, so where the hell

are we?

"Maven?" Everett checks.

He sounds bad, too.

Fighting through the residual heaviness of that impossibly deep sleep, I struggle against the claustrophobic tightness around me. I can't make this *thing* that I'm trapped inside budge an inch, but I hear chains rattling. Apparently, they tied more of those around whatever this shit is.

Thanks to the tape covering my lips, I can't curse out loud, but that doesn't stop me from growling in helpless frustration and trying harder.

Crypt swears before quickly explaining, "It's called a straitjacket, love. Careful not to fall off the sofa."

Sofa?

Where the fuck *are* we?

Finally, I'm able to half-swivel on the cushioned surface, which sure enough turns out to be a sofa. This room is excessively nice, complete with mirrors, sconces, chandeliers, rugs, a fireplace, a desk—

It's a suite, I realize. A completely colorless, expensive-looking one.

I'm on a couch facing a fireplace with a limited view of everything else, unable to see my matches. That's not going to fucking work, so despite Crypt's repeated worried warning, I intentionally fall off the couch so that I can roll on the notably charred carpet to see them.

Oh my fucking gods.

Everett is in a straitjacket like mine, minus the extra chains. A fabric bag is over his head. He's been left on his back on the massive bed.

Crypt is encased from the shoulders down in bronze—clearly the work of a skilled metal elemental. He's propped up against one wall with the mother of all syringes stuck into the side of his neck at an angle.

When my gorgeous Nightmare Prince sees me on the floor,

he tries for a smile that is more of a grimace. His mesmerizing violet eyes are a burst of color compared to the rest of this grayscale room, and his markings light up now and then.

"Whatever is in this damned syringe, it's kept me from plane-walking for the twenty-four hours we've been stuck in here. Luckily, it's not quite as vile as the smell of the drink they've been forcing down Frost's throat to nullify his abilities."

Twenty-four hours. I take it we were captured by someone with resources, but…

I'm momentarily distracted when a ghost passes through a wall. It's a young woman with bright blue hair. When she sees I'm awake, she looks excited before disappearing through another wall.

Straining on the ground, I try to see into the other corners of this extensive suite. Baelfire has to be here, somewhere. And Silas.

They *have* to be here, because if I lost them again—

"They put our necromancer in isolation," Crypt offers, still sounding pained even though he's trying to hide it. "Decimus was dragged out a bit ago for starting fires again. Not to worry, darling. They always bring him back quickly."

"We're still in New York," Everett adds. "At my parents' favorite luxury hotel, across the street from Arati's high temple. They're the *they* Crypt mentioned."

He sums things up quickly as I try to worm toward the nearest wall so I can sit up while still keeping a view of them. Apparently, we were captured at Arati's temple while I was passed out. Aside from Silas, we've been kept in this room the entire time, but even though Everett hasn't been let out to see the place, he's positive this is where the cowardly elite legacies disappeared to once the Divide fell and all hell broke loose.

"A void is posted outside," he finishes bitterly. "I haven't seen Asher Douglas since we were taken. He's probably dead."

"Such a shame," Crypt sighs.

Everett's bag-muffled voice is pure skepticism. "Uh-huh. Let me guess. You're only sad you weren't the one to kill him."

"Naturally. He shot Maven."

"I made him pay me back triple for that in blood when he showed up at Everbound wanting to work for me. You were there."

"Doesn't count, since I was too numb to enjoy it properly." Crypt looks back at me, concern and raw affection eclipsing everything else on his face. "You all right, love?"

I nod, still trying and failing to get some wiggle room in this godsdamned straitjacket. If it were any looser, I would try to get my arms over my head, but it's ridiculously tight, and that's *before* the chains they wrapped several times around me. It's a marvel that I could still breathe while unconscious in this thing.

As far as torture devices go, this one is quickly earning my respect. And the extra chain reinforcements? Honestly, the fact that they hindered me this thoroughly is flattering. It's almost like I killed some of the most powerful beings in the world to get to this point.

They must be terrified of me.

"I'll make you a bouquet of fingers from the soon-to-be fingerless legacy who dared confine you in that and put that fucking tape over your mouth," Crypt promises.

Gods, I missed his sweet violence.

My chest continues to burn. We sit in this lightly smoke-scented room for a quiet moment before there's a bang at the door. Someone yelps in pain, someone else snarls, and then Baelfire is shoved into the room before the door slams shut again.

And it's *actually* Baelfire.

His pupils are round as he adjusts to sit on the floor. Thick silver shackles immobilize his wrists and ankles. The collar I put on him is still there, as is the leash. His face is bruised, one eye blackened, nose quickly healing from an obvious break, and his ripped shorts are stained with an alarming amount of blood. More is dried all over his beautiful bare muscles.

He's also still holding the end of someone's bitten-off finger in his mouth.

When he spots me, his face lights up just like it always used to. Spitting the finger he just snagged aside, he beams.

My pulse flutters. Gods—there he is.

My sunshine mate is no less charming, all covered in blood. He's as ridiculously handsome as ever, his eyes sparkling, his smile bright.

But I can sense it right away—the change in his demeanor.

When I first met Baelfire, back when I was trying to reject my matches, he was so upbeat and guileless and…*good* compared to the rest of us. In a way, he seemed innocent, or at least as innocent as legacies can be.

Now? It's subtle, but there's a new edge to him, and not the kind that comes from his dragon.

Baelfire shuffles across the room to my side. As soon as he's close enough to me, he leans over to kiss my mouth through the tape.

"You okay, Raincloud? Gods, I was so fucking worried you wouldn't wake up," he rasps, kissing my jaw next.

He doesn't seem to remember there's someone else's blood on his face, but I'm so happy he's present that I'm not about to remind him. I've missed his singed cedar scent and those beautiful golden irises.

When Baelfire sees me drinking in the sight of him no longer feral and hissing, he looks sheepish. His broken nose has completely healed, and his bruises are starting to fade.

"My dragon is a godsdamned wimp. When anyone he considers a lesser being hurts us, and he can't come out to roast them, it's a huge blow to his pride. Only took a few beatings for me to get him in the back seat. For now," he adds with a slight grimace.

Beatings, constraints, my fae locked in isolation somewhere…

It's decided. I'll relish all the elite legacies' screams and pleas for mercy as I punish them for harming my quintet.

But for now, I'm ready to get this tape off my face. Leaning toward Baelfire, I lift my chin.

He immediately kisses my cheek, nuzzling my neck with a ragged sigh of relief. More flutters make me flush all over. His obvious excitement to be with me even in a situation like *this* is just…admittedly adorable.

I reluctantly pull away. Making sure Baelfire sees my purposeful expression, I tilt my face until he focuses on the tape.

"Oh, shit. Right. Hold still for me, baby."

It's quite the process, him nipping and pulling gently at the tape over my mouth. When it starts to peel away, my dragon shifter kisses each part of my face that's been uncovered.

When the tape finally falls away, I smile against his lips. "Good boy."

I'm not expecting the rough whimper that escapes him at those words, but *oh my gods,* it's hotter than I could have imagined.

Baelfire's warm lips are immediately moving against mine. His tongue drags against the seam of my lips until I open for him, and he growls as our mouths mingle.

He quickly gets more aggressive, tugging lightly on my upper lip before kissing down my neck, nipping it now and then. My head is spinning. When he gets to the mating mark he left on me, he groans.

"Hell yes. Right where it's always going to fucking be."

I can't help the exhilarated gasp that escapes when he roughly bites and then licks the scar to soothe it.

Everett swears under the bag on his head. "I'm missing something I want to see, aren't I?"

"Quite the little show," Crypt agrees, grinning.

When Baelfire adjusts to kiss the other side of my neck, I can feel his collar against me.

"Sorry about the collar," I manage.

He pulls back, raising his brows. "Hang on. You mean, they didn't put it on me? This was you?"

I nod and apologize again, but he groans and lets his head fall back on his shoulders.

"Damn, that makes me so hard."

Crypt's voice is strained. "Speaking of, they didn't leave any room for viewing pleasure in this fucking sarcophagus. So if you don't mind..."

I realize he's grimacing down at the bronze encasing him, too affected by our little make-out session. Everett hasn't said anything else, but he's tenting.

Oops. My poor voyeurs, minus one.

Finally being in a room with three of my matches coherent and conscious is amazing, but it makes Silas's absence painfully obvious. My empty stomach clenches painfully at the thought of what they might be doing to my necromancer.

"Don't be sorry, Maven. *I'm* sorry. So fucking sorry," Baelfire whispers, leaning his forehead against mine. "I don't remember everything from that night my dragon took you, but I—fucking gods, I *dropped* you."

"I stabbed you."

"So? I fucking dropped you and—"

I nip his lower lip to stop him from finishing that guilt-ridden statement before peering into his golden irises. "Who cares? That's nothing when we almost lost each other."

His molten gaze grows so uncharacteristically sorrowful and broken that it makes my chest twinge as he shakes his head, swallowing hard.

"Not right now. I can't talk about losing each other right now. Please. Because if I start to think about what happened six months ago, I—fuck, I *can't*," he rasps, shutting his eyes and shifting to rest the back of his head against the wall. He breathes in and out at a measured pace, trying to calm himself down. "Distract me with something. Anything. *Please.*"

I blurt out the first thing that comes to mind. "I was in Paradise. Not that I remember much of it yet."

He peeks one eye open. "Everett mentioned that."

"Syntyche is my mother."

"Yeah. He mentioned that, too."

Realizing that Baelfire knows what I am and is treating me exactly the same as before is such a relief that I beam at him.

His face lights up again, attention pinned to my mouth. "Holy fuck, I've missed that."

"Missed what?" Everett demands from the bed.

"None of your business, Popsicle Prick." Baelfire boops my nose with his. "When we get out of this Frosty shithole, I'm going to need a lot more of those from you, my cute little demigoddess."

I fix him with a firm look even as I try not to smile. "Not cute. I see ghosts and reap souls. I'm the daughter of Death."

"Sure, and you're also *so. Fucking. Cute.* I bet you look like a queen while you're reaping. *My* queen."

He kisses the tip of my nose, trailing more light kisses up and down my neck.

Gods, I've missed him and his persistent flirtiness.

But wait…

I tense, straightening as much as I can in this stupid, chained-up straitjacket. "Fuck. Where's my scythe?"

"Confiscated along with anything else they found on our person," Crypt says. His markings light up again, and he hisses in pain. "They took my lighter, too, and would have taken Decimus's self-discipline, if he had any left." He gives the shifter a pointed look. "Our girl is still exhausted. Give her space before your touch starts to bother her."

Baelfire pouts, but still hasn't moved away. "Is this bothering you yet, Mayflower?"

I want to tell him I'm more than fine with the touching—in fact, I'm craving anything I can get from my matches, after all that time I spent agonizing over whether they were still alive.

But before I can speak, the door to this suite opens and three people walk in. Two of them are legacies in fitted suits, and the third is a woman dressed impeccably well with a camera hanging from her neck.

Before I can register the fact that strangers have barged in, the woman snaps a picture of Baelfire's face pressed against my neck and my startled expression.

"Ah, good. The tape's already off. Maven Oakley," one of the suited men greets stiffly as he gestures at the big desk in the room surrounded by four chairs. "It's time for your pre-trial interview."

23

MAVEN

My what now?

The other suited man leans as if he's about to haul me to my feet since this straitjacket inhibits me. He smells like women's perfume.

But the second he gets close, Baelfire snarls and makes that odd noise deep in his throat before blue flames ignite the legacy's suit coat. The legacy shouts and flings off his coat, stomping it out and stumbling away from us.

"Try to touch her one more time, I fucking dare you," Bael warns, breathing out smoke as he speaks.

Gone is the charm he was just lavishing me with—now he looks ready to commit all kinds of murder.

Damn. Is it always this sexy when men literally breathe smoke? Thinking of how Crypt looks when he's smoking *reverium,* I decide the answer must be yes.

Then again, it's always sexy when they're murderous on my account.

The other suited man doesn't bother approaching. He just nods at the desk. "Fine. Join us, Miss Oakley."

When he starts to break into a sweat from the immovable

death stare I've perfected, the woman tsks and walks to the bed, reaching for the bottom strap of Everett's straitjacket.

No—her hands are going for Everett's pants.

"Maybe this will make her compliant," she coos, smirking over at me. "I bet the *telum* won't tolerate someone else playing with her prettiest toy."

Everett tenses on the bed, struggling uselessly as he realizes how close she's gotten to him.

Visceral rage floods me as my vision almost goes dark. I'm off the ground in a split second, crossing the room with all the inhuman speed I still possess until the top of my head slams into her throat. The bitch collapses immediately, flailing in panic when she can't draw in a full breath.

I glare down at her. "Get close to any of them again, and I will split your skull open, scoop out what little brain matter exists in there, and shove it in your mouth so you can taste how stupid you are for trying to fuck with me."

One of the suits shouts in alarm. He rushes over to help the idiot to her feet as she wheezes. I don't miss how handsy he is with her, but he's not the same guy who smelled like the perfume I just noticed on her.

They don't seem like quintet members, and these men seem extremely uninterested in each other, so they're probably not a throuple. An open relationship, maybe? Kenzie told me about those before. They happen sometimes with unbound legacies, and now and then among humans.

"Gods above, how I've missed your beautiful threats, darling," Crypt sighs from his bronze confinement.

The man guides the photographer away from me quickly. When he looks over his shoulder, I'm satisfied to see the fear I *should* evoke in these assholes written all over his blanched face.

"J—just sit down, now," he insists, pretending to still be in control. "We need to complete this interview, and then you can meet with the council executives before the official trial."

Trial? He's joking.

They're pretending the legacies who live here are civil and follow political procedures, but I know how the world of legacies works. They cull off the weak. They destroy their competition. They kill.

This so-called trial is nothing more than entertainment for the top-tier, spoiled legacies living in this secret "safe haven."

"If you don't do this interview with us, we'll kill the redhead," the other suit finally says, folding his arms.

Douglas?

Damn it. If they're not bluffing about him still being alive...

I arch a brow. "Show me proof of life first."

One of the suits pulls out a device I don't recognize. It's not a phone, and it plays static whenever he's not talking into it. Someone replies affirmatively before a big fae man throws open the door, dragging a brutally beaten Douglas into the room.

He's tossed aside, half-unconscious and bleeding, but he's still breathing. As much as I still don't fully trust him with my quintet, especially Crypt, there's something annoyingly likable about this unpolished mercenary. Letting him get killed by these idiots over a superfluous, fake interview would be a waste, especially since we'll need him to transport us back to Everbound.

Glaring at the suits, I finally move to sit across from them. The woman still looks shell-shocked, and her throat is already bruising nicely, but she sniffles and takes another picture of me sitting across from them before she moves to sit in the free chair beside me, scooting away slightly.

I blink away the spots left behind from the bright flash, ignoring when heat suffuses my chest again.

The suit on the left pulls documents and a little black box out of the desk. Clearing his throat, he pushes a button and the little device begins to blink with a light that is as sapped of color as everything else in this place.

"This is a recorder, Miss Oakley. You see, we would like to keep a perfect record of this pre-trial interview for future forensic psychiatrists to study, since you're quite the specimen.

The information we're about to gather from you, the defendant, will help the court decide your fate."

"What a motherfucking joke," Bael mutters from the floor behind us.

The legacy shoots him a dirty look before continuing professionally as he regards me. "My name is Nathan Thatcher, and this is my associate, Mr. Grant. Miss Bailey will be taking a few pictures to be published in our fantastic safe haven, which is, of course, buzzing with the news of your return."

As if on cue, the bitch snaps another shot of me. When I look at her, she scoots her chair further away, rubbing her throat.

"Please state your name for our record," Grant says.

When I roll my eyes, the big brute kicks Douglas hard in the stomach. Douglas wheezes in pain, curling in on himself.

Godsdamn it.

They want answers from me? Fine.

"Maven Oakley," I lie, letting my poker face slip on.

"Miss Oakley, where were you for the last six months?"

"Paradise."

Nathan Thatcher glances a bit too long at the photographer before giving me a chiding look. "Respectfully, I ask that you don't blaspheme during this interview and take it seriously."

"Respectfully, I ask that you eyeball Miss Bailey's cleavage later. You're getting drool on my straitjacket."

Crypt snorts in amusement, but otherwise, my matches listen quietly to this circus.

Thatcher's face reddens, and the woman shuffles uncomfortably. Her body language screams guilty. Mr. Grant glances between them and makes a face before adjusting the documents in front of him.

"Miss Oakley, is it true that you were raised in what was previously known as the Nether?" Grant asks.

"Yes."

"Isn't it true that you were also brought up by the Entity with the intention of your becoming the prophesied *telum?*"

"Obviously."

Thatcher takes over again, studying me. "And isn't it true that you assassinated every member of the Immortal Quintet to aid the Entity?"

"Sure, why not?"

It's not like my answers matter here, anyway.

My flippant reply ruffles Thatcher's feathers. "Is there something you disagree with in that statement, Miss Oakley? Please explain."

"You want me to pretend this is a real trial? All right. I was raised as Amadeus's scourge. I killed Somnus DeLune, Iker Del Mar, and Natalya Genovese. Go ahead and charge me with performing necromantic rituals, helping the Reformists, destroying the Divide, starting the Upheaval—you name it, I did it." I lean forward, fixing them with an earnest stare. "But never to aid Amadeus. Everything I did, I did to free the Nether humans."

They exchange glances. The idiot with the camera takes a picture of my profile.

Grant clears his throat. "So to be clear, you're pleading…?"

"Guilty as the hell I was raised in." I lean back, trying to adjust my arms in this unforgiving straitjacket. "Unless you want me contracting gangrene before the trial from blood loss to my arms, you should really loosen this."

"Without touching her," Everett adds in warning.

Nathan Thatcher folds his arms. "Not so fast, Miss Oakley. One last question before we take you to meet the new chief executives of the Legacy Council. Isn't it also true that you are one of the infernal beings known to this world as a demon?"

It's such an unexpected question that I blink. "What?"

"We know the truth. You can't fool us. You respawned after your death—the fact that you're sitting here in front of us is pure evidence of that!" Grant says as if this is an *aha, gotcha* moment. "Admit it. You are a demon, Maven Oakley."

Everett, Crypt, and Baelfire burst into laughter.

I start cracking up, too, but clear my throat to compose myself, shoving down the urge. Even though my guys haven't stopped laughing, I'm still not comfortable displaying strong emotions in front of strangers, let alone ones this clueless.

"Demon? With what horns?" I point out, smothering my laughter.

"Not all demons have horns," Thatcher replies confidently and completely incorrectly.

"Gods, you're both trying so hard and getting it so backwards," I sigh. "If you're this off the mark in your jobs, I pity anyone you lure into bed. Or whoever lures you both into theirs," I add, tossing a knowing look at Miss Bailey. "Between these two ass-scratching baboons, you must be accustomed to finishing the job yourself."

Her face goes red. Mr. Grant's head whips to look at her before he glowers at Nathan Thatcher, who pretends to be so busy scribbling on documents that he didn't hear me.

Baelfire whistles. "My mate is so damn observant."

Crypt hums in agreement even as his markings light up again. "Deliciously keen."

"Literally *divine,*" Everett hints pointedly, still chuckling.

"Enough of this," Mr. Grant scowls, standing to look down his nose at me. "We got the answers to everything we had doubts about. Your denial of your true nature will hold no water with the court. Rest assured that their final decision will be carefully weighed and just."

"*Just* a crock of shit," Crypt corrects.

"Prepare yourself to face the executives, *telum,*" the incensed legacy snaps. "Anton, give the Frost heir another dose for good measure."

The big fae guard by Douglas makes a face. "It's supposed to be a daily debilitant. I gave him some less than two hours ago—"

"Have you heard what that maniac's been doing on the front lines? Do you *feel* how cold it is in this fucking hotel? If this is what happens when he's not trying, we're not taking chances, you braindead dope. Just dose him again, and double it."

"Yes, sir," the fae grumbles.

Everett, being called a maniac? Interesting.

Nathan Thatcher quickly gathers up the documents before rushing out of the room. The flustered photographer takes another picture of me and hurries out with Mr. Grant right behind her. He's already starting a predictable argument before the door closes behind them.

Asher Douglas still isn't fully conscious, but Anton kicks the bounty hunter again before walking to a small kitchenette off to one side of the room to mix the concoction.

Fuck, Crypt was right. It smells like concentrated grass, gasoline, and sage blended with some other unpleasant herb. It's so awful for my regular sense of smell that I'm not surprised when Baelfire starts gagging loudly where he sits on the floor.

Moving to the bed, the fae shoves the cloth bag up Everett's face just enough to force my elemental to drink. Everett chokes on the overpowering concoction, unable to fight it. I grit my teeth when the fae roughly pinches Everett's nose until he's forced to swallow so he can breathe again.

He's still coughing when the fae replaces the bag, hauls him upright, and drags him off the bed and out of the room despite my shouted protests. Before the door closes behind him, another gruff-looking legacy with several intense facial tattoos strolls into the room, heading toward me.

My body tenses as instinct and training try to kick in. Restrained this intensely, it would be difficult to kill this guy, but I could still do some serious fucking damage.

But Tattoo Face is probably here to take me to wherever Everett was just dragged off to.

So for once, I force myself not to fight as he tosses me over his shoulder, carrying me out of our grayscale prison as Baelfire and Crypt spew impressive threats and more blue flames behind us.

24

MAVEN

This entire upscale hotel is colorless, but that doesn't diminish its wow factor as Tattoo Face steps out of an elevator and tosses me onto a cushioned chair.

I find myself in a much bigger, nicer room, glassed in at the top of the skyscraper. I think Kenzie called this setup a penthouse in a movie we watched once. Everything here looks ridiculously expensive, from the carpet to the modern chandeliers to the many decorative swords mounted on one wall.

Outside the window, gray skies serve as a foreboding backdrop for more colorless city stretching toward the dark ocean in the distance. This penthouse has a balcony overlooking the stunning view.

A dozen ravens are perched on the balcony's luxurious outdoor seats, watching me through the glass.

Everett sits on a couch nearby in his straitjacket, that bag still on his head. He looks unharmed, thank the fucking universe. A few ghosts drift into this room to watch me, including the blue-haired young woman I saw earlier.

I realize Tattoo Face just deposited me in front of a large, lit-up vanity. The mirror says I look the way I usually do: dark eyes, tangled black hair, and the same face. Only now, it's strange to know that I got my appearance directly from Syntyche, minus my much warmer skin tone and slightly more colorful dark irises.

The only difference is the slight shadows under my eyes, which isn't surprising. I'm still fucking exhausted after using all that holy power to rip through Syntyche's spell. I probably won't be able to use holy magic until I reap again, which makes me wonder about the now-consistent burning in my chest.

Tattoo Face gets a message through his static box before he leaves through a set of doors leading elsewhere in this skyscraper-top mansion.

"Maven?" Everett checks quietly.

"I'm here."

"Anyone else in here yet?"

"Aside from a few ghosts, no."

"Well, that's creepy. Thanks for the reminder that we're haunted." He takes a deep breath. "Okay. If you get the chance, kill them. Getting out of here is much more important than whatever idiotic hangups I might still have about the executives. Gods, I should've known they would use the Upheaval as a damn power grab."

I'm about to point out that killing our captors is the obvious choice, but the rest of his words sink in.

Oh, shit. He's saying that the so-called executives are…his family. Meaning, I'm about to finally meet the Frosts I've heard so much about from my matches.

A dark-skinned young woman with stunning features and gorgeous natural hair sweeps into the room before stopping beside me, fidgeting with a strange bag. Her eyes are wide as she looks me over, swallowing hard and then offering a smile.

I know nothing about her, but I'm pretty sure she's human.

"H—hello. You're…Maven Oakley, right?"

I study her, trying to determine how much of a threat she is.

She clears her throat, growing uncomfortable under my silent scrutiny. "I—I'm—"

"Reagan?" Everett asks from the couch, clearly recognizing her by her voice.

The girl, Reagan, looks relieved and offers me a shy smile. "Yes, I'm Reagan Bates. That name probably doesn't mean anything to you, since I know you're from…ahem. But before the Upheaval, I was a well-known actress—not nearly as famous as you are now, of course. I ran in a lot of the same circles as Everett. He was always very kind to me, so after everything happened, I went looking for him here, and his family took me in, and…"

Her smile fades, and she fidgets again. "They want me to make you look presentable before the trial. Their words, not mine. There will be more press, and you need to look—"

"She looks perfect," Everett interrupts. "Get the fuck out."

Reagan gets wide-eyed, obviously not used to my elemental's temper. But she stays, examining my face with objective interest as one of the more solid-looking ghosts tries to wave a hand in front of me for attention.

Fucking ghosts. This is not the time.

"You have fantastic skin. Nice, strong jaw. Honestly, there's something kind of…quietly interesting about your face. Especially your eyes—they're so pretty. Some mascara or even a bit of eyeliner would really make them pop. Mind if I touch things up a bit?"

Reagan's hand moves toward my face. Every nerve in my restrained body locks as I try not to flinch, bracing myself for the torture that always comes with strangers touching me.

"Lay a finger on her perfect face, and I will fucking kill you," Everett warns, his tone smooth and crisp as ice.

Reagan pulls back immediately, looking torn. It's clear she'll get in trouble for not doing this.

"Your parents—" she begins just as the double doors at the end of this grandiose room open.

"My parents can choke on Sachar's sweaty ballsack in the Beyond, for all I fucking care," he seethes just as a beautiful woman and a man who looks disturbingly like a middle-aged version of Everett stroll into the room, unknowingly passing through another ghostly onlooker.

"May Arati pardon you. All those years spent away from us have made you vulgar," the richest legacy in the world mutters, his glacial eyes sweeping to where I sit.

Alaric Frost's perfectly styled hair is just as white-blond as Everett's. He's in a flawless blue suit, has neatly trimmed gray facial hair, and looks incredibly refined as he examines me like I'm an endangered animal caged all for his fascinated perusal.

Everett tenses when he realizes who's here. "Fuck."

"Language," his mother scolds as she sits gracefully on the couch opposite him. "I wish you wouldn't make us go to such extreme lengths just to see you, son. You know, no matter how I tried to cater to you, you've ignored every single one of our dinner and event invitations for years. After the Upheaval, I decided I had to give up for my own mental health. It's awful to feel like your own son can't stand to be in the same room as you. Why put myself through more of that?"

She smooths her expensive-looking dress, ensures her updo is perfect, and finally looks over at me with narrowed eyes. Unlike Alaric, who looks exactly as wintry as his son, she looks more like the brief glimpse I got of Everett's sister in a photo long ago, with large brown eyes and pretty, soft features. But unlike her daughter, her hair is bleached crisp blonde, and she's missing the sweet smile.

Everett's mother wrinkles her nose at me. "Reagan, finish her makeup. She still looks like a corpse. Which I guess isn't too surprising, considering she should be dead."

"Watch your fucking mouth," Everett growls.

His parents exchange displeased looks.

Reagan shuffles. "I really don't think she wants me to—"

"Who cares what she wants? She'll be in a coffin soon, anyway," Daphne interrupts.

"Daphne," Alaric finally chides. "The *telum's* fate isn't final until we discuss things with her. Until then, mind your manners. This is our heir's renowned keeper, after all."

He strolls toward me with a fake, white smile. "At long last, here you are. I'm afraid the rest of my quintet is still preparing for the trial and could not join us for this little chat, but if you make the right choice, you'll have the privilege of meeting the rest of them later, over dinner."

He moves as if to help me up from the chair. I stand on my own, shoving the chair back as hard as possible with the backs of my legs so it topples over. Glaring at the asshole who voted for Amato's death sentence, I shuffle to the couch to sit beside Everett as well as I can in this fucking chained-up jacket.

The blue-haired female ghost I saw earlier drifts to stand directly beside Daphne Frost to wave at me. I ignore her.

When Reagan tries to leave the room, Daphne stops her.

"Wait. You might need to cover up my son's face if the garish stories we've heard are true. Alaric?"

Everett's father steps closer and pulls the bag off Everett's head, revealing his face.

Daphne full-on screams, utterly horrified.

Gods, I fucking hate her.

My elemental looks as ridiculously gorgeous as ever, staring down his mother with cold eyes and a smirk. That smirk is everything to me. Everett might worry about what I think of his appearance, but in this moment, it's clear that there was another reason he kept the scar.

If anything, it makes him look less like his father. Less like one of *them*.

"Gods on high, it's worse than I imagined," Alaric sighs as he sits beside his wife, rubbing his temple as if a headache is brewing.

Now Daphne is dramatically fanning away tears. "Leave at once, Reagan. Clearly, nothing can cover *that*. Arati have mercy, why did it have to be true? To think, I'm now the mother of two disfigured children!"

I don't know what she's talking about, but her words infuriate Everett. Despite the shit they forced down his throat to tamper with his abilities, snowflakes begin to fall in this room as the frost patterns on the windows grow.

Reagan rushes out of the room, smart enough to know not to stick around.

The look Everett gives his mother is pure savage contempt. "Pretend you were a mother to me all you want, but leave my sister out of this. Aside from birthing her and getting the hell out of her life, you never did a damn thing in Heidi's favor. She deserved better than this fucked-up family."

"Watch how you speak about our family," Alaric begins. "Frosts do not—"

"Frosts do not give a single flying fuck about anything except themselves," Everett snaps. "Frosts are shallow, spineless, corrupt, pathetic, whining little—"

His father strikes him across the face.

Hard.

I clench my teeth so hard they almost break as anger rushes hot and fast to the surface. I may be hindered now, but this asshole just signed his death certificate.

"Alaric!" Daphne protests. "His face—"

"Is a disgrace to the Frost name now, anyway," the elemental asshole huffs, straightening his tie and taking a deep breath for composure.

I'm ready to leap over the coffee table and shave his face off with my teeth, but Everett laughs. It's a cold, hard sound that shuts his parents up as he looks back at them.

"The Frost name, huh? Yeah, I'm done with that. When this is over, I swear on the fucking gods that I'll legally take my keeper's last name."

His parents look appalled that he would use blasphemous language, let alone suggest not wanting to be a Frost.

Meanwhile, the thought of Everett Amato makes me smile.

When Daphne sees my expression, she looks even more

disgusted. "No surprise that you are enjoying this crude behavior. You're clearly the one who taught it to him. Turned my beautiful, innocent son into a filthy, blasphemous deviant."

"Especially in bed," I agree.

Everett turns bright red at exactly the same time his mother does. His father begins coughing in a fit, avoiding eye contact. In another situation, their discomfort would make me laugh out loud. If his family weren't doomed for everything they put him through, they would be just as much fun to tease as he is.

The ghost behind the couch is gripping her stomach, laughing without sound. A few more ghosts have wandered into this room to watch this exchange.

"I—I cannot—Alaric, surely we are not going to offer this sick, atrocious little pervert a way out of what she so clearly deserves!" Daphne finally rages, so flustered and furious that when she tries to primp her hair, she accidentally pulls it partially out of the updo.

Sick, atrocious little pervert only makes me grin more.

Alaric clears his throat, moving on quickly as he finally faces me seriously. "Maven Oakley, we've wanted to meet you for quite some time. We always knew you would be an incomparable force of nature. In fact, we've wanted you as an ally ever since the *telum* was mentioned in our son's prophecy years ago—"

"The one you had falsely translated to manipulate him," I point out, my amusement long gone.

He brushes it off. "The prophet said the true translation was too complex to be completed, anyway. What good is an incomplete prophecy? We only wanted to temper his expectations appropriately. It was for his own good."

"You are such a fucking—" Everett begins angrily, but Alaric cuts him off.

"The real reason you're in this room is because we would like to offer you a deal, *telum*. As you can see from the lack of color here, this elite safe haven is located well behind the borders of the ever-expanding regions conquered by your creator."

If he thinks Amadeus is my creator, he's pathetically unaware of the facts. Unsurprising, since he's been sitting on his ass eating off silver spoons from the safety of his affluent little bubble, pleased with his own imagined position of authority.

"What we want from you is—"

"I know what you want," I cut in.

"Oh, please," Daphne huffs, admiring her perfect nails. "You can't possibly understand the complexity of our unique situation in the short time you've—"

"Amadeus knows you're here," I surmise smoothly. "You use a stolen shielding spell to keep out the worst of the fiends, but in order to ensure better safety for the so-called elite—who I'm sure practically worship you for giving them a luxurious safe place to laze around in—you must also be working with someone highly ranked in Amadeus's court. A lich, or a necromancer, or even a well-trusted monster."

They exchange glances before Alaric frowns at me. "A vampire, in fact."

"For my *'creator'* to allow you to live here, he would require something in return from you," I go on. "Wealth and fine things are useless to him, but despite his inhuman nature, Amadeus still owns a barbaric sense of humor. He enjoys tormenting the living as much as he can enjoy anything. My guess is that in exchange for being left alone, you've stooped down to sending him tributes—probably from the very people who show up asking to stay in this safe haven. Legacies. Humans. Animals. Anything he would enjoy torturing and pitting to the death in his arena for his court to mock."

Everett glares at his parents, incredulous. "Seriously? You're paying a blood tribute to the fucking Entity himself?"

The blue-haired young woman ghost with clearer features nods and flips off the Frosts, furious. Other ghosts shake their fists or appear to be silently cursing out the couple sitting on the couch.

Interesting. Are they ghosts of those tributes, come back to haunt the people who sentenced them to that fate?

Daphne lifts her chin, sniffing as if this topic is unpleasant. "As if it's something to clutch your pearls over. We've heard the rumors about your barbaric methods on the front lines. This is no different! It has always been the way of legacies to cull the weak. Of course, we took advantage of this chance, but—"

"But you don't like living under his sadistic thumb," I finish for her. I get it. I've been there, but that doesn't excuse the Frosts for this. "So when you caught me, you considered your new options. Whether it's possible or not, you decided maybe the *telum* could fix your problems. Meaning, you're offering to spare my life if I agree to end Amadeus and get you out of your rotten deal unscathed. Anything I'm missing?"

Alaric looks almost impressed by how much I've read between the lines, but Daphne glowers at me for calling them out.

Everett shakes his head, muttering, "This is disgusting. You seriously expect Maven to take out the Entity? No one even knows how he came to exist. He's been shrouded in mystery for thousands of years—and *that* is who you decided to barter with? You've been making shady deals for way too fucking long. You caught it in the ass this time, so deal with the consequences and leave my keeper the hell out of it."

Daphne starts to scold his language again, but Alaric holds up a hand as he examines me. "Is it possible? Ending the Entity?"

If there's anything I've learned in this brutal world, it's that every monster, legacy, human, god, and immortal has a weak spot.

My quintet has become mine.

Amadeus must have something I can use to bring him down. Whether it's a true death or just a steep fall from power, I'll do whatever it takes to find a way to defeat him. No one will endanger my future with my men ever again, but least of all him.

But the Frosts don't need to know that we have a mutual interest.

"Even if it was," I say, fixing them with my most deranged death glare and enunciating well so they won't miss this. "I will watch Amadeus's power consume this world and everything in it before I lift a single fucking finger to help megalomaniacal cowards as morally repugnant and soulless as you two."

For a moment, they stare at me in wide-eyed, fearful disbelief. A few of the ghosts applaud my string of insults. The blue-haired girl tries to punch through Daphne's face, but of course only passes harmlessly through the unwitting socialite.

Everett beams at me.

Godsdamn, that one dimple is just so fucking kissable.

Finally, Daphne sputters, "Surely, you don't mean that."

"Every fucking word."

"But this is your one chance to avoid public humiliation and a death sentence at the trial," she protests. "You must suffer from insanity!"

"Not really. Most of the time, I enjoy it." I tip my head. "Speaking of insanity, where is my fae? If he's been harmed at all, you'll need to arrange for your funerals before the fake trial begins."

"You dare threaten me in my own safe haven?" Alaric barks.

"You laid a hand on what's mine. *Safe* no longer exists for you," I darkly inform him.

Someone knocks on the door, interrupting whatever the Frosts would have sputtered next. When the very irritated Alaric calls for them to come in, the door opens and—

Oh, my fucking gods. No way.

Bertram.

25

MAVEN

WITH HIS SPRAY OF FRECKLES, handsome features, and that shock of red hair, the vampire who caused my failure six months ago is unmistakable as he dashes into the room with vampiric speed, dressed in a sharp suit. He whispers something in Alaric's ear, unaware of the nearby ghosts who lean close to hear whatever he's saying.

This is the vampire they're using to contact Amadeus?

Obviously, he's one hell of a bargainer if he outlived his usefulness to the Entity long enough to set all of this up, prove his value, and therefore be kept alive. He has the survival skills of a bright red, unbelievably fucking annoying cockroach.

I stare down the bloodsucker who killed his immortal lover to save his skin until he finishes speaking quietly with Alaric and straightens. He makes direct eye contact with me and has the nerve to fucking smile.

To everyone else, it looks pleasant.

To me, it's pure mocking.

"You must be the *telum*," he says in a light accent.

I smile back, conveying that I'll rip his head off once I'm out of this contraption. "Bertram."

Daphne's brows go up as she looks between us. "I see no

introductions are in order. Have you met the *telum* before, Bertram?"

"Not at all, *madame. Pardonne-moi,*" he adds before leaving the room just as swiftly.

Godsdamn it. He's going to run. He knows this place is compromised since I'm about to rain down hell on the assholes living here when I figure out how to escape. With survival skills that good, Bertram will disappear long before I have the chance to add him to the piled-up bodies.

When I swear under my breath, Everett leans as much as he can in his straitjacket to catch my eye.

"What is it?" he whispers.

"Later."

Gods, I desperately miss our telepathic connection.

Alaric Frost stands, re-buttoning his expensive suit as he looks coldly down at me. "It's a shame you couldn't get past your pride and agree to such a mutually beneficial agreement, *telum*. Even more of a shame that such a potent weapon will meet its end here. What a waste."

Everett bristles at how his father speaks about me like I'm not a person, but Daphne gives me the fakest smile in the world. It looks beautiful and classy like the rest of her, but there's no getting past the nasty undertone.

"Yes, what a shame. No matter. I'll be sure to have Reagan do your post-mortem makeup for your open casket viewing in a couple of days. That should please the press. But then, they're already over the moon about this little scoop. They're even broadcasting it outside our safe haven for anyone left out there watching."

"Soon the entire world will see what a favor we're doing them," Alaric agrees, striding to the glass windows overlooking the gray city below. "Frosts have always understood how influential spectacles can be. And why not honor the gods while we're at it? Arati will be very pleased."

I don't know why he's talking about my aunt, but this entire interaction with Everett's parents has been eye-opening. Everything my quintet has said about the Frosts is obviously true. How odd that such beautiful people can be so revolting, especially in the way they treat their son.

I wonder which is worse—growing up fending for yourself with no family at all, or growing up emotionally battered and manipulated by the people who should have been protecting you.

No wonder Everett was so standoffish and torn when I met him. No wonder he's so fucking hard on himself. They taught him all that self-loathing. Constantly being in the public eye, continually being pressured to be perfect, his appearance picked apart, every move he made held up in comparison to the Frost name, the verbal slights and social games…

My poor snow angel has gone through more than he'll admit.

Not that I'm one to talk, but still. Fuck them.

I'm distracted by loathing the Frosts until Tattoo Face reemerges through the double doors and nods to Alaric Frost.

"Everything is ready, sir."

"They've gathered?"

"Yes, sir."

Alaric seems pleased before motioning at me. Tattoo Face doesn't hesitate to throw me over his shoulder once again, and I fight back sudden nausea when his hand briefly touches the back of my bare neck. He starts walking back toward the elevator.

"Where are you taking her?" Everett demands.

He tries to rise to his feet despite the straitjacket, but he's suddenly frozen to the sofa as Alaric waves a hand. "No, no, son. You'll stay in here and watch the livestream of the trial with us. We certainly can't have that face of yours caught on camera until we find a way to fix it. It should be a quick proceeding anyway, but it's better to stay out of the smoke—which is what I told the rest of my quintet, but gods spare us, they wanted to have a front row seat."

We're being separated.

Shit.

Everett's shouts of furious protest cut off as the doors of the elevator close. I can tell we're descending, but my vision has blurred slightly. Even though Tattoo Face isn't touching my neck anymore, my body is still breaking out into sweat as I steady my breathing.

My view is an upside-down shot of this jerk's pants, but then the blue-haired ghost squats to smile and wave at me. She followed me into this elevator, along with a couple of other ghosts.

She tries communicating something to me with her hands, motioning from me to her and back, but I'm too dizzy and exhausted to piece it together before the elevator doors chime open.

The burly legacy carries me down a long hall before I'm suddenly set upright, facing revolving glass doors that lead outside. I squint through the glass, uneasiness running down my spine when I see all the people.

Two or three hundred well-dressed elite legacies and a few dozen humans wait on either side of the street, with a path cleared down the middle that lets me see something constructed in front of the steps leading up to Arati's temple. They almost look like—

Oh, shit.

Stakes. As in, the kind witches are burned at.

They clearly plan to burn me alive, but who is the other stake for?

The elite legacies and humans outside watch the door eagerly, waiting for my emergence. The Frosts have obviously taken time to prepare this spectacle in the grayscale streets of Manhattan, because at the end of this aisle of onlookers in front of Arati's temple is a full jury box, a robed judge at a podium, and a place for me to stand with cameras aimed at it.

There are also photographers waiting outside the revolving door, prepping their cameras. One of them is Miss Bailey from the fake pre-trial interview, who still looks pissy as she taps her foot and glowers at the door.

Oh, great. More pictures.

I'm starting to understand why Everett hates being on camera.

"It's time for the world to get their due from you, *telum*," Tattoo Face grunts.

He grips my shoulder too tightly and walks through the revolving doors, shoving me into the stormy daylight for my fake trial. The ghosts follow.

I'm immediately blinded by the flashes of cameras. They're so intense and so frequent that I turn my face away. They don't like that, though.

"Over here! Look over here, *telum!*"

"Maven Oakley! Eyes open, sweetheart! Look here!"

"Smile, Maven!"

Smile? At a fake trial? Whoever suggested that is fucking delusional. And whoever just called me *sweetheart* is about to have a broken nose.

Tattoo Face gets annoyed that I'm turning my face away from the photographers. He takes my chin in his hand, forcing my head to face the blinding flashes.

Immediately, my lungs deflate, and I can't pull in air. The rough, bare skin of his fingers drags across my jaw, squeezing and raw and absolutely fucking *unbearable*. Sweat beads on my forehead as my limbs lock. Panic pounds through my skull, reminding me of the countless times my body reacted this way in the citadel during my conditioning.

The scent of moldering corpses. Half-rotted Undead clawing at my skin.

Maggots.

So many maggots, trying to burrow under my skin as I screamed and clawed at the doors.

Gods, I'm starting to hyperventilate. I'm about to vomit in front of twenty cameras.

The camera flashes have slowed as they complain about me freezing up like this. Amid my haphephobic breakdown, the same blue-haired female ghost appears beside us. She glares at the legacy touching me, passes directly through me, and—

Tattoo Face screams, staggering back and *finally* fucking releasing me.

The crowds of onlookers gasp.

Someone shouts, "What was that? Did you see that?"

The photographers step away, but they're already snapping more pictures. I glance over my shoulder to see that the asshole who just had his hand on my face is now gripping his neck, choking and spasming on the ground until his eyes roll back into his head and foam drips from his mouth. He goes still.

"Get a healer!" someone shouts.

The photographers are still having a heyday as he's carried away. Two more legacy security members are immediately at my sides, gripping my straitjacketed arms and shoving me forward so I'll have to walk through the gawking elites. Most of them, including the judge and jury, are now watching me in disgusted terror as if *I* did that.

Did I?

It was the ghost, but it took passing through me for her to interact with the living. She targeted him for what he was doing to me. Are my demigoddess abilities more ghost-oriented than I realized?

Still reeling from the lingering horror of that touch, I'm forced to walk forward. Someone is wheeling a red-blinking camera several feet in front of me, showing all of this to anyone still out there.

I wonder if Kenzie is watching. Or Lillian.

The elite legacies I pass leer and gawk at me. Some take pictures on their phones, laughing and whispering to each other. Others chatter at full volume, wide-eyed as they see the *telum* reduced to this fucking morose parade. Many more of them flip me off, spit on me when they get the chance, and shout over the clamor of the crowd.

"Serves you right!"

"Suck my dick, you fucking demon!" another shouts.

"Go back to the Beyond where you belong!"

Usually, rubbing people the wrong way is its own kind of fun. This time, it's paired with the realization that I'm an object to these people—someone to be exploited for their entertainment.

I expect the staring. The smirks. Their abject fascination as they see the *telum* in the flesh for the first time, chained and straitjacketed to be the picture of defeat.

What I'm not expecting? That strange rush of peaceful magic that starts to course over my skin. It's similar to what I experience while reaping, and it begins to soothe the unpleasant burning sensation within my chest.

With all these eyes on me, it takes a second for me to remember Galene's words.

You see, we gods derive our power from worship.

I study the audience more closely as I pass. It's grown in number, but only because of all the ghosts gathering to watch.

Even when screaming out insults or taking videos on their phones, these legacies watch my every move with a strange sort of awe in their eyes. It's the same expression I saw on people fascinated by Everett in the past—people who thought of him as a celebrity.

Whether they like me or not, this qualifies as some form of worship. And wherever the big camera in my face is streaming to, the building rush of magic in my veins only grows until there is no pain in my chest. My pulse picks up, strong and furious.

Intriguing.

Finally, the assholes shove me to stand on the little pedestal in front of the fake jury and judge. They step away quickly, leaving me the center of attention. More cameras flash, but the ominous croaking of a raven draws my attention to the gray buildings surrounding this audience.

Everywhere I look, ravens are perched on the tops of buildings, watching.

The ghosts interspersed throughout the crowd are watching, too. Many of them look mad—but not at me.

I've just started formulating a plan when the revolving door I was pushed through opens again, and Crypt, Baelfire, and Silas are paraded outside.

My stomach lurches at the sight of them.

Crypt's face transforms to relief when he sees me, but he's gagged now. He's still mostly encased in bronze as they wheel him out, and that syringe is still in his neck. His markings light up constantly, proof that he's in pain that he won't show. Someone shouts that it's the Nightmare Prince, which induces more frenzied picture-taking and angry screaming. Plenty of the onlookers spit on him, too.

Baelfire is still in silver restraints, dragged by his leash as he snarls and snaps at everything. His irises are once again draconic slits that tell me he's not himself. The audience points and laughs, finding his cursed condition hysterical as someone in the jury loudly declares that he's Brigid Decimus's feral son.

And Silas—he's being dragged out by iron chains connected to iron shackles around his legs, arms, neck, and waist. My anger spikes to a dangerous level when I see that he's in a straitjacket covered in blood, struggling and shouting nonsense. He's fully descended into insanity again as he stumbles, collapsing to the street in crazed, panicked gibberish while everyone continues to laugh.

That's his own blood, covering him.

They were hurting my fae.

My empty chest clenches as hot moisture tries to rise into my eyes, seeing my ruby-eyed blood fae in this state. They must have confiscated his blood amulet.

Daphne was right. This is pure public humiliation for my quintet.

Obviously Not-Baelfire doesn't know that yet, but my stomach dips as I imagine how the real Baelfire will look when he realizes that everyone saw him collared like a feral fucking animal. My shifter is tied down near the steps of Arati's temple. Crypt is also left propped at the foot of the steps, facing me.

I realize it's so they'll get a front row seat to me burning alive.

If I wasn't seething to my very core and devising a plan to kill all these assholes, I would almost admire their barbarically sadistic appetite.

But this?

I've understood the magnitude of taking lives for a long time. I have a rule against harming or killing innocents—so I guess it's good that none of the elite legacies here fall under that umbrella.

Along with the holy magic, anger grows steadily in my veins, pulsing quicker and hotter as I turn to glower at the observers who are using my cursed quintet for entertainment. Everett isn't here. My elemental is probably still frozen to that sofa in the penthouse, also being forced to watch this.

Cameras flash as the so-called judge opens the trial, introducing me with dramatic flair before he calls up the two men who interviewed me earlier. They posture and preen as they talk at the jury and cameras, making a spectacle as they list everything I've been accused of. They present the "evidence" that I'm a demon, dramatically and incorrectly describe the ways I assassinated the Immortal Quintet, and generally make an ass of themselves for their rapt audience.

But I'm not listening to any of it, because the ghosts have gotten angrier.

There's nearly an equal amount of restless spirits here as there are living people. Finally, the same blue-haired ghost girl who attacked Tattoo Face leaves the crowd and drifts up to me, pointing at the skyscraper where the Frosts are watching before drawing a line across her neck.

I focus on her, speaking quietly. "You want revenge?"

She nods eagerly. So do many of the other nearby ghost spectators of this so-called trial.

"Good. I'll need my scythe."

"Silence, demon!" the judge snaps. "These two gentlemen are explaining your case to the court."

I ignore him and the additional stares his outburst has sent my way. The ghost girl nods, passing through me one more time. I don't feel any different, but she floats quickly toward the Frost tower, disappearing through one of the many windowed walls to search for my dagger.

At least, I hope that's what she's doing.

Crypt witnessed me talking to nothing. He catches my eye and tips his head curiously, still ignoring his swirling markings as they light up repeatedly.

I mouth, *Wait for it.*

This fake trial starts to wind to a close, with the live feed camera wheeling annoyingly close to get a shot of my face and everyone laughing when Not-Baelfire begins gnawing on his leash. I'm scanning the sky for the blue-haired ghost when a large raven flutters to perch on my shoulder.

I recognize this one. It's the same raven that helped Everett find me when Baelfire's dragon had me in the woods.

I study it before muttering, "When I make my move, peck out their eyes."

These imbeciles will lose much more than their eyes for this, but since all these laughing elite legacies are enjoying the sight of my quintet in this condition so much, I'm going to start by taking that sight away.

The raven croaks in agreement before fluttering off to perch on a building, squawking at the other ravens. No one present seems to notice all the ravens that have gathered to fixate on the eyeballs in the crowd, eager for their treats.

I know jack shit about legacy or human courtroom proceedings, but I'm not surprised when the jury votes and the judge rules without ever calling on me for a testimony.

"The jury is unanimous!" the judge booms, banging a shiny gavel on the table as more pictures are taken. "Maven Oakley, the Entity's demonic *telum* who murdered our beloved Immortal Quintet and brought about the end of our world, is hereby found guilty on all charges and sentenced to immediate death prior to Sachar's final judgment in the Beyond!"

The jury members and all the watching legacies applaud. One of the security members approaches me again. I hiss in surprised pain when he twists his hand near my scalp, dragging me by my hair to one of the towering, flammable stakes at the foot of Arati's temple.

Crypt sees that and shouts in helpless rage. Silas starts screaming again nearby, and as the asshole releases my hair, I realize my blood fae is being tied to the stake beside me. Not-Baelfire is still a laughingstock, and somewhere high above, Everett is being forced to watch all of this.

More holy power pumps through my veins, screaming at me to harness my fury and do something.

I will.

I'm just waiting for the right moment.

The fake judge bangs his gavel again to be heard over the excited legacies.

"Furthermore, as is our duty as legacies, and according to the landmark Sacredness of Life Act of 1742, the former blood fae known as Silas Crane is hereby found guilty of successful necromantic metamorphosis. To cleanse the world of his vile death magic, this necromancer shall also be exterminated expeditiously through traditional means."

That explains the wooden stakes.

The security asshole releases my hair and pulls out a key that finally drops the chains before loosening the arms of my straitjacket just enough to lift them high above my head. He starts tying my wrists to the stake using the ends of the straitjacket arms.

I don't fight it. Instead, I breathe at a measured pace, preparing for the right moment to unleash hell. Still, my stomach dips and twists with each minor brush of his skin against mine.

I'm fighting like hell to disassociate through this, but it catches me by surprise when cold gasoline crashes over my head, dousing me immediately. It starts to burn my skin, the pungent chemical scent searing my nose and throat. I sputter, spitting out the turpentine flavor. My eyes burn.

They must have doused Silas at the same time, because his nonsensical screams worsen. When I look over, he's thrashing despite his bound wrists, his blood-red eyes unseeing as his fangs descend. His blackened fingertips are on display, his hands tied over his head just like mine.

"Silas," I cough, desperate to comfort him even as the audience claps and cheers. Cameras are flashing again, but the jackasses who just tied us up like this have finally stepped back.

"Ei'thu leamsah head devil! *Thu occidere a'sai!"* he shrieks, choking on gasoline.

Most of that makes no sense, except the part where he might've called me a head devil.

"I'll fix this," I reassure him. Whether he can understand me or not, I can't take his panicked, paranoid screaming anymore. It hurts me more than the acrid gasoline burn in my throat. "I'm real. This is real, and it's about to be over. I promise. *Tha galeath."*

He stops fighting so hard for a brief second, rolling his head from side to side as his screaming turns into a prayer. It's the first time I've heard Silas pray, and I don't miss that he's praying to Arati.

It's fitting. We're in front of her temple. She's the goddess of fury, revenge, love, combat…pretty much everything we're about to need.

I glance at the sky, deciding it's not a bad idea. "From what I remember, you were a bitch. But so am I. Maybe we parted on good terms, so feel free to make yourself useful."

Nothing changes, but it doesn't matter. I don't need her when vengeance continues to rage inside me.

By the time a fire elemental moves to stand in front of the stakes, holy power is pumping so vigorously in my veins that I'm nearly shaking. Ravens look on. Ghosts are restless, drifting ever closer until the furious dead hover behind me, waiting.

Finally—fucking *finally*—the blue-haired ghost appears nearby with my etherium dagger in her hands. Only a couple of people in the audience notice the dagger floating toward me, and their eyes round in confusion.

"Maven Oakley," the judge booms, calling everyone to attention as cameras pan to me. "At the foot of Arati's temple, we now end your infernal existence as an offering to the gods. Say your final prayers to Syntyche, for the Reaper is known to be merciless and—"

I don't mean to burst into laughter.

Really, I don't.

It just bubbles up uncontrollably as everyone else falls quiet, uncomfortable with my humor. The jury and judge look annoyed. Photographers snap more pictures of my accidental bout of amusement as the fire elemental waiting to execute us looks around, unsure of what to do.

Crypt starts to smile as he watches me spook the audience. Not-Baelfire has stopped chewing on his leash. Even Silas has stopped screaming, leaving this colorless, crowded street quiet except for my laughter.

I was a fool, trying to keep my identity a secret until I was ready for the world to know. I thought it would give me time to adjust, but now?

Everyone watching needs to know exactly who they crossed.

"If you think Death is merciless, you haven't officially met her daughter," I warn the frightened onlookers as my laughter tapers off. I toss gasoline-soaked hair out of my face and smile as dark, murderous anticipation hums in the cold air around me. "Let's change that, shall we?"

The blue-haired ghost swipes my etherium blade through the straitjacket arms tying me to this stake in one fluid motion. The knife promptly falls out of her no-longer-solid grasp—and just like that, I'm free as my weapon transforms into a scythe in my hand, as ready as I am to reap.

Ghosts pour through me in a deluge, turning tangible as they flood into the mortal realm. Ravens descend as holy magic swirls around my fingertips, unleashed with my lost temper.

I smile as the beautiful screaming begins.

26

BAELFIRE

My dragon likes all the screaming.

He also likes chewing on his stupid fucking leash, which means that from the corner of our dark, shared mind where I barely manage to exist, all I get is a vague view of this moron chewing on leather.

Hey, Scales for Brains. Where the hell is Maven? I try to demand.

He ignores me easily.

Ever since my mate's scent started to make its way to me through the control of my dragon, she's all I can think about—besides trying to fight for dominance in my own head. But according to everything Everett told me earlier, that's been a losing battle for six months.

Six whole motherfucking months without her.

I push against my inner dragon, desperate to take over so I can look around for my mate and figure out what just happened to start all the screaming. I see some of what my dragon sees, but he sucks at paying attention to details. And his listening skills? Forget it.

The one and only thing I can thank the scaly alphahole for is his unique ability to sense Maven, no matter the distance. It's something to do with us being marked as mates, but only he picks up on it. Not to mention, it must not be a perfect skill, because the big scaly pain in my ass went and sniffed around an abandoned temple for hours on end before he went to hunt for Maven days ago.

Despite my inability to see or sense much trapped in my own head like this, I can still identify a barrage of smells. Gasoline. Smoke. Blood.

But most of all, the sour smell of fear, so fucking thick and powerful that it makes me think I'm missing something big.

Someone screams loudly in terror nearby before their pleas cut off.

"T—they're all ghosts!" another legacy shouts. "No! Mercy! Please, have mer—"

His voice cuts off as birds shriek somewhere nearby.

Ghosts? Are we in danger again?

Shit—is *she* in danger?

Godsdamn it, I need control. I need to get to her.

My dragon is suddenly restless and angry about something, but I can't get a fucking grip or sense anything happening in my own body until something slams into my head. I topple, pain rocking down my neck and spine as the world spins.

Just like that, the dragon retreats to hide from the pain that it can't shift to tolerate. I wrench back control and sit up, blinking at the chaos surrounding me. It looks like I was hit in the head by a chunk of Crypt's bronze enclosure that somehow shattered, but besides that…

Holy fucking fuck.

There are ravens and ghosts everywhere—at least, I'm pretty damn sure they're ghosts because they hover and fly around, are slightly see-through, and make my hair stand on end. But they're also able to touch the legacies who are screaming and trying to get away.

Some of the ghosts disappear into the bodies of elite legacies, who immediately fall to the street to writhe in agony with foaming mouths. Other ghosts taunt the people trying to flee, pulling them in strange directions, dancing creepily around them, or lifting them off the ground to drop them from high enough to break their legs.

I realize most of the elite fuckers can't see where to run because they don't have eyeballs anymore. Gawking, I watch a big raven attack the face of one of Everett's other snobby parents, pecking at his eyes as the well-dressed air elemental screams and thrashes, gusts of wind exploding uselessly from his hands.

Royal blue flames are devouring two huge wooden stakes nearby, proof that my dragon got involved. I get to my feet, turning and searching as my heart pounds—until I spot Maven and immediately break into a smile.

Hell, yes. That's my mate.

Tearing her way through the screaming legacies, my violent, sexy keeper looks every bit the daughter of Death as she reaps souls left and right. She's a fucking force of nature, with that spine-chilling smile on her beautiful face as ghosts and fluttering ravens surround her.

When a wolf shifter snarls and leaps at her, she gracefully dodges aside before her scythe cuts him clean in half. A magic attack is flung at her from some other panicked elite, but it bounces harmlessly off her when she bats it away with a softly glowing hand. She turns to swing her scythe again, moving like she's dancing as she and her otherworldly army slaughter everyone who hasn't managed to escape.

I'm ready to help my dark queen kick ass and take names in this black-and-white city all day, but I notice Silas sitting nearby, soaked with gasoline as he rocks himself, red magic hovering around his fingertips. One of his eyes twitches as blood drips steadily from his nose.

I glance at Maven demolishing our enemies with gleeful fury, then back at this fae, torn.

Finally, I sigh. Damn it. He needs to snap out of this.

I move toward him, lifting my hands to show I'm not a

threat, even though my head is starting to split as the dragon inside me writhes.

"Si. Hey, buddy. You in there?"

He startles and scrambles away from me. *"Nach ti'faieth!"*

"Gesundheit." I crouch beside him, grabbing his blackened-finger hands to stop him before he can fling magic at me. "You've gotta stop. Your nose is bleeding again."

Silas blinks at me several times before seeming to focus. A particularly shrill scream sounds nearby, drawing our attention to the chaos.

All the cameras have been destroyed. Several elite legacies are now fighting each other, which is odd until Crypt appears from Limbo, literally skipping as he enjoys the bloodbath. He kicks aside two shredded corpses, grins maniacally over at us, and triumphantly holds up…fingers.

A whole bundle of them.

Then he vanishes into Limbo again. Fucking psychopath.

"That's…real?" Silas checks, his voice slurring.

"The ghosts and birds and our stone-cold, badass demigoddess? You bet."

"Do demigoddesses berserk?" he frowns. "Should we be concerned?"

Hell if I know, but it's weird that *he's* the one asking *me* questions. My annoyingly smart quintet member clearly doesn't trust his own brain right now, if he thinks I have a clue what's going on.

My head pangs. I grimace through the dragon pushing for dominance before I clear my throat. "Nah, I'm pretty sure she's just really fucking mad about…something. Can't remember. When did we move outside, anyway?"

Silas doesn't notice my question as he squints at a puddle of blood nearby. "What about them?"

"Them, who?"

"The bloated faces in the blood. Are they real?"

"Nope, that's all in your creepy-ass brain. Come on."

I help him stand, trying not to wrinkle my sensitive nose at the overpowering smell of gasoline covering him. His breathing is rapid and he starts muttering fae shit I don't understand under his breath as we make our way through the aftermath of Maven's massacre.

Crypt finally steps out of Limbo to rejoin us, looking like he's having the time of his life as he rearranges his macabre bouquet. "Are we off to find wherever they have Frost next?"

I do a quick scan of our surroundings. Ghosts have slowly been vanishing, ravens are picking at the dead bodies, and the screaming has all but stopped. Maven stands perfectly still in the streets running with the blood of our enemies, her scythe in hand as she seems lost in thought—no, it must be memories. Everett mentioned that she's slowly remembering her time in Paradise.

But Crypt is right. Our elemental is nowhere to be seen, even though I spot a couple of the elite legacies in his parents' quintet lying motionless in their designer clothes nearby.

"Guess so," I grunt.

Just as we approach Maven, Crypt collapses onto the cold street. Silas and I both startle when the incubus gasps in pain, face contorting as all of his markings light up brightly several times in a row, like a warning.

I've never seen Crypt so obviously affected by his curse, but Silas and I exchange a look. He must realize what I'm also putting together: the fun little fact that the Nightmare Prince's curse can't be broken and is obviously worse than ever. Like all stewards of Limbo, his curse is slowly killing him.

Or maybe not so slowly, judging by the agony he's clearly in.

"Shit," I mutter.

"Shit," Silas agrees before flinching away from nothing and swearing in fae. "That not ever as how the leprechaun use is to spirits. *Daingeath,* singing head devils."

Yeah, never mind. He can't even string a sentence together.

I'm on my own here.

Seeing that Maven is still in her trance, I stoop to talk to Crypt. "Where can we get *reverium* for you?"

"Up your scaly ass," he snaps before grimacing again. "I'm fine."

"Yeah, you look fine," I retort.

The pain on his face slowly subsides until he takes a shaky breath, glowering at the stormy sky above as the burning stakes cast a blue glow on this gruesome setting. "Neither of you will breathe a word about this to our girl."

I scowl, gripping his arm to haul him to his feet. That makes him accidentally drop a finger, which he quickly retrieves like he's just picking up loose change as I gripe at him.

"Fuck that. Weren't you the one who said you didn't want to keep secrets from her?"

"Shove off, Decimus."

"No. I'm telling Maven—"

He straightens to level me with a violet glare as ravens squawk and flutter nearby. "Telling our keeper that while she was stuck in Paradise sacrificing gods-know-what to get back to us, I was doing my damned best to snuff out through my curse requires a tact you've never possessed, you fucking lizard."

It takes a second for that to sink in, and…

I kind of get it.

But I'm also beyond pissed. "If you're on death's doorstep, she has the right to know—"

"I know."

We all pause, realizing that Maven is now watching us. Her gaze is steady, her dark hair a mess, and the straitjacket those assholes put her in is ripped and stained with blood—but gods, my mate is so strong and beautiful that it's hard to breathe. Her scythe transforms into a clear dagger she stashes in her boot.

Crypt swallows. His markings light up again. "Forgive me, darling."

She gives him a hard look that is definitely a *no,* not bothering to hide the emotions warring under her surface. Gods, I want to pull her into a hug and promise that we'll figure out how to keep her creepy incubus, but she quickly turns and strides toward the Frost tower.

"I'll find a way to fix it. Come on."

The three of us follow her toward the revolving doors, with Silas talking to the voices in his head.

My inner dragon abruptly wrenches back control, shoving me back into the tiny corner in my head as I black out and he takes over.

It's so fucking disorienting every time.

I finally come to and try to get my bearings, but all I can figure out is that we're indoors. It still smells like gasoline, so I must still be near Silas and Maven.

Where is she? I demand.

Covet. Taste, my dragon growls back, senseless and feral as fuck.

"I'm not going to hurt you," Maven says from somewhere nearby.

Hurt me, I try to insist, needing that pain to get control back.

I have no control over my body, so I can't get the words out. Fuck, I miss our telepathic connection. If anything, I could've asked Silas or Crypt or Everett to whack me upside the head to snap me out of it, and they would've been all too ready to volunteer. Probably would've argued for who had the honor.

I pick up on the sharp scent of fear again before a woman speaks.

"Oh my gods, y—you're a…a—"

"She's a breathtaking demigoddess," Crypt supplies from close beside me.

The woman hiccups. "But you just killed all those l—legacies and…"

"Reagan. Focus. Is Everett still on the top floor?" my mate asks, gentle but firm.

"In the penthouse," the woman agrees, sounding terrified.

Someone pulls hard on the leash around my neck. I sense my

dragon's irritation before the taste of blood fills my mouth, telling me the asshole just bit someone really fucking hard. Crypt swears viciously, but when Maven starts to say something, his voice is all reassurance.

"Don't worry yourself, love. It's not the first time this feral tosser's taken a bite out of me. Better to get Frost back before the new wisps you just introduced to Limbo break free."

27

EVERETT

I NEVER WANTED to learn fencing.

When I was six years old, I figured out I could make snowballs in my bare hands whenever I felt like it. Whenever I got bored during my first year of private tutoring, I'd throw a snowball at the tutor.

I thought it would be fine. After all, the tutor was nicer than most other adults in the mansion I was raised in, probably because she was a human who came from nothing who believed kids should be allowed to be kids.

She thought my snowball pranks were funny the first few times. But eventually, she mentioned my newfound playfulness to my parents' quintet.

They punished me by making me watch as they severely reprimanded her, fired her without pay, and kicked her out the door while she was still sobbing. Then they hired a fire elemental tutor who melted anything I dared create during class.

Corbin, one of my father's quintet members, called me an undisciplined, rambunctious rascal and said the best way for me to get out my "godsforsaken childish energy" was if I had an outlet for it—fencing, they decided.

The first few practices were brutal. The equipment was

heavy. The private instructor shouted at me the entire time. I left sore, bruised, and frustrated. I wasn't good at it, so I started to hate it.

When Alaric learned I was shit at fencing at the grand old age of six, he sat me down and calmly explained that he would find a competent heir somewhere else if I kept turning out to be an embarrassment to the Frost name. Back then, I still cared about making my family proud. It was all I was taught to care about, so I returned to my fencing class the next day and kept my mouth shut when I left with welts and bruises.

A couple of years later, they added swordfighting to my fencing lessons.

Every day, I worked to become the best. Even long after I realized how much I hated my last name and everything that came with it, I practiced out of spite. Twenty-one years later, whether I'm holding a sword or an épée, it becomes an extension of me.

But I never enjoyed it.

Until now.

With a flick of my wrist, the tip of my sword slashes through Alaric's face, leaving a cut that's almost a perfect mirror to the scar marring my face.

He swears, choking as he covers his face. He's lying on the floor, scrambling back toward the floor-to-ceiling glass wall as this penthouse filled with ice continues to frost over. After Maven's revelatory words and the divine fury she began raining down on the elite legacies in front of Arati's temple, my parents freaked out.

They were ready to run and leave me frozen to the couch, but ghosts—fucking visible *ghosts*—appeared out of nowhere and furiously swarmed my mother. She's now dead on the ground several yards away, foam frozen around her mouth as she stares sightlessly at the ceiling.

Whatever gave them the ability to end my mother, the ghosts vanished—except for the one that freed me. I nearly had a damn heart attack when one of them passed into me next, but all it did was shatter the ice and rip through the straitjacket, freeing me.

I'd grabbed a sword off the wall to stop Alaric from making a run for the elevator, and it quickly became Frost against Frost.

He's been putting up one hell of a fight, for someone who just lost his quintet bond. Even though I still can't summon ice, I've barely been able to melt each of his attacks. Now I stand over him, glowering down as he clutches his bleeding face and wheezes, sweat breaking out on his forehead as he shakes and swears.

I'll never forget what it felt like to lose my bond to Maven. It's the moment all my nightmares are made of. As a keeper with four freshly broken bonds, he must be in agony.

Good.

Spitting out blood, my father sneers up at me. For once in my life, he doesn't look perfectly polished. "Enough. You wouldn't kill me, so put down the sword."

I scoff, letting the tip of my sword bend the flesh at his neck. "I'll show you how wrong you are as soon as you tell me where the stolen etherium for your safe haven's shield is."

The second they live streamed my keeper's face to the rest of the surviving world to prove she was back, I realized shit is about to hit the fan if we survive this. People were already way too fucking comfortable talking about my dead keeper and feeding off her posthumous fame.

Now, news of her return and her true identity will spread like wildfire. Countless people will be trying to get to my snowdrop—to see her for themselves, to attack her, to marvel at her…whatever the fuck it will be, they'll want to get close to her.

Which means it's only a matter of time before the news of her reaches the Entity.

I want another shield to keep her extra safe from it all, once we get back.

Alaric grips at the center of his chest as the pain from losing his quintet continues to sink in. His cold, pale gaze is almost wild with desperation. "You want it, you have to spare my life."

The smile I give him is humorless. "So you can live for what? Your safe haven? Your quintet? Your precious Frost name? That's all gone now. Come to think of it, I can just look for the etherium myself, so if you have nothing else to say—"

I move my sword, fully ready to slit his throat, wipe my hands clean of the Frosts entirely, and go looking for Maven. But Alaric shouts in alarm, holding up his hands. I don't miss that he tries to summon ice again in one last attempt to harm me, but he's too weakened from losing his matches and tapped out from our fight.

I smirk when he's left panting, scrambling back until his back hits the frosted glass. I follow, replacing my sword at his neck as he splutters, making one last desperate attempt to survive me.

"Y—your sister!" he sputters.

That makes me halt, unease settling in my gut.

After the chaos of the Upheaval, I had been so lost to soul-crushing grief and depression that I didn't go looking for Heidi until four months ago. Even after sending Douglas and his hell-hound to track her, I was never able to find her—or Ian, for that matter. The vampire I've known since childhood was fully aware that my sister has always been my top priority for him to keep an eye on, but he was no longer in Hawaii, where he went into hiding after faking his death.

Aside from searching for Crypt, I've spent months looking for my sister and worrying about what I would find.

And my father must know it, because he has that *gotcha* look on his bleeding face.

I narrow my eyes. "What about her?"

The doors of the elevator ding softly, but I don't take my eyes off Alaric as he lifts his chin. "I'll tell you where she is if I walk free."

I weigh my options as snowflakes pepper the air around us. The odds that Alaric is just throwing Heidi out as a bluff are extremely high. He knows how protective I am of her. And whether I like it or not, the odds that Heidi has actually survived this long with everything going on are…

Low. Nauseatingly low.

Heidi isn't a fighter like most legacies are born to be. For one thing, she's a type four empath, which is the most extreme and rare level of empathic abilities. I was relieved when my sweet, sunshiney sister finally admitted to me she would rather never attend Everbound and instead pretend to be a human.

During the Upheaval, she would have struggled to defend herself on account of the skittish, non-predator animal living inside her.

But even though it's unlikely, if there's a chance she survived and could be out there…

I glare at Alaric, moving the point of my sword to hover beside his ear. "Forget walking free. You'll tell me where she is or—"

"Or *what?*" my father spits, still shaking and gripping his chest where his heart hurts. "As you pointed out, your sick, twisted keeper already took my quintet away. I have no safe haven left. If you kill me, you'll never know where she is. There is nothing you can threaten me with, you hideous fucking disgrace."

Someone growls nearby. That confuses me enough to barely glance over and realize that Baelfire, Crypt, Silas, and Maven have ventured into this frozen penthouse. Baelfire is the one growling, his teeth bared at Alaric. Silas is staring at the bare wall like it's the biggest danger in the room, and Crypt is holding…fingers?

Oh, right. That freak made a promise to Maven. Gross.

Meanwhile, Maven's dark eyes are on my father, angry and unforgiving, but it's like an anvil lifts off my chest. Fucking gods above, I just can't breathe whenever I'm not around her. Remembering her tied to that stake, ridiculed and filmed and laughed at as gasoline was poured over her head—

Searing anger makes me turn back to Alaric and swipe my sword.

His ear comes off. He screams.

I leave his other one intact so that he'll hear my furious demand. "Where is she?"

"I–I won't tell you," he chokes out. "Frosts do not—"

I slash across my father's other cheek, and he howls, clutching his ruined face. Tired of this slow process, I toss aside the sword and haul my father up by his blood-soaked lapels, slamming him against the frost-patterned glass wall overlooking the gray cityscape outside.

"Last chance," I warn him, years of anger at the way they mistreated my sister welling inside me. Despite the debilitant they gave me, frost begins to climb steadily up my forearms as my curse reacts to my anger.

Alaric coughs blood in my face on purpose, trying to distract me. Past me would have fallen for it, but if he thinks blood is going to put me off now, it means he's not getting the fucking message. Releasing one of his lapels, I slam my elbow into Alaric's face, satisfied with the crack of his nose as he shouts in pain again.

"You're right. I can't threaten your quintet or your safe haven, so it's a good thing you still have what you really care about—your own damn hide," I point out. "You think I'd let you walk away after you fucking *broadcasted* humiliating my keeper? No. You have two choices. Tell me where my sister is, and I'll make it quick. Keep annoying the hell out of me, and I'll drag this on, kill you anyway, and rip this entire place apart until I find clues—and I know there will be something, because *Frosts always keep impeccable records,*" I mock his voice.

He glares at me, but it's unimpressive thanks to the blood, gashes, and pain all over his face. "You're really going to kill me? Your own father? You son of a bitch."

"Yeah, well, it's not my fault Mom was a bitch. Now choose."

Alaric seethes for a long moment before looking defeated.

Maybe it's from losing his quintet, or maybe it's because I bested him, but his shoulders slouch as he stares at me.

"She showed up over a month ago, looking for safety. It's the way of legacies and Frosts to cull the weak, and we couldn't have her weakening our safe haven."

"What the hell does that—" I begin.

"We turned her away—her and that little human friend of hers who brought her here. They were left to the fiends outside my safe haven to fend for themselves."

Horror and fury hit me so hard and fast that I freeze up as his words sink in.

He turned her away.

My parents fucking turned their own daughter away.

If Heidi had been desperate enough to come to my parents looking for safety, they would have treated her as they always have—like someone with no significant value. She's not a powerful legacy, and my mother, being the appearance-obsessed woman she's always been, wouldn't have wanted people here to find out Heidi was their daughter.

If they refused to take in Heidi left her to fend for herself—

There's no way she survived. She's dead.

My sister is dead.

My lungs feel like they're collapsing. Oh, my fucking gods. I failed her. I was too caught up in my grief after losing Maven to think clearly. I failed to protect her from our family. She probably died terrified and alone in some horrific circumstances, and—

Too late, I see the gleam of freshly summoned ice in my father's hand. It's sharp as a dagger, and he's already thrusting it up toward my chest when something blurs between us, roughly knocking me aside.

Glass shatters. Alaric shouts as he's tackled through the window by none other than Baelfire.

Who is now falling to his own death.

Maven shouts in frantic alarm, and that sound makes my chest clench painfully. I'm still in shock when Crypt swears and races forward to leap out the window next, dropping into Limbo immediately.

I scramble to the edge of the penthouse, my heart pounding as I watch Baelfire's careening form getting smaller the further he falls. Godsdamn it, he can't shift to save himself. Even a shifter can't survive a fall from this distance—

But like a blip, Crypt appears, grabs Baelfire, and then they both disappear before they can hit the ground.

I exhale, relief flooding me so quickly that I get lightheaded.

When I hear Maven breathe out in equal relief beside me, I realize how closely and fearlessly she's standing next to the ledge. I immediately grip her around the waist to pull her away from danger. Silas is still zoned out in his insanity, etching runes into one of the shards of ice nearby and whispering to the voices in his head.

Maven protests my fussiness, insisting she's fine, but I'm too busy taking stock of every inch of her. She's covered in gasoline, dirt, blood, and soot. Her wrists are red from how tightly they tied her to the stake, but despite the rips and tears in her strait-jacket and clothes, she's okay.

"Everett," she murmurs, making me realize she's been repeating my name as I've been analyzing any tiny nicks or cuts on her. She cups my face, making me look at her. My chest squeezes again, seeing the gentleness in her gaze. That bound-less concern. "Are you okay?"

"You just had your identity revealed on live television. You were laughed at and wrongly convicted, and then you were almost burned at the stake for the entire remaining world to see," I point out angrily. "Of course, I'm not fucking okay. I need to get you back to Everbound. Back to safety. If Douglas is still alive, we'll have him transport us back immediately, and I'll send a team here to raid the place for anything useful, including the etherium shielding—"

"I meant your parents," she interrupts gently, glancing at my mother's motionless body. "I know your relationship with your family wasn't ideal, but..."

Oh. She thinks their deaths are upsetting me.

At one time, years ago, I would have been heartbroken. Back then, I thought family meant family, no matter how cruel, and people owed each other just for sharing blood. In a warped, manipulated way, I loved my parents and their quintet and did anything I could to make them happy. To be a perfect heir.

Now? I haven't had them twisting my arm in so long that I can see why Silas and Baelfire and even Crypt constantly criticized my family while we were growing up.

Whenever my parents took me to the Decimuses to "make allies" with other strong legacy children, I pretended not to notice how different Baelfire's family was from mine. Still, he never missed the chance to point out how awfully my family treated me in comparison. A long time ago, before it ever entered my mind to go off on my own, Silas was the one who first suggested I get myself emancipated early.

They knew. It took years, but I get it now.

I shared blood with the Frosts, and I looked like my father, but I'm not them. And now that my sister is gone, I have only one person to mourn and no family to speak of.

I'm...whatever my quintet is.

A mess, basically.

But one I'm proud of.

I kiss Maven's forehead, using one of my straitjacket sleeves to wipe gasoline and soot from her pretty face. "One less thing to threaten our quintet. I'm fine, Snowdrop."

She studies me for a moment before her lips curl up slightly. "I was right. Angry Everett is definitely a sight to behold."

Crypt finally steps out of Limbo into the frozen penthouse, letting Baelfire stumble into one of the nearby walls. The Nightmare Prince immediately stoops to pick up those godsdamned fingers that he apparently dropped before turning and offering them to Maven, entirely earnest as he gazes at her hopefully.

"Forgive me now, love?"

I gag at the sight of the bloody fingers this disturbed freak is pretending are flowers. Meanwhile, Maven's lips twitch like she's charmed and trying not to smile.

"We'll talk about that later," she tells him, not that I know what she's talking about. "More importantly, you took Baelfire into Limbo again. Is he—"

"I'm fine," Baelfire reassures us. "I closed my eyes, so it probably didn't fuck up my head more than it already is."

I turn my face toward him in surprise. When I do, the shifter gets an eyeful of my face for the first time since he went feral. His golden eyes get round with surprise.

"Holy shit, your face is so fucking—"

I hold up a hand, not in the mood to deal with his big, fat mouth. "You have thirty seconds to get all comments about my face out of your system. If you say another word after that, I'll freeze your tongue, snap it off, and shove it up your ass."

Crypt grins, pointing at me with one of the dismembered fingers. "Good gods! Is this a version of Frost I could actually get on with?"

Baelfire raises his brows, glancing at the others. "Someone's cranky."

"We're all cranky," Silas snaps nearby, startling everyone. He's sitting with his back against a wall now, rubbing his temples before swatting at nothing once again. "I'm with Everett. I'd rather not listen to you crack amateur jokes about his complexion for however long we manage to live."

"Yeah, yeah. *Chill out* about your face, Frosty," Baelfire jokes, slapping my shoulder good-naturedly. "It's better this way, anyway. Makes you look less like the assfaced douchebag I just took care of for you."

I pause, a new realization setting in. "Wait. Did *you* do that to protect me, or was it your dragon?"

"You think my dragon gives a single flying fuck about you?

Nah, that moron would've pushed you out the window and then jumped himself," he snorts. "Brains aren't his strong suit."

"Remind me what other moron just jumped out a window sans plan," Crypt drawls pointedly.

"Oh, come on. I knew you'd jump out a window for me anytime, *buddy*," the shifter teases.

Baelfire just saved my life. On purpose.

That's weird, but I guess no weirder than Crypt rescuing the oversized lizard.

When I notice that Maven is quietly grinning at us, I sigh.

"I know what you're thinking, but it's not because—"

"It is *absolutely* because you're all a bunch of fucking softies," she inserts. "Incredibly sexy softies, but softies nonetheless."

Crypt huffs at that idea, as displeased as ever at the thought of getting along with us, but then he looks at me seriously. He looks almost…sad. "My condolences, Frost. Heidi deserved better."

Bael frowns. "Who's Heidi?"

"Frost's sister," Crypt supplies easily.

"What?" Silas and Baelfire ask in synchrony, both askance.

"Hold the fucking phone. You mean, there's another Frost running around out there?" Baelfire adds, looking between all of us with wide gold eyes, like that idea is horrible.

"Not anymore," I say, my voice suddenly too thick for the words to sound right. "Heidi isn't—*wasn't* a normal legacy. If my parents sent her away, she's—"

I cut off, turning to stare at Crypt as the entire conversation with my father replays in my head. I know for a fact that neither of us said her name out loud. Frost spreads further up my arms as I take a step toward him.

"Crypt. How the hell did you know my sister's name?" I demand.

He absentmindedly rubs the place where they previously had a syringe in his neck. His markings light up repeatedly, his gaze drifting to the broken window.

"Suppose that ginger mercenary is still alive?"

He's clearly trying to brush off this topic. Not about to let him, I test my powers again for the first time, raising a hand. A blunt shard of ice appears, jutting out from the floor and sending Crypt crashing into the wall. Before I can pin him there and demand how he knew about my sister, something big and way too fucking warm slams into my side.

Suddenly, *I'm* the one pinned to the wall by a very annoyed Baelfire.

"Don't hurt Crypt right now," he snaps. "He can't take it."

What the hell? "When did you start caring so much about that psychopath?"

Silas pipes up from where he sits on the floor, watching as he rocks himself. "What Baelfire means to say is that even more than the rest of us, Crypt is fragile at the moment."

The Nightmare Prince is more insulted than I've ever seen as he straightens from the wall to glower at the three of us. "*Fragile?* Need I remind you, I'm half actual monster, so you can piss right off, you fucking—"

His markings light up again. Pain crosses his face as his legs give out, but Maven reacts faster than any of us. She's immediately cradling his upper half on her lap on the ground, emotion raw on her face as she watches Crypt squeeze his eyes shut. He spasms and grits his teeth like his entire body hurts, sweat beading on his face.

The grief, anger, and tension drop from my shoulders as I realize the incubus is finally starting to get what he worked so hard to achieve while our keeper was gone.

And Maven is trying not to cry, because she knows it, too.

Seeing my strong, resilient keeper on the verge of tears is a sign of how much she's actually struggling with our curses. It rips my fucking heart out.

"Damn you, Crypt," I sigh, striding toward the elevator.

"Where are you going, Scarface?" Baelfire demands.

Throwing my arm back, I don't have to look to know I just

froze his mouth shut successfully. "To hopefully find Douglas still breathing so we can transport out of this shithole."

28

SILAS

FORTUNATELY FOR US, the leprechaun was still alive, and Everett found everything that was confiscated from us.

Unfortunately for me, my curse grew severe enough to take me in and out of consciousness until we returned to Everbound. Even now, back in our quintet apartment for the first time in six months, standing under the warm spray of a shower washing away all the gasoline and horrors of the day, I feel the madness crawling over my limbs like wet, hairy, long-legged spiders.

They bite and crawl and spin their vindictive, cruel webs all over my flesh until I scramble out of the water, scratching furiously at my skin as I try to catch my breath.

Blood, a voice in my head suggests. *Blood would fix this. Blood fixes everything.*

You need to strengthen yourself, my father agrees. *All the world knows what you turned yourself into for that Undead harlot—and now they'll come for you. They'll slaughter you in your sleep. You must prepare yourself to use blood magic!*

I dig my fingers into my wet hair, trying to breathe as I glare at my own naked reflection in the hall bathroom mirror. My reflection smiles viciously back at me, making the sign with his hands that fae use to ward off evil intent.

The voices are right on one count. I need Maven's blood.

I crave it so much that just thinking about it makes my teeth ache, eager for my fangs to descend.

But aside from the beguiling, *incredible* flavor, it soothes my curse and makes me ever so slightly less dangerous to my keeper. It's nighttime now at Everbound, and we're all exhausted from Crypt's rescue mission that quickly turned into brutal, near-death public humiliation.

Not to mention, torture.

So much pain, the demons in my head agree with a shudder. *So much.*

While the Frosts kept me separate from the others, they had a purple-haired fae caster practice "simple interrogation techniques" on me in one of the high-end hotel rooms. They were all amateur spells, and the caster herself was unimpressive at both attack and healing incantations. Still, although her techniques would have made the Garnet Wizard laugh in her face, it hurt enough to send the voices in my head into a tizzy of mad panic, dragging me under repeatedly.

I'm sure my blood blossom already suspects what they were doing to a necromancer like me. There's no need to tell her about it when it would upset her.

And gods above, she's already so upset.

Merely the thought of Maven holding back tears while Crypt suffered from his curse makes me groan in frustration, tearing at my hair once again. I loathe seeing my keeper unhappy, but I loathe how useless I am to her right now far more. If I were in my right mind, perhaps I could think of ways to lessen the others' curses until we figure things out.

Figure things out, figure things out, figure things—

"Shut up," I tell the voices as I storm out of the bathroom and into Maven's large, quintet-sized room.

She's not in here, but Crypt is on the bed, freshly showered and dressed in his usual attire minus the leather jacket as his markings remain lit up. His face is pinched, but when he sees me, he snorts.

"Forget something, Crane?"

"Reverium," I blurt impatiently. "That helps your curse, so go and fucking get some. Don't you see how *iomadh thu*—much you are upsetting our keeper?" I correct, scowling.

Baelfire opens the door of the bathroom connected to Maven's room, wearing nothing but a towel, his collar and leash, and shimmering green goo. He sees me and laughs.

"So what, did you finally decide shifters are right about clothes being stupid? Are we all going to start hanging out in our birthday suits from now on?"

I realize I'm stark naked, but I'm so worked up that I just snap, "At least I'm not covered in slime, you fucking slob."

Crypt barely holds back laughter. "The necromancer's right, Decimus. Back to the shower your slimy self goes."

Damn it all. I grimace. "That's in my head, isn't it?"

"Whatever it is, yes," Everett mutters, striding into the room in those ridiculous silk pajamas he always wears. He's showered, as well, and looks exhausted, but he tenses when he looks around. "Where's Maven?"

"She went to shower with you in your office," I frown.

"She told me she would shower in here." He swears, looking around for shoes as he's clearly about to go look for her.

But there's no need for him to go, because I hear Maven whisper from somewhere in this room. "You're going to hurt me, Silas."

"No, *ima sangfluir*," I say quickly, which makes Everett pause as he realizes I'm talking to her. "I swear I won't."

My assurance is useless, and I know it. How could the words of a madman comfort anyone?

"You already hurt me before," she points out. "I know you'll do it again. It's just a matter of time. Look—you're about to hurt me right now!"

I turn to face where her frightened voice is coming from and

—gods above, she looks terrified of me. I choke, staggering away and dragging Baelfire in front of me as the realization that I might hurt her cuts me to the bone.

"Stop me. Injure me if that's what it takes."

He's puzzled, reaching up to tug at his collar absentmindedly. "What the fuck are you talking about?"

"Injure me now so I don't hurt *ima thanafluir!"* I shout, my panic mounting as my heart races.

Crypt's markings have stopped glowing. He shrugs, sliding out of the quintet-sized bed. "Well, if he insists—"

Baelfire casually shoves the incubus back onto the bed before folding his arms to face me. "Tempting, but Maven isn't even in here right now, buddy."

I check the spot where she just stood. Sure enough, there's nothing.

"*Daingeath,*" I mutter. "I'm fucking insane."

Baelfire and Crypt both look amused, but when Everett catches my eye, it's far worse.

It's *sympathy.*

"Don't pity me," I warn him.

"Too late. I always have," he says quietly, looking away.

Scowling, I regard the three of them. "If our keeper ever *is* in the room, and I pose a risk to her, do whatever it takes to keep her safe. If necessary, kill me."

That sobers the other two before Crypt hums. "Our loon's on the right track. From this point on, be it from ourselves or from something else, keeping Maven safe is what we do."

Baelfire tugs at his collar. "Whatever it takes."

"We won't lose her again," Everett agrees quietly.

All four of us grow silent, but there's an understanding. It's an unspoken thing between us, the four cursed fools who somehow fucked up so badly as a quintet that we lost our precious keeper. Whatever differences we've had in the past, and despite the curses now plaguing us, protecting Maven from any and every threat is more important than anything.

As if you are capable of protecting her, my father's voice scoffs. *You don't even know where she is.*

I turn toward the door, batting several tiny floating cherubs out of my way. "I'll find her. Baelfire, if you don't go back to being a leash-chewing lizard-brained beast, scrounge up something for Maven to eat when I bring her back."

"Who the hell put you in charge?" he scoffs.

I ignore him, knowing he won't be able to resist his bone-deep instincts to take care of his "mate" now that I've brought up food. "Everett, make this room less godsdamned freezing so our keeper won't catch hypothermia when I bring her back. Crypt, go get *reverium* from Limbo to ease your curse or I'll hex your cock with impotency so you won't be able to please our keeper for weeks."

"As if there aren't plenty of ways to please our girl without a fucking cock, you obtuse bloodsucker," he calls after me.

I can hear him swearing in irritation before I leave, the front door of the apartment closing behind me. I stride down the hall, ignoring every looming shadow and the paranoia my mind is steeped in. If Everett thought Maven was with us, and we thought she was with him, she obviously made us all believe something different so she could do something without our knowing.

Probably to keep us from worrying.

As if that's fucking possible.

I'll worry about Maven until my final breath. My beautifully vicious blood blossom will just have to grow accustomed to us being overprotective, hovering, anxiously attached madmen for the rest of our lives.

If space is what she wants, she'll have to use her godly powers to separate us from her.

A giant spider made of shadows crawls past in this frozen corridor. I pause, trying to decide if that was real. Since I can't be sure and suffocating suspicion is slowly climbing up my throat, I decide it's best to conceal myself.

Yes, hide, the voices in my head hiss.

Calling on the remainder of my blood magic from the last time I fed on Maven, I shroud myself in a simple but effective cloaking charm and pass through the empty halls unseen.

According to Everett, there are dozens upon dozens of people camping outside Everbound Castle's front doors. I didn't see them when we arrived because I was in the thrall of my curse, but Nether humans, Reformists, reporters, and several others were gathered outside, hoping to get a glimpse of the demigoddess who was just revealed on live television.

We managed to get in unseen through an ancient servants' entrance that Maven knew about. Still, it irks me to know so many await her outside.

Not her. They're here to kill you, demons in my head whisper and titter, echoing on repeat.

Soft whistling and the glow of a lantern catch my attention. Lillian rounds the corner, bundled heavily against the cold as she seems lost in thought. She passes me on her way back to her rooms for the night, but I decide it's likely she was just speaking with Maven, so I follow the direction she just came from.

It's not long before I pick up on two voices. My blood blossom's, and Kenzie Baird's.

"—you going to actually use all this salt Lillian brought you?" Kenzie is asking.

"Salt wards off ghosts," Maven explains. "They're everywhere here. I grew up listening to the whispers and wails of restless spirits every night, but tonight I just want to sleep."

"Oh, my gods. That gave me secondhand PTSD just now, monk."

"That's not traumatic," Maven grumbles. "What's traumatic is having the freshly dead parents of one of your quintet members haunting you and trying to get sent to the Beyond. The Frosts are so fucking entitled, even in death."

Still cloaked and invisible, I emerge into an alcove where Maven and Kenzie both sit on an old stone bench beside a flickering lantern. Maven is freshly showered, hair still damp despite the wintry chill, and she holds a large bag of salt. She glances at a place in the cold alcove where I see Everett's birth parents and several other strangers standing and glowering at her.

Either their ghosts followed her here, or they're in my head, too.

Everyone in this alcove, living or dead, is plotting against you, my father whispers. *Pathetic, useless son. You've signed your death in your own blood.*

You'll bring me down with you when you fall, Maven's voice whispers in my head.

I rub my temples, resisting the urge to snap back at the voices.

The blond, curly-haired shifter is eyeing the bag in Maven's lap. "Is it weird that I'm craving salt like no one's fucking business, now that it's staring at me?"

"Be my guest."

Kenzie opens the bag, tastes the salt, gags, and hands it back to Maven. "Never mind. Gods, I still cannot believe you were almost burned at the stake on live TV by your rich in-laws. I'm so fucking glad you went all demigoddess on their asses because watching that stupid fake trial was *awful.* You would not believe how much I was crying—and Vivienne was a total wreck, too. But now that everyone knows you're back, my quintet and I are fielding a bajillion questions and trying to keep all of the Halfton refugees from storming the castle and…oof. It's just pure chaos. Felix was right that people are not handling your return well. I mean, a lot of them are thrilled you're back, but they're being so weird about it, too. I'm pretty sure some of them are trying to, like…worship you."

Maven makes a face and pulls her etherium knife from her boot to fidget with it. "Thanks for dealing with the shit show."

"Anything for you," Kenzie answers brightly, tossing her hair and adjusting her scarf. "Besides, I'm willing to take one for the team. Now that you have all of your guys back, you probably need to get back to having wild, unhinged sex with them, right? Come on, spill the deets," she teases, elbowing my keeper lightly. "Crazy person sex is the best sex—how nasty do you guys get in bed now that they're missing a few marbles?"

Maven spins her knife, glaring at the ghosts in the corner again. "I wish I knew. But too much just happened, and they need time to process. No matter how much I'm aching for them, I can't just jump their bones whenever I feel like it."

29

SILAS

SHE'S *ACHING?*

Thank the gods. That makes five of us.

Even with my fragmented ability to piece things together at the moment, I haven't missed the way my other quintet members have been stealing looks at Maven, aching for her despite our conditions. We've all been reigning ourselves in.

Personally, I've managed to keep my hands off her for this long because I remind myself I'm a threat to her, but I'm honestly impressed the others have behaved themselves.

Even with our curses and the fiasco we've been going through, after six months, it's a fucking miracle we haven't ripped her clothes off yet.

But if our keeper has also been holding back, I may as well share the good news with the others.

Filthy, deviant abomination to the living, someone whispers in my head.

My birth mother's voice makes a rare appearance. *How lascivious you have become, son.*

"Not to mention, they're all in such rough shape," Maven goes on with a sigh. "And I have a plan to follow, so now isn't—"

Kenzie holds up a hand. "Hang on. You just got your quintet of Maven-obsessed, sanity-lacking, gorgeous-albeit-cursed, morally *super dark grey* matches back, and you haven't started fucking the ever-living daylights out of them every tiny chance you get? Girl. What the hell are you doing? I'll ward off the weirdos outside as long as you need me to, but go get on that pronto—and by *that,* I mean their penises."

Their conversation is creating an excited thrum in my veins that moves steadily lower as I observe my blood blossom fidget, clearly flustered as she clears her throat.

She'll be the death of you, a voice reminds me.

I ignore it.

"The timing is wrong," Maven mutters.

"The timing is wrong?" Kenzie bursts, throwing her manicured hands in the air before making a sound like a buzzer going off. "Excuse denied! Look, no matter what my quintet and I have gone through so far, we've prioritized our bond and staying intimate in every way, and that's made us so much stronger and everything else so much fucking better. Your quintet needs to feel close to their keeper, and you need it, too, you traumatized little reaper baby. I promise. Now go get some DP action going or something. Rile them up, explore some kinks, and celebrate having them all back!"

The shifter's first suggestion makes me so flushed that I break out into a small sweat despite the cold and the fact that I never remembered to put on clothes. I'm practically leaning forward to gauge Maven's reaction to that erotic idea, but she just tips her head with a slight frown.

"DP?"

Godsdamn it all, she has no idea.

So excited over sharing a whore, someone scowls inside my head. *How depraved are you?*

Very depraved. And very thirsty for my blood blossom in every way possible, especially if I get to watch her pleasured twice over at once. My slowly growing erection is proof of my desire.

The shifter gasps, hand going to her chest. "*What?* Oh, my sweet summer child. My innocent little demigoddess—"

"Innocent? I just massacred the elites," Maven points out dryly.

"—it's the best thing ever," Kenzie goes on without losing the dramatic flair. "One guy in front. One guy behind—but *use lube*. And if you're feeling extra saucy, one ding dong in the hand and one in the mouth," she winks.

Maven is thoughtful. "If that's what DP is, I had a dream about it once. Does it stand for double penis?"

My blood blossom is adorable.

I know I am, Maven's voice says in my head. *You don't deserve me.*

"Shh," I silence the voice that I'm almost certain isn't real.

Luckily, my shushing is covered by Kenzie's cackle, which can probably be heard all the way from my quintet's apartment. "It means double penetration. And again, if you do it, use lube—in fact, before everything went to hell at Everbound, I actually bought a ton of new, unused toys and flavored lube and stuff like that. I think it's still stashed in my quintet's old apartment, so maybe I can track something down for you. Anyway—take your time, and don't rush. And it's *amazing*. Top-tier. Seriously, one time when I was sandwiched between Dirk and Luka, Dirk kept doing this thing where he reached around and played with Luka's—"

Maven throws up a hand. "Got it. No more details, or I won't be able to look your quintet in the eye anymore."

"You know, Dirk might prefer that. Even after watching you go all demigoddess on TV, he's still spooked over your Undead joke."

"Good," my keeper smirks.

Kenzie swats at her playfully before getting serious again. "Seriously, go get 'em, monk. Besides satisfying all that horniness you're pretending to ignore, it might help with getting your bond back, right? You mentioned that you bonded yourself to them after being intimate before because of your holy magic. Can't that happen again?"

Maven reaches up to rub her chest through her dark, oversized clean clothing. "It would if I had a heart for them to be bound to."

My breath catches as that sinks in. Gods above, how have I not thought of this? Her heart was ripped out and replaced by a shadow heart, but if that's gone and she's mysteriously returned...

She's Undead, a voice in my head decides. *You cannot sleep with a zombie.*

She's a devil. A wicked trollop.

Heartless, a final one whispers.

Kenzie looks just as surprised. "Wait. I thought you had a shadow heart?"

"Not anymore."

"Then...uh, not to be blunt, May, but how the fuck are you alive right now?"

Maven rubs her chest again. "My best guess is, I'm keeping myself alive with holy magic, kind of like a preservation or life extension spell. Or maybe it's something to do with people revering me—turns out, I get power from worship. Whatever it is...I'm not sure how long I can sustain it."

My throat starts closing in.

If she's being kept alive solely by her own magic...that's unstable. Dangerous. There's a reason life extension spells are considered so faulty.

It must be weakening her, too. What if she uses too much power at once, runs out of fuel, and drops dead again? Gods above, how close did she get to overextending herself during her awe-inspiring display of power in Manhattan?

No more. I refuse to leave her existence in this mortal world up to chance. I turn to leave, catching bits of their conversation echoed in the hall as I step over a slithering mass of glowing orange worms. Ducking under more cherubs, I quickly make my way back to our quintet apartment.

The second I burst into my keeper's room, the words are already leaving my mouth.

"Maven is heartless."

An absolute bitch, my father's voice agrees.

Other demons in my head chime in, complaining over one another loudly. The ringing in my ears increases in volume as I try to get my eye to stop twitching.

"Beautifully so," Crypt muses from where he sits, rolling fresh *reverium* into cigarettes at a desk.

The torn state of his clothes and a smear of blood on his neck tell me he put up with the dangers of Limbo to get the herb that will hopefully ease his pain and Maven's concerns.

Come to think of it, he's been merely smoking the substance. If I meddle with it, test it in spells or potions…

Perhaps I could amplify *reverium's* effects for the incubus. Anything it takes to not see my blood blossom on the verge of tears again.

Drawing myself back to the present, I flinch away from a luminescent bat that tries to land on my head before I focus on the others. Everett is on the bed studying a map, and Baelfire is setting some kind of steaming bean-and-rice dish on a small table in the room.

"I mean, she is *literally* heartless," I clarify.

Before Maven returns, I quickly explain what I overheard, omitting the arousing encouragements that I hope will give our keeper new filthy ideas.

When I finish, we're all quiet. Everett brushes frost off his hands as Baelfire grips his own head, scowling.

Crypt pulls out his enchanted lighter, flicking it open to study the flame. "Amadeus's head necromancer has Maven's heart. He went on the run with it when he deserted the Nether after the Divide fell."

We all stare at him.

"Hang on, her original heart still exists? How do you know that?" Everett demands.

"A little birdie told me."

"Share the true reason," I snap. "If it regards our keeper, it regards all of us."

Crypt glances at me and then away, pensive. "Like our girl said, her would-be-father owns a sadistic sense of humor. He preserved her heart and kept it on display on his mantle. She told me that herself," he mutters.

"On *display?*" Baelfire snarls, as incensed as the rest of us have quickly become.

Crypt nods. "It was what I went looking for last, before Syntyche hunted me down. I wanted to have every remaining trace of her here, at her honorary grave. Since Silas was useless, I persuaded another Nether escapee necromancer until he made me a spell to track her heart."

So that's what he was trying to get me to track when I was deep in the throes of insanity.

Baelfire snorts, looking at the incubus. "By persuaded, you mean tortured."

"Naturally."

"And you killed him the second he handed the spell over," Everett guesses.

"Of course," Crypt huffs. "What do you take me for? An amateur? At any rate, the spell led me on a wild goose chase. I pieced enough together to understand that Dagon was obsessed with what he called his *masterpiece.*"

Dagon.

I remember that name, from Crypt's memories of Maven's past nightmares. Recalling some of the horrors that obsessive necromancer inflicted on my blood blossom, I grit my teeth.

Crypt sees my ire and nods, his own expression darkening. "When he caught wind of what became of her, he stole her heart from Amadeus and went on the run with it. I had only barely scratched the surface of his true whereabouts when Syntyche caught up to me. Poor timing, that."

We're all quiet for a moment, considering this new information. I begin pacing, swatting aside a few imps as I think. But the more I think, the more my ire multiplies.

"That necromantic prick tortured Maven for years," I seethe. "He oversaw her entire experimental transformation into a revenant and enjoyed her pain."

"What?" Everett snaps as the room instantly grows colder.

Baelfire snarls in fury and quickly grips his head as agony crosses his features. It's clear that he's struggling to stay coherent instead of falling to the beast's control once more.

"How the fuck do you know that and more importantly, how are we going to kill this motherfucker?" he demands raggedly.

Crypt shoots me a warning look. It's easily interpreted as a violent threat to harm me if I breathe a word about seeing inside his past memories of Maven's dreams. So instead of expounding on the matter, I focus on Baelfire's latter question.

"We'll track him again," I decide, stopping my pacing. "If I use some of Maven's DNA to track her heart, we can—"

"English," Baelfire reminds me.

I realize that at some point, I swapped to something between the Nether-tongue and…I'm not even sure what that was. Probably a language the mocking fools inside my head devised. Carefully choosing my words this time, I look at each of my fellow quintet members.

"Maven would never ask this of us. She would handle it herself, alone, to prevent us from being in harm's way at the hands of this necromancer. But I will not allow that decrepit, twisted *scútráche* anywhere near her again. I'll cast the spell. We'll retrieve Maven's heart, and then we'll end his putrid existence."

They are all clearly in agreement, but our rare moment of unity is quickly dashed when Baelfire gives me a patronizing smile.

"I almost forgot you're insane off your fucking ass for a moment. Good job."

Asshole.

Before I can remind him that *he's* out of his mind most of the time as well, we all hear the front door of the quintet apartment open and close. This conversation is quickly shelved. As soon as Maven steps into this room, Baelfire has her scooped up and set on the bed, a spoon full of warm food in his hand as if he plans to feed her himself.

"We didn't have a lot of spices so it's kind of a crappy, plain meal. But I really need you to eat, Boo," he pleads.

She studies the rice and beans, takes a tentative bite, and nods. "It's good."

He practically preens. I roll my eyes at his predictable shifter pride in caring for a mate, but it's convenient that at least one of us knows the way around a kitchen.

"Good. Eat all of it, Mayflower."

She glances at Everett and me, eyes narrowing. "Where's your food? Are we all sharing this bowl?"

"I'd cut my tongue out before sharing a bowl with those asshats," Bael says brightly, booping her nose. "There wasn't much left here, but we're fine. We'll eat in the morning."

"You should all eat tonight," she argues.

"I certainly will, be it in your dreams or between your lovely thighs," Crypt winks.

Maven flushes and starts to protest the food situation again, but Everett cuts her off.

"Where the hell were you for so long?" he grouches, but his tone belies his actions as he slips into the bed beside Maven and begins gently detangling her damp hair.

She's in the middle of chewing another bite, but holds up the bag of salt as an answer.

"For the ghosts," Crypt understands with a nod, lighting one of his cigarettes and taking a drag.

He wanders to a window to crack it open, which is good

because that herb is strong when it's smoked. I'm fairly certain that's the first *reverium* hit he's had in months, since he's simply been taking the siphon approach to numbing pain until now.

Maven nods and stands like she's about to scatter salt at the perimeters of our abode, as I've heard must be done to repel ghosts. I quickly take the bag from her, flick an imp off the top of her head, and kiss her temple.

"Allow me. You eat."

"Sure, let the hallucinating madman be in charge of ghost duty," Everett mutters.

Flipping off the scarred elemental, I leave her room and get to work lining the perimeter of the entire apartment with salt. I only pause to examine my work when I'm done, and that's when I realize I'm back inside the bedroom and Maven is closely examining *me* now that she's done with her meal.

I smirk. "You don't seem to mind that I forgot where my clothes are, *thanafluir*."

She grins back. "Naked and insane does seem to be my type."

On cue, Baelfire quickly starts stripping out of the few clothes he has on, making our keeper laugh.

Gods, that sound is sublime.

It's the laugh of a lying, scheming, filthy little bitch, a voice snarls in my head.

"Shut the hell up," I mutter in fae.

Before the dragon shifter can strip completely, he hisses in pain, clutching his head and baring his teeth. Maven's amusement dies as she immediately cradles his head in her lap. The rest of us watch, tensed to see if his dragon is taking over. If so, we'll have to ensure he won't harm her.

But Bael pushes through, his breathing turning labored as he groans. "Fuck, I really hate that alphahole. Pretty sure everyone does, at this point."

Maven makes a face. "I don't hate your dragon. I hate your curse—I hate *all* of your curses. And to think, I once wanted to exploit them."

Baelfire's brows go up. "You did?"

"Yes. I needed you all to reject me to prevent…well, exactly what happened. You have me to thank for the last six months of hell."

Crypt scoffs, giving her a penetrating look. "The only person we'll be giving our very special thanks to is whoever killed Engela Zuma during the battle. Isn't that what happened, love?"

We all look at her for confirmation. She nods once, but she's focused on running her hands through Baelfire's hair as he continues to struggle with his curse.

"Maven," I prompt, already craving more information about the next enemy we'll demolish for her.

"Later. We're not on that step yet."

Step?

I see. My beautifully vicious minx must have another evolving plan we're yet unaware of. Something she hasn't shared with us yet.

But Everett doesn't let it go. His eyes narrow as he tips her face up to look at him. "The vampire. You knew his name. Is that why?"

Vampire? I know nothing of this.

She huffs. "I'll handle it."

"*We,*" I scowl, ripping through the blood-soaked vines dangling from the ceiling to crawl onto the bed toward her. With Everett on one side of her and Baelfire on her lap, I have no choice but to drag her away from them and into my arms to whisper against her ear. "*We* will handle it. Utilize us, Maven. Allow us to redeem ourselves. We lost you once because of our own ineptitude. You have my word that we will be much more useful monsters for you now."

30

SILAS

"WHO GIVES A FUCK ABOUT *USEFUL?*" Maven murmurs before capturing my lips with hers.

My head starts to spin, and whispers crowd my ears, but I ignore it all in favor of enjoying the way my blood blossom coaxes me with her delicious mouth.

She's divinity laced with sin, and I'm pure madness ready to worship at her altar.

But my stark madness becomes difficult to ignore when a scalding, tar-like wave of paranoia rakes across my skin, tensing every part of me so that even my fangs descend. Before I can pull away to try to get control over myself, Maven's teasing tongue flicks intentionally against one of my fangs, pricking it.

Her fucking *irresistible* flavor slams into the back of my throat, and a groan breaks from me as I lick more deeply into her mouth, eager for more. She hums, pleased with my reaction. My blood blossom is so fucking perfect for me. I crave her ability to claim every part of me—my darkness, my madness, my worship, my never-ending hunger for her.

And her blood.

Gods above, I want her blood.

When one of my hands moves to stroke the side of her throat, her lips curl against mine before she breaks our heated exchange to arch her beautiful, olive-toned neck in offering.

It's not right to bite her when I lack all control when it comes to her. I could harm her. But then again…the others who are watching know to stop me from truly harming our keeper.

And I need this blood. It soothes me unlike anything else in the world.

She soothes me.

Drink, drink, drink, drink, the voices in my head chant, an ode to the addictive perfection that is Maven's blood.

Without another thought, I bite into her neck, my fangs descending into her carotid artery. I can no more stop the moan that breaks free from me than I can stop the way my cock begins to ache, hard and desperate for this woman who puts my insanity to shame.

For a handspan of euphoric moments, I feed from Maven as the tension in this room builds with the carnal desperation of my quiet quintet members. My blood blossom became our center of gravity months ago—and now that she's here, gasping and clutching at my arm as I drink from her…

"Si," Baelfire says thickly, clutching the side of his head before a growl escapes like he can't help it. "We've all been fucking starving for her."

Don't let them near. They'll kill you. Trust no one, someone hisses in my head.

But no. The dragon is right.

Feeding from her is heavenly, but I want more.

Releasing Maven's neck, I lick up the last mouthwatering traces of blood from her neck before sliding my fingers down, dipping them below her pants and panties until I can feel how fucking soaked she is.

"Naen mahk," I whisper in fae against her throat as my cock throbs.

Good girl.

Maven is still panting from the pleasure-feeding. Crypt

moved to the end of the bed at some point to get a better view, and now his mouth curls up, his violet gaze wicked upon our keeper.

"What divine sounds she makes," he whispers.

"Fucking perfect," Everett agrees.

I can only nod, taking in the artwork of my keeper's flushed face. There's a large snake slithering beside us on the bed, but since no one else has noticed it, I decide it's another trick of my mind as I continue to focus on Maven.

Crypt hums and moves closer to brush her hair from her face, his voice silken despite his markings lighting up continually. "Let us worship you again, love."

Maven smiles. "As if I'd stop any of you."

I smirk back at her, loving the sound of that. "Then perhaps we should bind you to this bed and worship you until dawn, *ima sangfluir.*"

Her smile fades slightly, and she shakes her head. "No bondage. It brings back memories."

That's all our sexually adventurous keeper needs to say for us to realize how traumatic those *memories* must be. Now I cannot stop remembering the glimpses that I got of her past within the dreams in Crypt's memories. Bound to lab tables, chained in onyx cells, her wrists and ankles tied until they bled…

Everett tenses, swallowing hard. "Is that why you shut down when I was carrying you out of that combat zone, and I…"

Whatever his question is, he trails off, looking horrified.

Maven isn't having it. "I just don't want to be restrained. Don't make a thing out of it. I'm still waiting to be worshipped," she adds teasingly.

Everett moves quickly, scooting toward the middle of the bed and reaching to pull Maven away from me. She's suddenly between his thighs, leaning back against him as he strips her shirt and bra off in one smooth movement before roughly cupping one of her tits as his other hand wraps lightly around her neck.

My blood blossom gasps and arches her back, enjoying the sensation as I watch, palming my hardness.

"So fucking beautiful," Everett murmurs.

"And so fucking clothed. Why are my pants still on?" she asks us, arching a brow.

"You're so fucking right," Baelfire groans, moving until he's between her legs. "Fuck, your scent is driving me crazy. I just need a taste, baby. One taste of that fucking perfect pussy. Godsdamn."

As soon as he drags off the rest of her clothes and laps at her beautifully wet entrance, they both moan. My mouth goes dry as I watch, my heart pounding from the sheer beauty of Maven being pleasured.

Her moan is delectable as each one of us falls deeper under the spell her now-naked body is putting us under. Crypt scoots up the bed to play with Maven's other tit as he gazes at the gorgeous sight of her undone and so godsdamned needy. I'm equally transfixed, drowning myself in the sight of my keeper alive and basking in the pleasure we were always meant to give her.

"Gods, you taste so fucking *good*," Baelfire growls.

The feral dragon shifter grows more aggressive, groaning as he tries to press her thighs wider, desperate to lap up more of our keeper's delicious wetness.

But Maven's next cry is mingled with pain just as the scent of her ambrosian blood crashes into my nose.

"Decimus," Crypt hisses, shoving the shifter off the bed with murder in his voice. "Too far."

Bael is reeling as he gets to his feet and stares down, eyes widening in horror as he realizes what he just did. I move closer to see that in his fervor, he left claw marks on the insides of Maven's thighs that are already starting to drip blood.

Our keeper is trying to catch her breath to reconcile the pain with the fading pleasure. When she tries to move her legs closed, I quickly nudge Baelfire aside and slip between them to stop her.

Dipping my head, I lick away the blood as gently as possible.

Gods above, it's potent every time. I will never not crave this flavor. It's a haunting heaven that drives me to lick her other thigh, too, my own pulse crashing in my ears as raw need dizzies me.

"S—Silas," she manages, one of her hands tangling roughly in my hair.

It's the twinge of pain in her voice that reminds me to lift my hand, calling forth a simple healing spell to mend the broken skin I just licked clean. When I'm done with her other thigh, I heal that, too, and then I cannot stop myself from dragging my tongue through her soaked pussy.

Maven gasps and arches, hand tightening in my hair. Everett hums from his position behind her, murmuring something in her ear that makes her writhe again.

"Gods, I'm so sorry, Mayflower," Baelfire rasps, gripping one of her knees to spread her better for me as he looks like a kicked puppy. "Just can't fucking get enough of you."

"I—I want—" she begins.

I pinch her clit between my lips roughly enough that she cuts off with another exhilirated gasp. Each of her reactions is a perfection driving me further into this hunger-fueled delirium.

"You want what, darling?" Crypt whispers, caressing her beautiful bare skin as he languidly watches her pleasure build.

"Two of you at once," she manages.

That's enough to make me lift my head. Somewhere in the lust-addled haze of my ruined mind, I can sense voices and whispers vying for attention, angry that this beautiful woman has so much of my attention. But I focus determinedly on my keeper as Crypt, Baelfire, and Everett all go still, wondering if we're interpreting her words right.

"You mean..." Everett trails off, his voice unsteady and rough.

My blood blossom is flushed and determined all at once. "I mean, I want to take two of you at once. I want to try double penetration."

"Fuck me," Crypt swears, ignoring the glowing markings displayed on his body as he begins to strip all the way.

"Better idea. You fuck me in my ass right now," she shoots back.

Baelfire makes a choking sound before he has to brace himself on the edge of the bed. "Gods, baby, that is so *fucking hot*."

Maven surprises us all again when she sits up and turns to straddle Everett, taking charge as elegantly as she always does when she tugs his hair to tip his head back.

"I'm ready," she insists.

He makes a rough sound that can't possibly count as English before he clears his throat and shakes his head, his cheeks pink. "N—no."

"*No?* What the fucking hell is wrong with you?" Baelfire huffs, getting back onto the bed. He can't seem to take his eyes off Maven's perfect ass. "If you won't give her what she wants—"

"I meant, not yet," Everett snaps, closing his eyes in bliss when Maven begins kissing and nibbling one of his ears. "We'd need to prepare before trying that for the first time."

"Why bother?" Maven demands, pulling back. "Just spit and shove it in."

"No, love," Crypt cuts in. "That could hurt you."

"I have a high pain tolerance. I'll be fine. Now just—"

Everett's hand cracks against her ass, startling her and making me swear because *gods* her skin looks good with a handprint quickly forming on it. Maven is still reeling from the sharp contact and grinds slightly against him, but to his credit, the elemental still manages to get words out.

"You want two of us to fuck you at once? Fine. But we're

going to do it right—so you're going to wait until later, when we have you prepped and ready and fucking begging for it."

"She's already begging for it," Baelfire points out hoarsely. "Look at her—she's fucking soaked. *Gods,* Mayflower—do you have any fucking idea how sexy you are?"

"Not sexy enough, if you aren't going to fuck me," she mumbles.

Crypt growls and grips her ankles, yanking her down the bed before shoving her legs back.

"Who said we weren't going to fuck you?" he demands before thrusting his pierced, hard cock deeply into her.

Maven cries out, and that gorgeous sound makes me groan along with the rest of us as Crypt begins to fuck her hard and fast. Her back arches from the pleasure, but her dark, alluring gaze falls on me.

She licks her lips, her desire evident. "Silas—"

I'm already scrambling on the bed, grateful now that I never found my clothes as my cock brushes against her lips. Maven opens for me so beautifully, wrapping her warm, wet mouth around my length and sucking until I can't stop myself from pumping my hips.

Fucking gods, she feels amazing.

"Thanafluir," I moan.

Maven hums around my cock, sinking deeper on it as Crypt continues to slam into her. The rough sounds of their coupling serves as an erotic backdrop as Everett strokes himself and Baelfire sucks on one of Maven's tits.

When Crypt groans and reaches down to tease her clit at the same time, I know he's reaching his limit but refuses to finish before our keeper. I thrust deeper into her perfect mouth, that same mad dizziness sweeping over me as desperation takes hold, heat bearing down on my spine with the urge to fill her devious mouth.

But Crypt reaches his goal first and Maven pops off my cock to cry out as her orgasm rips through her. I swear and jerk myself off, unable to stop the rising tide of pleasure that crests over me as I watch her shake and arch and swear.

Baelfire is on her next, snarling and shoving himself deep as Maven gasps in renewed pleasure, her orgasm not yet done. He pinches her nipples and swears and praises her as he fucks her hard, and she's loving every second of it.

I groan at the sight of her being rutted so savagely by the big shifter, her hair a mess, her eyes squeezed shut, and all those delicious sounds falling from her lips.

She's a sight to behold. An insatiable, stunning marvel.

We're intoxicated, falling deeper under her spell with every sound, every taste—every cry and moan and gasp of her voice.

A dark shadow is creeping into my vision, mad voices hissing their displeasure as I continue to fight them off. I cannot have them here in this moment, when my keeper is again on the brink of orgasm.

Still, insanity dips into my mind, stealing moments away from me as I strive to remain in this sensual, perfect moment. One moment, I'm watching Baelfire rail her as Maven cries out, and then I find that Everett is between her legs, mercilessly stroking her clit as he breathes frost to stimulate her bare, reddened inner thigh.

Maven shudders as she grips the sheets on either side, gasping, "Wait, I—I can't take anymore."

"Too bad," Everett whispers, fingering her hard with two fingers to make her cry out. "We're not done with you yet."

Crypt is kissing her as another orgasm tears through her, violent and raw. My blurred gaze stays fixed on her beautiful face as she falls apart once again.

So fucking beautiful.

That's the face of your ruin, a voice snickers inside my head. Other voices chant and sing and drive me mad as I try like hell to hold on to sanity.

Everett still has not stopped wringing pleasure from Maven, fingering and frosting and slapping her pussy until my blood blossom is panting and swearing. She shakes in the sheets in a way that makes my cock thicken with renewed need.

"One more," Baelfire growls, licking her jaw and biting the mating mark on the left side of her neck. "Give us one more, hellion."

"I—I can't—"

"You can, and you certainly fucking will," Crypt purrs, kissing her other temple as he teases one of her dusky, pointed nipples.

She's so glorious like this. So *ours.* Moaning, gasping, telling us what she needs and how she needs it. I watch, adoring the sight of my blood blossom as she takes what she wants until everything becomes a blur of moans, pleasure, and desperation.

I want nothing more than to rejoin. To stay. But a violent panic is creeping over me as long centipedes trail across the bed toward me. The walls are dripping blood as whispers laugh from the shadows in this room.

My heart pounds as the madness creeps in.

It's not safe for me here.

No, *she's* not safe if I'm here. I'm a risk to her.

Any moment, I might snap or black out. I crave Maven in every way, including her pleasure, so I refuse to be the one to ruin it.

The voices in my head grow in volume, from a whisper to a shout to screams of deranged fury.

I can't breathe.

I can't stay.

Stumbling off the bed, I ignore my trembling hands and pounding heart as I race from the room to let the madness and shadows devour me whole.

31

BAELFIRE

ICE-COLD WATER CRASHES over my head, jolting me awake. My dragon snarls at the rude awakening as he rushes to take a backseat, extra fussy first thing in the morning.

Spluttering, I wipe water off my face and realize Crypt just dumped an entire fucking pitcher over my head where I was sleeping on the floor.

"What the—" I start to snarl.

He holds his fingers to his lips and glances at the bed, indicating that Maven is still asleep. But when I try to sit up to check on her, my leash tugs painfully, nearly choking me—and that's when I remember that I told Everett to tie me up overnight so my dragon wouldn't set the bed on fire for shits and giggles and fry my quintet in their sleep.

"You were starting fires thanks to your dream," Crypt mutters as an explanation, stomping out a couple of small blue embers dancing on the ground before he drops back into Limbo.

Probably to go back to snorting Maven's dreams like they're crack.

Trying to stay quiet, I untie the damn leash from the leg of the desk until I can finally stand and peek at the massive bed. A stupid grin crosses my face when I see my mate.

Naked in the sheets, covered in hickeys, and drop dead fucking gorgeous with her dark hair a mess around her peaceful, sleeping face. She's resting deeply, tucked snugly against Everett's chest as he keeps his arms around her like he's afraid to let go of her even while unconscious.

Meanwhile, her glass-like knife-scythe-thing is in her hand. I watch as she squirms slightly in her sleep before relaxing again, a soft sound escaping her pretty lips.

Godsdamn it, she always looks so good. And last night? Fuck. I bite back a groan, trying not to linger on the fact that she wants to take two of us at the same time. My little hellion is adventurous in bed and for the fucking life of me, I can never guess what she's going to say or do next.

This room is filled with the chill from Everett's presence and Maven's indescribable scent. It's light and sweet and just as teasing as my dark queen likes to be.

Gods, I fucking love the way she smells.

It's making me so damn hard and desperate, to the point that my skin feels like it's prickling with need for her touch. Maybe if I pull her away from Everett and get on my knees for her and she might let me wake her up by licking her pussy. She could yank on my leash and call me her good little pet with her raspy morning voice and bite my neck and drive me fucking insane and…

Oh. Shit.

This is more than just me drooling over my keeper. That obviously happens all the fucking time—but right now, I'm nearly trembling as I broil in the sight of her ridiculously fuckable body. I want to lick and bite and fuck her so much it hurts.

It's been months since I was in human form this long. I'm supposed to take extra-strength rut suppressants at least once a week. If I don't track some down soon…fuck. I already have next to no control, thanks to the asshole who's trying to erase me. Going into a rut right now is a huge hell no.

Still keeping as quiet as possible, I slip out and rummage

through my old room for a sweatshirt to go with the shorts I wore to sleep. Slipping into my shoes, I pause when I see my brown suede jacket nearby. As usual, I don't feel the cold, but it might cover my collar and leash a bit.

I don't mind that Maven put these on me. I get why she did it—I'm still pissed my dragon fucking dropped her in Everbound Forest and was practically hunting her. Taking away my ability to shift is the wisest course of action until we figure shit out.

But I can't help the humiliation I feel when other people see it.

Silas mentioned something about us being broadcast to the rest of the world when they were trying to burn him and Maven at the stake. I don't remember much of that nightmare, thanks to my dragon. Still, knowing so many people, especially other shifters, saw me collared and feral like a common fucking animal…

I huff and turn to leave the room, leaving the coat.

So, the collar's humiliating. So what?

People can think whatever they want to think about me, so long as my mate is safe and sound and in my arms.

For the next half an hour, as light starts to dawn outside, I raid one of the abandoned university stores, the healers' area, and even my wolf shifter friend Cody's old apartment. No rut suppressants to be found.

Irritated and cranky as hell to have to be away from my mate for this errand, I storm into the administration hallway, hoping a past instructor at Everbound might have stashed something here.

But I pause when a door creaks.

A woman with curly, blond, white-streaked hair pauses when she sees me. She's dressed in several colorful layers and a bright pink beanie and is holding a small tray full of steaming hot chocolate as she studies me.

She smiles brightly. "Baelfire, right?"

I resist the urge to tug at my collar as I realize who this must be. "Yeah. You must be Lillian."

Her blue eyes sparkle. "I see Maven talked about me. I'm still getting used to that."

"Her talking about you?"

"Her talking to other people at all." Lillian gets a far-off expression. "For years, I worried about how quiet she preferred to be. Even when she was speaking to me, it was difficult to get her to say more than a few words at a time." She looks at me and beams again. "But look where we are now. I'm happy I finally get to officially meet you, Baelfire. Maven is fiercely protective of you, you know."

I grin. "Yeah, I know. She's perfect like that. Hey—want some help?"

Lillian lets me take the tray of steaming mugs, but she tips her head. "I was just going to drop off hot chocolate for your quintet before I leave for Halfton. A lot of people have been arriving in the wake of news about Maven. It's gotten chaotic, so the Baird quintet asked me to help, but...did you come here looking for me?'

"Actually, I was—" I pause, clearing my throat. "Nah, it was nothing. Forget it."

She raises her brows. "They told me you were the most polite of her matches. I didn't think you would be shy, too."

Me, shy? Ha.

The truth is, if I ran into anyone besides Maven's oldest friend and caretaker this morning, there's a good chance I would've broken their nose if they tried to talk to me. If some walking waste of time got in the way of me getting back to my sexy little miracle of a keeper, I wouldn't have hesitated.

Lillian, though? She looked after Maven in the Nether. She's like family to her. She seems nice and down-to-earth, so maybe...

I smile sheepishly, hoping this won't weird her out. "Any chance you know where dragon-grade suppressants might be?"

"Dragon-grade..." She frowns slightly, and then it dawns. "Oh. Shifter suppressants. So that you don't go into heat. Right?"

Rut, heat, same difference. I nod, lifting the tray to sip at the edge of one of the fuller mugs of homemade hot chocolate brimming with whipped cream.

That's delicious. I want to pour it all over my naked body and beg Maven to lick it off. She could suck the whipped cream off my dick and then cover her tits in more cream and let me–

Godsdamn it, I'm getting hard again. I absolutely cannot pop a boner in front of Lillian, so I try to think about anything that'll kill the arousal. Everett. Crypt. Silas...

Damn it, this isn't helping because they were wringing all kinds of sexy sounds out of Maven last night, too. I've never been much of a voyeur, but holy fucking gods, I love it when my mate is being well-pleased and sated. And with all her talk about taking two of us at once—

Mayday, mayday. Tenting has begun.

Del Mar licking his own eyeballs. I force myself to think about that instead. Actually, thinking about any of the Immortal Quintet members and the shit they put us through is a good way to cool off.

Thankfully, Lillian hasn't noticed my struggle to de-hornify myself as she adjusts one of her scarves, rubbing her cold-pinkened nose. "Actually, I think I do know where some might be. We did a big sweep of Everbound Castle to bundle a lot of supplies for Halfton a while ago, and...wait right here."

I wait as she slips into one of the administrative staff rooms nearby. When she returns, it's possible one or two of the mugs have been completely drained.

Sue me. I'm fucking starving, and I'll take whatever I can get.

The blond human triumphantly offers me a small plastic bag full of extra-strength suppressants.

"Thank gods," I grin, thanking her as I accept the bag.

Just to be safe, I take two of the huge-ass pills as I walk with

Lillian toward my quintet's apartment. It'll take a few minutes for the effects to kick in, but—

My inner dragon snarls and hisses, furious that I would force an inferior substance down his throat. Agony pierces through my brain before I'm shoved hard into that corner of my mind where I can't function. I can't see and can't think clearly, but I do know one thing: I just became a danger to Lillian.

Shit. What if I turn her into a chunk of charcoal?

What if I burn the entire fucking castle down?

Let me out, I growl at my beast.

He growls mindlessly back. I fight against him with all I have, panic taking over as I once again realize just how helpless I am like this. If I stop fighting him for a moment, I'll disappear into my own head and never be found again.

I'm trying like hell to break free before my inner dragon hurts Lillian, but then the taste of blood fills my mouth. I can tell my dragon is biting hard, ripping at something, and then—

Ouch.

The vague nothingness I'm stuck in disappears as pain cuts through the dragon's hold. I startle and blink back to myself when I realize that I was just flung back into one of the stone walls by a violent blast of bright red magic. Silas is in this Everbound hallway now, gingerly helping Lillian get to her feet.

She's bleeding profusely from one of her shoulders since I apparently bit it repeatedly like some deranged, feral animal.

Maybe because I basically am one.

Godsfucking damn it.

I spit out the taste of her blood as my head pounds, my dragon throwing a world-class fit about the pain keeping him from being in control.

"I—I'm so fucking sorry, Lillian," I manage to say.

Even though she's putting pressure on her shoulder with strain on her face, she's quick to smile reassuringly at me. "You didn't mean to. And luckily, Asher is extremely gifted with healing. He's been resting in the apartment he claimed since you all returned last night, so I'll just swing by and ask for his help."

"We'll take you there," Silas offers.

I'm not surprised he doesn't offer to heal her himself. He's been finicky about using his magic, what with the voices in his head and seeing things and shit. Grimacing through more splitting pain in my head, I wipe blood off my chin and fall into step on Lillian's other side as we walk her to wherever Asher Douglas has been staying in Everbound.

"Sorry," I mutter again.

"I'm more upset about the spilled hot chocolate," she teases brightly.

Feeling like a piece of shit for hurting such a nice human, I glance over her head at where Silas stares straight ahead with shadows under his eyes. The fae looks like he didn't sleep a wink after his insanity drove him out of all the fun with our keeper last night.

"You could've asked Crypt for help sleeping," I point out. "Or better yet, you could've asked Maven to ask him. He would never say no to her."

"I would've, but the dyspeptic unicorns wouldn't let me leave my old dorm room."

"Oh, right," I laugh. "Forgot all about those pesky, deceptive unicorns."

"Dys*peptic*," Silas corrects, like *that's* the real problem here. He swats at something beside his head and glances down at Lillian as we turn another corner in this freezing castle. "I need to ask you for a favor you may not agree with."

"Why wouldn't I agree with it?" She stops in front of a dorm room door, knocking quietly with her uninjured arm.

"We need you to spend time with Maven while we...retrieve something."

Lillian looks between us as she puts what we're asking for together, and then she laughs. "I'm sorry, but you want me to *distract* Maven? Surely you boys know your keeper better than to think that will work with her. She'll figure out something is up immediately."

Silas and I exchange a glance. Lillian is right that Maven is sharp as hell—but we're going to get her heart back from Dagon, and there is no motherfucking way that necromantic creep is getting anywhere near our keeper again.

Leaving my mate for even a few hours is going to suck ass, but she's safer here at Everbound than anywhere else right now. Which is why we'll need help keeping her here, just for a while.

The door finally opens, and I snort at the sight of a sleep-rumpled, yawning Asher Douglas. "You look like shit."

His attention skips to Lillian's bloody shoulder and back to me. "You look like the feral dickhead who just took a bite out of a defenseless human. Come in and sit down, Lillian."

She slips into his room and perches on a small wooden chair near the fireplace, checking the bites on her shoulder. Silas and I follow her inside, and I quickly examine the tidy space. It's so clean that you'd barely suspect anyone was living in this dorm, except for the fire in the hearth and a gun being cleaned on the table.

Douglas's eyes glow green as he begins healing Lillian's shoulder, rolling one of his own after a second and shooting me a glare. After a second, Lillian relaxes with a soft sigh, tipping her head to smile at him.

"Thank you, Asher. I hope you're feeling better after everything that—"

"*Stad cantare ad'ihm!*" Silas shouts, whirling to glower at the empty kitchen with blood magic dancing on his fingertips.

"Si," I prompt quietly, gripping his shoulder so he'll stand down. "There's no one there."

His breathing is rapid until he finally drops into one of the spare wooden chairs near the fireplace to rest his head in his hands.

"It would only be for a few hours," he rasps, clearly talking to Lillian again as he deals with whatever is happening in his mind. "You know we wouldn't leave *ima sangfluir's* side unless we deemed it absolutely necessary."

Lillian studies him thoughtfully. Douglas finishes healing her and yawns again before folding his arms.

"You're seriously trying to ditch her for the day? In case you forgot, the last time your psychotic keeper got pissed off, she massacred most of the fat cat legacies with a smile on her face as her demon chickens pecked out everybody's eyeballs. I wouldn't ask for round two of that nasty temper if I were you."

"Her temper is perfect," I snarl as a rush of anger makes blue heat flicker under my skin. "Mine is the one to watch out for, so keep your motherfucking mouth shut when it comes to my mate. Besides, we're not ditching her, we're just going to get her heart so—"

Silas quickly sits up and kicks my shin to shut me up. Good thing, because I don't know who does or doesn't know about Maven's missing heart.

But Lillian must know, because her face transforms with realization as she rubs her now-healed shoulder. "Oh. I almost forgot he still had it. But if you go after it, you'll be traveling way too far into the reach of the Nether if it's still where it was—"

"It's not," Silas clarifies. "Dagon has it now."

She gets very pale and whispers a prayer to Arati. To Douglas's credit, he doesn't bother asking what we mean by *it*, or who Dagon is. Instead, he goes back to cleaning his gun like we're not even here.

Lillian stands and regards the two of us very seriously with her bright blue eyes. "All right. I'll distract Maven as well as I can, because frankly, I don't want *him* near her ever again. He's —he's just…a *scútráche,*" she finishes with surprising bitterness.

Silas's brows go up. It looks like he's trying not to smile, which makes me think that's some kind of fae curse that took him by surprise.

"You really did teach Maven her fae," he muses. Then he

stands to open the door for her. "We'll take care of the *scútráche*. Thank you, Lillian."

She smooths her bloodied outer jacket, looking between us one last time. "All right. But please come back safe and unharmed, because if you don't, she'll never forgive any of us."

"We'll be fine," I assure her, smiling. "Thanks again for the suppressants. And sorry again about biting you. When we get back, I'll make dinner for all of us to make it up to you."

"If all the people who are trying to get into Everbound to meet the demigoddess herself haven't destroyed the place by then, that is," Asher Douglas grumbles from the table.

Lillian says goodbye to us one more time and leaves. Silas is zoning out again despite his tight hold of the blood amulet around his neck, pupils blown as he mutters in fae under his breath. Not liking that he's in such bad shape with this mercenary asshole to see it, I decide to suffer Silas's wrath later and toss him over one of my shoulders to stroll out of the dorm.

Everbound Castle is completely empty. No Reformists, no mercenaries, nothing. It's starting to weird me out until Crypt appears out of fucking nowhere, startling me. He's leaned up against the hallway wall, smoking leisurely while his markings continue to light up.

"Frost had all his Reformists sent to stay in Halfton last night. No one but the Baird quintet is allowed in while we're away."

"Good," I grunt, shifting Silas's weight on my shoulder slightly as he starts rambling in fae. "Where's Maven?"

"Still fast asleep in Frost's bed after the rounds we put her through last night," the Nightmare Prince smirks before pushing off the wall to walk toward one of Everbound's nearby courtyard exits. "Frost is this way, waiting for the Nether caster to get here."

Nether caster? It takes a second for me to understand as I follow. "The one who helped the Nether humans escape? Francis or Finn or…what was his name?"

"How the hell would I know?"

I roll my eyes, finally setting Silas down when he starts to struggle. "Oh, I don't know—maybe you would have heard his name again at some point since you weren't trapped inside a twenty-five-ton scaly beast for the last six months."

"Even if I did, why would I bother remembering it?" he shrugs, exhaling more smoke.

"His name is Felix," Silas supplies hoarsely. The fae staggers a bit but smacks my hand away when I try to steady him. "Enough. I'm fine. Let's get this over with and get to *ima sangfluir ante fhada.*"

This time, when he realizes he's not using words we understand, he just tosses his hands in the air and storms through the doors into the courtyard with us right behind him. It's snowing outside, no fucking surprise there, but at least it's not as cloudy as it was in Manhattan. Everett is standing nearby, talking quietly with the same Nether-born caster I met briefly months ago.

Felix glances at the rest of us as we approach, keeping his face blank in a way that reminds me of Maven's tendency to hide her emotions from people she doesn't know. He looks less corpse-like after a few months in the mortal realm, but his skin is still sort of gray-ish, which I guess must be a Nether human thing.

I'm about to greet him when I run smack into Silas's back. He's stopped to glower at one of the many nearby ice sculptures.

"What did you just say?" he seethes.

Everett sighs. "No one said anything. They're frozen, remember?"

Frozen? Curious, I turn and take a closer look at one of the sculptures near me before my mouth drops open. He's right. There's a whole person in there.

"Holy fuck," I scoff. "You *froze* all these people and monsters and shit?"

Everett gives me a look like I'm slow. "What did you think they were?"

"I guess I thought you hired people to carve a ton of sculptures for your weird-ass high-end rich person taste in art," I shrug.

"That makes no sense."

"Makes more sense than you keeping a garden of living Popsicles."

Everett rolls his eyes at me before turning to Felix. "We're ready. Start the spell."

32

MAVEN

WAKING up alone is my first clue that something is going on. My quintet wouldn't leave my side unless they had a damn good reason, so I quickly set out to find what that reason could be.

I shower and dress to cover all the love bites I still wear as reminders of their vicious need last night. Tucking both my favorite daggers into the pocket of my sweater, I slip out into the empty castle. I want to find Silas first. My poor, tortured necromancer had to leave last night before I got to really enjoy him, thanks to his stupid fucking curse.

But before I get far, I run into Lillian sipping coffee and looking out one of the tall, gothic arched windows.

"Did the salt help?" she asks innocently.

Too innocently.

Still, if Lillian knows something is going on and isn't telling me, she must have a reason. Deciding not to interrogate her first thing in the morning, I nod and join her to see what she's looking at. It's the castle's largest courtyard, where the large greenhouse sits solitary and frosted over. Unlike the other courtyards I've seen, Everett doesn't keep anyone frozen here.

"Your grave is in there."

I blink at her. "I have a grave?"

Lillian smiles softly, but it's sad. "Everett put it together. He even had Asher enchant flowers around the honorary grave so they wouldn't wilt. He spent a lot of time in there, actually. Do you want to see it?"

My eyes narrow. On the one hand, I absolutely know Lillian must be using my morbid delights to distract me for a reason.

But on the other hand…

Well, who wouldn't want to see their own grave?

"Fine," I decide, since this will probably be fast.

She leads me down the hall until we descend a small set of stairs to exit into the courtyard. The snow is greatly disturbed here, like there's been some commotion. When Lillian sees me noticing it, she smiles.

"Asher often brings his hellhound here to play fetch."

Playing fetch with a hellhound? Not bad.

She says something about hoping the wards don't keep me out as she unlocks the greenhouse, but I'm distracted when three ravens land on the top of the greenhouse, peering down at me. The big one that I've started to take a liking to croaks low in its throat, tipping its head.

Finally, Lillian lets me into the greenhouse, and while I sense the wards ripple over my skin, they don't stop me. Stepping inside, I study the simple setup.

There's a headstone made out of dark blue nevermelt, carved with "Maven Amato" and dates showing my twenty-three years of not-life. A few random past belongings of mine sit at the foot of the headstone, like a pair of leather gloves, what's left of the massage oil Everett gifted me, and the tiny vials of kraken ink I used to use to speed up my episodes.

The rest of the greenhouse surrounding the headstone is filled with thriving, ethereal white flowers that droop almost like they're in mourning, too.

Snowdrops.

"Who knew he was poetic?" I grin, gently brushing one of the flowers with my finger. "I love it."

Lillian smiles. "I thought you might. Are you hungry? I can make breakfast."

I arch a brow knowingly. "Sure. Let's invite my quintet. Just point the way to them."

She knows the jig is up and sighs, glancing at my grave.

"They're good matches for you, you know. I was worried when I met them. They were suffering so much from their curses, but I just...I've always hoped you would find people who loved you as much as you deserved. I can see that goes both ways," she smiles. "It's nice to see you so smitten."

"Lillian. Where is my quintet?" I press, getting concerned.

She starts to answer, but a loud bark sounds outside, followed by vicious growling. Peeking out the greenhouse door, I see that Asher Douglas is fake wrestling a gigantic black hellhound that growls and snaps at him. He snaps back before tackling the infernal canine.

When Lillian looks out the door, her face brightens.

"I haven't seen Dev for days," she calls, slipping past me before I can stop and question her further. "I tried making dog treats for him. I'll go get them."

I protest, but she hurries out of the courtyard, leaving me to glower at the mercenary playing with his deadly pet. But speaking of deadly pets...

I have my own way of getting answers now.

Turning to the ravens still perched on the greenhouse, I focus on the big one. "Find out where my quintet is and report back."

All three ravens squawk and flutter before winging off into the wintry morning sky. When a loud bark sounds much closer, I turn to see that Douglas's hellhound is now standing in front of me. He tips his big, hound-like head, red eyes pinned on me as slobber drips from his razor-sharp bared teeth.

"Devil won't hurt you," Asher Douglas assures me without need. He brushes dirt and snow off his winter clothes and moves to stand near me, reaching up to rub behind the creature's ear. "He only kills whatever we're hunting on a job."

I examine the massive canine. Hellhounds are known for their single-minded focus, their near-perfect ability to track prey for miles, their unwavering loyalty to whoever they imprinted on, and their unmatched savagery even compared to other creatures from the Nether.

As far as pets go, I consider these ones an obvious choice.

But I'm not about to pet this thing when it was once hunting me across North America.

Glancing sideways at Douglas, I arch a brow. "My quintet and I almost got you killed in Manhattan. I expected you to quit. Why are you still working for Everett?"

"Money."

"There are less deadly positions out there for a caster of your talents," I point out.

"I like a challenge. Especially one with a fat paycheck."

I roll my eyes. "After Manhattan, you could have demanded an early paycheck, cut your losses, and been on your merry way by now. Which means there's another reason you're sticking around."

The redhead glances at me briefly before turning back to watch his hellhound chase his tail. "Okay, yeah. Maybe I thought about jumping ship after Manhattan, but I stayed because of Pietro."

I do a double-take. "Explain."

"I knew your dad," Douglas admits quietly. "More than knew him. He was like a father to me when mine was nothing but a dick. Pietro tried to save my mother and I from a fucked-up situation."

Oh.

Gods, who *didn't* my father know? A more sentimental person might see my paths crossing with so many lives he touched as fate, but to me, I'm starting to think my extroverted birth father needed to get a hobby or something.

Asher Douglas goes on. "Your dad and my mom were old friends, grew up in the same neighborhood and everything. She turned out to be an atypical caster but got knocked up with me as a teen and married my asshole father way too fucking young —before she was ever old enough to attend a Seeking." He shrugs. "The really early years were okay, not that I remember them much. But I do remember Pietro coming around to help my parents a lot. He took care of me whenever my mom was working and my dad was binge drinking. He'd do his med school homework at our kitchen table and tell me about how important it was to help people who were hurt. Taught me a lot about healing before I ever manifested a hint of magic."

I arch a brow. "I wouldn't have guessed you're an asscaster *and* a saint."

"Again, I'm not a saint, but that's another story. Anyway, the good days didn't last long, and my dad got a lot worse. He started taking out his problems on my mom and me. The next time Pietro came around, he saw the bruises and was furious. He got in a huge fight with my dad, who pretty much beat your dad to a fucking pulp and left him in a bathtub to die."

Douglas's face darkens as he watches his hellhound snap at a raven that flutters to perch nearby. "I honestly thought Pietro was a goner. My dad packed up my mom and me, and we moved in the middle of the night to a new shitty apartment in a new state with an even emptier pantry for his idea of a fresh start. I never saw Pietro again—until he was in the news years later for being executed by the Legacy Council." His green gaze flicks to me and away. "I had no idea he had a daughter, but honestly, I'm pretty fucking jealous. I would've given anything for him to be my dad instead of the asshole I got saddled with."

We're quiet as we watch Devil sniff and pace in the courtyard, massive tail wagging as he looks for another raven to target.

"This is the part where a normal person would express sympathy," Douglas deadpans.

I glance at him. "If it's any consolation, I missed out on having Amato as a father, too. I got Amadeus."

He grunts, rubbing his tattooed neck. "That does help, actually. Explains a lot about your freaky half-god ass, too. Zombie see, zombie do."

Angry whispering nearby draws my attention, and I realize the disheveled ghost of Daphne Frost is nearby, leering at me. Alaric's ghost is standing beside her, his nose wrinkled in disgust at the hellhound.

I wonder how Everett would feel if he knew his parents were literally haunting us.

Not to mention, the spirit of the blue-haired young woman who killed Daphne. She passes through the courtyard with a small wave at me, swaying like she's dancing to music in her ghostly head before she disappears through another wall.

I haven't been reaping the ghosts I come across, because I'm conducting a twofold experiment. If I don't reap them, I want to see if they will eventually leave me alone and go looking for Syntyche. I also want to see if I can repeatedly bring them into the mortal realm as I did at the Frost stronghold.

But when Daphne Frost's restless spirit continues glaring at me, I decide I don't need the Frosts for that experiment.

Pulling my etherium knife out, I watch as it extends into a full scythe. Douglas's hand immediately goes for where his rifle typically hangs on his back, and he takes a wary step away.

"The fuck are you doing?" he demands like he thinks I'm about to attack him. His wariness means he doesn't trust me still, which means we can't possibly be categorized as friends.

What a relief.

I don't bother answering him as I approach the whispering, discontented ghosts. Hoping Sachar assigns them a particularly shitty afterlife, I reap the souls of Everett's parents. No sooner has my scythe stopped glowing than I'm abruptly jerked into another memory.

• • •

"Very well," Arati's voice echoes again. "I will tell you how the divine may permanently return to mortality."

We're back in that strange, heavenly room again as her fierce temper abruptly cools. And now I remember why she was so pissed at me.

It's because for nearly three weeks, I did everything in my power to annoy the hell out of the gods so Arati would tell me how I could permanently return to the mortal realm. I stole the queen's golden armor and hid it in Pheli's never-ending wine cellar. I reorganized Koa's library based on how boring the titles sounded. I followed everything on the *Make Them Hate Me* list that I originally wrote for my own quintet—only with the gods, I had far more success stirring up drama.

I involved Paradisians, too. I convinced Pheli that his lover, Raan, was having an affair with one of the angels. I set fire to one of the forests, and everyone suspected the fire sprites. I even managed to track down some heavenly species of spider and filled Koa's pillows with its eggs.

I was an absolute bitch to make my point clear, and apparently, it worked.

Mostly.

Again, I find myself lifting my chin in this recollection. "Great. Then tell me."

"I will, on one condition. If you really want to return to your fate-given matches so desperately, it will come at a price you already well know. You must first exchange a blood oath with me."

Surprise courses through me.

The last time I made a blood oath, it was to tie my fate to the humans in the Nether and give them hope. It was done of my own accord, a brutal measure to ensure I kept my promise to free them. That oath is something I don't regret, but it did put my quintet in danger.

This would be an oath to get back to them.

The difference? Exchanging a blood oath means it goes both

ways. I would promise something of great significance to the queen of the gods, and she would do the same in return.

Memory Me weighs her options before, to my absolute horror, she nods.

"I accept."

Arati smiles. "I knew you would. As much a menace as you've been, my dear niece, your passion and depth of love have earned my respect. There's fire in you where fear should be. Let's hope you don't regret that later."

This memory shifts abruptly, billowing and changing until I find myself once again at the edge of a sea of clouds. Only this time, I'm looking down below with a hollow ache in my chest as the dark silhouette of something circles far below.

Round and round it goes.

In this memory, I sit up and pull out a knife. And when I cut my hand, instead of crimson, golden blood seeps from my broken skin as I let it drip onto something I can't see.

It reminds me of another vague memory. My golden blood—no, *ichor*—swirling into a bowl along with the golden blood of Arati as words I know too well slip from my lips.

"I swear this oath in my own blood, that should I survive my fall to mortality…"

I jolt back to myself with a gasp, my pulse racing despite my empty, burning chest.

"Fuck," I mutter, my grip tight on the scythe still in my hands.

"What was that about?" Douglas asks, sounding disturbed.

I don't have time for questions. I need to track down my guys and tell them that once again, I have royally fucked up.

Because I made another oath.

I exchanged a fucking *blood oath* with the queen of the gods, and I have no fucking clue what I swore to do or not to do. Breaking a blood oath means your essence is wiped from every plane of existence for all time, and yet I agreed to it—and now…

"Where are they?" I blurt.

Asher Douglas grunts. "For the record, I told them not to piss you off by going."

"Going *where?*"

"No fucking clue. They said something about getting something from a Dagon. Pretty sure someone mentioned your heart, which makes no fucking sense."

Oh, my gods.

If they survive Dagon, I'm going to fucking kill them.

33

EVERETT

"I CANNOT BELIEVE I actually miss hearing you *scútráchae* inside my head," Silas mutters. "It would be useful right now to telepathically communicate with Crypt, but gods only know I have enough moronic input bouncing around in my skull."

"And then there are all those pesky voices you have to deal with," Baelfire shoots back, gripping his own head with a growl as we stalk through this snowy, tree-filled landscape.

I don't bother jumping into the usual banter. We've been away from Maven for almost an hour, but already, it feels like my lungs are slowly collapsing. I pause in our trek to brace my frost-covered hands on my knees, trying to breathe as I spiral.

What if the wards on the castle fail, and all the people clamoring to see a demigoddess in the flesh manage to get inside? What if she realizes we excluded her from this and thinks it's because we doubt her abilities?

I remind myself that this is necessary. We needed to get her heart as soon as fucking possible, because the thought of her holy magic suddenly running out and her dropping dead again is strangling me.

Unless…

What if it's already happened, and this time I'm not even there to hold her while she dies?

Oh gods, oh gods, oh gods, oh—

"Hey. Breathe," Baelfire says, gripping my shoulder to pull me upright. "In. Out."

"I know how breathing works," I manage as snow begins to fall even thicker around us.

Felix is at the front of our group and pauses to turn around, calling, "Is he okay?"

"He's fine," Silas says quickly. I don't think he's aware that he steps slightly in front of me to keep Felix from seeing my spiraling hyperventilation. He's clearly still paranoid about our quintet being perceived as weak. "Mind your business and continue following the trail."

Silas is still holding one of Maven's sweatshirts that he used to perform some kind of necromantic tracking spell to lead us to her heart. That led to Felix transporting us here, to the colorless outskirts of the ever-spreading Nether border in West Virginia.

I've been here before. In fact, I think we're close to one of my more shameful battle sites.

Felix mutters something under his breath about how vile it is to be around necromantic magic, but he waits for us. After a moment, I can finally breathe again as I shove down every thought and focus instead on the asshole we're hunting.

Dagon.

According to Silas, he used to be Amadeus's head necromancer who experimented on Maven, torturing her for years until she became a revenant. Before Crypt slipped into Limbo to scout ahead, he briefly mentioned that Dagon often appears in Maven's nightmares.

He didn't give details, but he didn't need to. As much as we all want to bring her heart back, killing that twisted son of a bitch is also pretty fucking high on our priority list.

We continue trekking through this snowy terrain as Silas and Felix follow the magic Baelfire and I can't see. Sometimes Silas talks to people who aren't here, and Baelfire's head is obviously in pain, but at long last we get to the top of a big hill—and there it is, down below.

The small town I froze solid, people and all.

Baelfire blinks down at the macabre, ice-coated display. "Holy fuck. That's a lot of not-ice-sculptures."

Some humans are frozen while trying to run away. Others are encapsulated in ice inside their cars, or rushing out their front doors, or any number of things. Houses and town roads gleam under a thick layer of ice that is slowly being covered in a fresh layer of snow.

Felix looks at me, still expressionless, but there's no missing the accusation in his voice. "I heard about this. You seriously didn't even have the decency to unfreeze these innocent people?"

I wish I could.

I didn't mean to freeze anything. There was an unexpected surge of shadow fiends near this area months ago, and when I came with troops to defend it, things got ugly. I was injured badly and then hypnotized by a Nether siren whose song hooked deep into my brain, feeding off my emotions and compelling me to wreak havoc.

I don't even remember using my abilities. I woke up later with Asher Douglas tending to my injuries and an entire town of innocent humans frozen in time. The siren song must have affected my abilities somehow, because no matter how I've tried to melt the nevermelt, it stays.

Maybe if I had control of my abilities, I could undo what I did here. But even then, I don't know the survival rate for being trapped in nevermelt for months.

"Come on," I mutter, turning in the direction we were headed before.

"No," Felix snaps, though his expression remains inscrutable. "Those are innocent people. It's wrong to leave them like that. Whatever you asked me to bring you out here for, you need to go down and undo—"

Crypt materializes in front of us, blowing *reverium* smoke into the Nether caster's face as we all startle. "Don't bother with the lecture on morality. I found him," he adds, addressing the rest of us.

Felix coughs, waving away the smoke. "Him? Him who?"

"Dagon," Baelfire growls like he's already envisioning ripping the necromancer's head off.

For the first time, Felix's face morphs into something besides composure as he rears back. "Excuse me? You could've mentioned we were coming out here on a damned suicide mission. I would never have left Kenzie's side if I knew *he's* what you're out here for."

"Kenzie Baird?" Baelfire asks, confused before he catches on. "Oh, shit. You must be the missing caster in her quintet. Congrats—I didn't hear about that."

"Of course, you didn't. You've been too busy burning down the north as a winged monster," Felix huffs, turning to glare at me next. "What is this about? Revenge? Because, as much as I'd love to see Dagon or any of the other necromancers from Amadeus's court meet their end, you're all hardly in the best condition to take him on. I've only seen Dagon in person one time, and that was when a bunch of humans from my compound were forced to watch him sacrifice someone who manifested magic and bring them back as a lich. And by the way, bringing someone back as a lich requires an incredible amount of power and magical fortitude—"

"We get it," Baelfire yawns. "He's scary. Big whoop. No need to keep yapping."

The Nether caster rolls his eyes. "You're as bad as Maven. She once threatened to sew my mouth shut with my own shredded tongue if I didn't stop talking, and I'd barely even said ten words to her."

Crypt sighs wistfully, looking out over the white winter landscape like he wishes he could be at Everbound right now. "That's our girl."

"So damn violent," Baelfire grins.

"Unhinged," I agree, my cheeks warming since I can't help thinking about last night.

Felix throws his one arm in the air like he's had enough of this. "Gods above, you all really do belong together. Fine. If you're set on getting yourselves killed and turned into Undead puppets, I won't try to stop you—but I'm not risking my happily bonded life for this idiotic plan, so I'll be waiting here. If you die, I'm leaving."

Crypt stomps out his cigarette, shrugging. "Fair on all fronts."

He starts to say something else, but his markings light up brightly before he breaks into a sudden coughing fit, grimacing as he drops to his knees. His next cough sends a spray of bright red blood across the white snow.

I swear. So does Baelfire. Silas crouches beside the incubus as his coughing fit winds down. Crypt bats Silas away when he tries to help him up, and as he does, I can't help noticing that the swirling light and dark markings on his hands are gone.

Felix doesn't bother hiding his surprise. "What's happening to him?"

Crypt is…dying.

My other quintet members and I exchange solemn looks as that truth becomes more obvious than ever.

When we were younger, I could never figure out the Nightmare Prince's curse. Sometimes I thought maybe he didn't even have one. He was inhumanly ruthless, stronger than most incubi ever dream of being, and didn't give a shit about anything. Basically, he was untouchable.

But now, seeing him struggle to get to his feet as his curse wracks his body?

I almost can't watch.

"You good?" I check quietly.

Crypt wipes blood off his mouth, completely ignoring my question and everyone's concerned looks. Instead, he gestures in the direction Silas's spell was leading us.

"The prick's in an abandoned cabin that way," he rasps. "Before we pop in, I'll weaken him."

"Enough with the blasted singing!" Silas hisses at one of the nearby trees before he frowns at Crypt. "Weaken him, how?"

"Wisps. Keep up, but don't go in until the screaming stops," he offers vaguely before vanishing back into Limbo.

Felix stays there as our meeting point to travel back, but the rest of us continue to follow the tracking spell that only Silas can see. As we trudge toward a cabin in the distance that I can barely make out through the snowfall, a low croak nearby makes me look around.

Three ravens just perched on a nearby tree to watch us.

Those beady-eyed birds used to torment me. I loathed them and saw them as a sign that the gods were mocking me.

Now that I know it was Maven all along, keeping an eye on me all the way from Paradise…

Godsdamn me, I adore her.

"Maven's ravens will tell her where we are soon," I murmur, looking ahead again.

Baelfire barks a laugh. "Maven's Ravens sounds like a band. Don't worry. We'll be picking up this asshole's charred bones and bringing them back to her before she can try following us into danger."

Silas jumps through the snow like he's crossing a chasm of some kind. I don't have the heart to tell the lunatic that this is the flattest, safest terrain we've come across so far.

"Why bring back his bones?" Silas frowns.

"Why the hell not?" Baelfire shrugs. "Just picture Maven's face when she sees them."

That's true. I can already imagine that morbid, beautiful smile curling her lips. Our keeper would love a vengeful, gruesome gift like that.

As we near the snow-lined cabin ahead, Silas holds out an arm to stop us.

"Wait. There are several severe magic snares laid here that I need to disarm first."

Bael rubs his temples, cursing at his dragon. "You sure they're actually there, or are you just…you know. Seeing shit?"

Silas considers that, stoops to pick up a branch nearby, and tosses it a couple of yards in front of us. The second it touches the snowy ground, it explodes into dust.

"Damn. I'm still not sure," the blood fae frowns. "If the stick had exploded, I would have had my answer, but it's clearly unharmed."

I rub my scarred face. "Fucking gods, we are so screwed."

Baelfire pats Silas's shoulder. "The stick is gone, Si. Do your thing before the asshole in there stops screaming."

Sometimes I envy shifters for their heightened senses. I don't get to hear the necromancer's suffering from this distance from whatever the wisps are doing to him.

Silas calls blood magic into his hands and makes quick work of the magic snare spells, now and then snapping at the voices in his head or flinching away from nothing. Once he's finished, we hurry closer to the cabin, and I finally start to hear it.

Hoarse, frantic screaming. Glass shattering. And then, after a few more seconds, abrupt silence.

Without speaking, we move as a cohesive team. Baelfire breaks down the door at the same time Silas throws up a protective spell around us for good measure. The second we step into the ransacked, shredded interior of the cabin, I freeze the gray-skinned necromancer from the neck down.

Dagon is covered in lacerations that ooze dark, inky sludge, like his blood is congealed. He's missing an ear that was slashed off. It looks like a whirlwind of knives just blew through here, and I realize Crypt must have let wisps loose in here.

I don't see the incubus, but there are two mummified corpses laying on the massive kitchen table near this living room. Those poor humans probably owned this remote cabin before the runaway necromancer decided to go into hiding here.

Dagon begins chanting in a strange language, sending darkness flooding into the room. Silas throws out a counter spell that pushes back the dark mist, but the other necromancer is already hissing something else that makes the ice around him crack and shatter completely.

Damn it. I tried to make it nevermelt.

Dagon makes a strange motion with his hands, and mirage-like images of him fill the room, ghostly optical illusions that crowd around us as he limps quickly toward a door.

As soon as one of the optical illusions touches me, my skin starts to bubble and blister, quickly darkening. I shout in pain as it starts to spread—but this sadistic freak of nature made a mistake in thinking I'd let him go, after everything he did to Maven.

I'm not fucking around. The metaphorical gloves are coming off.

Before he can reach the door, I swipe my blistering arm through the air, concentrating to make my rampant abilities as accurate as possible.

A wickedly sharp blade of ice cuts through the air. Dagon screams as he falls to the hardwood floor, his dismembered legs twitching nearby.

A wave of blood-red magic surges from Silas, dispelling the mirage copies of Dagon. It clearly takes a lot out of the fae, because his nose starts to drip blood. Meanwhile, Baelfire stoops to grip our now-legless enemy by the throat, dragging him closer.

Dagon reaches up to claw at Baelfire's arm with blackened fingertips. When some kind of dark magic begins gathering in his hands as he prepares to attack again, I decide to nip that shit in the bud and summon a nevermelt blade.

With two flourishes of my wrist, Dagon's blackened hands drop to the floor, too. He screams and swears in a language I don't understand. When Baelfire roughly shoves the heavily injured necromancer into a wooden chair nearby, I finally get a good look at him.

Dagon is bony as hell and dressed in gray robes like he stepped out of a time gone by. His skin is ashier than Felix's, and his hood has fallen back to reveal a bald head covered in dark runes. His eyes are sunken and completely colorless, just pale pools of soulless, gleaming malice.

He looks even worse when an unhinged grin bares his sharpened, yellowed teeth. *"In te olfaca palmarius me ume. Im telum,"* he hisses in laughter.

Silas scowls. "He said he can smell his masterpiece on us. His scourge."

"She's not your anything," I correct, pointing my blade at his throat.

"She returned," Dagon manages in heavily accented English, his face beading with sweat as his dark, thick, inhuman blood begins to drip onto the hardwood floor below. "I always suspected she was more than merely mortal. My masterpiece was destined for more than my lord's plan. I made her what she is."

Baelfire snarls, "Shut your nasty fucking mouth and tell us where her heart is."

Dagon just laughs again, the sound an airy hiss as he struggles in the wooden seat.

Crypt appears in the room finally. Shit—the wisps clearly got to him, too. His clothes are pockmarked with still-bleeding cuts. There's a particularly bad one on his chest.

Still, he throws down several items as he stares down Dagon. It takes a second of frowning at the items before I figure out what the hell I'm looking at.

There are a couple of braids of silky black hair. *Maven's* hair. Beside them are old, crusty, bloodstained bandages that Silas reacts to strongly enough for me to decide they must be covered in our keeper's blood. There's a vial of more blood, two heavily sketched-in leather-bound journals, a broken dagger, and other odds and ends that Crypt rounded up from this abandoned cabin.

This fucking creepy necromancer has been collecting all kinds of shit related to my snowdrop.

Crypt was right. He's clearly obsessed with her.

Irritated, I bury the tip of my blade in one of Dagon's upper shoulders. He shouts in pain as I lean down to meet his disgusting eyes.

"Where is the heart?" I demand.

His breath stutters before he starts laughing again, hysterical as he bleeds out. Since he's being difficult, Silas turns and calls more magic to his hands, casting a spell to find it faster. Meanwhile, Crypt stalks over to the limbless necromancer, a dangerous smile on his face.

"Amused, are we? I've seen everything you put her through, you feculent swine. The torture. The damned *screaming*."

"Such beautiful screams," Dagon wheezes, still laughing nonsensically. Then his gaze slips to the mummified corpses nearby. *"Vivere rursus ad mortem!"*

Dark magic pulses through the air, dropping the temperature in this abandoned cabin even further. All at once, the corpses on the table lurch upright, moving with the unnatural speed of the Undead as they dart toward us.

One of them tackles Crypt immediately, bringing down the already-weakened incubus as Dagon collapses. The other Undead sinks broken teeth into my already injured arm. The shock of the pain makes me drop my blade of ice as I struggle to shake off the aggressive fiend.

Crypt shouts in pain just before a bright blast of Silas's red magic illuminates the space, disintegrating the Undead attacking the Nightmare Prince. I finally kick off the one biting me and scramble to retrieve my ice sword, slashing quickly to cut the damn thing in half. Both of its halves are still trying to get to me, but I ignore them and turn to see that Baelfire is now gripping Dagon by the front of his robes, hauling him high in the air.

"What are the chances we can find Maven's heart without having to ask this sick fucker another godsdamned question?" Baelfire snarls.

Silas wipes blood from his nose. "I'd say high, because my tracking spell leads into the basement."

"Good." A strange sound rumbles low in Baelfire's throat before the shifter breathes blue fire that quickly ignites the necromancer.

Dagon's screaming is different this time. He's in more pain, thrashing helplessly as the flames consume him and a horrific smell fills the room, almost strong enough to turn my stomach.

And the entire time that Maven's old tormentor burns, Baelfire holds him high in the air, watching with pure, satisfied menace on his typically smiley face.

34

BAELFIRE

IT ALWAYS HURTS, breathing fire in human form. I used to avoid it when I could, because it burns my insides, and my shifter healing has to work triple time to undo the damage.

But this time? So fucking worth it.

Watching the scumbag who tortured my mate turn into ash as I hold him is satisfying. My feral inner dragon enjoys it, too, so for one long, blissful minute, he isn't vying for control of my brain and body.

Once Dagon's screaming cuts off and he's nothing more than a smoldering lump of good-for-nothing charcoal, I drop him to the cabin floor and brush off my hands.

Good fucking riddance.

When I turn back to the others, expecting them to be on top of the ball and already looking for Maven's heart, I instead realize they're all watching me. Silas's brows are raised, and Crypt is outright grinning. Even the previously uptight Frost looks pleasantly surprised.

"Not bad, Decimus," Crypt laughs despite his glowing markings and slowly-healing cuts.

"Go fuck yourself," I huff, not interested in praise if it doesn't come from the sexiest woman in the world, who I can't fucking wait to get back to. Ignoring the furious blue flames still licking under my skin, I turn toward the basement door. "Come on. I'm done keeping Maven waiting."

Searching the basement takes too damn long. I'm fighting tooth and claw here to stay inside my own head as we rummage through dusty storage bins, spiderweb-covered wooden chests, and a bunch of other creepy shit that looks like it belongs in an old black-and-white movie about treasure-hunters.

Finally, I lose the battle as I'm shoved back into the little corner I can barely even call home.

It's frustrating as hell, knowing my dragon is either going to hurt someone or fuck around and enjoy his dominance over me, all while my mate is probably upset that we left her side.

You're an asshole, I grumble at my dragon.

Tasty spiders.

Excuse me? He had better not be shoving spiders in my mouth while I have no control over my body. Fucking nasty.

I can't tell how much time has passed when pain cuts through the blurry haze of my half-existence. I find myself standing in thick snow, not far from the place Felix said he'd wait for us. Blinking in confusion, I realize Silas just shocked me with magic.

"Thanks for snapping me out of it," I mutter, relieved to be mostly in my head again as I tug at the collar around my throat.

"It wasn't a favor. I had to frighten your ear leeches away," he says like that sentence makes perfect sense.

Crypt and Everett are standing beside us, having stopped the trek back to Felix to see what's going on. Everett looks impatient as frost clings to his trench coat, but my attention immediately drops to the glass apothecary jar in Crypt's hands.

Inside the jar is a softly beating heart surrounded by dark, swirling magic.

Oh, my gods.

That belongs inside my keeper.

I'm both disturbed and relieved. My own heart pounds as I stare at the mesmerizing, morbid display. "Fuck. Just…fuck."

"Articulate as ever, Decimus," Crypt drawls, but there's an undertone of pain as his markings light up over and over.

"Maybe you shouldn't be the one holding that," I frown. "If you collapse again—"

"I'd sooner rip out my own heart than let anything happen to this, and you know it."

He turns to continue down the faint path left behind from our journey to the cabin, though so much snow has fallen that our tracks have practically been buried already. The rest of us follow, with a few ravens fluttering alone, cawing at us like spooky little reminders of my adorably spooky mate. A few minutes later, we find Felix sitting on a fallen log as he communicates with someone through the scrying brand on his arm.

As soon as he glimpses us, he stands and adjusts his thick coat, shivering in the cold. "Oh, good. I won't have to tell Maven you're all dead. You were gone long enough that I—" His gaze slips to the heart Crypt is carrying, and the breath whooshes out of him. He swallows audibly, eyes comically wide with something between fear and fascination. "So that's what you really came here for. I mean, I heard he ripped it out of her, but I had no idea it was still—"

"Is there even the tiniest possibility that a transportation spell would harm it?" Everett demands. He's clearly done with the small talk and as desperate to get back to her as I am.

Felix seems unable to take his eyes off Maven's heart as he frowns. "No, I highly doubt it. That looks like an extremely powerful preservation spell, so it should be fine. Plus, if Dagon brought it here, he probably transported with it multiple times. Rumor has it that a lot of necromancers fled Amadeus's kingdom after the Upheaval because he began permanently killing off a lot of his court as he began his conquest of the mortal realm. Dagon must have—"

"Dagon, Shmagon," I cut in, gesturing at the glass jar. "We

have a heart to return to the sexiest, deadliest demigoddess in the world, so chop chop, Grayscale."

He glowers at me. "Kenzie once described you as a giant, friendly golden retriever with a bit of a temper. Personally, I understand why they keep a hulking beast like you in a collar."

Jackass.

As the caster begins laying the transportation spell, I notice Silas take a hand out of his coat pocket. A fucking *hand.* Based on the blackened fingertips, it's probably Dagon's, but still. What a creep.

"Si," I begin like I'm talking to a toddler, holding out my hand. "Whatever the voices in your head are telling you, you don't need to hoard a creepy-ass dismembered hand. Give it."

He surprises me by giving me a very non-insane-Silas look, like he thinks I'm a moron. "We *do* need it, because the jar is sealed with the same spell as is laid on that nifty collar around your neck. Without Dagon's hand, it would be impossible our naught we *cridhe dhi.*"

It's the weirdest thing. One second he sounds sharp as a tack, and the next I have no fucking idea what he's trying to communicate as he smacks away creatures that don't exist.

At long last, Felix is ready and we all move close until we're in a huddle touching each other's arms. A bright flash of green light turns my world inside out before suddenly, we're standing just outside the ancient servants' entrance into Everbound Castle.

The trouble is, this entrance is no longer being ignored. I realize we just transported into the middle of dozens of humans, legacies, and Nether humans who are literally camping outside the stronghold. Our unexpected entrance makes them gasp and shout in excitement.

Before we have time to react, camera flashes begin blinding all five of us.

"Is it true that the *telum* is divine?" someone shouts. "How did she come back from the dead?"

"Where is the demigoddess now?"

Someone else shoves forward, almost jostling Crypt, who quickly shields the jar with his ripped leather jacket to keep it out of the camera's view as more flashes blind us.

"I need a miracle! Please, can I meet the daughter of the reaper? I'm begging you!"

"We're building a temple for Maven Oakley! We need to measure her for a statue in her honor, so please—"

The overwhelming barrage of insanity cuts off when dozens of ravens shriek and caw, descending from above like a swarm of bees out of an angry hive. Obviously, the demigoddess-obsessed people gathered here saw the Frosts' broadcast, including the ravens pecking out eyeballs, because their overwhelming excitement quickly turns into terror. They turn and run, trying to take cover from the hostile birds.

The door of the servants' entrance creaks open—

And there Maven stands, arms folded as she stares at the five of us with no expression.

I'm pretty sure that means she's pissed.

But holy fuck, she's so gorgeous and perfect and *mine*. I break into a big smile, because damn, I was blessed with the best keeper in the entire fucking universe.

"Hi, Boo."

One of the people trying to hide from the ravens spots her and lifts his phone to take a picture. He's immediately frozen solid as Everett shakes off the shock of the ambush of frenzied fans. He steps inside, gently moving Maven away from the doorway so she'll be out of sight. The rest of us follow them inside quickly, including Felix.

Once we're all in the narrow hallway and the door is closed, I can't help remembering the first time I cornered my keeper in this very spot. She had just punched me in the face after combat training while soaking wet and wearing my shirt. *Gods,* I'll never forget scenting Maven's arousal for the first time.

So much has changed since then, including me. But one thing

that hasn't changed? My heart still goes fucking berserk every time I'm around my strong, incredible mate.

Maven's dark gaze moves to the jar in Crypt's hands. Her jaw clenches before she looks at Felix. "That was on Amadeus's mantle. Did you take my quintet into the citadel?"

"No, Snowdrop. We only went—" Everett begins, trying to soothe her.

"Were they behind enemy lines?" she demands, still looking at Felix.

"Yes," the atypical caster admits.

"In danger?"

"Yes."

"And you *agreed* to take them into danger without me knowing?" she seethes, the full force of her livid glare making Felix shuffle and swallow uncomfortably.

Damn, I forgot how fucking scary she can be. I almost feel bad that he's getting the full force of her wrath right now.

"Hellion—" I try, but she cuts me off, too.

"Thank Kenzie when you see her, because you being in her quintet is the one and *only* reason your heart is still beating inside your motherfucking chest," Maven says smoothly, still not looking at the rest of us. "That will change if you ever go behind my back again. Understand?"

Felix is unreadable as he nods. Then the corner of his lips lifts ever so slightly, and the smile is almost...*brotherly*.

"Look at you, caring so much. If someone told me a year ago that the terrifying girl who made a blood oath to free us would someday become hopelessly infatuated with four legacies, I never would have believed them."

The rest of my quintet and I exchange looks, all clearly expecting his amusement to irritate Maven enough for her to *actually* rip out his heart.

But the second he mentions the blood oath she made, she looks away, and some of her anger visibly leaves her. "Get out of the castle before I kill you."

Felix doesn't take his chances any longer. The moment he's gone, Silas moves forward to pull Maven close, kissing her neck. I'm ready to enjoy watching her flip him like a pancake, but she just embraces him back.

"Thank the gods," Silas breathes.

"Again, it's more effective to thank me," she mutters, pulling back enough to study him. She touches the blood amulet hanging around his neck. "How are you?"

"Deeply disturbed, but more yours than ever, *thanafluir*. The abysmal state of my mind is nothing compared to being apart from you."

So fucking sappy.

I mean, I get it a hundred percent, but still.

As Maven brushes dark curls out of his face, I tip my head. "Huh. So you were just mad at Felix, and not us? That's a relief, because I thought—"

Her glare cuts me off. "I'm fucking furious at all of you."

"Way to remind her," Everett sighs.

Crypt's markings light up, and he carefully hands me the jar holding Maven's heart. He pulls her close next, kissing her deeply before whispering something in her ear too quiet even for me to hear. Whatever it is, it makes her grin and kiss him again.

"You're smiling," I point out, hopeful. "So you can't be that mad at us, right?"

She pulls back from Crypt and huffs, sliding out of his arms to look between the four of us. Crypt mouths, *I'll fucking kill you,* at me for ending his sweet welcome home.

"I'm mad," Maven mutters, "but I also want to fuck all of you seven ways to the Beyond. Juggling emotions is such a pain in the ass." She arches a brow, looking at each of us with an unexpected, adorable smirk. "But speaking of my ass..."

I groan, immediately hot and bothered at the reminder. Maven's ass is *phenomenal.* Knowing she's eager to try more things in bed—godsdamn. How did I get so lucky?

Crypt grins wickedly at her. "Go on and ask us, darling. Frost can't possibly resist a second time."

"Maven." Everett pinches the bridge of his nose even though his cheeks are definitely pinker in the faint glow of the mage lights in this hallway. "That's not—"

"Kenzie dropped off lubricant and a couple of unopened toys that she thought would be helpful while you four ditched me here," she adds innocently.

Fuck. Using toys on Maven sounds like heaven.

But Everett is three times as flushed now as he sputters, looking for the right words before blurting, "Fucking gods, now is not the time to talk about *that* when we just brought *this* back." He gestures at the jar I'm holding as carefully as fucking possible.

Silas glances at our keeper, surprisingly gentle as he murmurs, "She knows. *Ima sangfluir* is trying to distract herself and the rest of us from it because she's nervous."

I look at her, too, surprised. "Is that true, Raincloud?"

Maven's lips press together as she looks at the jar in my hands. Whatever she's thinking about, she's careful not to show it on her face, but one of her hands absentmindedly goes to her chest.

"Having my own heartbeat again will be…strange," she admits quietly.

There's the tiniest bit of wariness in her voice that immediately has me turning to offer Everett her magically preserved heart. He takes a step back, holding up his frost-covered hands as a clear warning that he's not sure it's safe for him to handle it. Giving it to Silas instead, I scoop our keeper up and bury my face in her neck, kissing her there.

"Having your own heartbeat will just mean there's no chance your holy magic will dip out and take you away from me again," I remind her quietly, still not able to linger on that moment, even in my head. I pull back to study her face, realizing her guard is finally down and she looks...well, more than nervous. "Hey. Pretty little Angel of Death. What else is bothering you?"

She shakes her head, looking back at the jar. "One thing at a time. Silas, do you think you could...?"

His red gaze turns deeply regretful. "I barely trust myself to be near you, *sangfluir,* let alone reaching into your chest with the spell this will require. I know I'm useless to you right now, but I swear—"

"For such an intelligent fae, you believe some really stupid things," she says gently before taking a deep breath. "I was only asking out of cowardice. I'm pretty damn sure I can do it myself, I just..."

Aww. She's more anxious about it than she's letting on.

Deciding to get my mate somewhere she'll be more comfortable to face this, I carry her out of the narrow passageway and up a flight of stairs. The others follow. When my dragon hisses inside my head, slowly deciding he wants to take over again, I stub my toes several times on purpose to remind him I'll take as much pain as needed to keep him out of my head for a few minutes.

As soon as we reach our quintet apartment and slip into her room, I set Maven on the massive bed. I sit beside her to kiss her nose, cheeks, and those soft lips before smiling at her.

"Hey. We have a surprise you'll like. Silas, show her."

He frowns. "Show her what?"

"You know. The thing in your pocket."

He continues to look mystified.

Maven tips her head. "Is that an innuendo? Is the thing in his pocket his cock?"

"No," I sigh, standing to approach Silas. "Your fae is just fucking delusional right now. Silas. Give it."

I reach for his jacket pocket, but he grabs my hand to stop me, scowling. "What the hell are you—"

"Just take it out," I snap.

He clearly thinks *I'm* the one who's lost my mind. Crypt is openly laughing as he enjoys watching all of this, while Everett looks like he's questioning how his life brought him to this exact moment.

Using my shifter speed to move quicker than Silas, I snatch the necromancer's hand out of his pocket before he can stop me again. I hold it up triumphantly. Maven's eyes widen.

And then, just like I was aching for, a dark grin slips over her pretty face.

"That's..." she begins.

"Dagon's hand," Silas remembers abruptly examining the morbid souvenir as he gently sets the glass jar holding Maven's heart on the bed beside her to take the hand from me.

Oh, sure, *now* he remembers. Fucking insane blood fae.

"I wanted to bring you his charred bones, but not as much as I wanted to get back to you fast," I admit.

"How violent of you. I love it anyway."

We all watch, holding our breaths as Silas cautiously places the necromancer's hand on top of the jar resting on the bed. He clamps the lifeless, blackened fingers around the lid, whispers words I don't understand, and squeezes, twisting.

The jar opens.

We all remain quiet, so the only sound in this room is the quiet beating of her preserved heart that I'm not even sure the others can hear. No one seems to know what to say until Maven takes an unsteady breath, lifting her chin as she reaches into the jar.

"This is probably going to hurt like a motherfucker, so it's better to get it over with."

My mate is trying to put on a brave front, but I've never seen her look so shaken as her fingers close around the shadow-cloaked heart, pulling it from its glass cage. For a moment, she stares at it in her hand, her face unreadable. Meanwhile, we all stare at her, gathered around the bed. The tension in the room is thick enough to almost taste.

Our keeper looks at Everett. "Mind holding it for a second?"

"N—no, I can't. You shouldn't let me. I might hurt it if I—"

"You won't. Here," she says, placing it in the elemental's hand.

He gets even paler as he gawks at the beating heart in his frosted, bare hands—but I'm immediately distracted when Maven strips off her dark jacket, oversized black T-shirt, and black bra. When she pulls her etherium knife out of nowhere and places the tip against her chest with a determined expression on her face, my vision almost blacks out.

"No!" I snap, wrapping my hand over hers on the handle to stop her. "Fuck, no."

"Baelfire. I have to put it inside my chest," she says, trying to reason with me.

I knew she'd have to do something with the heart, but I didn't think about the logistics of it. When I glance at the others for help with this impossible situation, they look as torn and frustrated by the idea of her having to hurt herself as I am.

Finally, Silas moves to Maven's side on the bed. He carefully takes the etherium blade from her hands, looking like the weight of the world is on his shoulders as he does what's necessary.

"I already have your blood on my hands. At least this time, it will help you."

"You can't tell what's real from your own shadow right now," Everett points out, still holding Maven's heart like it's the most precious thing in the world—because it is. "Are you seriously about to perform godsdamned surgery on her?"

Silas takes a deep breath, looking into her eyes. "I know this is real. *Tha galeath.*"

"Tha galeath," she whispers back, bracing herself.

The scent of my mate's blood slams into me as he carefully makes an incision with the knife her mother gifted her. I don't realize I'm snarling until Crypt grips my shoulder to stop me from rushing forward. Blood drips steadily from Maven's chest until Silas finally drops the knife, his hands shaking, but our keeper is already taking her heart back from Everett.

"Maven," he chokes as snowflakes begin to fall inside this room.

She's in pain, but begins chanting anyway. I don't understand any of it—or maybe I do and it's all just a blur because I can't fucking *breathe* as I watch glowing light gradually replace the shadows swirling around Maven's heart.

Just as she sways from the tax of the spell, Maven plunges the heart back into her chest. Her cry of agony cuts through my very soul before she collapses on the bed.

"Maven!" I shout, panic taking over.

I can hear the others' alarm, too, but darkness claws savagely at my vision as my dragon seizes control once again. He pushes me toward that stupid fucking corner. I push back. I fight with everything in me, but I still lose as I'm suffocated in the beast once again.

Maven.

The spell has to work. She has to wake up. If I just lost her again—

No. I barely survived losing her the first time. She came back from fucking *Paradise* to reunite our quintet and have a future together. My mate is a damn demigoddess and the strongest person I've ever met. She has to survive.

I cling to that hope for all I'm worth until something pierces through the overwhelming control my inner dragon has over me. Shaking out of the beast's grasp, I find that I'm tied by my leash to a desk in the corner of Everett's room.

Crypt sits beside me on the floor. I've never seen the incubus look so downcast before, but he's holding Maven's etherium knife and clearly just cut my arm with it.

I rub my quickly-healing arm, disoriented as I look around the ice-covered room. Everett is pacing, leaving more ice with every footstep. Silas is rocking himself in the chair by the bed, clutching at his hair as he mutters to voices in his head.

My stomach drops and churns so quickly that I don't know if

I'm about to throw up or break into a thousand pieces as I look at Crypt.

"How long have I...how long has *she*—"

"Two hours," he rasps.

I look over at Silas, my heart struggling to beat. "Si. With the spell she did, how long is it supposed to take?"

He doesn't respond as he continues to rock.

"Everett—" I try next, scrambling to get my stupid fucking leash untied.

"I don't know," he snaps, stopping his pacing to cover his face. He looks a breath away from shattering. "I just...I don't fucking know."

I'm immediately on the bed beside Maven, panicked as I look her over. The puddle of blood from Silas cutting her open has stained the foot of the bed, but they clearly repositioned her. Her head is on the pillow, hair carefully brushed aside, a blanket pulled up to her waist. The fresh injury on her chest has closed, and someone must have wiped up the blood, but my mate is lying so still.

So. Fucking. Still.

She's not breathing.

As gently as possible, I press my ear against Maven's twice-scarred chest, squeezing my eyes shut as I wait and pray to all six gods that they won't do this to me again. Even they can't be that cruel.

"You promised you wouldn't leave me again," I remind her quietly.

Seconds pass. Minutes. Almost another half an hour.

And then finally—*fucking finally*—I hear it.

The faint flutter of a renewed heartbeat.

PART II

THE BOUND

35

MAVEN

Ba-dum.

Ba-dum.

Ba-dum.

The heat in my chest is different now. It's transformed into a rhythmic, steady beat.

"Go get Frost and Crane," a lyrical voice rasps nearby. "She'll wake soon."

Someone else says something quietly, but it feels a million miles away as unnatural drowsiness continues to toy with my consciousness, pulling me under again. It's not the same kind of restfulness I get from my Nightmare Prince. This is something I did to myself. It's the result of a heavy anesthesia-like fae spell I tried to weave into the necromantic-inspired revival spell I recited before—

Before putting my heart back where it belongs.

Oh, my fucking gods.

I have a heart again. That's what the unfamiliar rhythm in my chest is.

Fighting the lingering effects of my own spell is a serious fucking challenge. I tried to channel all my holy magic before I passed out, and *holy hell,* it hurt almost as much as the moment Amadeus ripped my heart out.

But now, I feel good. Scratch that—I feel better than I can ever remember feeling.

Aside from the anesthesia-level drowsiness, that is.

"She's awake?" Everett's frantic voice works its way through the heaviness of my mind. He sounds out of breath, like he ran here.

"Getting there," Baelfire agrees before something warm presses against my temple. "Come on, Angel of Death. Two days is way too fucking long to go without seeing your pretty eyes."

Two days.

That's not great news. Mostly because with the news of my return raging like a wildfire, Amadeus definitely knows by now. He's going to make a move soon. I have no way of telling what that move will be, but I don't like that my matches were left without my protection while I was out.

A coolness settles on my chest before I hear the most relieved sigh in the world from my elemental. The stress has seeped out of his voice. "I could listen to her heartbeat all day."

"Why didn't Crane return with you?" Crypt asks Everett as gentle fingertips trace my jaw.

"He's on his way. Took me a while to get through to him, but not as long as it took trying to get away from that godsdamned war meeting," he mutters. "The Reformists are gathering here out of hope, but I swear on the gods, if one more person requests entrance to Everbound, I'll leave them frozen from the waist down on the front lines for the fiends to snack on."

So violent. I always enjoy when my matches speak my language, but I don't realize it's showing up on my face until Baelfire's breathing catches.

"She can hear us. She just almost smiled."

"Ima sangfluir?" Silas asks gently. His fingertips skim my temple before he makes an irritated sound. "She's still working through the spell. Crypt, maybe if you—"

"I've tried for two days straight, Crane. Whatever holy magic she used, it's kept me out of her beautiful mind." His voice turns into a soft whisper near my ear. "I'm ravenous for you, love. Come back to us."

Determined to shake off the lingering effects, I focus on the lack of holy magic burning in my chest. If I'm not using it to stay alive anymore, then I should be stronger. I should be able to—

I'm not sure how I do it, but the harder I focus, the more an etherial, warm sensation sweeps throughout my body. It burns away the rest of the exhaustion until I can finally open my eyes and sit up.

Gods, what a sight. Four overwhelmingly attractive legacies, all smiling at me. Baelfire is beaming. Everett's one remaining dimple is on full display. Crypt's purple gaze sparkles, and Silas gazes intensely at me from the side of the bed where he sits.

Looking at them stirs something unbearably powerful and tender inside me, but it also makes the rhythm in my chest abruptly turn choppy.

I frown at the fucking bizarre sensation. "Ugh. What the fuck?"

"Ouch. Do we really look that bad?" Everett sighs, instinctively reaching up to feel the scar on his face.

His assumption is so preposterous that it draws a surprised laugh from me. If I thought they looked happy to see me awake before, now my entire quintet looks delighted to see me laughing.

"Not even remotely," I clarify, not bothering to hide my smile. I tap my extra-scarred chest, which I'm not surprised to still find bare. To be fair, I would keep my guys naked all the fucking time, if I could. "I'm just not used to…whatever the fuck it's doing."

Baelfire frowns and leans down to listen to my heart. It picks up even more as soon as he touches me, which continues to freak me out until he straightens with a big smile.

"Baby, that's what hearts do when you get excited or

nervous. That's your body telling you that you want mine all over it."

"Or it's her body reminding her how godsdamned stressful you are," Everett rolls his eyes.

"It feels weird." I feel the new scar, glancing down at it. It still bothers me that my chest doesn't show their marks anymore—

But wait.

I can get them back now.

I look up, making eye contact with each of my matches. Their smiles and amusement have vanished as they catch on to where my thoughts have headed. Our hive mind is once again full steam ahead as I grin wickedly at them.

Everett's swallow is audible, but his blue gaze is piercing. "We should give you more time to recover."

"Pass. Any other objections?"

Crypt is the first to pounce, pinning me to the bed with a consuming kiss. His lips are demanding as they move against mine, his tongue teasing my own as he uses one of his knees to push one of my legs, spreading me wide.

By the time he begins kissing down my neck and kissing my nipples, I'm gasping for breath. I realize Baelfire and Everett are on either side of me as Crypt works further down my body—and I jolt when my Nightmare Prince's tongue teases my clit in a light circle.

Baelfire's lips are pressing along my throat, branding me with his heat while Everett's cool fingers skim over my tits, teasing my nipples with a chill that leaves me gasping. Bael groans and turns my face so he can kiss me with feral hunger—and an instant later, Everett is the one kissing me gently.

Meanwhile, Crypt does absolutely fucking *wicked* things with his tongue. He laps and groans and feasts on me, his tongue delving deeper to hunt for every last taste of me as he grips my thighs.

"Should've known you were divine," he breathes, sucking on

my clit before pinning me with hunger-darkened, silver-flecked purple eyes. "You always did taste like ambrosia."

In between the way I'm being devoured, I manage to catch a glimpse of Silas. He's sitting at the end of the bed beside Crypt's sprawled form, watching with dilated pupils as I begin to pant and arch my back from the pleasure they're giving me.

When I reach for him, gasping again from one of Everett's rough pinches to my tits, Silas moves around to take my hand. He kisses the back of it almost reverently, but then lets it go to glance at Everett.

"Where are they?"

"Bottom drawer," Everett says, going back to kissing me as Crypt moans and finally pulls away from the way he's been mercilessly teasing me down there.

I want to ask what they're looking for, but my question is answered a second later when my gorgeous matches stop their barrage of kisses and I see that Silas is holding the tube of lubricant and one of the unopened butt plugs that Kenzie dropped off while my quintet was gone.

My new heart jolts as I realize they're going to do this with me. I'm going to have two of my matches fucking me at once, and just that thought has heat breaking out all over my spine as I try to swallow.

Gods, yes. I'm so fucking excited. And my heart is still doing weird shit in my chest, but I'm going to pretend that's normal.

"On all fours, love," Crypt murmurs, his gaze sparkling.

I smile and turn to get on all fours, showing off my ass. All four of them groan in the most delicious fucking harmony. I hear a bottle get popped open before suddenly, Crypt emerges from Limbo directly below me, facing up so he can watch my face closely.

"I'm putting it in, *sangfluir,*" Silas says, his voice hoarse.

I nod, breathless. A moment later, something cold but well-lubricated gently presses against my back door. Silas isn't trying to press it in. He's just teasing me with it—prepping me.

Crypt must like the look on my face because he hums. "Give her more, Crane."

Silas presses harder, and then harder. There's resistance, but he's still not pressing hard enough to fill me with the plug. I try to feel out whether I like this and decide I do. A lot. I'm ready to be done with the toy so I can have one of my matches back there.

"Just stick it in," I insist, frustrated by all the teasing.

Crypt tuts. "We don't want to harm you, darling."

If they're treating me like glass because I just got my heart back, I'm over it. The next time Silas presses against my ass with the plug, I press back against him until it pops in. He inhales sharply, and Everett and Baelfire both groan.

"Look at that," Baelfire growls. "Fuck, our goddess looks so damn good."

"How do you feel?" Everett checks.

"Like I want to get fucked in both holes," I say pointedly, looking at him over my shoulder. "And I want you in my ass first."

His cheeks flush and he swallows hard, but he moves behind me to squeeze and rub my ass cheeks, his bare chest heaving up and down. Crypt turns my head to kiss me while Everett toys with the plug in me, twisting and moving it in and out as he makes sure I'm really ready.

And I am. So fucking ready.

"Fuck me," I demand, breaking away from Crypt's lips to arch my back impatiently.

"You're right. She hates edging," Everett laughs, clearly talking to Silas—but his voice is breathless and thick with want.

A moment later, I finally feel the plug being removed. I shudder in anticipation as cool air touches the stretch left behind —and then I feel something warm and much thicker than the plug rubbing against it.

I jolt and groan. *"Yes."*

"First, more lube," Silas tells Everett, handing him the bottle.

I feel more cool liquid dripped around my back end before

equally cool fingers rub and tease and toy with my ass—but I still feel the head of Everett's cock teasing, wet now from lube as he rubs it against me.

"If you want both of us, it may be easier to start with Crypt," Everett finally manages.

Crypt doesn't hesitate. He leans up to kiss me while simultaneously lining himself up with my pussy and thrusting up. I gasp at how fucking hard and thick he is before his piercings drag out and back in.

"Fuck, darling," he groans, dropping his head back to the pillow as he reaches up to pinch and squeeze my tits. "Godsdamn me, your cunt is heavenly."

I swear when he thrusts again—and already, I feel that tingling release slowly building inside me. I want both of them in me when I come, so I look over my shoulder again and see that Everett is transfixed watching from behind like the other two as Crypt slides really fucking deep and back out.

"Everett," I rasp, needing more.

His arctic gaze moves to me and turns unexpectedly blistering before he moves forward again, gripping one of my hips in one hand and using the other to guide his straining erection back to my ass.

"Fuck, let me in," he groans, rubbing and pressing himself against me. "Fuck, you're so godsdamned tight, I can't..."

"Easy does it, Frost," Crypt manages.

He's too busy struggling to fit into me to respond, but just the sensation of having Everett trying to enter my ass while Crypt is slowly pumping in and out of my pussy makes my breathing ragged. I rest my forehead against Crypt's, wanting to grind and push until I get what I want.

My Nightmare Prince brushes my hair from my face, peppering kisses across my cheek, jaw, and lips. "Bear down back there, love."

I'm not sure what that's supposed to mean, but I try.

The tip of Everett's cock pops in, and he lets out a strangled swear. Crypt also inhales sharply, his hands gripping my tits harder as he feels the elemental slowly move into me.

My mouth drops open. Oh, my gods. That feels…different.

Different, but really fucking good.

My elemental goes perfectly still, still panting. "Am I hurting you?"

"No. More," I demand, already trying to press back against him. "Fuck, I like this."

"Thank the fucking gods," Everett groans. "Hold still, Snowdrop. Tell me if you're hurting, and I'll stop."

"Don't stop. Just fuck me," I huff, aware of how much I'm soaking Crypt's cock from the sheer pleasure of even this much.

Everett works his way into me slowly, pulling out and pushing back in and occasionally stopping to add more lubricant. Crypt is no longer moving as my elemental makes progress, but he's gazing up at me like I'm the center of his existence.

When Everett gets even deeper, I gasp, clenching on accident. Crypt jolts, thrusting instinctively, and we all groan as new sensations wash over us.

"Look how beautiful she is stuffed full like that," Silas groans from the foot of the bed.

When Everett is all the way in, I'm actually fucking *trembling* at how full and fucking incredible I feel.

"Are you okay?" Everett chokes.

I shake my head.

"Words, darling." Crypt rocks into me again like he can't help himself.

"No. I'm fucking *amazing,*" I finally manage to whisper. "More. I want more."

Baelfire swears. "Gods, look at you, baby. So fucking greedy and perfect."

Everett slowly pulls out as Crypt presses in. Then they switch, Crypt withdrawing while Everett presses so deep into me from behind that I lose my breath. For a moment, they're just getting the hang of the rhythm—and then suddenly they have it down, and both of them are fucking me in tandem, careful and slow but relentless in their desire to claim me.

I cry out. The sensation of their cocks sliding against each other with me caught in between is overwhelming and divine. The constant stimulation of being filled and fucked and worshipped makes my chest burn as my lungs sieze from pleasure. The euphoria of release is quickly catching up to me as Crypt pinches one of my nipples again and Everett grows rougher, swearing and smacking one of my ass cheeks.

Yes, yes, yes. I love this.

"Gods above," Crypt swears, his thrusting getting even more brutal.

I make eye contact with him and bask in the consuming obsession I see there.

He smirks wickedly. "See where that beautiful, sinful cunt has gotten you, darling? Stretched open like the fucking goddess you are for us—just as you were always meant to be."

Shifting my weight to one arm, I reach down with the other to slide the tips of my fingers through all the wetness gathering around his cock as it plunges in and out of me. Holding Crypt's gaze, I circle my nipples with the moisture.

He jerks inside of me, swearing before he lifts his head to suck on my nipples, lapping at ambrosia I left on them for him.

Silas and Baelfire are at the head of the bed now, cocks already hard and aching on either side of me. I reach for Baelfire first with my free hand, and he groans, bracing one hand against the headboard as I stroke him. Silas swears as I turn my head to close my lips around his hard erection. When I turn back to Baelfire and bob on his straining need, he makes a hoarse sound.

"Gods, I love the way you suck my cock, baby. So fucking warm and perfect for me. Fuck."

For a moment, I'm in pure heaven as my entire quintet fucks me at once. I swap between sucking Baelfire and sucking Silas, enjoying their pants and moans and the way Everett is quickly losing control behind me.

"Damn it," he swears, desperation dripping from his voice.

"Having trouble lasting, Frost?" Crypt teases, watching my every microexpression with desire written all over his face.

"Fuck off," Everett snaps, but I don't miss how his cock twitches inside me.

I gasp again when my elemental leans forward, licking along my spine before blowing cool breath over it. It turns into ice immediately, sending a shock of pleasant chill through my body.

The next time I bob down on Silas, trying to take more of him, I manage to get him into my throat—and he shouts, his hips jerking as warmth spurts, flooding my mouth. The surprised, pleased moan that leaves me has Baelfire cursing and tangling a hand in my hair, desperate for me again.

"You're gonna fucking kill us, baby," he says raggedly when my lips close around him.

"I'm—I'm—" I struggle to talk as all the addictive sensations make my mind go blank.

"Fuck, yes," Crypt whispers. "Come for us, darling. Show us how stunning you are when you fall apart."

My chest starts to burn—not from pain, but from something bright and right and whole. Abruptly, I realize it's holy magic, searing through my entire body as my pleasure comes to a sharp and sudden peak.

And then everything breaks open and clicks into place, all at once.

Pleasure hits me so hard I can't breathe, and the rest of them are right behind me. My heart pounds, surging with power as the bond sweeps over us once again—an eternal tether pulling them tighter to me with every cry, thrust, and moan.

As each of them finishes, the heat in my chest only magnifies until I'm really damn sure my fucking chest is on fire. Magic pours through me in one great flood before I collapse on top of Crypt, shaking.

For one long moment of breathless euphoria, I just stay here and feel my heart pounding. Finally, the heat in my chest fades and *oh my gods.*

It's official. Group bonding is unparalleled.

The incomparable rush of bonding all at once has left us all a breathless, euphoric mess crowded on the bed. I'm still on top of Crypt. As his hands smooth soothingly over my back, I can feel his heart pounding in sync with mine.

It's going to take time to get used to that.

Despite the post-coital satiated buzz lulling me, I sit up, still straddling my incubus. Five sets of eyes, including my own, immediately go to my scarred chest. Elation floods me so fast and hard that it takes my breath away for a second time.

I did it.

There they are. The emblems of my quintet, perfectly overlaid to create the same pattern as before down the center of my chest.

Gods, I missed this.

That's met with four incredibly sexy groans at once. Crypt's fingertips dig into my sides, his hips rocking slightly like he can't help it, his violet gaze consuming.

Everett tests the telepathic bond next. *So have I.*

Hell yes, we're back, Baelfire beams, sitting up to pull me off of Crypt. He cradles me, scattering little kisses all over my face and neck until I'm left laughing.

Silas sits up, too. His ruby irises trail over the length of me, lingering on my new emblems and then once again on the apex of my thighs, where I can feel them dripping from me.

"Ut ath'ann lei fhuil, la'restituas orm ais d'chal," he says with a wicked smile.

Which means, *What a beautiful sight that welcomes me back to sanity.*

Realizing he's right and some of their loathsome curses were broken just now, my heart just…stops for a second.

Yikes. Is that normal?

I pause, trying to feel it out. "I might be dying."

Everett bolts upright, alarm written all over his beautiful, scarred face. "What? Fuck—are you in pain? Is it your heart? What do you mean? What's going on? Why—"

Baelfire bursts into laughter, kissing my forehead. "Relax, I heard it happen. Her heart just skipped a beat. That happens sometimes, too, Mayflower. As much as I love watching you give Professor Popsicle an aneurysm, you'll live."

Silas and Crypt are equally amused, but Everett exhales, rubbing the right side of his face.

"Godsdamn it, Maven. *Context.* We just got you back. Have some mercy on my nerves."

Grinning, I maneuver out of Baelfire's arms to kneel on the bed beside Everett, kissing him. My position puts me right beside Crypt, who takes the opportunity to cup and squeeze my bare ass, humming in approval.

"Fuck me, that's beautiful. Are you sore, love? Or shall we continue to ravage you?"

I pull away from Everett's kiss to look at them. All four of my matches are gazing at me with a throat-clogging amount of adoration. Even though they're not pressuring me, it's hard to miss the fact that they're all getting hard again.

Part of me knows I should tell them about the blood oath I made to Arati in Paradise. I don't remember what it was, but they still need to know.

A much more dominant part of me decides that conversation can wait. After all, the newlybound pull to my unfairly attractive quintet members is way too fucking strong to ignore right now. Even though I honestly am a bit sore, I'm more than ready to make up for some lost time with them.

"What's a realistic amount of time we can stay in bed without the world ending?" I check, already kissing down Everett's jaw as Crypt's hand ventures around my leg to drag teasingly through my dripping pussy.

"Screw realistic," Everett groans when I bite his neck none too gently. "Let the world end."

36

MAVEN

TURNS OUT, you can fuck around in bed for a long time when you're actively ignoring anything waiting outside the front door.

It helps that, in between making me scream his name, Crypt has slipped away several times through Limbo and returned to our quintet apartment with stolen food items and anything else we've needed. Between the mind-melting pleasure of fucking my quintet until we pass out—except for Crypt, who has avoided sleep since waking up from Syntyche's spell—only for it to start again when we wake up, interspersed with a few steamy showers, short meals, and near-constant cuddling...

Gods, I've almost lost track of time.

I've also started to struggle with all the constant touching.

I'm not going to breathe a word about it, not when I just got these gorgeous legacies back. Being newly bonded and so extremely well sated is fucking *amazing*. I still want to touch and adore each of them as much as I can, no matter what my stupid past conditioning wants to remind me of.

But the jig is up when Crypt, who's currently spooning me as the rest of us sleep off another fuckfest, starts to trail languid kisses over the back of my neck.

I don't mean to tense up. When I do, he immediately goes still.

"I'm good," I say quickly.

But it's too late. He's already putting space between us. When I roll over to look at him, he's gazing dreamily at me despite his lit-up markings.

"Take all the moments you need, love."

"I'm perfectly fine," I insist again.

I thought Baelfire was still asleep, but he turns over on my other side, propping his head up as he studies me sleepily. "No, Boo, we've been selfish. And rough. Godsdamn, look at all those love bites," he adds, almost smiling. He starts to reach for me and then pulls back, checking himself.

I scowl. "Touch me. I can handle it."

"It's not about you handling it, darling. It's about you *enjoying* it," Crypt points out.

I still want to protest, but his markings light up brightly several times in a row. I only glimpse a brief flash of pain on his face before he vanishes into Limbo.

My heart twinges.

Gods, what a fucking horrible new sensation.

I know my Nightmare Prince is in pain. His curse has bothered him less since we rebonded, but it hasn't and *can't* be broken. I would bet anything he's only going into Limbo to hide the worst of it from me.

As heavenly as it's been to bask in my rebonded quintet, this is like a shock of cold water being poured over my head. I *hate* when I can't protect what's mine.

No. I'll find a way to fix it, I think.

I didn't mean to communicate through the quintet bond, but it apparently wakes Everett because his arm encircles me from behind. He was lying on the other side of Crypt in this massive bed, but now he pulls me against his chest and kisses my temple with refreshingly cool lips.

"We'll find a way," he corrects softly.

I nod, take a deep breath, and gently extricate myself from his arms to slip off the bed. Maybe I *do* need space, because that niggling discomfort crawling over my spine finally calms down.

Realizing the air no longer has the same cold bite to it as it did before, I glance at one of the windows and find that it's no longer coated in layers of ice and frost. In fact, it's almost a normal temperature in this room.

Silas wakes and sits up, his crimson gaze trailing over me as a smirk curls his lips. "I'm beginning to understand why shifters enjoy marking their mates so much. You're stunning, *ima sangfluir.*"

Since they're all unabashedly checking out my love-mark-covered body, I can't help the impish urge to tease them. Turning, I stroll to the corner where my clothes and knives were discarded at some point. When I bend over, giving them a full view of my bare ass as I reach for my things, I'm rewarded with three beautifully tortured groans.

But when my hand grazes the handle of the etherium knife, another surge of memories crashes over me, stronger than ever before.

"Just because you can read my mind doesn't mean you can change it," Memory Me warns.

I'm back in that idyllic, sunlight-dappled forest, walking side-by-side with Galene. Her golden hair gleams in the lighting, her ever-changing irises shifting from purple to blue to green as she glances at me.

"As I once told you, my fearless one, I know you far better than you might think. I'm aware how futile it would be to try to change your mind," she says softly. "I also know what you wish to ask next."

I ask anyway. "Why did Arati call me your secret earlier?"

Galene speaks slowly, as if she's not sure how to break more news. "You are my secret because I am the reason you came to be."

Remembering Iker Del Mar's words about my existence being orchestrated, I make some quick deductions and take a stab at it.

"Let me guess. Once you realized the Immortal Quintet sacrificed humans to suffer like animals in the Nether, you looked into the future and decided that the way to fix it was by sending me into the Nether."

Galene gives me a sad, almost *guilty* smile. "Not quite. The truth is, I foresaw you long before the Immortal Quintet. You see…it was my fault that Amadeus conquered and corrupted the Nether in the first place. He was one of my chosen saints, back in his mortal days long ago."

I pause to stare at her as that sinks in. I suppose if Amadeus got his abilities from Galene, the goddess of prophecy, that does explain his foresight.

But Amadeus being a saint, even when he was human? That's…

"Hard to believe now," the goddess agrees quietly. She looks away as if she's looking back through time. "Millennia ago, the Nether teemed with life. It was the land of the fae and of wild magic, and though it could be dangerous for humans because of the monsters there, those monsters mostly kept to themselves and caused no harm. I often descended from Paradise to admire that land. That is where I met Amadeus, in one of my temples that the fae had built. He was a pure soul then, one who desired little more than having a family of his own one day."

Her expression darkens as she looks back at me in this memory. "They call me The Knowing, but I am not omniscient. I cannot see everything at all times. I thought Amadeus admired me just as any mortal revered the gods. But after nearly two decades serving as my saint, his worship of me grew strange. Lewd. I realized he desired me, and nothing would deter him from believing he deserved a place at my side in Paradise."

She gestures around us at the ridiculously beautiful woods as we begin walking again. Fairies flit about through the treetops, and constellations continue to dance in the perfect sky overhead. It smells like crisp fall woods, but the temperature remains perfect.

I want to hate it here, but I can't stop staring when a herd of pure white deer amble across the path ahead of us. They're followed by two giggling girls who look like they're literally made of leaves and wood. They bow when they see us before skipping away, holding hands.

"Dryads," Galene supplies, running her hand over tall golden ferns as we pass them. "You're right that it is easy to love Paradise. In fact, I can see you finding a form of happiness here, far in the future, if you decide to stay."

Not interested.

"You were just about to tell me how you rejected Amadeus. Let me guess. He didn't take it well and retaliated by becoming the king of the Undead," I muse.

She looks sad again. "In greatly simplified terms, yes, that is what happened. Once a saint is selected, their holy powers cannot be taken away. But after I spurned him, Amadeus wanted nothing to do with holy matters. In an abominable dark ritual unlike anything I have seen before, he corrupted his powers and sacrificed his own heart in order to gain his immortality and necromantic powers."

Yep. That sounds much more like my dear wannabe father.

Galene nods in agreement. "Amadeus then used his life force to corrupt the Nether, slaughtering the fae until they fled by the masses to the mortal realm to start a new existence there. Times grew exceedingly dark until the Great Wars, when we finally put the Divide in place. The Nether had already become the terrible dimension of darkness it is now—I could no longer even see into that dark place, nor could we gods hear prayers from that place. We have no power in that realm. By the time we realized that humans were suffering so heavily there, it was too late. They were out of our reach."

I consider that. "You didn't think about just popping back down into the mortal realm and killing Amadeus yourself?"

We come to a place where the path splits. The goddess of knowing turns left as she sighs, shaking her head.

"We gods are explicitly forbidden from meddling directly with the workings of the mortal world, unless fate so decrees it. We can only send messages, servants, and the like. Any deity who meddles without permission simply ceases to exist. My own meddling to bring you and your quintet to fruition was slight, but enough that the other gods were quite terrified I would vanish."

Galene turns to face me, her expression brightening. "But fate knows best, for one fateful midnight, I had a particularly powerful vision. I saw Syntyche freeing the humans of the Nether. I witnessed great bloodshed and horrors just before a time of unrivaled peace unlike the world had seen in ages. The vision confused me until I later foresaw Amato and realized it was not Syntyche ending the reign of Amadeus, but *you*. Of course…"

She pauses and looks sheepish. "It is quite difficult for humans and gods to conceive together. Not to mention, the other gods frown upon such unions. I could not tell them any of this, not until Amato became an admirable doctor in the mortal realm. Finally, I told Syntyche, because the only future in which I saw Amadeus defeated and the Nether cleansed was the one in which you existed." She laughs lightly. "And so it came to pass that the goddess of life asked the goddess of death for a favor."

A favor.

As in, Galene asked Syntyche to conceive me with Amato. *I'm* the favor.

Damn. My existence really *was* orchestrated. I was born to be a means to an end.

Galene shakes her head quickly, her pretty face distressed.

"No, Maven. You were born for far more than that. I could not observe you in the Nether, but I know there were a great many chances for you to give up or act selfishly. There was no certainty that you would do what needed to be done, but look at what you accomplished. Think of all the future human lives you have given a brand new existence to. What I see going forward is so much brighter, thanks to you."

Ignoring all the pretty words she's throwing at me, I squint at her. "What did Syntyche get in exchange for getting knocked up by a mortal?"

"Nothing yet. I still owe your mother a great favor of her choosing, whenever she wishes to call it in."

Still. She basically pimped out the goddess of death to fix her ancient mistake.

How classy.

Galene's laugh is pure amusement. "No one could 'pimp' Syntyche out, I assure you. Though your mother will never admit it, I sensed how deeply she respected Pietro. She was fond of him. Years later, when a noble act nearly took Pietro's life, he became one of the few mortals whom she has ever pardoned from a true brush with death. He deeply cherished and adored her, even knowing who and what she is. It wasn't the type of love most know, but it was the nearest thing to it that your mother has ever experienced."

Her soft, echoed words evaporate along with the surge of memories. I jolt back to myself and quickly realize I'm back inside the oversized hoodie I stashed my to-do list in last. I'm straddling Crypt's lap, facing him as he holds me in one of the wooden chairs in our quintet apartment kitchen. Just like the bedroom, it's far less cold everywhere in our quintet apartment.

A sign that Everett's curse is gone. Everything is slowly thawing.

The others are in here, too. Baelfire is dressed only in shorts as he stirs something on the stove. Silas is carefully combining potion ingredients at the table beside us, and Everett is on the opposite end of the table wearing his adorable-as-fuck reading glasses as he rubs his temple, scowling down at a handwritten letter.

The moment Crypt sees that I'm out of the trance, he grins. "There's our girl. How was your latest stroll down memory lane, darling?"

I'm still reeling from all the information returned to my brain. Amadeus's mysterious past, the gods' limits, how I came to be...

It doesn't take a mathematician to run the numbers and realize Syntyche must have spared Pietro Amato's life right after he took a beating for trying to stop Asher Douglas's father. If there wasn't such a high chance that Douglas's father was already dead, I'd consider tracking him down to kill him myself. Maybe I'll ask the mercenary about it later.

Refocusing on Crypt, I start to answer his question, but my gaze locks onto his neck. There are still light and dark swirls there, but…there used to be more. I noticed it during sex, too. Several markings are missing on his hands, legs, and torso.

I give him a stare-down, speaking only to him telepathically. *Where are the rest of your markings?*

He studies me for a moment before kissing my forehead. *Later, love. There's enough going on as is.*

That's a fucking brush-off if I've ever heard one.

We're interrupted when Baelfire blurs to our side, holding the stirring spoon in one hand and gently tipping my chin up with his other so he can have my attention. Damn, he looks good in a collar. All of his delicious golden muscles are on display as he smiles down at me. There's no more pain or feral gleam in his molten amber eyes—just the characteristic excitement of my charming match.

"You were out of it for a while. How're you feeling, Raincloud?"

Honestly? Aside from the memories still settling in my head, I feel incredible. Powerful.

Like I'm *theirs* again.

With the heart pumping steadily in my emblem-marked chest, I feel stronger, too. The difference is so clear to me now that it's no wonder I felt like my holy magic was so weak. It was all going toward keeping me alive.

But now that I have my matches back, a heart beats in my chest, we're bound again, and I've fucked them senseless for hours on end…it may be time to address the bad news I've been trying like hell not to think about.

It's only fair to warn them.

I clear my throat. "We may have a problem."

"What else is new?" Everett deadpans, glancing up from the letter he's been reading.

"I made a blood oath."

Silas nods as he discreetly de-stems *reverium* to add to the potion ingredients. How odd. Is he making something for Crypt? I don't think my incubus notices.

"We know, *sangfluir*. The Nether humans are free thanks to that oath."

"Another one," I clarify. "I made another blood oath."

Four heads whip toward me so fast it would be comical if my quintet didn't look half shocked and half livid.

"What?" Everett sputters, ripping off his reading glasses to give me the full force of his penetrating blue stare. "When? And who the hell did you make the oath to?"

"Arati."

"What?" they all shout at once as Baelfire accidentally snaps the stirring spoon in half.

Their voices are surprisingly harmonious together, but now probably isn't the time to mention it when they're all swearing and reacting so strongly.

"And what *exactly* did you swear to do this time?" Crypt demands, his violet eyes hard as they search mine.

"If it puts you in danger, I swear on the fucking gods..." Everett trails off dangerously before shoving his seat away from the table and standing to pace.

Silas's red stare is inescapable as Baelfire tosses aside the broken spoon, all traces of his smile gone. Their angry scrutiny doesn't budge as the oven timer goes off.

"I don't remember. Yet," I add, like that one word is the good news.

"Godsdamn it all, Maven," Silas sighs, exasperated. "You can't keep doing this to us."

"At this point, I'm going to make you make a fucking blood oath to stop *making* blood oaths," Baelfire grits, storming back to the oven to turn off the timer.

Their reactions are justified. Considering the hell I've put them through, I'm a little surprised they haven't tried tying me up in one of the rooms to make sure I never step foot outside the door again. But as irritated as I am that I can't remember what oath I made, I do know one thing.

"Whatever happened in Paradise, I chose you four," I tell them quietly. "I would never swear an oath that would put you in danger."

"Us? You think we're worried about *us?*" Baelfire growls.

He pulls a casserole of some kind out of the oven with his bare hand before slamming the oven door shut and whirling to stalk toward me again. I forgot how impressive Baelfire's temper is, but...gods. He can be kind of scary when he's this mad, with blue fire flickering ominously under his tanned skin.

"We'd live for you. We'd die for you. We're *yours*—so do whatever the fuck you want with us. That's not the problem," he snaps. "The problem is, you're too fucking self-sacrificing. You literally went through hell to get humans you didn't even know out of the Nether. What if your blood oath had to do with getting back here, huh? How much more would you choose to suffer just to return to us?"

"A lot more," I agree without missing a beat, getting off of

Crypt's lap so I can stand and glare up at my furious, towering shifter better. "You're right. I would have done anything—*except* hurting you four. So whatever price I agreed to pay, it would have been with full intent to stay here with you. It worked, because I'm back and we're bound and so fucking help me, nothing and no one will stop me from finally enjoying a long, peaceful life with the men I lo—"

I catch myself and press my lips together.

Shit. I've told each of them individually, but saying it out loud in front of my complete, bound quintet is different.

Silas raises his brows, his frustration starting to dissipate as he smirks at me on the other side of the table. "Yes? The men you…?"

"You know," I mumble.

"We know, but we'd like to hear it," Crypt grins. "Come on, darling. Confess."

I decide this conversation has been productive enough and turn to study the food Baelfire just made. Whatever it is, it has potatoes and cheese in it and smells amazing. "That masterpiece is going to get cold."

"How is it possible that you fell from fucking *Paradise* to get back to us, and you still think it's weird to say the *'L-word'* out loud?" Everett asks, baffled.

Before I can pretend the potato casserole has my full attention, Baelfire envelops me in his strong, warm arms. He kisses the top of my head, sighing as his shifter temper subsides as quickly as it was riled.

"You know, Cutie Pie, it's really fucking hard to stay mad when I know you just do stupid shit out of love. But if you get all your memories back and we find out this blood oath is going to cause you pain, I'll..." He stops, considering.

I tip my head back to smirk at him. "I love a good threat, so go ahead. You'll what?"

He makes up his mind. "I'll only serve you green Jell-O for the rest of our lives."

Now that's just cruel.

37

SILAS

BEING BOUND to my blood blossom is different this time.

It's the difference between being bound to Maven's shadow heart and being bound to her *actual* heart. I doubt our stunning demigoddess is even aware of the effect it's had on the rest of us yet, but the difference from our last bonding is staggering.

Before, it was incredible. The best thing to ever happen to me.

This time, when the bond snapped into place, it instantly became an unrivaled, ethereal epiphany. A divine lightning strike directly to the soul, sealing my heart and fate to Maven's.

The newlybound urges are far stronger this time, too. Despite the last day and a half spent relishing Maven and enjoying every moment of her pleasure, whether it was caused by me or my quintet members, I'm still aching for more of her. The only madness that remains from my curse is the insanity she inspires in me.

Yet once again, my curse is *finally* gone.

It's poignant, this sensation of sanity. Even something as simple as eating with my quintet is blessedly peaceful as we gather around the table to eat the casserole Baelfire made—except for Crypt, who takes to studying Maven's new etherium blade.

Although his markings have been lighting up as his curse affects him, I've noted that it's been less frequent since we were rebound to our keeper. Considering the almost unmanageable boost in power I can sense racing inside my veins, I've decided he must also be stronger overall and suffering slightly less.

Still, I don't envy him for his unbreakable curse, hence why I've been meddling with a *reverium* potion. He just so happened to leave his leather jacket on the floor unattended yesterday while he was fucking our gorgeous keeper, and I just so happened to find several sprigs of the colorless herb in one of the pockets.

Soothing the pain from his curse is his only reprieve. Perhaps I feel I owe him that, knowing what I now know of the Nightmare Prince's nightmarish past.

Having my curse gone again…gods above, I feel like myself again for the first time in six long, wretched months. No more voices ripping my head apart. No more glowing herons or imps or other figments of my imagination fluttering about. All that remains is the same burning thirst for Maven and her delectably powerful blood—but then, my perfectly vicious keeper doesn't mind that, so neither do I.

I bask in the simple pleasure of owning my own mind as we eat, the others exchanging small talk until there's a firm knock on the front door. Baelfire uses his shifter speed to open it quickly, revealing Asher Douglas. The mercenary is no longer bundled in as many winter clothes, since the temperatures are slowly returning to normal in the wake of Everett's curse being broken.

Douglas is fully recovered from everything that happened at the elite safe haven and doesn't spare the rest of us a passing glance as he looks over Baelfire's shoulder at Everett.

"Well?" he asks pointedly, nodding at the letter Everett was reading.

Everett sighs. "Just kill him and be done with it."

"Kill who?" I frown.

"The crackpot caster who's obsessed with your keeper," Douglas huffs. "He's been gathering followers outside the castle ever since she decided to fucking broadcast her true nature on live television. Which, by the way, what a reckless way to—"

"Hold up," Baelfire cuts him off with a glare. "Someone else is obsessed with Maven? Fuck that—my mate already has four obsessive freaks. We don't have room for more. Who is this caster?"

Douglas notices the food we're eating and glances into the kitchen, though he still can't enter thanks to the wards remaining in place. "Got any leftovers? I'm starving."

"No," I say at the same time as the others—except for Maven, who arches a brow.

"We do have food leftover, though," she points out.

Crypt finally sets down the etherium knife. "That's for you, love. I didn't go searching for the potatoes you like just to have them shoved down the gullet of someone who shot you."

"I apologized for that," Douglas grumbles. "Over-apologized, if you ask me."

"We didn't," Everett says coldly. Then the elemental sighs and replaces his reading glasses to skim the letter again, his brow furrowed as he addresses the rest of us. "Lillian slipped this under the door for me. The crackpot Douglas is talking about is a cult leader named Orlando Coates. She met him before, a long time ago, when he and his cult members tried to take up residence in one of Syntyche's temples. He's apparently obsessed with Syntyche and teaches his followers that since she was the firstborn of the celestial triplets, she should be the queen of Paradise and ruler of the world and a bunch of other lunatic shit like that. Lillian wrote this to warn me that Coates is beginning to resort to desperate lengths to get our attention so he can finally meet you," Everett adds, glancing at Maven.

She tips her head. "Define desperate lengths."

"He's telling all his followers and the other people who've gathered to Everbound's safe haven that he's going to make some big sacrifice at noon in your honor," Asher Douglas grunts from the doorway, still eyeing the casserole on the stove. "He's also building a temple for you."

"For *me?*"

The mercenary nods, scratching the tattoo on the column of his throat. "Yep."

"He's fucking insane."

"Yep." Asher looks back at Everett. "Killing Orlando Coates will piss off his surprisingly large cult. They might stir up the other Reformists and Nether humans, too. You guys can only hole up in here for so long."

"Then kill the cult off, too," Everett shrugs, indifferent.

"Before they become more of a problem," Crypt agrees easily, spinning Maven's etherium knife on the table.

My brows go up, and I exchange a look with Baelfire, who looks equally surprised. Gods above. *These* are the two who were running the show while we were out of order? I've gathered that Everett changed a bit over the last six months, but a full extermination order is extreme, even for us.

Meanwhile, my blood blossom examines Everett without giving away her thoughts.

"You're fucked up," Douglas scowls. "I'm not killing off an entire cult just because you don't like the idea of them near your keeper."

Everett takes off his glasses again. "You said yourself that they're obsessed with her. Obsession makes people dangerous."

"No shit. Exhibit A," the mercenary scoffs, gesturing at our entire quintet from the threshold where he still can't enter.

"I'll meet him," Maven decides, standing from the table.

We all stand, too, our immediate protests echoing through the quintet bond as we talk over each other. But she cuts it all off with one firm look, and then she speaks telepathically to us.

The cult leader could be useful. I'm not turning down allies before we take down Amadeus.

Take down Amadeus? That leaves us all staring at her in

surprise as she tells Asher Douglas we'll be right out and shuts the door. By the time she turns back toward us, I've caught up.

"You've only said you returned for us. In truth, you want to kill the Entity?" I check.

Maven pulls a folded-up piece of paper out of her pocket and unfolds it, handing it to me to pass around as she confidently says, "I need to end him if we want any kind of permanent future together. Which I do."

Crypt, Everett, Baelfire, and I gather around to get a good look at this list.

Crypt grins. "Written in crayon, as all good hit lists are."

My attention slips to the end, and I nearly laugh. "*Sangfluir,* 'rest in peace' is a phrase typically used to describe the fate of someone who died."

"Someone did," she grins, gesturing at herself like it's funny.

Gods above.

Crypt coughs like he would laugh if the situation were different. Baelfire and I stare at her, and I'm positive that, like me, he's considering the possibility that we may *actually* need to get her into therapy.

Everett pinches the bridge of his nose. "Nope. Too soon."

Our reactions to her tasteless joke don't dampen her amusement. My blood blossom just grins wider as she folds the paper back up, giving us a brief glimpse of an intricate sketch of a map on the back before it disappears back into one of her hoodie pockets.

Then Maven grows serious. "Aside from protecting ourselves, defeating Amadeus will change everything for legacies and humans. The Nether can return to what it once was, and monsters wouldn't try to flee into the mortal realm anymore. It would bring peace for everyone, but especially us."

She briefly explains some of her most recently returned memories—everything Galene told her about how Amadeus came to be, and how that, in turn, brought about Maven herself.

When she finishes, she waits expectantly for us to agree or

disagree about taking on Amadeus, but I'm distracted. Some of her wording makes me wonder if she believes…

"You are far more than a machination of the gods, *ima sangfluir*," I murmur. "Tell me you know this."

She looks away, quiet for a moment before she looks back at us with that beautifully fierce determination that is pure Maven.

"Maybe I was born for a purpose, but I don't fucking care. No matter how I came to exist, I choose my own fate now. And I choose us. Killing Amadeus is just a fringe benefit and the best way to protect the legacies I love—" She sees our excited expressions and quickly tacks on, "to fuck."

Such a stubborn ending to such a serious, beautiful statement draws surprised laughs from us. Baelfire wraps his arms around our keeper, spinning her around like a giddy fool.

"Stop being so fucking cute," he groans, setting Maven down to kiss her forehead. "It's making me hard."

I roll my eyes. "Everything she does makes you hard, you oversexed lizard."

"Like you're any better, you horny bloodsucker," Everett scoffs.

Crypt grins. "Now, now. Let's not pretend any of our cocks aren't utterly mesmerized by our lovely keeper."

Baelfire shakes his head. "Way to word it. You say the weirdest fucking shit."

"Him?" Everett gawks at Baelfire. "Seriously? Am I imagining the time you opened your big fat mouth to ask about the temperature of my sperm, or do you just have no self-awareness at all?"

Maven's laughter takes all of our attention at once, and my heart picks up its pace when I see the smile curving her beautiful lips. "He asked about your what now?"

Everett's face pinkens. "It was nothing. Your shifter just doesn't have a fucking filter."

"I, for one, still await your answer to Baelfire's very reasonable question," Crypt says, patting Everett's shoulder.

Everett slaps his hand away, growing redder. "Shut *up*."

"Boo, tell me once and for all," Bael begins. "When his popsicle pops off, is it like—"

Everett freezes Baelfire's mouth, huffing and adjusting his coat before he faces Maven. "*Anyway*, back to the topic at hand."

"Your sperm," I suggest, unable to resist.

The scarred elemental glares menacingly at me before turning a far softer look on our keeper. "You really want to kill Amadeus?"

Maven is still grinning about our antics, but nods. "Or whatever the closest thing to death is for him at this point. So long as his reign ends and you four are safe from him."

She'd be safer, too, Crypt reasons through the bond, but only to me, Everett, and Baelfire.

My thoughts exactly, Everett replies. *We're nothing to the Entity. He would only hurt us to get to her. He must know she's back now, so it's only a matter of time before he makes a move.*

If he dares try to harm her in any way, his fate is signed in blood, I chip in, irritated by the very idea of Maven's Undead would-be father figure trying to get to her ever again.

Baelfire nods.

Our keeper looks between each of us, obviously aware that we're communicating without her. She's always been impressively observant, and none of us is particularly gifted at hiding our emotions the way she is, so I'm not surprised when she looks satisfied, easily deciphering our feelings on the matter.

"Good. Then let's get another pawn on the board."

She means the cult leader.

As much as I adore my blood blossom's brutal practicality, I still don't like the idea of her leaving this apartment. Whether it's because of my far stronger newlybound urges, or because we've just barely started to recover from a hellish six months, I want to keep Maven spirited away here. Here, we are guarded by wards, and we can adore and tend to her to our heart's content.

Out there…

"If any of the freaks out there *do* try to hurt you, can I light them all on fire?" Baelfire checks.

"They won't," she says confidently, leaving the kitchen to go look for more clothes and boots in her room.

When she's out of earshot, the rest of my quintet and I regard one another.

Baelfire shrugs. "Fuck it. If anyone makes a move toward her that we don't like—"

"If they even so much as *look* at her in a way we don't like," Crypt corrects, glaring out one of the windows as his markings light up repeatedly.

"They're dead," Everett agrees.

I nod.

38

MAVEN

As soon as we step outside our salt-protected apartment, I'm greeted by several dozen ghosts waiting in the hallway. Most look fresh, though some of them are slightly blurry—like the blue-haired young woman ghost who waves at me like we're good friends as she drifts past.

She doesn't seem in a hurry to get reaped and move on. I tried telling her my plan to see how long they'll stick around the other day, when my quintet took off to get my heart without me. I'm not sure how much of my plan was lost in translation, but it seems like she's been explaining the situation to the other ghosts, because none of them are particularly impatient as they haunt Everbound.

My entire quintet is dressed in regular clothes as we stroll through the hall. Although I appreciate the warmer temperature, I miss Everett's beautiful frost patterns decorating the windows.

Pausing our trek through the halls, I look out of one of the vaulted castle windows.

Gods. That's a lot of people gathered outside.

The refugee tent city surrounding Halfton has now spread to surround Everbound Castle. Now that the wintry weather is finally letting up, everyone camped outside seems to be in a good mood. Some of them look like refugees from other areas, here to take cover within Everbound's etherium-powered wards. Other campers are Nether humans with muted gray skin tones, who are helping one another and sticking to themselves.

Further out, closer to the twisted Everbound Forest, the tents are all black. The figures I see walking around out there are dressed in black, too. Cult members, probably.

And then there are the human reporters.

I know they're reporters because of all the cameras they're holding, but also because Lillian stands out there in a light jacket. It's obvious that she's asking them to leave as nicely as she can.

One of the photographers says something and flips her off. The others laugh.

I don't realize how hard I'm glowering at him until Crypt rests his chin on one of my shoulders.

"Shall I make an example of him, love?" he asks, kissing my cheek.

I glance at him, taking a moment to admire the silver flecks in those deep violet irises. He's just so fucking *handsome,* but it irks me when I note the few remaining light and dark swirls decorating his neck. If I ask about his missing marks again, I fully expect another brush-off, and now is not the time.

Knowing how much my gorgeous incubus craves our deeper connection, I speak telepathically to just him. *I don't like it when people disrespect Lillian. Scare him, but don't kill him.*

His gaze transforms into a deliciously dark smirk before he vanishes. A moment later, the rest of my quintet and I watch as the Nightmare Prince appears just beside Lillian. He reaches out as if to shake the disrespectful reporter's hand. The man is so shocked and wide-eyed that he extends his own hand as if on autopilot, his mouth hanging open.

As soon as Crypt grips the human's hand, they both vanish.

The other photographers freak out. Meanwhile, Lillian

glances back at the castle with a perturbed frown. I'm not sure if she can see us from this one window, but I wave anyway.

Crypt doesn't reappear below, but the reporter does. He staggers out of Limbo, shoves his way out of the crowd of reporters, and throws up before falling to the ground in a shaking, sobbing mess.

"Sadist," Everett murmurs, brushing my cheek with the back of his cool fingers to point out that I'm smiling.

"He deserved it," I defend before sighing. "We'll have to deal with the rest of them before getting to the cultists."

"Easily done," Silas says, raising his blackened fingertips glowing with blood magic at the ready. "I'll hex them any way you like."

"Freezing them takes less time," Everett points out.

Baelfire shrugs. "Sure, but I bet lighting those intrusive, rude fuckers on fire and listening to them scream would make our little goddess smile again."

Oh, my gods. Not a single hesitation to jump to extremes. They're all so fucking *unhinged* now.

I love it.

But as much as I loathe the idea of being in front of more cameras, the reporters below are just another piece on the metaphorical chessboard.

When I was seven years old and so isolated in my hovel outside Amadeus's citadel that I sometimes forgot what it was like to speak out loud, Lillian taught me chess. She carved the game pieces out of dead pieces of wood, drew a makeshift board with charcoal on the floor of my hovel, and taught me everything she knew. She said that her fae ex-husband had loved chess, and told me that if I looked at life like it was a chess game, I would be able to predict things and strategize much better.

Whenever I wasn't playing chess with Lillian, I played it with myself. It taught me to analyze both my opponent and myself and look for every possible future attack and outcome. Those skills translated into outthinking and outmaneuvering anyone I faced during my training, and later on in Amadeus's arena.

Once Amadeus has fallen and my quintet and I are left in peace, the reporters will have more to focus on as the world begins to repair itself. But for now, their biggest focus is going to be on me, whether I like it or not. Killing them off or harming them will lead to retaliations—or worse, it may lead to my quintet being compared to the vindictive, selfish Immortal Quintet. I'd rather staple my tongue to another stake and get set on fire than be anything like those immortal assholes.

Right now, the world is overexcited about my return and will gobble up any detail these reporters feed to them, whether it's true or false.

I'd rather they get the truth directly from the source.

"We won't hurt them," I decide just as Crypt appears back in the hallway. "I'll answer a few questions and move on to the cultists."

Everett grimaces. "Snowdrop, I've dealt with paparazzi and cameras for years. Trust me, they won't be fine with just a few questions or pictures. They'll try to get too close to you."

"Then I'll introduce them to my ravens. Or ghosts. Or you guys. Or my new knife," I list on my fingers before grinning at my worried quintet.

Baelfire squints. "How about…Cuttrina?"

"What?"

"You named your other dagger Pierce, so you'll need a name for your scythe-knife thing, right?" he points out. "This one can be Pierce's girlfriend, Cuttrina."

I grin. "Are we naming all my weapons now?"

"Why not, hellion? You can name all our cocks while you're at it," he flirts, brows bouncing.

Everett scoffs, cheeks turning pink already. "That's a no. We're not doing that."

"Though if she did, she'd also have to name mine Pierce," Crypt teases, blowing a kiss at me. "For obvious reasons."

Asher Douglas gags loudly from beside us, making me realize he turned into this corridor while we were distracted. The big bounty hunter is making a face of disgust about what he just unwillingly learned about Crypt's dick as the blue-haired girl ghost hovers up and pretends to kiss his cheek.

"I just came to see if you five finally dragged yourselves out of bed before the cult leader does something stupid," he grumbles. "But please, for the love of all the gods, just stop being the fucking weirdest quintet I've ever had the displeasure of working for."

Seeing him so uncomfortable, I can't help but grin again. "Prude."

"Hardly. I just really do not need to know anything about your quintet's junk," he shudders, gagging again before he turns to stalk out of this hallway.

As he does, I notice the top of a strange, shimmering golden tattoo peeking out from under the long-sleeved combat gear he's wearing. The ginger has other smaller tattoos visible, but that one draws my attention. There's just something about it.

Baelfire notices where my attention is lingering. "If you like ink, I'll get some. Anything you want. I'll even get all those weird, swirly tats Crypt has that you like so much."

"For the last fucking time, they are not tattoos," Crypt drawls, taking my hand as we continue strolling down the hall. His markings light up several times, but he carefully avoids showing any pain.

I still want to know what's happening to them, I remind him telepathically.

Later, love. First things first, let's deal with all your unwelcome admirers.

The moment we step outside of Everbound Castle's main western exit, it's an uproar. Nether humans clap and cheer, cameras go off, and people try to swarm closer to us. Luckily, hundreds of ravens have gathered on the tops of the castle. When the sinister birds see me outside, several dozen of them flock to me while the big one I'm fond of perches on my shoulder once again.

It's an adequate reminder. The onlookers quickly step back to give us a wider berth as we stroll through the encampment toward the cluster of photographers already rushing to greet us.

Walking through an awed, excited crowd is strange after everything we were subjected to in the elite safe haven. Instead of people swearing, screaming, and spitting on me in repulsion, these humans and Reformists have fascination all over their features as they watch my quintet and me walk past. Some look excited, while others watch on in fearful awe.

The fresh rush of power inside my veins reminds me that aside from reaping spirits, my holy magic is now fueled by them revering me like this. But even more notably, my heart is pounding *a lot* as we walk through all these stares.

Stop doing that, I scowl at it inside my head.

Baelfire grins, scanning the awed crowd for any sign of danger toward me. *She's talking to her heart again.*

Aww. Feeling nervous? Everett teases, moving to my side opposite Crypt to hold my other hand.

Is this what nervous feels like with a heart?

Ugh. Hearts are such fucking drama queens.

Finally, the reporters and photographers encircle us as closely as they dare to with my entire quintet and a conspiracy of ravens glaring at them in warning.

"Maven Oakley!" one of them shouts. "Over here! Give us a smile!"

Again, with the smiling shit? I look at that one, ignoring the flashing cameras as I let him know with my expression just how stupid he is for making that suggestion. He flusters and hides behind other reporters who call for my attention, talking over each other in frantic excitement.

"Are you happy to be back with your quintet?"

"Were you the cause of the Upheaval?"

"Is it true that you're a demigoddess?" a third shouts.

Gods. Do they always ask such obvious questions?

"Someone ask something that we don't all already know the answer to," I sigh.

That was apparently the wrong prompt to give, because a woman steps forward who isn't even trying to hide the fact that she's checking out my quintet. She clears her throat, shoving a microphone toward me as she keeps her gaze on my four gorgeous matches the entire time.

"Maven Oakley. You belong to a nightmare-devouring half-monster, a prodigy turned necromancer, a dragon that breathes the hottest fire known to mankind, and a rich, nevermelt-wielding general. That's quite the impressive quintet, not to mention their looks! You're very lucky. How does it feel to have such raw power at your beck and call? Is your connection to Paradise the reason the gods blessed you so extremely generously with your matches?"

Hold the fucking phone, Baelfire growls through the bond. *Did this bitch really just bring up all of our abilities except yours? Is she just ignoring the fact that you're a fucking demigoddess?*

I don't have to look to know that the rest of my quintet is equally irritated by her wording, but I couldn't care less about someone overlooking me.

Her real mistake is that she's still drooling over my quintet.

Covering the microphone and moving it away so I can speak only to the woman, I give her a misleadingly sweet smile. "I don't blame you for lusting over them, but if you look at what belongs to me again, I'll hex you to piss shards of glass for the rest of your rapidly shortening lifetime."

Her eyes widen and she retreats like her ass is on fire.

So possessive, thanafluir, Silas chuckles through the bond.

With threats like yours, who needs poetry? Crypt tacks on, squeezing my hand affectionately.

I'm struck with a sudden, strong urge to drag one or both of them aside to kiss them. Baelfire is still glowering over the people admiring us, and *gods,* I love his dangerous side. Everett, too, has my attention as he completely ignores the photographers subtly trying to take pictures of his beautiful, scarred face.

Pleasant heat tingles in my lower stomach. Maybe it's because we were just all bound together again, but I'm already so fucking ready to be done with this so I can jump their bones again. It's not like I can resist them for long when they're so protective and handsome and *mine.*

Gods, I smell that and it's fucking divine, Baelfire groans through the bond just to me.

Someone else steps forward to interrupt my possessive thoughts, eyeing the ravens around us nervously as he lifts a microphone toward me.

"M—Maven Oakley, we've heard quite a lot of rumors about you for six months. Some of those rumors have been clearly false, but with your recent return and the unexpected surges and attacks at the fringes of the ever-growing Nether—"

I check to make sure my etherium knife is still in my boot where I left it, pulling it out to study the beautiful, clear blade. "Get to the point."

Several of the reporters turn and run.

That made it seem like I was threatening them again, didn't it? I realize.

Maybe don't pull knives out in casual conversation, Everett suggests.

He's clearly amused, as are the others. Crypt is outright laughing at me, kissing the back of my hand.

Finally, the reporter extending his microphone grows a pair, clears his throat, and asks, "Is it true that you've returned to bring about the end of the Upheaval?"

"Something like that."

The reporters get excited, taking pictures and repeating variations of that question until one of them spits out, "How are we supposed to trust you? Aren't you still the Entity's scourge?"

I look at that one. "I don't give a fuck if you trust me, but I am not Amadeus's scourge anymore. I'm his reckoning."

They're still going wild over that when I spot Lillian approaching, trying to peek over the reporters to see me better. Deciding the world will have to make do with whatever pictures and shit they just got, I move forward, trying to get to Lillian. When one of the excited photographers gets too close for a close-up shot of my face, I instinctively flinch back from the threat of physical contact.

He's immediately frozen in place, encased in such thick ice that it doesn't shatter when Everett kicks over his newest ice sculpture and turns to glare at the cameras.

"Get out of my sight before you join him," my elemental warns the reporters.

Gods, his scar makes him look so fucking savage. It makes my heartbeat pick up and makes me remember again all the deliciously wicked things he and the rest of my matches have spent the last day and a half doing to me in bed.

I want more of that already.

My ravens croak happily, fluttering about as the reporters scatter, fleeing to hide in their tents or getting lost in the rest of the makeshift living spaces surrounding the castle. Lillian is quick to move to my side as soon as the way is clear. Today, she's dressed in a bright pink jacket and hand-painted, colorful floral jeans, along with colorful shoes.

Gods, she wasn't kidding about missing color. My eyes hurt a little.

She sees me squinting at her and laughs, completely ignoring all of our fascinated onlookers as she reaches out to adjust some of my messy hair. "I'm not surprised you didn't fall in love with colors as soon as you entered the mortal realm. You always did prefer plain black clothing."

"Must be hereditary."

Lillian laughs, but then turns more serious as she examines my quintet and me. They don't know her as well as I do, but I can see she's putting together how much better three of my matches are doing—and if their curses are broken, it can only mean one thing.

"You have your heart again," she murmurs, beaming at me. "Good. These rascals left me completely in the dark after they returned, you know—they just kept saying you were resting as they spiraled out of control."

"They're hopeless like that," I tease, earning a gentle poke in the side from Baelfire. "I'm fine, though. Better than fine—I just feel…right."

"Being newly bonded probably helps with that," Lillian notes before looking pointedly at my neck as if to remind me of something.

Oh, right. I forgot about the love bites I'm covered in from hours in bed with my matches.

An obsessive part of me loves that I'm wearing proof of my quintet's attraction to me. I don't care that it's immortalized on camera. I don't want everyone in the world in our business, but since they butted in, they get to know just how much I adore my quintet.

There's no judgment in Lillian's expression as she smiles at my entire quintet. "Now I can get to know all of you without those pesky curses. Oh—Baelfire, are you too warm in that jacket?" she adds with a frown.

I realize she's right. My always-toasty dragon shifter is dressed in a brown jacket despite the spring-like weather finally thawing the outside world. Frowning, I start to ask why he put the jacket on, but then it hits me.

It hides his collar.

The one I put on him. The one shifters find so fucking humiliating.

Gods, am I the worst keeper ever? I should have noticed sooner.

Glancing at the refugees still watching us from their tents, I step closer to him. "Lean down. I'll take it off."

"Nah."

"Baelfire, I should have taken it off sooner. Just—"

Raincloud, I like *wearing a collar you put on me,* he says just to me through our bond, his golden gaze burning me. *I like the leash, too. They make me feel more like I'm yours, as long as no one else sees them. Besides, with the newlybound urges so fucking bad this time around, I think it's helping to calm me down since I can't have you naked in bed for a little bit longer.*

His newlybound urges are worse, too?

I wonder if the others have been experiencing the same thing. Before I can ask, Crypt disappears into Limbo without another word.

39

CRYPT

SYNTYCHE'S SCYTHE, *everything* hurts.

I loathe that my muse has been left concerned in the distorted mortal realm as I retreat here for the worst of it. But as little as I care for the opinions of others, collapsing in pain in full view of the refugees gathered here would have caused a commotion that Maven shouldn't have to deal with.

Not to mention, those pretty tears she held back the last time she saw me like this hurt almost as much as my curse. I'll do anything to spare her more tears than I know she'll one day shed for me.

Curling in on myself, I grimace as the pain repeatedly wracks through me. My limbs burn. My lungs can't pull in oxygen as a sensation like millions of needles burrows inside my veins. When I can finally breathe again, it quickly turns into coughing —and up comes more blood.

It's less severe than it was before my heart was rebound to Maven's, but in the end, there is no help for it.

It won't be long now before this curse of mine takes me away from her again. My guess is a week or two, or maybe days. Whatever Sachar has in mind for my afterlife sentence in the

Beyond, it will be nothing in comparison to being ripped away from my obsession again.

Unless…

My darling reaps souls now. Perhaps she would not reap mine. Perhaps she would instead allow me to haunt her until the end.

Come back. Stop hiding from me when you're in pain, Maven's frustrated voice pleads through the bond.

If only she would ask me for anything else. I'd steal each and every one of the fucking stars from the night sky for her, if it would make up for my past actions catching up to us.

I'll be fine, darling, I insist, sitting up in Limbo to spit more blood out of my mouth.

Liar.

I'm searching for a way to put her mind at ease when Crane frowns in the mortal world, his distorted image glancing down at the very spot where I sit. He's almost looking me in the eye.

Hang on. Can he see me? Is this some result of his previously being inside my head?

"I almost feel as if Crypt is…" he trails off.

"Oh, thank fuck—I thought *I* was crazy this time," Frost huffs, gesturing at the exact place I sit. "You feel like he's there, right?"

Decimus nods, his hand sweeping around the vicinity where my head is. "Yeah, here-ish. Sitting."

Gods above.

Does this mean the rest of them can sense me in Limbo now? Perhaps this is a result of our stronger bonding this time around. What a fucking nightmare—not to mention, it spoils all the fun of dropping out of Limbo to scare those three bastards.

As I stand and fight to regain the last of my breath so I can step back into the mortal world and reassure Maven, Lillian looks at the spot Decimus gestured to.

"Is he okay?"

"It's his curse," Decimus explains quietly.

"I thought those were broken," she frowns, brushing a wind-blown strand of curly pale hair back behind her ear.

"Yeah, but Crypt's curse is different because it's actually more like a—"

Fucking gods, is that lizard seriously about to just spill everything he knows about my curse *again?* Stepping out of Limbo, I elbow the blabbermouth hard in the gut so he shuts up and remembers that even if his curse is gone, mine deserves some privacy.

"Asshole," he grumbles, rubbing his stomach.

"Loudmouth." I glance at Maven, immediately transfixed by her dark gaze as something in my chest melts. "See? I'm fine enough, love."

Her expression is utterly blank as she observes me, and then she turns to stride toward the cultists' section of the encampment.

"We'll catch up with you later," she calls over her shoulder to Lillian, who will not be venturing with us into the cultist area.

Maven knows you're not fine, Crane warns telepathically, pinning me in his ruby stare. *You know how much she's already struggling with it. Lying to her for false comfort won't help.*

Piss off, I shoot back, irritated as I fall into step behind the muse who owns every facet of my being.

If all I can give her is false comfort right now, then I'll give it all the same.

As soon as our quintet draws nearer to the black-tent section of the encampment, there's a clear difference in how we're received. Where the Nether humans and Reformists cheered, clapped, and looked on in excited, curious fascination, these black-clad cultists stop what they're doing and bow deeply to my keeper. They appear to all be legacies, and though many are older, a few of them can't be older than Decimus.

It's almost noon, Frost points out telepathically. *Where is their psychotic leader so we can stop his sacrifice?*

We turn into a new area of their encampment and pause,

taking in the view. Another giant wooden stake has been constructed here. Surrounding it are more cultists who are assembling a feast of some kind—one heavily dependent on smoked meat skewers, by the looks of things. Animal carcasses are strung up to bleed out, and several other cultists are painting canvases with scenes of death and graveyards using the animal blood.

As soon as these cultists see Maven, they also bow. When another of them emerges from a big tent behind the massive wooden stake, there's no mistaking that he must be Orlando Coates. His eyes light up with unnatural obsession as soon as he sees my muse.

The middle-aged caster with slightly graying hair immediately drops to his knees, pressing animal-blood-covered hands over his heart as he gawks at her. "Daughter of Syntyche! You are so beautiful, I could die."

"Please do," she mutters without missing a beat, making me grin. Her attention moves to the wooden stake. "Who are you sacrificing?"

"Only a creature that will please your dark appetite," he promises.

He snaps his fingers at some of his nearby followers, who rush quickly into one of the tents. A moment later, they pull out a changeling. At first, it's in its true changeling form, horns and all. It hisses and struggles against its many bindings while they drag it toward the stake.

But as it draws closer, the skin of the Nether creature rapidly morphs and ripples, changing until the changeling now resembles a blue-haired young woman who leers at my keeper.

I don't miss that both Maven and Crane glance from the creature to a spot where no one stands and back again, almost as if they are drawing comparisons to something I cannot see. A ghost, perhaps.

My suspicion is confirmed when Crane telepathically muses,

This changeling must have seen her before she died. In the Nether, perhaps.

So she was a tribute sent to Amadeus by the Frosts after all, Maven agrees.

"Veriba pateris thui da'tib!" the blue-haired falsity snarls even as it's dragged toward the stake.

I understand none of it, but Crane speaks through the bond. *That is Nether tongue. It's saying it has a message from her 'father.'*

"Enough, enough. Take it to the stake so that its life may be a suitable offering," Coates orders, snapping his fingers more quickly when the changeling continues to shriek.

I know how much my muse dislikes changelings, but she's studying this one curiously. "No. Let it speak first."

The cultists glance at their leader, who looks unsure but orders them to halt. The changeling again fixes Maven with a cold, inhuman glare that makes me fantasize about ripping each of its horns off and stuffing them down its gullet.

"Imperrat teb pateris, ut retheas ad illum, recipiet semel dedit. Cavo, mon'neth gemas, telum," the creature hisses.

Translation, Frost demands through the bond.

Crane doesn't hesitate as he glares at the changeling. *It said, 'Your father orders you to return to him, else he will take that which he once gifted you. Heed this warning or weep, scourge.'*

This creature is threatening my muse?

"Before we kill it, let's harvest its vocal cords as a memento of the stupidest shit we've ever heard," I suggest to my quintet, already stepping toward the changeling.

The others agree immediately as Coates looks hopefully at Maven. "Indeed! Would you prefer the honor of reaping its life yourself?"

"No. We're not killing it," Maven adds, making me sigh wistfully. She looks at the cultists again. "Give the changeling to my matches."

Crane gives her a curious look, speaking through the bond. *What do you have in mind,* ima sangfluir?

It's not a full plan yet, but this changeling might be useful. Everett, is there somewhere in the castle where we can hold it until later?

He nods. *The dungeons.*

Those are cushy training rooms now, Decimus points out.

No, I turned them into dungeons again while you were a feral beast, Frost explains. *Dungeons are way more useful than training rooms when the world is being conquered.*

The cultists shove the tied-up changeling toward us, and Decimus holds on to the struggling creature easily as Maven turns back to Orlando Coates. I dislike the way his beady eyes are so fixated on my keeper. I hope he says something we don't like so I can tear those eyeballs out to keep him from looking at my muse ever again.

"Then, oh great demigoddess, who shall we sacrifice to earn your approval?" Coates asks, clasping his hands together like a plea as he remains on his knees.

"No one. Stand up." Maven looks at all the other cultists. "Everyone, get up."

They obey at once, and Coates takes a few steps closer as his gaze remains affixed to my keeper's beautiful face. I'm clearly not the only one his avid attention is rubbing the wrong way, because both Frost and Decimus step in front of Maven, brushing elbows so she's hidden behind them.

"You mustn't worry!" the cult leader says quickly. "I would never harm the demigoddess. She is a great blessing upon our world. She will guide us into a new and peaceful future!"

The other cultists cheer, many of them bowing again to revere Maven.

Although she keeps a poker face, I know my keeper is uncomfortable with all this blatant worship. She didn't enjoy getting recognized and stared at while attending Everbound, either. Her aversion to being the center of attention is understandable, considering her adorably antisocial tendencies.

"Take the stake down," Crane tells Coates, glaring at the wooden structure.

"Not unless the daughter of Syntyche demands it," Coates says, bowing to Maven. "For we are here to honor her as all past demigods and demigoddesses have been honored. My dear demigoddess, I am a historian at heart. Long have I studied the histories and instances of precious and rare divinities upon the earth, such as yourself. For this purpose, we have come for your blessing and to build a suitable temple for your comfort, for I know you derive holy magic from the formal worship of mortals."

Crane's attention slips to Maven. *Is that true?*

Yes, unfortunately, she replies through the bond, still studying Coates. *Though with everyone so damned invested in my return, I don't need a fucking temple or formal anything.*

"I'll give my blessing if you leave," she says out loud to the cultists.

The other cultists whisper in excitement. Orlando Coates straightens, clasping his blood-stained hands together once again as he supplicates her.

"We would indeed seek your blessing, but please do not send us away before we finish constructing your temple! It shall be complete by midnight. We wish to offer it to you during a grand celebration tomorrow evening. Anyone who wishes to honor you is welcome. We are already preparing a feast," he adds, gesturing at the meat skewers slowly roasting over fire pits off to one side of the encampment.

"No thanks," Maven makes a face.

"But—" Coates looks out of his depth before looking at the stake. "It must be because we have not honored you to Syntyche's liking. I know she would prefer us to sacrifice someone in your honor. Phoebe!"

One of the cultists, a young woman, rushes forward to bow. "Yes, my leader?"

"Tie yourself to the stake."

"Don't tie yourself to the stake, Phoebe," Maven counters, staring down the cult leader as ravens croak ominously nearby.

Meanwhile, Phoebe looks at several other cultists in wide-eyed excitement, whispering, "She knows my name!"

Surely your mother— Crane pauses that telepathic thought to shudder slightly—*doesn't truly want someone sacrificed in your honor. Right?*

Maven's answer is matter-of-fact. *From what I remember of her so far, she wouldn't* not *want it.*

Frost is thoughtful as he considers the cultists we're surrounded by. *Several of the Reformist leaders suggested something for morale. A formal introduction of you to the troops, or a war gala of some kind. Something to take the edge off before whatever comes next.*

"So what?" Decimus asks, forgetting to use the bond.

So maybe their temple celebration shit could be useful, Maven surmises, tipping her head. *Kenzie did mention how hopeless things have been. And we* are *about to prepare to end Amadeus, once I've finished coming up with a decent plan to attack someone with future sight. I guess it's just as logical to celebrate the start of a battle as it is to celebrate the end of one.*

Decimus grins. *So you're saying we get to have a wild party before we launch an attack against the asshole who ripped your heart out? As long as those stupid fucking reporters aren't invited, I'm all in, Boo.*

Not to mention, it would serve as a celebration for our new bond, Crane adds.

The rest of us nod in agreement.

Maven lifts her chin as she addresses Orlando Coates. "I accept. We'll attend the celebration, as long as you don't sacrifice anyone or pull any weird cult shit on me."

Coates is chuffed to bits at this news. The cult members cheer again, bowing and chattering to each other in fresh excitement. The changeling struggles against its bonds again, hissing in Decimus's secure grip.

"Everyone! The demigoddess will now give us her blessing," the cult leader announces.

Everyone falls silent, looking at Maven with wide eyes. She rubs one of her hands as if wishing she could adjust her gloves, and I quickly make a mental note to track some down for her once we return to the castle. She doesn't need them around us anymore, but it's an extra measure of protection for my muse against unwanted touch whenever we're around others.

"Right. I hereby bless you," Maven deadpans, waving one hand in a big arc.

It's apparent to everyone here that her gesture did nothing. Decimus barely holds back a snort of laughter. I'm no better, fighting my amusement as Frost shakes his head. Crane keeps a straight face, but gives our keeper a side eye.

"Oh, no, my dear demigoddess," Coates says, moving just in front of her and getting on his knees again. "A proper blessing may only be completed by you laying your hand upon our heads."

Just like that, all my amusement is gone.

"She's not fucking touching you," I say darkly, giving this caster his only warning.

"It's fine," Maven mutters, again going to adjust gloves that aren't there before she clears her throat.

Decimus growls quietly, and I grit my teeth as she lays her hand on Coates' head. Again, she makes her face unreadable—and again, I know my muse is hiding her discomfort. I can't fucking stand her being anything but sated, content, and safely away from the unfamiliar touch of anyone outside our quintet.

Orlando Coates' eyes widen and quickly fill with tears the instant Maven touches his head. She jerks her hand away, obviously creeped out by his show of emotion, but the cult leader bows to her again.

"Such peace. Thank you, Daughter of Syntyche. Thank you!" he sobs.

I suppose it comes as no surprise that a cult leader is full of shit, Crane huffs telepathically.

I tip my head, recalling what she did to me before she broke me out of Syntyche's punishment. *He's telling the truth. Our girl can spread peace through her mere touch now. One of her new abilities,*

I believe—and it feels almost more incredible than every other touch she gives.

I did notice something like that, Frost frowns.

Maven looks at her own bare hand, studying it curiously. *My mother said something about me bringing pain and peace. If I can create peace just by a touch, it must be the same with pain—maybe that's how I got Baelfire to shift out of dragon form so easily. Kenzie, too.*

That's exactly what happened, Decimus agrees. *My dragon's a scared little bitch when it comes to pain.*

Curious as a cat, Crane moves between Maven and Coates and tips his head down. "*Tha mi a'faire pacem.*"

I don't speak a word of fae, but he's clearly asking to experience Maven's touch next. She says something back to him in fae. When she touches his cheek affectionately, tension flees Crane's entire body. Emotion floods his face, and he exhales sharply before pulling her close, burying his face in her neck so no one will see him in such a vulnerable state.

I don't bother teasing him about it, and neither do the others. The lot of us have rarely, if ever, experienced peace like the kind my stunning muse now wields with a mere brush of her hand.

The cultists are buzzing with excitement as they begin lining up, prepared to see what has their leader still openly weeping. I'm not keen on the idea of Maven touching any of them, but I also know her well enough to understand that if I protest, she'll hand me my ass along with a reminder that she's in full control of her autonomy.

Crane finally straightens, not meeting anyone's eye as he rejoins the rest of our quintet. Before more of the blessings begin, Maven glances at Frost.

"If we're going to have a celebration of sorts tomorrow, we should invite the other Reformist leaders. You mentioned something about them being here at Everbound, right?"

"Most of them are here, actually," he says, rubbing his neck. "They started to rally to this safe haven while you were recovering from getting your heart back. The Decimuses are the last to join us. Brigid said they'd be here tomorrow morning for a war room meeting."

"Really?" Decimus perks up.

Maven smiles. "Good. Then get that changeling somewhere it won't escape. I already have an idea of how it will come in handy, but I may be here a while."

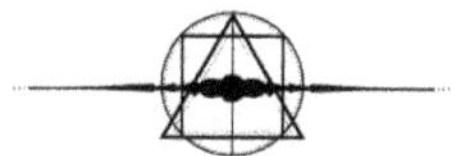

It took until nearly nightfall for Maven to briefly touch the heads of each of those obsessive, reverent cult members. She missed dinner to get it over with, which made Decimus incredibly sulky. By the time it was all done, I was nearly suffocating with the overwhelming newlybound urge to have my muse in bed again, safe and sound and stuffed with cock until she wept with pleasure.

Which is precisely what happened.

Now, most of my quintet snoozes peacefully on the quintet-sized bed in our apartment—except for Crane, who's meddling with some potion in the kitchen.

Maven sleeps deeply and peacefully beside me, as irresistible as ever as her restful body draws me like the most captivated moth to the most beautifully twisted flame. The memory of her whispered admission of love is enough to make my heart bang about my chest in giddy chaos.

In life or death or in between, you're all mine.

She has no idea what words that pretty do to an already-rampant obsession like mine. I would blissfully fall under her spell for the rest of time, were it an option for us. Dreaming of and with her for eternity is a luxury I would do anything to experience.

Technically, I could sleep now, if I wanted to. When Maven made herself my muse, it granted me the ability to rest whenever she does. I can now open my psyche to hers and bask in her subconscious as she experiences my own. They say for incubi, it's an unparalleled pleasure.

But I was trapped in a nightmarish, sleep-like hell for three months. Not to mention, no matter what kind of permanent future I crave at her side, I only have so many moments remaining in this plane of existence.

Therefore, I'll be staying in the mortal realm to hold Maven as much as I can get away with, until the end finds me.

Gently running my hand over Maven's naked body, I relish the soft, smooth feel of her bare back as her head rests on the pillow beside mine. My beautiful dreamer needed no help from me to fall asleep tonight. Although blessing all those people didn't seem to affect her, she must still be recovering from the spell that sealed her heart back inside her lovely chest.

My quiet adoration of the woman I love is interrupted when I sense a nightmare unfurling quickly nearby. Even though I'm in the mortal realm, I can sense the acrid heaviness of it. The cold, heart-rending fury.

I've sensed this same dream before. Frost used to get it almost every night, after the battle. At the time, I was too numbed and empty to do a thing about it if I ever came across it —instead, I carried on with my murderous plight.

But knowing he's reliving the moment he lost her, all over again…

With a quiet sigh, I kiss Maven's forehead and fall back into Limbo, allowing her to go on resting comfortably on the bed. Turning, I grasp the tendrils of the raging nightmare beside us and delve into Frost's nightmare.

He's holding her as the world plunges into ice and snow. Nearby, Crane is going mad. I'm somewhere in this recollection, and royal blue flames are quickly eating up the battlefield in the distance as Decimus goes feral.

I know this is just a dream of a memory, but I still can't bring myself to look at Maven's motionless body again. I recall that moment all too clearly—returning with the head of the one who hurt Frost, only to find my dark darling cold and lifeless in his arms.

This horrific memory haunted me, too, inside of Syntyche's punishment.

Frost's agony is making this dream tremble as he tries to wake himself. His subconscious is doused in the grief and helpless despair I saw in him every day after she was gone. Deciding to be done with it, I ignore the pain in my limbs and the clenching in my lungs as I twist his dream, reframing and reweaving it.

Finally, Frost is left blinking as he finds us back in the small cabin where he first bonded with our keeper, back when our quintet was on the run.

"Feels like an eternity since we were really here," I note, flicking one of the branches of the small tree we'd brought inside for Maven's first Starfall Eve.

I can tell he's caught up to his new surroundings when he sighs hoarsely, rubbing his scarred face. "Fuck. Thanks."

I could leave, but then again…I owe him something.

Getting around to it is more difficult than I thought, so I end up sniffing the air and frowning. "You must have a strong memory because your dreams are oddly crisp. Fresh as a mint."

Frost shoots me a look. "I didn't ask. Now, are you going to say whatever shit you're sticking around in my head to say, or what?"

He's right. Better to get this over with.

I look him in the eye. "If you hadn't sent me on errant missions to fill my time, I would have made it to the Beyond far sooner to look for her there. So, th…" I trail off and sigh, trying again. "You have my th…"

Frost rolls his eyes. "Don't hurt yourself."

"Let's just call it even," I finally decide.

"Even?"

"You once broke Maven's heart in a woefully misguided

attempt to protect her. However, you're also the reason I get a bit more time with her. So we'll call things even, and I'll retire the idea of slowly driving you mad in your dreams for the next few decades."

He stares at me. "You were planning on driving me insane?"

"Of course. You hurt her," I shrug.

Next thing I know, I've been kicked out of Frost's subconscious as he finally rouses himself back into the mortal realm, looking around frantically. When he sees Maven now cuddled up against Decimus, he exhales with relief.

"Fucking incubus," he mutters, glaring at the exact spot where I'm sitting on the bed in Limbo.

How annoying that the others can tell precisely where I am now.

Crane slips into the room, his attention also going to where I sit in Limbo. "I have something for your curse that may help temporarily."

Curious, I appear back in the mortal realm. Immediately, pain rips through my body. I choke, swallowing blood back down as my markings light up, searing my skin. When it finally stops, I can feel the familiar, strange coldness on my right arm as I've felt other places. One quick glance confirms that another one of my markings has vanished entirely.

Ignoring the lingering pain, I look at Crane. "Only *reverium* soothes it."

Crane nods, stepping forward to hold out a syringe full of strange gray liquid. "I know. I took what you had left in your jacket. Just trust me and inject this intravenously."

"A Crane, helping me freely?" I scoff. "When has that ever happened before?"

His expression turns almost sad before he shakes his head. "Never, but I can't excuse my family. Just take the damn injection, Crypt. It will help."

"Yes or no. Is this about appeasing your misplaced guilt after whatever you saw in my past?"

The fae who cannot fib easily deflects. "This will give Maven peace of mind. If you won't take it as my apology for blaming you for my family's demise all my life, then take it for the woman we're eternally bound to, you prick."

I glance at Maven, who looks as fucking amazing as ever as she rests peacefully.

She hates seeing me in pain.

With a sigh, I take the syringe from Crane and jam the damn thing into my arm.

40

BAELFIRE

WHAT'S MORE embarrassing than turning into a stupid, mindless beast for six months and roasting countless people for no good fucking reason?

The fact that my family witnessed all of it.

Everett gave me the rundown on how my dragon spent the last six months. Eating, burning shit, sleeping in caves, burning shit, killing people and—big surprise, setting fire to more shit. I was out of hand. Feral. I must have driven my entire family up the wall, since they took it upon themselves to try and protect me from hunters and anyone else trying to exterminate the threat I became.

Having my curse broken is fantastic. It means I'm in perfect harmony with my inner dragon again, but a part of me still wants to wring his scaly neck for everything he did over the last six months.

I can already picture how my mom will look at me when they arrive. She'll be happy to see me back in my own head, but there's no fucking way my stalwart commander mother won't also get overwhelmed by her shifter emotions and cry a bit. My dads or brothers might crack a joke about something to try to make me feel like things are back to normal, but with how bad I was for the last six months…

There's not really a normal for me to go back to.

As relieved as I am that they've all been okay during the Upheaval, I can't lie. I'm dreading seeing them again—especially because I'm not the same nice, happy Baelfire they're used to.

I can be nice, sure. I can still be charming, if necessary.

But mostly, I'm over being a people person. Pretty sure none of my many "friends" from the good old days did anything but gawk at me with the rest of the world when I went feral and wound up in international headlines. My family would never say it to me, but I did a number on our family name—and still, only they and my quintet members tried to help me when I was barely surviving in my own head.

So fuck being nice to everyone just for the sake of it. I'm much more interested in burning anyone who gets close to Maven without her permission.

I guess being trapped inside a monster for six fucking months changes a guy.

This morning is the war meeting Maven called for before the temple celebration shit tonight—but my family will get here before the meeting, which feels really fucking soon.

I'm pacing inside my old room in the quintet apartment when Maven knocks gently on the door, like she's not sure if she's allowed in. Which is fucking insane. It's like she hasn't fully realized that I'd gladly spend the rest of my life with her wrapped around me like a koala with absolutely no space between us ever again, if I could.

I pull her into the room, wrap her in my arms, and kiss her forehead. "Hey there, Mayflower. I like this," I add, flicking her ponytail. "And I *love* this," I add with a grin, squeezing her perfect ass.

"You mean all those times I've caught you staring at my ass like you wanted to take a bite out of it wasn't because you were completely indifferent? I'm shocked." She stands on her tiptoes to kiss my chin. Then she examines my eyes with a knowing look. "You're nervous about seeing your family."

"I'm just in my head about it. I know they still love me and shit, but…" I grimace. "I can only remember blips over the last six months, and in most of those memories, I was roasting people. Not a great look for the Decimus family."

"They care more about you than the family image."

I know that. Still…

"This is going to be rough," I sigh, burying my nose in the side of her neck to inhale her scent. How it's so fucking soothing and yet so arousing at once is beyond me.

But if I thought that was arousing, it's nothing compared to the moment Maven tugs playfully on my leash.

Holy shit. Does she have any idea how hot that is? Is she trying to drive me insane?

When I pull away, the breath whooshes out of my lungs when I see the mischievous sparkle in her eyes.

Oh, fuck. She is absolutely aware of what she's doing to me.

But when her fingers trace the edge of my collar and she fidgets with the latch, my heart sinks so fast I can barely keep up. I swallow hard and try to play it cool—which is *not* my strong suit. I'm pretty sure no shifter in the world can play things cool, let alone godsdamned dragon shifters. We're too fucking hot-blooded and emotional.

"Did you just come in here to take this off of me?" I check, trying not to sound brutally disappointed.

"Yes," she murmurs, trailing her fingers lightly down my bare chest before she smirks wickedly up at me. "But not until I'm done with you. You once offered to be my free use fuck toy. If that still stands—"

"It does," I blurt, heat crawling over my skin as my breathing picks up. "Always. Literally anytime. You can use me any way you want or just—"

Maven pulls on my leash again, much rougher this time, so

I'm forced to lean down to her eye level. My heart pounds painfully as the delicious rush of her taking charge sets in.

"You interrupted me," she warns, still playful.

"Sorry," I breathe, but I'm really not sorry because *fuck*, I love her pulling my leash.

"Show me how sorry. Get on your knees, pet."

Pet.

Oh, hell fucking *yes*. I love it when she calls me that.

Obediently, I get to my knees, which puts me just barely below her eye level because I'm a big motherfucker and she's the perfect size for me in every single way. I'm already getting hard in my shorts, but I don't dare take them off without her permission. The tenting only gets worse when Maven reaches out to gently trace the mating mark she left on my neck months ago.

"I love that you marked me," I whisper.

"I had to," she murmurs, leaning to kiss just beside my mouth to drive me nuts. "Since I can't have you collared like this all the time, I had to have a way of showing off that you're mine."

"All yours," I agree, trying to kiss her, but she pulls away just enough to taunt me. "Doesn't matter what I'm wearing or how you mark me—if anyone else touches me, they're dead. Only my queen can touch me. My goddess. My mate. Fuck, *please* let me kiss you."

That *please* is what she was waiting for, and I'm rewarded when her sweet, warm lips press against mine. The kiss quickly deepens until her tongue is trailing against mine. When I get greedy, trying to slip my tongue further into her mouth, she bites it. Not enough to really hurt, but enough to make me moan.

By the time we're both panting, Maven pulls away to look me over like she's deciding the best way to devour me. Whatever she wants, I'm all in. I'm so fucking excited that she's taking control and teasing me with this dynamic that I'll do anything she wants. If she tells me to get on my hands and knees while she sits on my back for hours, just pretending I'm her throne—

I mean, it's not as mouthwatering as her sitting on my face, but fuck me, I'll do it.

"Lie on the bed," she whispers.

I immediately obey as my heart crashes in my chest, my cock straining against my shorts as I try to calm my breathing. It's no use, though. I'm way too fucking excited to calm anything down right now.

Good thing Maven likes how worked up I get. She crawls onto the bed between my legs and smirks down at me, a delicious glimmer in her dark eyes.

"Gods, look at you. My mate is so fucking sexy."

That praise is already turning my brain to happy mush, but when she trails her hand teasingly over my erection, I whimper.

Fucking *whimper*.

I don't think I've ever done that in bed, but I'm losing my mind here. I'm desperate for anything I can get from my mate. I'm dying to covet her.

"I'd look even better naked," I try.

"When I'm ready," she muses, still looking me over.

She's perfectly in control in a way that just makes me even more of a mess for her. Her hand finds the end of my leash again, and my heart jolts as I expect her to tug it, but she leaves it right where it is, like she was just making a note of where to find it for the next time she needs it.

Maven's beautiful gaze finds mine again. "Three rules, this time. You don't touch me—I touch you."

Not touching her is always torture, but I nod.

"You don't come until I say you can."

That almost makes me whimper again, but I nod again as eager heat curls slowly along my spine.

"And the others might overhear when they get back from their supply run, so you can't make a single sound. Got it?"

"Yes," I whisper, swallowing hard as I decide to break the third rule already to get more of what I want. "Please touch me. Use me. Fuck, baby, I just need—"

She jerks my leash hard to one side—enough that it almost chokes me for a second, and for that second, I swear my eyes almost roll back.

Note to self: Ask her to choke me more. I might be onto something.

"I know what you need," Maven reminds me, letting up on my leash before she leans down to kiss my lower stomach. "Just hold still and stay quiet for me."

Gods, I love this new game.

Her explorative kissing is just pleasant at first, but another jolt of heated arousal pulses straight to my rock-hard cock when Maven's tongue drags along the ridges in my stomach. She keeps licking my abs and teasing, making her way lower and lower until *finally* my shorts are dragged off.

She hums at the sight of my straining, desperate cock. "So damn hard and ready for me. Already leaking, too. Good boy."

Just like before, when those words sink in—fuck, they do something to me I can't even put into words. My breathing turns ragged as my hips rock of their own damn will. I'm falling apart and she's barely even fucking touched me yet.

Please, I groan through the bond, just to her. *I need you. Gods, please touch me.*

"No using the bond," she whispers. "That's cheating."

And then my gorgeous, devious, fucking cruel mate laps at the head of my cock like my precum is her favorite treat. The hoarse sound that escapes me would be embarrassing, if it wasn't quickly followed by another and another as more of my inches sink into the hot, wet, fucking *perfect* suction of Maven's mouth.

She's struggling a little bit with my size, but that only drives me more insane. I grip the sheets on either side of me for dear life and try to keep my moans to a minimum. But when she gets most of me into her mouth and throat and swallows around my length, that mind-melting sensation makes me curse.

Maven immediately pulls off of my cock to arch a brow at me.

"Fuck. Sorry. Fuck, *please* don't stop," I beg, panting as my hips rock again.

"You agreed you wouldn't be too loud," she sighs, getting off the bed.

Alarm has me sitting up, panicked that she's seriously about to walk out and leave me with a raging boner from hell. "Wait. No. I'm sorry, I'll be better about—"

The words die in my throat as I watch her slip out of her pants and then gently step out of a simple pair of black panties next. She moves with such speed that it takes my breath away when she shoves me back into a lying position on the bed.

Her gaze is pure, dark, delicious desire. "Don't be sorry. Just open your mouth for me."

I open it without a second thought. Obeying her is satisfying as hell, so why would I resist?

When Maven gently stuffs her panties into my mouth, I get lightheaded. They smell clean, barely worn—but there's the barest scent of her on them, too. I can taste a hint of her fresh arousal perfuming my mouth now, and it makes me groan like a dying man.

I don't know how she knew I would be so into this, but *oh my gods.*

So. Fucking. Hot.

When my moan is still too loud for this game we're playing, Maven covers my panty-stuffed mouth with her hand and smirks down at me. "Shh. I'm still playing with my toy."

Her sultry, teasing tone and all these soft little touches and the scent of her arousal is going to fucking kill me. As she lowers back down to suck my cock deeper and deeper into her hot, wet mouth, I can barely think straight.

And holy *shit*, my mate gives one hell of a blowjob. Probably helps that she can read me like I'm a fucking book, and each time she can tell I'm getting closer to the edge, she pulls back and goes back to teasing me. For someone who hates being edged, she's painfully good at edging.

Over and over, she drives me almost to the finish line until every inch of my skin is flushed with heat. I'm left panting and moaning, despite the third rule. The need to come is so fucking bad that I desperately work her panties out of my mouth and gasp, "Please. Fuck. Please, can I come?"

She pops off my cock to murmur, "Not yet."

"Maven, *plea—*"

She squeezes my balls and goes back to sucking me off again.

Oh fuck oh fuck oh fuck oh fuck—

Not making another sound is impossible. I bite my fist, ignoring the taste of my blood.

I've never fought an orgasm this hard before, but I almost choke on the next wave of unbearable pleasure when she swallows around me again, massaging my cock in simultaneously the best and worst way possible. My balls ache, so full they hurt. I'm pretty damn sure I'm still leaking precum. Moisture trickles over my temples as I squeeze my eyes shut, so fucking desperate to be good for my mate.

She's edging me until I fucking *cry,* and I still can't stop begging for more. My mate hums around me, pleased with the mess she's turned me into.

But *oh my gods,* that humming. It makes it all worse until I can barely manage to choke out, "Please. Please. Godsdamn it, fuck—please can I—"

"Such a perfect, greedy mate. Come for me," Maven whispers, stroking my cock hard as she gently squeezes my balls again.

I explode.

The release takes me so hard and fast that I shout in both agony and relief, pleasure searing me as I come like I've never orgasmed a day in my life. The entire time, Maven strokes me the way she knows I like, until I'm left mindless and panting, staring up at the ceiling as my head spins.

"Fuck. Just…holy *fuck,*" I moan, words slurring.

Maven tugs lightly on my leash, just enough to get my attention as she adjusts, moving higher up on the bed. "Need another minute, or is it my turn?"

"Your turn," I say immediately, my mouth already watering as I realize what she has in mind.

Soon, her thighs are on either side of my head as her pussy presses against my mouth. The scent of her arousal envelops me as I lap at her entrance. She's so damn soaked—and I *love* the way she tastes, almost as much as I love my mate dominating me in bed.

When she tugs on my leash insistently this time, it's positioned beneath my chin so she's tipping my head back, forcing my mouth tighter against her pussy. I groan raggedly against her, adoring every second of this.

She makes a breathless, needy sound, sending another rush of arousal crashing through me. I lap and suck and nip, focusing on her clit when she starts to grind against my face.

"Baelfire," she gasps, her thighs clenching around my head.

Fuck it. I can't stand not touching her anymore.

My hands immediately go to spread her thighs as wide as possible so she'll put her full weight on me. I suck on her clit again, living for every one of Maven's small sounds of pleasure as she builds toward her release.

She finally cries out, her pussy convulsing slightly, and I groan as more of her divine arousal drips for me to lap up.

"Tastes so good," I moan against her. "My mate comes so fucking pretty. Godsdamn."

My mate is right. I *am* greedy, and I'm still craving more when she tries to move off my face. Gripping her ass, I keep her there for another moment to finish my dessert while she swears and moans, fingers tangling in my hair.

Finally, she grips one of my wrists in a quiet plea to let her go. With a contented sigh, I do, and Maven adjusts to lay beside me on the bed.

As I slowly come down from the potent high, Maven leans into my neck and teasingly bites my old mating mark. She licks it gently, almost like a shifter might do to soothe their mate as her arm goes around me.

Fuck, I'm so in love with her.

But Maven's touch isn't just calming me down after all that intensity—it's stronger than that. I don't think she's even aware, but she's emanating peace. Contentment. She's using her abilities to soothe me without even realizing it, and it's heavenly.

"I love it when you bite me," I murmur happily.

Maven pulls back to smile at me. I'm one thousand percent sure she has no idea her smiles sweep me off my feet every single time.

"I love teasing such a sexy mate."

Sexy mate.

I melt at the extra dose of praise, turning and pressing my face to her neck to deeply inhale her scent again. I'm so addicted. Once all this fighting and shit is over, I can't wait to hold her and love her for hours on end with no more interruptions.

As I'm still basking in the afterglow, Maven gently reaches up and unclasps the collar around my neck. It slips off easily for her to toss onto the nightstand.

I sigh wistfully. "It'll be nice having that off, but still…"

Maven laughs. "Come on, let's get dressed. They'll be here soon. I'll get you a better collar later, for whenever it's just us."

It's official. I'm the luckiest dragon in the entire fucking universe.

Thirty minutes later, I'm trying not to look nervous as my entire quintet waits in the western library for my family to walk in. When the doors finally open, I'm not surprised that my mother is the first one to storm through them, scanning the room with her remaining eye like a woman on a mission until she spots me.

At once, she's crashing into me with shifter speed, wrapping her arms around me, and—

Gods, why was I dreading this?

I hug my mom back tightly, letting out a shuddering breath and praying my voice doesn't crack as all kinds of emotions crash over me. "Hey, Mom."

"Baelfire Finbar Decimus," she sniffs, pulling back to glare at me. There's no real heat to it. In fact, her eye is teared up. "How dare—you can't just—Decimuses don't—"

It's the first time in my life I've ever seen my strong, decisive, militant mother struggling so much with her own emotions. My lion shifter birth father, Oscar, is the next to blur to my side, wrapping both of us in his big hug, which cuts her off.

"Thank all six gods. We were so worried about you, son," he breathes.

"Bael!" Declan calls with a giant grin as he strolls into the library.

Cace is right behind him, along with several members of their quintets and the rest of my parents. I'm suddenly swarmed with nearly two dozen grinning, overly emotional Decimuses, all hugging me and welcoming me back.

Even Quinn is here, beaming as she runs up to hug my leg. She's tiny for a seven-year-old, but her volume more than makes up for her height.

"Uncle Baelfire! You're not a big meanie dragon setting Grandma's house on fire anymore!"

I look at my mom. "Shit. I'm sorry. I didn't mean to—"

"Of course, you didn't. The house is mostly fine and none of us would give two shits if it wasn't, anyway. What's important is that you're still—" My mom cuts off with a sniff, trying and failing to compose herself. "You know that I just care about my baby. Even when he scares the hell out of me and makes me lose sleep for months and then doesn't find a way to reach out and reassure me after his curse is broken and he's finally back in his own head," she adds pointedly.

She's right. I should have thought about reassuring my family, but—damn, everything's just been happening so fast.

Besides, I can tell she's not actually upset about it. My mom's good at understanding circumstances.

"Sorry," I say anyway, before adding, "For everything."

Declan throws an arm around my shoulders. "Wasn't your fault, little bro."

My mother wipes her eye before clearing her throat, trying to compose herself. "Thank all six gods that you have such a strong quintet. I can't even tell you how often Everett's aid answered my prayers, or how many times Crypt took care of the hunters before we could get there in time."

Crypt was looking out for me while I was feral? I didn't know that. I glance over at my quintet standing nearby, where the incubus is listening to Quinn as she chatters happily at him.

You were checking in on me? I ask only Crypt through the bond.

No.

Kinda seems like you were.

He looks at me like I'm a giant wart. *Don't flatter yourself into thinking I was even capable of concern for your idiotic hide over the last six months. I was numb. Whenever I grew bored between targets, hunters were merely an entertainment for me to kill off.*

It's hard not to snort out loud. *Uh-huh. Sure. So it had nothing to do with protecting my scaly ass.*

Get over yourself, lizard.

"Maven," my mom says, interrupting our telepathic exchange as she disengages from the Decimus family huddle and approaches my gorgeous mate.

My mom is ten times more observant and intuitive than I ever hope to be, so I'm not surprised when she doesn't try to hug Maven. She must have picked up on how uncomfortable it made my mate the last time they met.

Still, I can tell my keeper is trying to hide her nervousness as the rest of my family's attention moves from me to the demigoddess in the room. I really have no fucking idea how they'll react to her half-divine status, but luckily the ice is broken when Cace gets an eyeful of Everett's face for the first time.

"Holy shit, would you look at that!"

Quinn sees it, too, and gasps. "Oh, no! The old geezer man hurt his face."

Silas coughs to try hiding his laughter.

Everett sighs as he speaks telepathically. *I forgot that big mouths run in your family.*

Crypt is the one who taught her that, I point out.

My mom shoots Cace and Quinn a look that shuts them up before she turns back to Everett, tapping the edge of her eyepatch. "Ignore them. I've told you before, and I'll tell you again—battle scars are a privilege. They're permanent trophies for proving ourselves and surviving shit we never thought we could survive."

"Plus, it's sexy," Maven adds without missing a beat.

I grin. That's my mate. I can't tell if her playfulness makes me want to kiss her or bite her hard enough to leave another mark showing the entire world how much she's mine.

Several of my family members burst into surprised laughter at her unabashed statement while Everett turns bright red. Quinn turns to ask one of Cace's quintet members why a scar is sexy, which just makes more of them laugh.

The nervous tension of how my family will handle Maven being a demigoddess is long gone. I breathe out in relief when I see my mother smiling at my mate with nothing short of pure pride and motherly affection.

"I didn't say it wasn't dope-looking," Cace chuckles, turning back to Everett. "I was just surprised, since your family's so big on image and since…well, you know. You're a Frost."

Everett glances at Maven, still red-faced as he speaks telepathically. *Not for long.*

That piques Crypt's interest. *Are we taking Maven's last name?*

I am. Get your own thing, Everett scowls.

Cace must think Everett is scowling at him, because he starts apologizing again and quickly makes it worse as he compares Everett's scar to a scrape from silver he once got on his ass.

"Careful or Snowflake will freeze you and add you to his collection," I warn Cace.

Declan slaps my shoulder good-naturedly as he lowers his voice. "Careful, or I'll have to remind you that you should've taken a long, thorough shower. Some of us are shifters, Bael."

Oh. Shit. He means he can scent what Maven and I were up to before this, and most likely so can my parents.

I'm pretty sure I'm blushing as hard as Everett now.

41

MAVEN

My quintet and the Decimus family walk together through the halls toward the castle's main dining hall, where we decided to hold the Reformist meeting since apparently it will be a pretty large group.

Unreaped ghosts trail through the halls with us, including the blue-haired young woman who waves at me again before she passes through one of Baelfire's unwitting fathers. Silas sees it, though, and mutters something about ghosts in fae.

Baelfire's brother, Cace, catches up to glance sideways at me. "So, you're like…an actual demigoddess? Half god, half human?"

"Yes."

"And *the* Syntyche is your mother?"

"I'll introduce you, if you want."

He recoils and falls back to walk with the rest of the Decimuses, which makes Silas laugh darkly from where he walks on my left side.

"Finally, a fitting reaction," the fae murmurs. "With all due respect, your mother is acutely terrifying."

"Thanks."

Meanwhile, Baelfire is laughing and chatting with his family as they stroll behind us. The last few months have affected him a lot, but I'm happy to hear my sexy dragon shifter sounding almost as cheerful as he used to be.

Just as we approach the double doors of the dining hall, Kenzie and her quintet turn into this hallway from another corridor. Kenzie spots me and squeals as she hurries to my side, gearing up for a hug. I brace myself, because she's one of the very few outside my quintet whom I would like to grow accustomed to affection from—

But Everett steps in front of me to act as a shield at the last moment.

"Mind her boundaries," he firmly reminds the lioness shifter.

As far as shifters go, Kenzie is fairly good at controlling her intense, swinging emotions most of the time—which is why I startle when she loses her temper and snarls loudly at him.

"I've been worried out of my fucking mind about my best friend, so get your bossy, frozen, scarred ass out of my way!" she hisses, baring her teeth.

Whoa.

Ghosts scatter nearby, speaking in hushed, unintelligible tones like they don't want to be too close to the angry shifter. I quickly check to make sure her pupils are round and I'm not dealing with another changeling Kenzie—but no, this is her.

"Hey." Baelfire slows his stride, stopping beside the rest of us to address Kenzie as the rest of the Decimus family goes into the dining hall ahead of us. "What'd Snowflake do to piss you off?"

The rest of my quintet is just as baffled as they face the Baird quintet. Vivienne takes one of Kenzie's hands, rubbing the back of it soothingly.

The typically bubbly lion shifter grimaces as she realizes we're all confused about her strong reaction. "Gods, I'm so fucking sorry, Everett—I shouldn't have gone off on you like that. That's embarrassing. Feel free to bury me in snow or something."

She's so contrite that my testy elemental brushes off the interaction as he glances down at me. "I'll be inside organizing the chaos for you."

I nod. *Thanks.*

Silas kisses my cheek as he goes in ahead of me, too, sidestepping several ghosts drifting through the vaulted hallway.

Baelfire and Crypt remain out here with me. Dirk strikes up a conversation with Baelfire, and Vivienne pretends to tune in. My Nightmare Prince slips easily into Limbo to give Kenzie and me the illusion of privacy, even though I can clearly sense him standing beside us.

Since Kenzie's quintet has also given us a tiny semblance of privacy, she gives me a sheepish smile. "Sorry again about that. And gods, I'm so fucking sorry I haven't been here more—I've just been going through something huge and unexpected. I know you were asleep for a couple of days, and I heard that there was a whole thing with those weird cultist people camping outside, but…fuck, May, I'm so sorry I've been MIA. I just got you back, and we've barely had time to talk. I'm like, the worst best friend ever—you're even rebonded to your guys and everything! I missed it," she huffs, getting teary-eyed out of nowhere.

Okay, I'm missing something. What the hell is up with her crying so much more than usual?

I note the way her quintet members keep obsessively glancing at her like they're making sure she's okay. It's normal for quintets to become highly possessive and protective of their keeper, but Kenzie isn't made of glass. There's no reason they'd be so worried about her, unless…

When I look at Kenzie again, it hits me hard.

Oh, shit.

"You're pregnant."

Kenzie's mouth drops open. "How did you—"

"You're experiencing stronger emotions," I point out as my heart pounds in that strange, unfamiliar way. According to my quintet, that means I'm either anxious or excited. "You said you were going through something big and unexpected, and your quintet is far more protective than normal. Also, your boobs are bigger."

"Hell yeah, they are," she laughs before beaming at me. "And yeah. I'm pregnant!"

"Holy shit—congratulations!" Baelfire grins at Dirk and the rest of Kenzie's quintet. They're all over the moon as Vivienne bounces with excitement, Dirk preens with pride, and Luka looks at Kenzie like she's the center of his existence.

What's delayed you, my blood blossom? Silas checks through the bond.

Kenzie is pregnant, I explain.

No wonder she almost bit my head off, Everett grumbles. *Gods-damned pregnant legacy hormones.*

I smile at the lioness shifter. "You'll be a badass mother," I inform her.

Kenzie bursts into tears and throws her arms around me, careful not to touch my skin.

"Fuck, I really hope so," she half-laughs, half-cries before launching into a slew of words so fast I barely catch them all. "I've always wanted a quintet and babies and the whole nine yards but now that I have a little crotch goblin baking in my oven, I'm so excited but it's also so fucking *terrifying*—like what if this baby takes after me? I don't remember a lot, but I know from stories and my old journals that I was such a rebellious little punk when I was a kid, and I put my parents through so much stress, and if this cute little goblin does the same things to us once it pops out of my oven—"

Oh, my gods. I'm running out of breath just listening to her.

When I awkwardly reach up to pat her head as a sign of comfort, Kenzie's flurry of frantic panic slows.

"*Whoa.* Okay, total meltdown averted. Whatever you just did, it helps. I'm going to make you hold my baby all the time when it's crying because you'll soothe it, and I have no idea how to soothe a baby. Or change a diaper. Or deal with other baby things. Oh my gods, I'm going to have to read so many parenting books, and I hate reading. Maybe I'll just skip the books, and then my crotch goblin will grow up all undisciplined and feral and—"

Felix gently pries Kenzie away from me, since he knows I'm pretty much the worst possible person to comfort anyone, ever, for any reason. The caster wraps his arm around Kenzie and kisses her cheek, smiling at her. I haven't seen him smile much, or maybe ever, but it's just a reminder of how much he's changed in the mortal realm.

"Our *crotch goblin,* as you put it, will be perfect. Especially if they take after you."

That only makes the lioness shifter cry harder. Her quintet gathers around as they try to comfort their pregnant keeper.

It's absolute hell to have you out of sight, Snowdrop, Everett says to only me through the bond. *Tell Kenzie to take a ticket and stand in line and then get your ass next to me so I can breathe again.*

So needy, I tease.

You have no fucking idea.

Deciding I'll talk to Kenzie later, I give the Baird quintet some space and move quietly away. Crypt quickly re-materializes beside me, grinning.

"Have I mentioned how entertaining it is to watch you around anyone in tears, darling?"

"Their faces are leaking. What the fuck am I supposed to do with that?" I point out, shuddering.

He laughs at me before extending something in his hands. They're gloves, I realize. A pair of my favorite gloves that I thought I lost while on the run. And even though the chances are low of anyone being stupid enough to lay a finger on me, wearing gloves just makes me feel secure.

It's a psychological comfort that I didn't realize I was missing so much until this instant.

I look at him, accepting the thoughtful gesture. *As if I wasn't already obsessed enough with you,* I tease only him through the bond.

His humor fades as he gives me the most intense look. *Forgive me now?*

No. I don't.

If anything, each time I remember that his time here is limited, it gets more painful.

I slip on my gloves as we finally move toward the double doors.

"I'm so fucking excited for them," Baelfire says, falling into step beside us. "That baby's going to be so damn spoiled—especially because it'll have the most badass aunt in the entire world."

"I don't think Kenzie has siblings."

"You, Boo," he grins. "I'm talking about you."

"Oh."

There's a thought.

I wasn't there when Kenzie was bonded with her quintet and her curse was broken, but if I manage to bring down Amadeus and right the world, there's no way in hell I'm missing this. Pretty much all I know about babies is how they're made, the fact that they're bizarrely fragile, and that they cry a lot.

But still. I'm a quick learner. Baelfire is right—as long as I don't drop the baby, maybe Kenzie will let me be part of her kid's life.

As we step through the double doors, I realize just how crowded this long, spacious room has gotten with the Reformists who have gathered. They're all chattering and talking loudly with each other. Everett stands at the end of the room beside Silas as they both talk quietly with Brigid Decimus and a couple of other Reformists.

There are also quite a few ghosts in the mix. I watch the blue-haired young woman ghost pretend to kiss one of the unwitting female legacies.

I'm surprised by how many people I recognize here.

Monica, the asscaster empath, is here with a couple of her quintet members. So is Professor Crowley, one of my former professors who apparently survived Everbound University's chaotic fall into ruin. On the other side of the room, Amelia Lykoudis chats with Harlow Carter and a few serious-looking ex-mercenaries whom I'm positive I've seen before.

There are even more Reformists I don't know. It's such a crowded, chaotic space, but at least that means not everyone is staring at me yet. As Baelfire, Crypt, and I pass by a small group of Reformists dressed in their combat gear, one of them spots us and hurries over. He looks around my age, with dark skin, faded hair, and an easy, bright white smile.

"Finally! Maven Oakley. Godsdamn, you are so much more stunning than people kept telling me you were. Much better in person than in all those pictures I keep seeing of you everywhere on the news. It's a pleasure to finally meet you, but I hope that's not the only pleasure we'll share together," he grins, reaching for my hand as if to shake it.

Crypt snatches his hand and twists it hard until something breaks, making the stranger yelp in pain. The Nightmare Prince keeps his voice misleadingly calm. "From one incubus to another, I will skin you alive and feed your rotting entrails to the wisps if you ever try to touch *my muse* again."

When Crypt releases the stranger, he's quick to shake off the pain in his healing hand and looks at me somewhat awkwardly. "Shit. Muse? Okay, *clearly*, your quintet is not nearly as platonic as a friend told me it was. Really sorry about that. I'm Collins."

"The orgy guy," I recall.

He sighs like he gets this all the time. "I mean. I'm now a highly decorated captain leading troops against the worst of the wraith attacks in South America, but…sure. Yeah. I also threw some orgies, back in the day. Good times, right, Bael?" he grins at my shifter like they're old pals.

Baelfire makes a face of disgust, wrapping his arm possessively around me. "Don't fucking remind me."

"By the heavens," a familiar voice mutters nearby. When I glance over, it's Ross—one of the Garnet Wizard's acolytes from the Sanctuary. The one with the third eye, which is still magically concealed as he gawks at me. He bows, but it seems more out of fear than respect. "I heard so much about your return, but... good gods on high, you really are back."

"Disappointed?" I smirk.

He practically trips over himself trying to assure me that he's thrilled to have me back, but he's interrupted when someone clears their throat loudly behind me.

Turning, I come face to face with both Amelia Lykoudis and Harlow Carter. The two high-ranking legacies are eyeing me almost as intensely as they did on my first day at Everbound—only now, they're not assessing how much of a threat I am. Instead, they're studying me the way everyone else is starting to: like I'm some otherworldly being they've never seen before.

"Carter. Lykoudis," Baelfire greets flatly with narrowed eyes, clearly not a fan of them.

Harlow's previously colorful hair is now shorn completely, which is a damn good look on her. The tough legacy folds her arms, shaking her head at me with a grin. "Wow. You really put the bitch in obituary, don't you?"

Ross chokes nearby like he thinks she just signed her death warrant. Baelfire snarls.

"I think that's supposed to be a compliment," I clarify quickly, holding up a hand to keep Crypt from stepping forward and ripping out her spine or whatever beautiful punishment he had in mind.

"It is," Harlow agrees quickly, glancing at the Nightmare Prince with an appropriate amount of fear.

Amelia Lykoudis sniffs as she studies me. "You know, I lead the northeastern pack of wolf shifters now. After my dad was murdered, they put me in charge, even though I'm not a shifter. I'm the first non-shifter to be in their pack, let alone lead it. It's a huge honor."

"That's nice." I don't know what else to say, because none of this is relevant to me.

"Funny thing about my father's death, though. Turns out, someone ripped his heart straight out of his chest. Exactly the same way Iker Del Mar's was ripped out and wound up all over the news. Got something to say to me?"

"Nothing you haven't already figured out on your own."

Amelia huffs. "I knew it. Listen, I don't believe you're a demigoddess. The ravens and coming back to life and weird shit you do—there has to be another dark, disturbing reason for all of it. A lot of Reformists here, including Harlow, say you started the Upheaval with good intentions—but guess what? A lot of people in this room and all over the world hate you for what you've done, and they always will."

Let me rip her jealous, weak little psyche to pieces, love, Crypt pleads. *It will only take a moment.*

His words trigger Silas to speak through the bond next. *Is someone bothering Maven?*

My fae and Everett start scanning the room from where they stand, glowering when they see the people gathered around Baelfire, Crypt, and me.

I ignore my pissed-off matches and the way Ross and Harlow are glaring at Amelia as I regard her. "Good. I'm not here to make friends. My inner circle is overcrowded enough as it is."

The next person to join this annoyingly close group gathering around me is Asher Douglas, who shoves Ross aside and starts shooing people away. "Hey. Commander Decimus is about to officially start the meeting. Get your asses into chairs and shut your faces."

A couple of the people he's shooing away don't move at all as they continue to stare at him.

"You missed some," I point out, gesturing toward them.

He looks where I'm pointing and then back at me like I just grew a second head. "What are you talking about? There's no one there."

Oh. "Never mind. Those are just the fresh ghosts."

The expression of deeply disturbed incredulity that crosses

the burly ginger's face is a fantastic addition to my day as I walk away with my quintet members.

Old dining room tables and chairs have been moved to line the perimeter of the room, facing inward so everyone can see each other. As Reformists file to take their seats, Baelfire takes my hand and guides me through the chaos while Crypt glowers at anyone who gets close so they'll give us space.

Soon, I sit on the same end of the room as Brigid Decimus and several other higher-ranked leaders. Everett sits on my left and takes my hand. Baelfire is on his other side, and Silas takes the chair to my right.

Crypt ignores his empty chair altogether and leans against a nearby wall to light a *reverium* cigarette.

No smoking inside, Everett says through the bond.

Crypt flips him off and exhales smoke.

Silas's telepathic voice is distracted as he observes the room with careful calculation. *Let him. The injection didn't work as well as I wanted.*

I take it the injection is whatever he was working on for Crypt. The idea that it barely helped my incubus makes my heart throb unpleasantly in my chest, but I try to focus as Brigid Decimus finally stands and addresses the room.

For such a petite legacy, her presence is powerful. She has no problem commanding everyone's attention.

"Reformists. We are entering the next, and hopefully the *final,* stage of defending the mortal realm from the Entity's advances. Whether or not you fully appreciate everything my daughter-in-law has done for the Nether humans and the rest of the world, no one here can possibly argue with her abilities. Her very presence here was all it took for so many people to rally to the front lines. Now that she's here, the rumors about *why* she has returned can end."

She glances at me, offering the tiniest bit of a smile for encouragement. "Maven. The floor is yours."

Dozens of pairs of eyes shift to me. I nod and stand, but pause.

Oh, gods.

What the fuck is happening in my chest? My heart is going berserk.

My heart might be broken, I inform my quintet.

You're just nervous, Baelfire says, smiling reassuringly at me. *It's normal because public speaking is a bag of ass. But you've got this, Raincloud.*

I'm starting to really regret getting my heart put back since it won't fucking calm down as I stand to look over the room. Everyone is expectant, fascinated, reverent, or even frightened as they watch me. A few look disgusted, like Amelia Lykoudis. Several ghosts watch on, including the blue-haired ghost who is shaking her invisible ass at one of the good-looking ex bounty hunters in here.

My psychotic pulse slows ever so slightly when I see Kenzie waving at me from one of the chairs on the other end of the room. Her quintet is seated beside her, but so are a handful of legacies I don't recognize.

She points at them and mouths, *My parents love you! Go Monk!*

Someone clears their throat impatiently. Ignoring them, I finally address the room.

42

MAVEN

"You know why you're here," I tell the Reformists. "I'm not going to waste your time or lie to you. I came back to reunite with my quintet, but now it's time to end Amadeus and remove his hold over the Nether."

Reformists exchange whispered murmurs.

I go on. "You're here because you want to help defend the mortal world. I'm not asking for anything more than that. Instead of just defending yourselves, we'll launch an attack into the bounds of what used to be the Nether. It will be as bloody and death-filled as any other battle you've seen, but no worse than the future of the mortal world will be if we don't stop Amadeus's advances. And after everything this plane of existence has been through, it deserves peace."

"Hasn't the mortal world gone through so much because of *you?*" one of the legacies sitting near Amelia Lykoudis points out.

Baelfire growls quietly, as irritated as I'm sure the rest of my quintet is by that statement.

"Yeah—the reason we have to make a stand against the Entity at all is because you're his scourge!" another one scoffs, shaking their head at me.

The blue-haired girl ghost flips them off, but I can't help snorting. Their claim is fucking ironic now that I know I was literally designed to fix the problem they're blaming me for.

"She thinks being the cause of all our problems is funny," Amelia Lykoudis scowls.

"The cause of all your problems?" I repeat. I take a step forward to make this point loud and clear, looking at all the faces in this room. "Does anyone here seriously believe all the problems with legacies and humans started with me, a twenty-three-year-old you never even heard of until six months ago? Did you approve of the way the Legacy Council and Immortal Quintet ran things, treating legacies like second-class citizens who didn't deserve a place in this world unless they were willing to lay down their lives at the Divide the second they graduated?"

A lot of the Reformists are shaking their head, proving my point. Even the legacies sitting near Amelia frown, paying more attention.

Amelia folds her arms, looking away. "You could at least apologize."

"You could choke on a bag of dicks," Baelfire grumbles, earning snickers from nearby legacies.

I shrug one shoulder, still addressing the room and not her directly. "Blame me for the Upheaval all you want, but this world was a shitstorm well before I came along. Humans in the Nether deserved a shot at freedom, so I took that shot, and I would take it again. I won't apologize for something I'm not sorry for. I'm only here to find out who's joining the final attack on the Nether, and who's out. This meeting is happening because this is where the cowards need to leave us. Trust me, there's a big difference between fighting off fiends that stray into the mortal realm and trespassing in the realm of the Undead."

Reformists exchange glances. Some look uncomfortable, but no one leaves. Even Amelia Lykoudis shuts her mouth and acquiesces.

"Came back from where?" Ross pipes up from where he fidgets in his seat.

"What?"

"You said you came back to reunite with your quintet. If I may ask, my lady, where exactly did you come back from? Was it the Beyond, or…?"

He clearly suspects where I was. Dozens of curious eyes turn back to me.

"Doesn't matter," I decide, adjusting my gloves. I'm extremely ready to be done with all this attention and the stupid fucking pounding of my heart.

"Pretty sure it does," Harlow Carter disagrees loudly. "Some people are still wondering if you're a demon like those suits in the elite safe haven claimed you are—before you slaughtered all of them. Kinda like a demon would. I mean, how are we supposed to follow you into battle if we don't even know where you were for the last six months while the world went to shit?"

Pot stirrer.

"Fine. I came back from Paradise," I admit before quickly turning to take my seat beside Everett again.

Reformists gasp and chatter about that, exchanging newfound shock. Even Brigid Decimus's eyebrows bounce up before she looks at Baelfire for confirmation. He nods before taking my hand and whispering that I did great. Everett is scowling at the room like he wants to freeze everyone who was doubting me. Crypt stomps out his cigarette as he looks equally irritated.

Meanwhile, Silas is deep in thought as he examines the present ghosts and the legacies as if he's still scheming something.

Legacies ask questions in quick succession, some standing in their excitement.

"What was Paradise like? Did you meet the gods?"

"How is it possible for you to ascend and then come back? Isn't that permanent?"

"How can you prove that you're a demigoddess?"

There are plenty more questions, but I'm distracted when I notice Monica looking sick in her seat on the edge of the room. When more of the legacies stand, talking over each other at me as reactions in the room continue to mount, Monica passes out. One of her quintet members quickly pulls the empath onto his lap, scowling at the rest of the overexcited Reformists like he blames them.

I've seen something like that before.

When I was fifteen years old, Amadeus brought me and the few remaining other contenders for becoming his *telum* into his private balcony overlooking his arena outside the citadel. He said all his subjects were to observe a special treat. The necromancers dragged a scrawny incubus with shredded wings and a cut-off tail into the arena as the monsters of Amadeus's court watched on.

Dagon was there, too. He excitedly explained that this incubus had turned out to be an empath—a rare mutation occurring in monsters, legacies, and manifested casters that the Undead absolutely loved to use for their version of amusement.

We were made to watch as other creatures were tortured near the incubus, who suffered all of their pain without a single blow falling on him. Everyone there thought it was fascinating and laughable, even some of the other kids I sat beside. Only Gideon seemed as bothered as I was by the display.

Eventually, the incubus passed out, paralyzed from the sheer magnitude of the emotions he felt from everyone he was exposed to. Dagon called it an empathic overload. Amadeus was very pleased when the incubus didn't survive it.

"Hellion?" Baelfire whispers, kissing my temple.

I'm in his lap. When did that happen?

With a start, I realize I disassociated at some point while I spaced out thinking about my past life in the Nether. Now, Brigid Decimus has called the room back to order. Reformist leaders are giving detailed reports of the combat zones they're in charge of, though some of them are still glancing at me curiously. It's obvious that their unanswered questions will come up again the second they get another chance.

Monica is awake again, looking much better as she listens to the reporting. I don't know her well, but I can't fucking imagine what a nightmare it must be to constantly experience so many emotions at once. It's bad enough having so many of my *own* emotions, let alone other people's.

Thinking about empaths reminds me of Everett's sister, Heidi. The one who was cast out into the reaches of the Nether by her own cruel family. Everett is still probably mourning her in secret.

I glance at my elemental and realize he was already staring at me with concern.

Are you okay? he checks, anxious. *You zoned out. Were you remembering something in Paradise?*

Not exactly. I'm fine, I reassure them.

Just a few more minutes of this, ima sangfluir, *and we'll leave before anyone here can bother you again,* Silas promises through the bond. *You missed that every single Reformist leader pledged their aid during the attack on the Nether.*

Good.

Then, after we celebrate with the cultists at the temple tonight, I'll polish my plan.

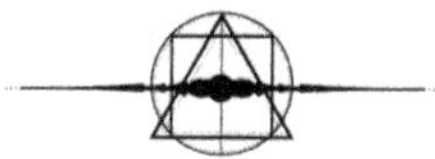

This was a terrible idea, Everett broods through the bond.

Dreadful, Crypt agrees. *Just have her take down the dreamcatchers, love. You'll barely notice I'm in there.*

Or just come back to our apartment, Baelfire chips in. *We'll help you get ready.*

I quietly roll my eyes at them as Kenzie curls another section of my hair. We're in the attached bathroom of the dorm room we used to share what feels like an eternity ago. As soon as the newly pregnant lioness shifter caught wind of a celebration later, she practically dragged me out of the Reformist meeting as it started to wind down so we could get ready together.

I was on board because it means I won't get pulled into unwanted conversations after the meeting, but also because I've missed my lioness shifter.

According to Kenzie, we're going to treat this "creepy weirdo cult party" like a replacement for the time she couldn't get ready with me for the Matched Ball months ago. She's so excited she's practically bouncing as she curls another section of my hair and blasts music I don't recognize from her phone resting on the bathroom counter.

I can't get ready there, I pointedly tell my quintet through the bond.

Why not? Everett demands.

Because you're all much better at getting me out of clothes than into them.

Our keeper is right, Silas muses. *We'd fuck her seven ways to the Beyond and bring her to the celebration with cum dripping between her thighs to remind everyone who we belong to.*

That vivid image makes my heart pound wildly as the other three vehemently agree. I temporarily shut out my quintet for now since A, I'm here to spend time with Kenzie, and B, she's a shifter who might sniff out when I'm getting too turned on by my telepathic conversation.

"My parents wouldn't stop gushing about you during the Reformist meeting," Kenzie tells me as she adjusts one of my curls. "I mean, obviously they've heard a lot about you from me, but they were just so thrilled to finally see the daughter of Pietro Amato himself—and Syntyche," she adds. "But I mean…mostly Pietro. I'm honestly surprised more people don't know he was your dad."

"I don't advertise it."

My birth father made his mark on the world in a big way and helped a lot of people. I don't see why I need to add an asterisk to his memory that he also had a daughter with a goddess and she turned out to be the *telum*. Being associated with me might taint how fondly people remember Amato.

Ready for a topic change, especially because I can sense my guys trying to get through the barrier keeping them from communicating inside my head, I glance at Kenzie. "So… pregnant."

"Yeah. I'll start bloating like a fresh corpse soon," she sniffs.

"Actually, corpses bloat when they're not fresh. Around the three to five day mark."

She sighs. "May. I'm lamenting the temporary future loss of my *spectacular* physique. Now is not the time to remind me of how thoroughly traumatized you are, you poor, short reaper baby."

I'm average-sized, not short. I also don't see how that statement of fact was indicative of my past trauma, but I grin at her anyway. "We both know you're going to look adorable as a pregnant lady."

Kenzie looks at me hopefully, pouting out her lower lip. "We do?"

"Absolutely. Your quintet won't be able to keep their hands off you."

"Well, sure, but when do they ever…"

"And you can buy all those cute maternity clothes you used to point out when you took me shopping."

She makes a face. "I mean, if the world goes back to normal and stores reopen before the baby comes, I guess…"

"If they don't, I'll ask Crypt to steal all the cute baby clothes you need."

Kenzie bursts into tears again.

"This is just so fucking *nice!* Oh my gods, May, you'd steal baby clothes for me? Gods, I missed you so much," she sniffles, wiping her face. "Ugh, I hate crying all the damn time. Good thing I didn't do my makeup yet—but we do need to start on yours because your hair's all done and you're going to look so fucking stunning. I have a few dresses you could borrow. If they're too long, I'll cut off the hems. Thank gods the winter is finally ending so we won't have to cover up how sexy we are with jackets. I'm going to make you look amazing—not that it's difficult," she adds, still half-crying as she finally unplugs the curling iron.

I forget to monitor my expression as I watch her blow her nose and wipe her leaking eyes. When Kenzie catches me looking, she bursts into laughter.

"Oh, my gods. Your face! Don't worry, May, I'm sure you'll be much more level-headed when you get knocked up."

I look into the mirror, studying the way my hair has been curled. Maybe I'll remember how to do this again later, if I ever decide to dress up for my quintet on my own. Kenzie is like family to me, so it's better to let her know now.

I may not be a revenant anymore, and I have my heart back, but that doesn't reverse what my body went through in the past. All that experimentation took a toll. They were thorough and extremely practical about turning me into the perfect weapon.

I can still hear Dagon's chilling voice as he cut me open years ago. *"You will become a perfect weapon. My masterpiece. But masterpieces do not bleed."*

Shaking off the dark memory, I clear my throat.

"Actually, I can't have kids."

"Oh." Then Kenzie's bright blue eyes get wider, and she puts both hands on her cheeks. *"Oh,* right. It's because you're a demigoddess, right? I heard that it's extremely difficult for gods to have children with humans, which is why there haven't been many demigods or demigoddesses throughout history. That makes you kind of a miracle, but that would probably make it extra hard for you to—"

"I'm sterile," I clarify. "It happened when necromancers were experimenting on me in the Nether. My quintet already knows."

Kenzie starts to fight back tears.

Oh, gods.

"I don't think I'm the kid-having type," I add quickly, trying to get ahead of the rainstorm.

"Ugh, Monk, that is so not the point," she huffs, leading me out of the bathroom so she can rummage through the few dress bags she brought from her quintet's temporary living space. "I just forgot for a second all the shit you went through. It's one thing to choose not to have kids and another thing if someone else took the choice away from you completely. Stupid motherfucking necromancers," she snarls, throwing one of the dress bags at a wall.

I hear snarling, Crypt's alarmed voice finally breaks through into my head. *Gods above, is that psychotic, hormonal pregnant woman attacking you?*

I'm not even going to comment on the irony of you *calling someone else psychotic.*

You beat me to it by barely a second, Boo, Baelfire laughs. *But seriously, Kenzie sounds pissed. You okay?*

I'm fine.

We're not *fine,* Everett groans. *You always look gorgeous, Snowdrop. Just come outside.*

Hang on. *You're not all just waiting around out there in the hallway, are you?*

Would you rather this, or us ripping each other apart in the apartment? Silas asks. *Because we're the furthest thing from good company for each other whenever you're away.*

Gods. They're ridiculous.

I'm fighting a smile as I focus on Kenzie again, deciding to change the topic since this upset her so much. "Which dress are you wearing?"

"I don't have 'momnesia' yet, so don't think that conversation is one-and-done. We're coming back to it another time," she huffs in warning before her entire face brightens, and she holds up the first dress she's pulled out. "This one is mine. What do you think?"

"I think someone stole the rest of the dress."

"Nope. That's all of it," she bounces her eyebrows. "Look, I have to show off while I still can, before I turn into a total fucking blimp and the best curve on my body is my baby bump."

I laugh at her melodrama. "For the last time, you're going to keep looking gorgeous."

"Thanks," she sighs. "Logically, I know I'll be fine, but *gods,* I don't know how my vanity is going to survive this pregnancy. Not to mention, my dignity. Did you know some women shit themselves when they give birth? *They shit themselves,* May. Ugh! My quintet will never look at me the same again."

"The baby will probably be cute," I try, not used to this whole optimistic shtick.

"Probably?" Kenzie practically shrieks, gesturing wildly at her face to make her point.

"Definitely," I amend quickly. "The cutest baby ever."

Did she just yell at you? Baelfire growls through the bond. *I heard a raised voice.*

Maybe you should break the door down again, Silas deadpans.

Do it, Everett says, taking that suggestion completely seriously.

Oh my fucking gods.

You four need a hobby.

I have *a hobby,* Crypt sighs wistfully. *But I can't enjoy it properly with those damned dreamcatchers up.*

Stalking doesn't count as a hobby, Everett grouches.

Our keeper would disagree. Wouldn't you, darling?

All right. That's it.

I'm not letting my quintet pout around in a hallway, I tell them firmly through the bond. *Get your sexy asses dressed, go to the cultist celebration, and wait for me there. Kenzie and I are running late, anyway.*

To say they're unhappy with this arrangement is an understatement, but I block out their protests so I can help Kenzie pick out a pair of shoes. Soon, she's dressed in the glittery, strappy, short dress with multiple cutouts to show off her back, stomach, and her quintet emblems on one tricep.

When she does a twirl, I smile. "You're the most inappropriately stunning and stunningly inappropriate pregnant lioness shifter I've ever seen."

She claps and unzips two more dress bags. "Okay! So, I had this little black number. Very elegant, but also very safe. Then there's this red one. I think you'd look stunning in red, but it is a little bit long…"

She continues chatting about the dresses, but I'm struck with an abrupt pang of missing my guys already, now that they're not all nagging me. Realizing that I have an entire party to get through before I can be alone with my guys again…

Gut me with a fucking spoon.

Being around people I don't know is exhausting. Still, I'm sure the bizarrely worshipful cultists will be fine with me showing up briefly. We can just be there for a little bit. Or better yet, if I could find an excuse to leave the celebration early…

I glance at the other unopened bags.

"Do you have something that will drive my quintet insane?"

Kenzie beams. "I love the way your sadistic little mind works, monk. I did bring something a bit more scandalous that could fit you."

She unzips another bag and holds up the gown. "I wasn't sure about it, since I know you usually avoid anything too low-cut."

I shake my head, studying it. "It's perfect."

Several minutes later, once makeup has been brushed on, we both stand in front of the bathroom mirror for a final check.

I take in her reflection. "Someone should warn your quintet. You look dangerously good."

"Thank you," she gushes. "You look like some divine, otherworldly being who's about to lure her quintet to bed and devour their souls."

Aww.

43

BAELFIRE

WELL, I'll be damned. Turns out, cultists know how to throw a party.

I take in the shindig as Silas, Everett, and I step through the protective wards into the massive clearing in Everbound Forest where the ruins of an old castle used to sit. Dead trees have been cleared to make room for this event.

Multiple tables have been laid out with meat skewers, wine glasses, and bottles of red wine. Several miniature bonfires line this place, illuminating it as the sun sets and providing extra warmth despite the snowless, Spring-like weather.

Most of the cultists here are still wearing black like they're in mourning, but they're a much less morose group than they were yesterday. They chow down on the feast and dance to instrumental music being played through some kind of magic charm.

Several dozen Reformists are here in combat attire, toasting each other, drinking wine, and waiting to officially meet my keeper. Some Nether humans are in attendance, too, but they're a lot more mellow and quiet where they stick to the corners and observe like they're not sure what to do at a celebration.

Cultists also know how to build a temple in record time.

I examine the new construction in one corner. It's a small

temple partially constructed from the old ruins. It looks more like a cathedral than a temple and reminds me of Syntyche's ruined temple that my dragon randomly dragged me to before it tracked down Maven.

Gothic architecture. Kind of sinister. Covered in dozens of ominous ravens perched near the steeples as they stare out with beady eyes like the creepy little fuckers are warning everyone away.

"Maven's gonna love that," I grin.

Everett nods, but he's repeatedly adjusting his sharp suit coat as his nerves get to him in the absence of our keeper. All three of us are wearing suits, but I skipped the coat because it's already plenty warm for a dragon shifter like me.

Silas is frowning at the wards we just passed through. "Whoever put up those wards, they're a fucking joke. I doubt they'll keep out mosquitoes, let alone the nefarious creatures that may be lurking in these woods. I'll have to reinforce them before—"

"Uncle Baelfire!" Quinn's voice calls.

I break into a smile when I see my niece racing toward me, dragging Lillian along behind her. The little water elemental is wearing a blue dress with white bows in her hair as she beams at us. She looks a lot like my brother Grady's quintet members, her birth parents. My mom mentioned that Grady and Aidan were dealing with an urgent outbreak of ghouls near some pretty severe Limbo Zones somewhere in eastern Canada, or else they would've come here to see me, too.

"Nice dress, Quinn," I greet, glancing at Lillian, who's laughing at my niece's antics. "Looks like you found a friend."

"Yeah! She's super nice and she read me books all day in the library today, and her name is Lilly," Quinn incorrectly introduces. She looks at Lillian and points at Everett. "His hair's white and his scar is sexy."

Silas and I burst into laughter at the look on Lillian's face, which is almost as good as the completely appalled expression the scarred ice elemental is wearing.

"It's—that's not—" Everett sputters before pinching the bridge of his nose. "Godsdamn it, Baelfire, your family needs some filters."

"She learned it from our keeper, not them," I laugh before squatting to smile at Quinn. "Where's your grandma?"

She shrugs, scrubbing at her cheek like it itches. "I dunno. I took Lilly and knocked on the door of the room in the big castle where Grandma's staying to tell her the party was starting, and Grandma said through the door that they're busy and they'll be here later."

I frown. My mom isn't the type to blow off anything.

I'm concerned until Lillian clears her throat, seeming embarrassed. "Your parents were preoccupied."

But still, it's not like them to—

Oh. She means *preoccupied*.

I gag at the same time Silas and Everett pull faces. None of us needed to know that little tidbit.

If you think that's off-putting, don't check behind the temple, Crypt suggests through the bond just as I can vaguely sense him somewhere nearby. *Not unless you want to see the three-eyed acolyte shagging the Carter girl. I, unfortunately, will never have the ability to unsee all three of his eyes rolling back in pleasure.*

Yuck. Why'd you have to provide that *detail?* I grimace.

It will haunt your dreams tonight. You're welcome.

Everett frowns. *Why the hell are you here instead of keeping an eye out in the castle to let us know when Maven is coming, like I told you to?*

Did you? I must've tuned that out along with most everything else you say.

Crypt— Everett starts, frustrated.

"He's not going to just prance around here ignoring Maven," Silas points out. "Flighty as he is, we can always count on the fact that he's as hopelessly transfixed by her as we are. He'll go back."

Obviously, Crypt agrees through the bond. *I had to scout this celebration to see if the cultists had something untoward planned for our keeper. I dislike it when others are almost as obsessed with her as I am.*

Get used to it, because we're right there with you, I point out.

He makes no other reply, leaving us to focus on Quinn excitedly pointing out the small bonfires to Lillian. Quinn sees a cultist set grapes down on one of the feast tables and quickly drags Lillian there next. The blue-eyed human smiles and waves goodbye at us, clearly happy to spend time with the little water elemental.

The celebration is hitting its stride as we end up wandering to one of the feast tables. I try one of the meat skewers as I ignore anyone who waves at me. I'm sure plenty of people are surprised to see me back and eager to chat, but my inner dragon and I are just getting petulant the longer we go without being around Maven.

Silas and Everett look just as pouty as Silas samples the wine. When Asher Douglas shows up with a few other ex-bounty hunters, Everett tells them to quickly scout the area before joining the celebration. Douglas reassures Everett that his pet hellhound, along with a few other hellhounds belonging to the other hunters, are hanging out in these woods, so there should be no problem.

Once we're left alone again, I try reaching out to Maven through the bond again. She still has us closed off.

So fucking stubborn.

I get that she needs space and time to talk to her friend, but godsdamn it—can't she just chat with Kenzie while I hold my mate in my lap and never let her go?

Fucking gods above, Crypt's voice rasps through the bond.

What? Everett demands.

The incubus doesn't respond, but a few minutes later, I sense him nearby again. It's pretty damn nice to not have the ever-living shit scared out of me anymore when Crypt appears.

So when the Nightmare Prince steps out of Limbo beside the

meat-skewer-and-wine table we're standing beside, I'm not surprised to see him.

But I *am* surprised to see how flustered he is. Like the rest of us, he's in some variation of a suit. It's the first time I've ever seen the incubus even remotely dressed up, but he quickly loosens and flings off his tie before rolling up his suit sleeves like he's overheated.

"What's wrong? More importantly, is Maven headed this way yet?" Everett demands impatiently.

Crypt huffs and grabs one of the many glasses, pouring wine and downing it all in one go before he scowls. "This celebration will have to be rescheduled."

"Why?" I frown.

"Because our perfect, merciless keeper is just begging for us to fuck her into insanity for the next week straight," Crypt rasps, scowling again when his markings light up a couple of times. "You've been forewarned."

When he downs another cup of wine, Silas snorts. "Really? I can't wait to see what you mea—"

The fae's voice cuts off on a choke, and I realize his attention has snagged on something at the edge of the clearing. And when I glance over to where he's looking—

Oh.

Holy. Fucking. Gods.

That dress. That *woman*.

And I thought I was feral before.

Crypt is right. There's no fucking way we can let her out of bed if she's showing up in public like…like…

"Oh, *fuck* me," Silas whispers, subtly adjusting himself as Maven steps into the cultist party.

Vaguely, I'm aware of the cultists cheering at her arrival, along with several other Reformist attendees clapping and gazing at her in awe. Kenzie is somewhere near my keeper, talking to her, but all I can focus on is Maven.

She's wearing white. A pure white dress with a slit in the

skirt that goes nearly to her hip. Every time she takes a step, I get a mouthwatering glimpse of her toned leg and a pair of simple flats.

But the real kicker is the gown's plunging neckline. It's so low-cut that it dips almost to her belly button, boldly and intentionally displaying the scar down the center of her chest…and all four of our quintet emblems.

She's showing off her killer body and our claim to her all at once.

"She's—" Everett has to stop and try speaking again, his voice is so hoarse as he shakily turns and pours his own cup of wine. "She's not even wearing a godsdamned *bra*. That dress should be fucking illegal, showing off her nipples like that—and with all these people staring at her," he groans.

Silas loosens his own tie as he speaks in fae, his voice thick. *"Vitiosus minxe."*

I nod in a haze like I understood that, but I'm also pretty sure I'm on the verge of openly panting. Not like I can help it. I've never seen Maven in white before, but in contrast to her warm olive-toned skin and black hair, she's striking as hell. I want to rip that dress off my mate, pin her to the ground, and fuck her right on the forest ground to punish her for looking so damn good.

When Maven looks over and sees how much she's torturing us, her lips curve up.

"Gods above, that's it," Crypt grits, more worked up as he shoves off his suit coat, his hungry gaze following her as she walks toward us. "I'll take her back to the quintet apartment through Limbo. The rest of you wankers can either meet us there or go fuck yourselves—I really don't care."

Maven must overhear the end of his frustration as she approaches, because she responds through the quintet bond. Whatever she says, it goes right over my head because I'm way too distracted watching the sway of her sexy, biteable hips as she walks. The silky white fabric clings to her, showing off her graceful movements so well that it's hard to swallow.

"Of course, we know you want to stay," Silas growls in reply to whatever she said, moving closer to toy with the ends of Maven's curled hair. "You enjoy torturing us like this. It's too cruel, *sangfluir*. Even your small army of ghosts agrees with me."

He gestures at nothing off to the side of the clearing. If I didn't know Maven could see the spirits too, I'd assume Silas was sinking back into insanity.

Our keeper grins. "Thirty minutes, and we'll leave."

"Five," Everett snaps, his eyes trailing over her again. "That's more than enough time for people here to gawk at you. They're lucky I don't freeze them all here in nevermelt as an eternal reminder that no one outside our quintet should see you looking so—so—"

When he can't find the right words, he swears and drinks the rest of his wine.

"Fifteen minutes," Maven decides, grinning when Crypt can't stop himself from reaching out to trace his emblem on the center of her chest.

"Very well," the incubus says in a much softer, far more dangerous tone than his recently flustered one. He smiles darkly at her. "Enjoy those fifteen minutes, darling. Because after that, you'll be weeping with arousal and pleading for mercy as four monsters wring every single ounce of pleasure from your teasing little cunt for as long as we like."

Yes to everything he just said.

Our keeper grins and leans closer to stage-whisper beside his ear, just loud enough that we can all hear her. "Promise?"

He swears. Silas mutters something in fae. I'm pretty sure Everett is now seriously considering freezing everyone here just so we can get our keeper alone sooner.

"Fourteen fucking minutes left, Raincloud," I warn her, having to turn away from everyone else in the celebration so they won't see the raging hard-on torturing me.

"Maven Oakley!" someone calls.

It's Orlando Coates, the cult leader. He quickly hurries to Maven before dropping to his knees in a low bow.

"Our demigoddess, you came!"

No, but she will *be coming,* I scowl through the bond. *Again and again, thanks to me.*

Silas hums. *Just two orgasms? Or was that three? Either way, I'll give her far more.*

Just not as many as I will, Everett chips in, beginning to pace with impatient arousal.

Another bet, then, Crypt suggests as his eyes remain pinned on our keeper. *This one has no deadline or prize aside from proving who can worship our girl the best.*

I'm in, I say almost at the same time as the others.

Despite our telepathic thirsting over her, Maven's face stays perfectly blank as the cult leader beams at her.

"So many of our guests here tonight are just dying to meet you," Coates says.

"Literally?" she checks, looking around for another giant wooden stake.

He laughs like that's a funny joke and not a reminder of the extreme lengths he was ready to go to just to see her. "No, no—they merely wish to be graced with the honor of meeting you individually."

Fuck, no, Everett says immediately, glaring out over the sea of people here. *That will take longer than the twelve minutes and forty-two seconds you have left, and I need to be in you* now.

Maven smirks and waves coyly at the ice elemental before following the cult leader to the first group of people he wants to introduce her to. Crypt follows her, and Silas is right behind him.

"She's so fucking mean," I sigh.

Everett agrees, grumbling, "It's annoying how damn sexy that is."

I nod and then examine him. "So what, you're a masochist *and* a voyeur?"

"You know, I didn't freeze Silas because I worried what it might do to his brain in the long run." He looks me over. "You? Wouldn't even hesitate. Hell, you might even come out smarter. Maybe then you'd mind some boundaries."

Dick.

Our attention is drawn away when Coates guides Maven back to the table full of food.

"Please, eat," he invites with excitement. "We made these meat sticks just for you."

"Thanks, but no," she mutters, eyeing the sauce-drenched meat.

"The only meat stick she likes is mine," I inform him seriously.

Everett chokes. Maven barely holds in a laugh, amusement sparkling in her dark eyes. And seeing her right in front of me again, with all that beautiful bare skin and her scent and my biting mark and emblem so proudly on display…

Damn it. I'm hard again.

How much longer until we can pounce on Maven? I ask only Everett.

Can't remember. Whatever it is, it's too fucking long, he scowls through the bond.

I'm not sure if he even knows how hard he's checking her out, but it's not like I'm any better.

Nearby, I hear a raven croak and realize a few of the glossy black birds have fluttered over here from the temple to carefully watch over the daughter of the reaper goddess. I've always thought ravens were ominous little featherballs, but knowing that Maven can influence them makes me wonder if they're here because she called them or if they're just…here.

Six minutes, Crypt warns Maven.

I don't see him anywhere in the party when I do a quick scan, so he must be in Limbo. Silas is standing on the opposite side of the party now, drinking another cup of wine as he watches Orlando Coates lead Maven back to the center of the party.

I'm just as transfixed by my mate's every move until Coates calls out, "And now, we will present the goddess with her gift! As in times of old, we hereby gift this temple to the demigoddess in our midst. Daughter of the Reaper, please enter and inspect the temple we have built and dedicated in your honor. We shall not leave this place, nor shall we stop feasting and celebrating your presence in this world until you tell us we have won your favor!"

I'm not sure if he's pulling all of this out of his ass or if he really did study a shit-ton of history books about how past demigods and demigoddesses were treated. Either way, everyone claps and whistles. Even the shy Nether humans look happy for her.

Maven thanks Coates and turns to saunter toward the temple, but her beckoning voice echoes through the quintet bond to the rest of us.

Well? Come on. This temple isn't going to defile itself.

44

EVERETT

My heart pounds as I follow the woman I love into the temple built for her.

She's been teasing us. Tormenting us.

I need her so fucking badly, it hurts. I can't tear my eyes off of the sway of her ass as she walks in front of me.

The echo of distant celebration still hums beyond the stone, but here in the temple, it's all pristine stone floors and wooden pews with flickering candles left out to light the space dimly. It's a small temple, but definitely nice enough for a god, let alone a demigoddess—

I stop when I see the altar at the end of the pews.

It's a big altar.

Big enough for me to start fantasizing like the fucking blasphemous sinner I am. But is it really blasphemy if I want to worship the new owner of this temple on her own altar?

I may never be worthy of her, but I'd still adore her anywhere, anytime if she would only let me—but especially here.

As if Maven can read my mind, she doesn't stop until she's turned and perched on the altar, facing her quintet as we enter. She looks absolutely fucking irresistible in that dress, and I'm pretty sure she knows it because she smiles wickedly and leans back, parting her thighs so the slit of her dress opens.

It shows us she's not wearing panties.

Oh, my gods. She was out there walking around, meeting all those fucking Reformists without wearing a bra *or* panties?

My palm itches. I want to smack her ass so bad to remind her that nobody outside our quintet gets to see her without a stitch of underwear on—but when she arches a brow and speaks with a voice like velvet, I'm helpless.

"Kneel," she says simply, spreading herself further.

The four of us drop like worshippers, obedient and ravenous. Crypt is smiling, Baelfire looks like he's about to start drooling, and Silas's stare is so damn intense, I'm surprised Maven's face hasn't burst into flame.

My eyes drag over my keeper—all that bare, beautiful skin glowing in the candlelight, her black hair falling in curls, her dark gaze trained on us. When her fingers slide down her belly, teasing lower and lower, my mouth waters.

Baelfire swears hoarsely when Maven's fingers finally slip through her pussy, teasing us as she closes her eyes and exhales sharply. My entire world seems to narrow on the way her body is responding so fucking beautifully—to us—and finally, I move forward and lean in.

I don't ask. I just devour.

Maven gasps when my eager tongue drags through the wet perfection between her thighs. Her taste explodes across my tongue, subtle and heady at once. I groan against her, gripping her thighs and spreading them wider until my tongue can trace tight circles on her clit.

Soon, she's swearing and grinding against my face, desperate.

I love seeing her desperate.

I love everything about this, even the fact that my cock is now straining painfully inside my pants.

"Look at you, soaking this altar," I whisper as I slip a finger into her tight pussy, my voice rough with awe. "So fucking beautiful and ready for us to worship."

"Gods," Maven groans, breathless with pleasure as she glances at the rest of our rapt quintet.

Baelfire's already shucked down his pants and has started stroking himself, eyes half-lidded as he watches Maven writhe. Silas stands, his eyes hungry on Maven as he, too, begins to unzip.

Crypt is done waiting. He stands and moves closer, stripping as his markings glow slightly purple among the candlelight of this temple. He reaches out to caress Maven's face, but despite his gentle movements, his voice is all savage need.

"Lie back, love. It's time for the defiling to begin."

I stand, too, desperately working my clothes off as Maven gracefully swivels until she's laying on the altar, her head hanging slightly off one end and the slit in her skirt still leaving access to her fucking perfect pussy.

Crypt moves to where our keeper's head hangs off the edge of the altar. He first stoops to kiss her aggressively before standing and rubbing the head of his pierced cock over her bottom lip, smearing pre-cum that she licks away with a hum.

"Such a filthy fucking goddess," he murmurs raggedly.

Maven doesn't hesitate to take the incubus's stiffness into her mouth, deep and smooth. He gasps, hand fisting in her dark hair —and godsdamn it, I'm already seconds from coming just from watching the way she worships him back.

Heat grips my spine as I move between my snowdrop's legs, but I don't move to fuck her. I'm enjoying the show way too fucking much. Silas steps up next, tracing his blackened-finger hands gently over Maven's spread thighs before lining himself up and thrusting into Maven, hard and fast. He groans like it physically hurts to be inside her, but we all know it's because of how fucking good and right it feels to be with the one we're bound to.

Maven's next moan around Crypt's pumping cock fills the

space as Baelfire also stands beside the altar, his breathing labored. I'm stroking myself now, too, fisting my cock slowly as I try like hell to wait. But gods, watching her like this—

Our keeper's back arches off the altar, and her breathing gets choppy. Crypt swears and comes in her perfect, eager mouth just as Silas begins to slam harder into her. The fae swears and grips Maven's hips as he fucks her, reaching down to pinch her clit until finally, her first orgasm has her crying out.

The sound is so fucking beautiful, I hope it echoes in this temple forever.

"That's one," Silas manages, voice strained before he loses himself, too. He jerks and swears in fae as he comes inside our keeper.

I wanted inside Maven's gorgeous pussy, but now I can't take my eyes off of the way her tits look as she tries to catch her breath. Her dress has shifted so they're both out in the open now, cradling the sides of our emblems and her scar—all on display and teasing me to insanity just like when we were out in that fucking party.

Gods, I love my keeper's tits so much. Deciding I want to come all over those, I walk around the altar and gently brush her hair away from her face, marveling at how fucking gorgeous she is.

Maven smirks at me and accepts me into her mouth. I groan when her tongue flicks under the head of my cock, teasing and exploring at once. She's so greedy for it, taking more each time I thrust.

Pleasure is gripping my balls like a godsdamned vice as she moans and sucks me—and when she swallows around me, I barely hold back my shout. Pulling myself quickly out of the slick perfection of her mouth, I stroke myself until my release paints her beautiful chest over and over.

When I'm done, I still can't take my eyes off of how beautiful she is when we've made such a mess of her.

"Gods above, you're so radiant, love," Crypt breathes, as enchanted by our sexy, divine keeper as I am.

But Baelfire hasn't had his turn. He's already stepping up, blue flames flickering under his skin as a sign of how worked up he is. The normally jovial shifter flips Maven over on the altar with gentle ease, kissing one of her ass cheeks and spreading her until he can push into her soaking pussy from behind.

When he shoves all the way in, the sound she makes goes straight to my balls. Baelfire is so lost to the feeling of being in her that he begins fucking her hard and fast, until the sound of slapping skin fills the temple along with their moans and gasps.

"Fuck me," Maven pleads, clutching the sides of the altar so he doesn't knock her off with the force of how hard he's slamming into her. "Fuck me, fuck me, fuck me—"

She's so close to her next release that she's completely undone, sweat-drenched and gasping as the dragon shifter grips her hips tightly, swearing as he gives her what she needs.

When Maven finally buries her face in one of her arms, trying to muffle her cry of euphoric release, I groan right alongside Baelfire. His head drops back on his shoulders and he falls off that cliff with her, pumping slowly and swearing until finally, the temple stops echoing with the sex sounds that make me so damn horny.

"That's two," I mutter, voice thick as I watch Baelfire pull out.

Silas and Crypt both swear as cum drips from between Maven's reddened thighs. She adjusts to sit upright on the altar and notices where we're looking. My heart stutters and my cock throbs with arousal when my devious keeper reaches down, swipes up some of the release dripping between her legs, and brings it to her lips for a taste.

Oh my gods.

"Have some fucking mercy on us," Crypt half-laughs, half-groans. "We're only mortals, love."

"I won't hold it against you," Maven teases, licking her lips.

Silas looks as near-feral as I'm starting to feel as he adjusts himself, eyes pinned on her. "Another round, *ima sangfluir?*"

Maven's lips curl up, but she pauses, considering. "Not here. One of those cultists could just walk in any moment and get an eyeful." Then she glances at me, smirking. "Not all of us would enjoy that as much as others."

I fight a smile. She's right. I don't mind an audience.

However, the idea of someone seeing *her* looking so fucking incredible makes me want to freeze someone's innards.

"Let's say goodbye to the party and move this to our apartment," I suggest.

We're all in agreement. As the rest of us get redressed, Crypt gingerly helps Maven off the altar. He cups her face to kiss our keeper slowly while his markings light up. Once he releases her, my gorgeous keeper straightens her dress, uses my discarded jacket I offer her to clean up our cum, and starts detangling her curled hair.

Gods, I love the way she looks when she's flushed and freshly fucked.

I'm ready to keep this up for the next few hours—or if our keeper needs a break, I'll massage her tired muscles and shampoo her hair for her and anything else she wants. So much has been going on, I've barely had time to pamper my snowdrop the way she deserves.

We're all taking our time, lingering in a haze of post-sex bliss until Maven tenses.

"Fuck," she whispers.

"Boo?" Baelfire frowns, his attention moving to her chest. "I hear your heart pounding again. What's going on?"

She whirls to face the entrance of the temple, her throat constricting as a sign of fear.

"Wraiths."

I've only heard this undertone of terror in her voice once before. I quickly realize what it means and swear.

"Gideon is here," I announce.

On cue, screams ascend from outside the temple.

45

EVERETT

THE SCREAMING OUTSIDE IS loud enough to be heard despite the thick stone walls. Maven withdraws her etherium knife, which quickly transforms into a scythe as she darts out of the temple with her unnatural speed. The rest of us are right behind her.

As soon as I throw open the double doors, the sound of terrified chaos magnifies.

Everyone at the celebration is reacting in real time to their greatest fears. Many of them run, blind from whatever they see in their heads as they crash into each other or trees. Many cultists and Reformists are attacking each other. Ex-bounty hunters shout nonsense as they race out of the clearing like they're being chased by demons.

Felix is trying to pull a coyote that I can only assume is Dirk off of another of his quintet members. Kenzie throws a half-eaten meat skewer into a cultist's eye to keep them from attacking her in their panic-induced insanity.

Other Reformists lie sobbing, paralyzed with sheer terror as the whispers of that mutated, sickening wraith taunt the living from the shadows of this dead forest. Several loud gunshots go off somewhere in the distance before hellhounds begin to howl.

My attention zips to Maven in time to see her dodge an

insane Reformist, vault over a feast table, and swing her scythe in a glowing arc. It whistles, cutting through the center of a wraith that howls and hisses even louder than the rest of the screams permeating this forest.

The hissing laughter of another wraith echoes nearby, just barely audible above the screams permeating this forest.

There's still fear in Maven's voice as she speaks through the bond, which tells me Gideon is still here somewhere. *The wards that Coates put up aren't strong enough to protect these people. Silas, these people need—*

Protection. He's already running down the steps of the temple and veering toward the edge of the clearing, throwing blood magic that annihilates several shifting shadows. *Leave it to me.*

A stark scream of pain nearby catches my attention as she cuts off. A fear-blinded Orlando Coates just unwittingly wandered through one of the small fire pits. Now he's on fire as he runs through the clearing, bumping into other terrified people.

Raising my hand, I freeze him and unfreeze him in a matter of seconds, putting out the flames. The cultist leader slumps to the ground, passed out. I glance at my hand. I almost forgot how accurate I am with my element when my curse is broken.

I spent most of my life being complimented on my abilities and taking those compliments as empty flattery, since I was obviously lacking.

Now? I've never felt this strong.

"No! *Maven!*"

Baelfire's roar from beside me sends fear and panic hurtling through my system. Godsdamn it, is she hurt? Is she dying again? Where is she? I rush down into the chaos of the shadow-plagued, ruined celebration, quickly growing desperate when I can't see my snowdrop.

Darling, Crypt chokes from wherever he is in Limbo. *What happened to your eyes? Gods above, you're bleeding everywhere. Crane, get over here and—*

Maven swears through the bond. *Whatever you guys are seeing, it's the wraiths getting to you. I'm perfectly fine.*

As if to prove her point, the agonized shriek of another wraith echoes in the woods surrounding the clearing. Maven emerges between the trees, still gripping her scythe, her beautiful white dress splattered with the dark blood of these intangible, fear-wielding shadow fiends.

Relief makes me weak for a second before a fear-blinded cultist slams into my side, taking me down. My head smacks against something hard, making my ears ring. When the cultist tries to claw at my skin in their blind horror, I freeze her solid and shove her off of me, getting back to my feet.

My vision is blurry from hitting my head, and I'm even more disoriented as I hear more gunshots being fired somewhere far away. But I go still as an otherworldly hissing voice fills my ears.

"Favored, ye walk alone…"

Those words send goosebumps over my skin. It was never fully translated, but those lines are from my personal prophecy. Fear clots in my throat, and I can't move as my heart's pace increases to a dangerous rate.

Suddenly, all I can see is Maven, dead in my arms.

Gone.

I was always destined to fail her. To be alone.

Everett, get down, her beautiful voice tells me.

But I barely register that warning, because her perfect body is limp in my arms. The emptiness in her lifeless eyes breaks something in me all over again. Tears drip down my cheeks, freezing along with everything else I touch.

"Telum-*cursed…vice of keeper dead,*" the whispers mock, still reciting the prophecy that's tormented me for years. *"Deaths to five…"*

Something slams into me again. It's disconcerting as hell because all I can see is the worst moment of my life on replay, but I'm aware someone just tackled my physical body. A whistle cuts through the air before a furious screech assaults my ears—

And suddenly, I'm blinking up at the darkening twilight sky.

Maven just slayed the final wraith that was tormenting everyone in this clearing. Crypt tackled me to move me out of the way so she could cut the damn thing in half. A lot of the screaming in the clearing begins to taper off as the wraiths' influence dies with it.

I exhale, shakily wiping the moisture off my temples as I get to my feet. Maven sees and immediately steps close to embrace me.

I don't care that she's covered in wraith blood. I pull her tightly against me for a second, internally reminding myself over and over that she's here and she's alive and we're bound again. That was just another godsdamned wraith getting inside my head.

Still…

I'm pretty sure the thought of losing my entire world all over again will always haunt me.

Tell me again, I plead with Maven, only speaking to her telepathically.

She knows exactly what I mean as she peers up at me. Despite slaying wraiths, she's still so breathtaking that it fucking hurts as she stands on her tiptoes to kiss my jaw.

I love you, and I'm not going anywhere.

Those words are my lifeline.

Crypt tips Maven's chin back, studying her face to reassure himself that her eyes are still where they're supposed to be. Then he grins. "You wear the blood of fiends so well, darling. Any chance you'd let me give your scythe a swing? Seems fun."

"It is," our keeper smiles back before turning serious again, her determined gaze sweeping over the clearing. "But we have a problem. None of the wraiths I just killed were Gideon. He's playing his favorite game."

Hide and seek. I remember the fiendish asshole taunting her about it the first time we crossed paths with him. For the last six months, I haven't seen a single fucking glimpse of this asshole—I'd hoped Maven killed him in Alaska after all.

Clearly, we're not that lucky.

The celebration is in shambles as everyone slowly comes out of the fear-induced hysteria. The Baird quintet hovers protectively around Kenzie while cultists tend to their burnt, unconscious leader. Reformists check on each other, still on edge as they examine their surroundings fearfully.

There are a lot of injuries, but no one is dead. They probably have my keeper's quick response time to thank for that.

I'm eyeing all nearby shadows as Silas and Baelfire rejoin us. Baelfire is smeared with blood that isn't his own. Other than looking incredibly guilt-ridden, Silas is fine.

"I should have reinforced the wards the moment we arrived. Forgive me, *sangfluir.* This was my fault," he tells Maven.

"Believing that doesn't make it true," she mutters, still clutching her scythe tightly as she looks for signs of the worst of the wraiths. "Besides, if Gideon was able to get through the Divide before, you changing the wards wouldn't have kept him out of—"

Three gunshots fire off from far out in the woods, drawing our attention.

"Someone needs help," Baelfire realizes. Then he looks quickly over the aftermath of the wraith attack, and the blood inexplicably drains from his face. "Hang on. Where's…"

My attention is called by Felix, who's been healing coyote bites on Vivienne's leg.

"Commander." Felix holds up his arm to show that his Reformist scrying brand is glowing. "It's a distress signal. Douglas just set it off."

"Quinn," Baelfire chokes, already stumbling toward the edge of the newly-warded clearing. "She's missing. So is Lillian."

Shit.

The rest of us don't hesitate to rush after him. Even though I want to beg Maven to stay behind in the clearing and help the others recuperate after the horrors of the wraiths, I know my keeper would never willingly send us off into danger and stay behind.

The woods are filled with twisted, dead trees and swirling mist. As twilight shifts fully into nightfall, darkness presses in as the five of us stay close together, running and scanning for signs of anyone.

"Lillian!" Baelfire shouts. "Quinnie?"

The rest of us call for them, too. But finally, I come to a screeching stop when I catch a glimpse of a dead ex-mercenary slumped on the ground nearby.

"Over here," I tell the others.

When I reach the motionless legacy, I realize others are scattered on the ground, either dead or severely wounded in this thickly wooded area. Two hellhounds are slumped lifelessly to the ground here, too.

With the way some of these people were bitten multiple times and flung around like ragdolls, I'm not surprised when I see Asher's pet hellhound, Devil, curled up on himself nearby. It looks like he was shot once or twice, but he's still breathing.

Other motionless ex bounty hunters were clearly shot, too.

"Gideon is nearby," Maven murmurs beside me, scanning the dark woods beyond the light spell she's summoned into her hands.

Silas eyes the shadows as he steps over one of the dead bodies, calling his own light spell that glows red. "Either he got into these legacies' heads, or he got into Asher Douglas's. If it's the latter, the mercenary's distress signal may have been a trap arranged for us by the wraith."

Godsdamn it. He's right.

"Nope, no traps. Just me getting ambushed by my friends thanks to that shadowy motherfucker."

We're all surprised to see Asher Douglas shirtless, slumped against a tree behind some overgrown shrubbery. He grimaces as he tries to dig a bullet out of one of his shins. It's not the only bullet in him—he was clearly shot a few times. He's covered in so much blood, it's almost difficult to make out all the other tattoos covering his bare torso.

When Maven sees the state he's in, she glances at Silas. That's all she needs to do before he crouches to help Asher heal some of the more serious bullet wounds. The mercenary exhales in relief as his body slowly begins to mend under the fae's blood magic.

"What happened here?" I ask, wary.

What if this is just another wraith trick?

"Saw Lillian and a few others running out of the clearing, so I followed to see what was going on. Didn't know they were being influenced by a wraith," Douglas grunts. "My friends went out of their fucking minds as soon as we got into the woods. Dev and I tried to stop them, so now we're both Swiss cheese. That's all I know."

Baelfire squints at him. "And we're supposed to believe the wraith didn't affect you at all?"

Douglas can't answer as he winces in pain when Silas leans him forward to pick out another bullet lodged high in one of his shoulders. Maven tips her head to study the golden phoenix covering most of the burly ex-bounty hunter's bloodied, bare back.

"So that's why the wraith didn't get to you," she muses. "That's a blessing, not a tattoo. You were touched by Arati."

"Way to make the queen of the gods sound perverted."

"I'm related to her. Of course, she's perverted." She straightens, looking around again as ravens croak somewhere in these trees. "Where are Lillian and Quinn?"

The mercenary glances over at his curled-up, bloodied, massive hellhound and whistles. "Dev. Good boy. Let her go."

The hellhound's red eyes move to us before he huffs and uncurls his body, moving his dark tail out of the way, too. As soon as Baelfire sees his niece unconscious, huddled against the hellhound's side, he hurries to her side to check her pulse, ignoring the hellhound's warning growl.

"Is she hurt?" Crypt demands, looking back at Douglas.

Douglas swears when Silas finally digs the bullet out of his shoulder. "She tripped and hit her head on something when she was chasing after Lillian. Probably just a concussion. She's safe with Dev and me until we can get her back to Commander Decimus. Dev has orders to guard her with his life."

That surprises me. That damn hellhound is the only thing this mercenary cares about, besides food, sleep, and money.

"Thank the fucking gods. I owe you," Baelfire manages as he stands, letting the hellhound guard the little water elemental again.

"Chasing after Lillian?" Maven repeats the mercenary's words. "Where did Lillian go?"

His face falls. "She didn't go willingly. The shadows came to life out of fucking nowhere and dragged her away—that way," he adds, nodding with his chin before looking surprisingly sympathetic. "Her screams cut off before I could finish handling these guys. I'm sorry."

Fucking gods.

I turn to Maven, already reaching for her, but her inscrutable mask slides on. She turns and takes off through the dark woods in the direction he indicated.

"Maven!" Silas shouts as we race after her.

Even Baelfire is struggling to keep up with our keeper's pace as she dodges trees, leaps over fallen logs, and scours this part of the woods for Lillian. The light spell in her hands and Silas's red glow from beside me cast a dim, disturbing glow all around. They're just barely keeping the shadows at bay.

The darkness in these woods feels almost palpable as Maven veers suddenly to the right, tracking Gideon using her ability to sense fiends. Chills prickle over my entire body when I hear a hissing whisper somewhere in the dead trees surrounding us.

Maven goes perfectly still. The rest of us surround her in the quintet formation we were taught at Everbound, silent and scanning.

"I'll stay and search for her," Crypt tries, glancing at Maven. "But if you stay, it's exactly what he wants. He's after you, love. Baiting you."

"I know. He can have me. Not Lillian," she grits, her face lit ominously by the light in her hands.

"No," I snap, glaring at her. "Crypt is right. We're in the perfect place for him to attack. This asshole wants to feed on your fear, but if you leave—"

"I'm not leaving until I find her."

I want to protest again, but we all hear the slight tremble in Maven's voice. It's killing me to hear her like this.

But we're not letting Gideon anywhere near her. The things he put me through inside my head in Alaska were fucking sickening. I loathe that he was ever inside my keeper's mind at all. There's no way in hell any of us are letting him torment her ever again.

"Boo—" Baelfire begins, equally desperate to get her out of here.

But his words cut off as the shadows thicken and come alive around us within a split second. Darkness crashes over us like a wave of viscous black smoke, concealing everything from sight and snuffing out the light spells Maven and Silas were just holding.

Instinctively, I fling ice toward a shadow I see moving toward Maven, but Crypt shouts in pain instead. Fuck. Baelfire snarls, my keeper gasps, and then the most awfully sickening sound of flesh and ligaments ripping and tearing echoes around us—

And then warm liquid splatters on my face.

I've been in battle on the front lines enough times to know by now that's what a spray of someone else's blood feels like.

Oh my gods. Oh my gods. No.

Maven.

I can't even speak or focus enough to send it through the bond. I'm frozen in horror as blood drips down my face. But I didn't feel the bond break. So what the hell just happened?

"Maven—" Silas starts to shout, just as alarmed and confused as I am.

"Sweet raven, sweeter fear, finder's keepers ends here," whispers sing, echoing around the dark forest. *"Never liked her liking you. Time to see the tears."*

Silas begins reciting another spell, but he cries out in pain just as something barbaric hooks into my skull, twisting and wrenching until it slides deeply into my brain.

I collapse as stomach-churning images flood my vision. A younger version of Maven, sobbing and thrashing helplessly on the floor of a gnarled forest a lot like this one as her nose bleeds. Gutted monsters hung up on display outside of large, foreboding gates made of onyx. Young teenagers fighting each other to the death inside a massive, ornate arena, blood pooling on the stone floor as grisly-looking spectators watch.

But unlike the last time this wraith got into my head, it only lasts a fraction of a second before Maven shouts in a language I don't understand. A flash of holy magic light blinds me for a moment, extinguishes any darkness left in this section of Everbound Forest. I'm sure a flare of light this strong can be spotted all the way from the castle.

Her spell completely drives that sick asshole out of my head as the shadows completely retreat as a glow like midday light lingers in the forest. We're left alone in this space so suddenly, it's disorienting.

For a brief second, I'm grateful for Maven's powerful magic.

And then my attention drops to the grisly scene that was just lit up to highlight every detail.

Oh my fucking gods.

My heart cracks when Maven's knees hit the forest floor as she numbly takes in this sickening scene.

Lillian is literally in pieces. Her blood drips from nearby tree trunks and is splattered all over mine and the rest of my quintet's horrified faces. Gore and body parts are strewn around the forest floor. The human's head is nearby, her blond curly hair stained with blood.

I quickly look away as nausea threatens to rise up my throat.

I've never seen Maven break the way she does now. In the shocked silence of this haunting forest, her first cry of grief tears my heart clean in two. For the first time since I met my resilient, strong keeper, she breaks down into heart-rending tears.

This was her caretaker. Her oldest friend. The only person who helped Maven survive hell before helping me survive my own version of it over the last six months. Maven just barely got Lillian back into her life. Out of all the things that motherfucking wraith could have done to hurt her, this is the worst.

For one horrible moment that seems to last forever, none of us knows what to say to comfort our devastated keeper.

I can't breathe.

Finally, Baelfire gets on his knees in front of Maven and pulls her against his chest, carefully blocking the ghastly view. I glance at the others for the first time and see that Crypt's side is still healing from where I accidentally cut him with a spike of ice in the darkness. Otherwise, my quintet is unharmed as we face this new horror of Maven facing a loss so deep.

We need to get her to safety, Silas finally says through the bond, carefully leaving our keeper out of it as he glances at the spell around us. *This will fade and that damned wraith will come back to taunt her.*

Yes, get her to safety and I'll hunt down that godsforsaken fucking wraith myself, Crypt grits telepathically.

You can't kill him without blessed bone, I remind him before looking at Baelfire.

Bael nods and tries to brush tears off Maven's face without letting her see past his big frame. "Come on, Raincloud," he murmurs softly, trying to move her. "Let's get out of here."

"No," she resists, wiping at the tears that drip off her cheeks and chin. "I'm waiting for her."

Silas's expression is dark as he once again glances at the awful scene before us. "Her spirit isn't here, *sangfluir.*"

"Not L—Lillian," she manages, her voice raspy from crying. "My mother. I prayed, so she has to come. I have to fix this."

Does she think Syntyche will bring Lillian back? I feel so fucking helpless, watching the woman I love in such pain.

And Silas is right. The light spell is slowly fading around us as darkness creeps back into this area of Everbound Forest. I don't want Maven anywhere near shadows right now—not when that piece of shit could try to get to her again. She needs time to mourn, but her safety is my biggest priority for the rest of my life.

Waiting for Syntyche isn't an option.

"Snowdrop," I murmur, picking up the etherium knife she dropped. "It's time to go."

"No," she sobs.

"We'll give her a proper burial tomorrow, darling," Crypt promises gently, crouching beside her to cradle her face. He looks as tortured as the rest of us to see her like this. "In the daylight. She'll be laid to rest beside your headstone, if you like, but we need to get you out of here."

"No."

Even in the depths of mourning, she's the most stubborn person I've ever met. Baelfire is just holding her as she weeps. Silas has silently begun using magic to clean up the worst of the macabre scene, trying to spare her from seeing more of this tragedy.

One moment, Maven is inconsolable as she's wrapped tightly in Baelfire's arms. But just as her spell begins to finally fade and I hear fiendish, chilling laughter from gods know where, her rage takes over. Maven promptly rips herself out of Baelfire's arms, holding her hand toward me for her knife.

Silas sees and shakes his head. "No, *sangfluir.* Now is not the time—"

"Now is the only time," she seethes. "He came to carry out

Amadeus's warning. He's only lingering to feed on my fear, and then he'll disappear again. I'm not waiting to avenge her."

"Maven—" I begin to protest, panic squeezing my heart at the thought of that twisted bastard getting anywhere close to her.

She silences my words with a look that shows me all the raw fury hiding beneath her broken exterior.

I let my argument die. After all, my keeper found a way back from fucking *Paradise* when the gods insisted she had to stay. If the gods themselves couldn't stop her from accomplishing what she put her mind to, how the hell do I stand a chance?

But I'm not leaving her side.

Never fucking doing that again.

We're all tense and silent as the last of her holy magic spell slowly evaporates, leaving nothing but the dim glow from Crypt's lit-up markings behind. Maven holds her etherium dagger, twisting it slowly in her hand as she bides her time.

Gideon's chilling whispers dance through the darkness, mocking. *"Little goddess, broken bird, weeping daughter, never heard. No more chess for you."*

He hisses with laughter.

She remains quiet, waiting as her poker face hides her pain.

My jaw clenches as I remain close to my keeper, frost called to my fingertips as I prepare to do—I don't even know what. Unlike other wraiths, he's tangible, but my ice won't hurt him.

"Such delicious fear, sweetest raven Maven," Gideon sings.

Baelfire is pissed off. Blue flames flicker beneath his skin as he looks around. "Come out, you motherfucking coward."

More otherworldly laughter bounces between the trees as the experimental wraith toys with us. Shadows shift, swirling and solidifying occasionally around the place we stand at the ready.

Crypt. Go into Limbo. He can't see you there, Maven says telepathically.

He drops into it immediately.

"Hunting me, hunting you. Back from a grave to mourn at a

grave," the wraith taunts. *"If she never loved you, she would have survived. They who love you must die."*

To underline his point, the wraith finally makes his next move. Shadows lurch towards Baelfire, but the shifter dodges aside just in time. My attention is pinned on the swirling, tactile shadows. I barely have time to notice the vague, dark figure rising up behind Silas before Maven's etherium blade is hurtling toward it.

Her knife whooshes just over Silas's head and plunges into the center of the wraith. Gideon's hiss of pain fills the air as shadows wrap around Silas's neck and yank out the knife all at once. The blade twists down, aiming at the fae's chest as he's being strangled—

Until Crypt drops out of Limbo and slashes his own sword upward, knocking her knife free of the shadows.

Maven capitalizes on the wraith's temporary confusion, moving faster than my eyes can register as she catches the spiraling blade and darts forward. Suddenly, I'm watching Maven bury the etherium blade into the fiend.

Gideon shrieks, and his tangible shadows try to swarm around Maven like thousands of wickedly sharp knives—but she shouts something that makes holy magic flare around her. Her spell punctures through every one of his attempts to harm her as she stabs him again, black wraith blood gushing.

Over and over and over, she stabs it.

The shrieks are deafening as what's left of Gideon falls to the forest floor, writhing in a mass of dying shadows. Maven doesn't let up even after the writhing stops, but once the wraith evaporates like all the others, my snowdrop looks exhausted.

Silas is still trying to catch his breath after nearly getting strangled, but Baelfire helps him up as Crypt and I immediately crouch beside Maven.

Fresh tears are on her pretty face as I pull her close, quietly repeating that everything will be okay.

"He's dead," Baelfire assures her softly, glancing down at the place the wraith just was.

"You avenged her beautifully," Crypt adds, brushing hair out of her tear-stained face.

"So she did," a woman's voice murmurs beside us.

I don't even have words for the kind of terror that floods me just with those three words. This is a completely different kind of fear from the blind panic wraiths wield. It's controlled. Absolute. The kind of primordial fright that haunts you when you least expect it.

With my heart pounding in my throat, I peer over Maven's head to see my mother-in-law in the flesh for the first time.

46

MAVEN

THE LAST FEW minutes have been such a blur that I've only processed three things.

One, I killed Gideon.

Two, my mother is here.

Three, Lillian is dead.

Or maybe I haven't processed that last one yet, because my heart is still doing something horrible inside my chest. I'm suffocating from the surreality of the sight of her ripped to pieces.

She died in fear. I know that much.

And I wasn't here to help her.

Death has always been a part of my life. I've been surrounded by it for as long as I can remember. I've always been able to sense it, too–like a heavy tide going out, taking with it the spark of life.

But sensing it this time is different. It hurts. I didn't see Lillian's spirit or feel her move on or say goodbye.

I *need* that goodbye. If I can't go back in time and change the fact that I wasn't here to protect her, I need to at least see her again. Which is why I sucked up my pride and prayed for the first time in who knows how long when.

Now I sense all four of my matches are tense with fear as my mother stands nearby. Her hood of shadows is up, completely concealing her face as she looms over us in these eerie, blood-stained woods. Another scythe rests on her shoulder, almost a copy of the one she gifted me.

"You came," I finally manage.

Syntyche dips her concealed head, her voice as smooth and quiet as I remember. "Amusing as it is, I advise against including threats in your future prayers, spoken aloud or not."

She's the furthest thing from a warm presence, but I don't miss the way my quintet members all flinch away from her voice. Even Crypt looks like he's having great difficulty adjusting to her presence or looking directly at her.

Silas isn't even trying. He's frozen in place, crimson eyes wide as he pointedly looks in the opposite direction of the reaper goddess.

They're terrified of her.

I don't sense anything, but I've heard she's the goddess of fear. Maybe that affects them. But I'm too numb from the pain in my chest to try reassuring them. Instead, I look back at Syntyche.

"I need to say goodbye to Lillian."

"So you mentioned, in between all the threats."

I stare at the hooded figure. She makes no sound or movement.

"There must be something you can do," I finally insist, half afraid I might break down again if this plight doesn't work.

"There is. You just haven't asked."

What is it with the gods trying to get a *please* out of me? First Galene, now her?

"*Please,*" I grit, desperate enough to give in.

Syntyche considers for a moment in the dark silence before her hood dips forward again.

"I shall take you into the vestibule between the two lowest planes of existence. The vestibule is the halfway point where the spirits I reap await my brother to lead them to their respective afterlives. You may only be there briefly, for only a fully divine being can linger there without consequence."

"Consequence?" Crypt enunciates, finally looking at the hooded figure as he gets over the fear she emanates. "No. She stays."

Syntyche's hood turns toward him, distaste in her voice. *"No?"*

"She's not going anywhere without us," Everett clarifies, managing to look at my mother again. "Especially not if it's dangerous."

"She will likely return," the goddess muses.

That makes Silas frown, and he finally glances over his shoulder at the hooded figure, too.

Baelfire scowls. "What do you mean, *likely?* There's no fucking way we're about to risk—"

Syntyche throws her hood back, and for a fraction of a second, her face is a skeletal mask so disturbing that it makes all of us flinch away in surprise. Her face returns to normal immediately, like that was just a horrific warning. She looks down at my quintet with no expression at all, but there is menace in her voice.

"I will wipe all memories of you four from existence and watch your mortal corpses molder upon the steeples of my ruined temples if you dare question me again."

They all go pale from her threat that she delivers more expertly than any I've heard before. But that doesn't stop Baelfire from speaking through the bond.

Holy fuck, Mayflower. You look just like…

The resemblance… Everett starts to agree before trailing off in equal terrified fascination.

Silas has whipped around to face the other way again, holding perfectly still like he thinks that will help him avoid his mother-in-law's attention. Meanwhile, Crypt's jaw is clenched tightly as he glowers back at Syntyche. His markings are lighting up again, but he ignores it completely.

Don't go, darling, he whispers inside my head. *I can't follow you there. Don't do this to me again.*

My chest pangs even more. Leaving them alone in this plane of existence for even a moment will hurt, but…

I need to see her one more time. I swear on my beating heart that I'll be back.

He studies me for a moment before looking down at some of the bloodstains left behind despite Silas's quick work. Finally, he murmurs through the bond again. *Give Lillian my thanks.*

And mine, Everett adds. *She did more for me than she ever needed to.*

She deserves all our gratitude, Silas agrees, still not looking at my mother.

Baelfire squeezes my hand for comfort. *Give Lillian a big hug for me, get your goodbye with her, and then get back here before we lose our fucking minds again. Please.*

I nod and pull away from my quintet to face Syntyche. "Take me to the vestibule."

She moves gracefully, twisting her scythe as a hollow whistling sound fills the air. Softly glowing holy magic runes follow the path of her scythe as it swings in an arc, tearing through the fabric of this plane so that now I have a view into… nothing.

Pure white emptiness.

I analyze it, unsure what I'm looking at. When I glance over my shoulder to see how my quintet is reacting to this, I realize they're all in the exact positions they were a moment ago. They're not even breathing as time holds perfectly still.

"Once you return, I will release them from this suspension in time," Syntyche says, apparently done waiting for me as she steps into the vestibule of the Beyond. "As mortals, they cannot glimpse into the fringes of the Beyond without being irreversibly drawn to it. Come."

Ignoring whatever the hell my heart is doing, I step through the rip between planes of existence. As soon as I step into the empty white void, I feel…light. The crushing weight of Lillian's death lifts from my shoulders and chest as I walk after my mother.

I look around, noting how scentless and silent it is here. It's perfectly temperate as we walk across a white sand-like substance through all the nothingness.

"Is this what the Beyond looks like?"

"No. The vestibule allows spirits to review their past helps and harms done to others so they may better understand my brother's final verdict of their afterlife." She stops and motions at more nothingness with her scythe, glancing down at me with her pure black irises. "Your caretaker has been re-experiencing some of her most noble moments. Now she waits for you. I have a favor to discuss with my brother before I return."

She walks away without another word, leaving me to venture tentatively into what looks like more empty whiteness. But as I step forward, my surroundings change and transform.

Almost within the blink of an eye, I'm standing in my old hovel in the Nether again. It's where I spent so many lonely days and stayed up most nights listening to ghosts weep, whisper, and wail outside.

Sitting on the floor beside a makeshift fireplace is Lillian, carefully sketching out a chessboard with a piece of charcoal. She's so focused that she hasn't seen me yet, but emotions clog my throat so fast that I can't stop the small sound I make.

Gods, it's so nice to see her like this again. Alive and in one piece, she glances up and smiles brightly, both shocked and elated.

"Maven!" She stands and moves toward me, brushing charcoal off her hands before she stops in front of me. As always, she doesn't go for the hug without me initiating it.

And I do.

Of course, I do.

I don't care that my nerves clench when her arms wrap

around me so tightly. I don't fucking care about anything except for the fact that I get to hug Lillian one more time.

"I'm sorry," I choke. "I'm so fucking sorry."

Sorry that she died in fear. Sorry that I was the cause of it. Sorry for all the shit I've put her through.

Lillian pulls back, and I see tears in her bright blue eyes. She smiles. "No, little raven. No more blaming yourself. Nothing that happened was your fault."

"Gideon wouldn't have hurt you if he weren't trying to get to me. Amadeus would never have sent him if I—"

"Shh," she soothes before glancing at the makeshift board. "Is now a good time for that game you mentioned? Your mother told me you couldn't stay too long."

Glancing down, I see the same hand carved pieces she and I played with for years. The ones she gifted me for one of my "birthdays" so long ago.

Oh, my fucking gods.

I'm about to burst into tears just like Kenzie.

I manage to hold it together and nod my head. Lillian and I sit on the floor of the hovel just like we used to. Except, unlike old times, daylight filters in through the windows, illuminating this rickety old space as if this is now a happy place.

Silently, I arrange my side of the board, and she does the same. I make a move. She makes a move. I make another.

Finally, I can't take it anymore. I look at her. "Did it work?"

She tips her head, sending a pale corkscrew curl bouncing out of her braid. "Did what work?"

"You accepted Galene's mission in order to redeem yourself." I pause, looking over my shabby old hovel before examining her. "Will you get to see Annabel again?"

Lillian studies the chessboard, moving another piece. "I don't know yet. Sachar may decide I didn't do enough. My past may be more checkered than you realize."

I clench my teeth, looking down at the game. She's always

been good at chess, which is nice because it offers a small distraction as I have to think about my next move.

Moving one of my knights, I look at her again. "I'll make sure you get to her. I'll talk to Sachar."

"Maven."

"No," I huff, shaking my head. "After everything you've been through? It's absolute manticore shit if you don't get what Galene promised. That's it. No matter what it takes, I'm going to—"

"Enough!" Lillian snaps with enough surprising volume that I shut up. Her bright blue eyes are unyielding. "Everything *I've* been through? Maven Amato, it's time for you to start thinking about yourself. I made my choices, so whatever afterlife I'm assigned to, I have no regrets anymore. But I've watched you for years and years, and do you know what I saw?"

I move another piece after she makes a quick move. "A demigoddess with no fucking clue about her true nature?"

She shakes her head, huffing at me. "I saw a brilliant, fiercely determined girl who put others ahead of herself every time and never asked for anything in exchange. You didn't sit around feeling sorry for yourself, even on the worst days when it was killing me to see everything they put you through. You just took it on the chin and survived so that you could do the very thing you were chosen to do—even if you had no idea about that," she adds.

Implying I was chosen instead of specifically made to kill Amadeus is a nice thought.

Lillian moves one of her pieces again, and I frown when I realize she's a lot closer to checkmate than I thought.

"But mostly, I saw a girl who forgot that she deserves to be happy," she finally murmurs, looking at me again. "You were always so busy preparing for a tragic ending. You survived for others, but it's time you stopped putting everyone else first. It's time you live for *you*. I need you to promise me that you'll live and love and be happy without always putting others ahead of yourself, because you deserve that and so much more. *Promise.*"

I consider everything she's saying.

In my past life, I was a survivor. I made most of my choices based on necessity. The one time I really felt like I was taking matters into my own hands was when I decided to leverage my unique position as the *telum* to free the Nether humans.

Maybe that's why learning about my orchestrated existence bothered me so much. It felt like that choice was just another given—another thing I was simply made to do.

But now? Lillian is right.

I already survived the tragic fate I always anticipated. And even though I didn't stick the landing, I'm really fucking proud of the fact that the Nether humans are free. I already know what future happiness I'm fighting for—a lifetime with my quintet.

They will always be my priority, but besides that...I wouldn't mind being a little more selfish.

After all, a demigoddess bitch deserves a break now and then.

"I promise," I smile at her.

Lillian looks relieved before she knocks over one of my pieces. "Checkmate."

Damn it.

She laughs at my expression. When a strange bell begins to toll somewhere in the distance, Lillian stands, brushing more charcoal off her hands and beaming at me as I also get to my feet.

"That bell is mine. It means Sachar is ready for me. If you don't mind seeing me off..."

I nod and then pause, glancing down at the makeshift chessboard that was such a big part of my melancholy childhood. "Can you take things from the vestibule into the Beyond?"

"I'm not sure."

Worth a try anyway. I grab both queens from the chessboard, pocketing one and offering the other to her. "Something so you won't forget me in the Beyond," I mutter, feeling ridiculously sentimental.

Lillian laughs as we leave the hovel and walk back out into white nothingness.

"You're not very forgettable, Maven. But if I can take it with me, I'll treasure—"

"Mom!" a girl's voice shouts in the distance.

Lillian's eyes widen and fill with fresh tears as she whirls to face the direction from which we heard the voice. A moment later, the same curly-haired girl from the picture I saw on her nightstand skips into view, a big grin on her face.

She's walking beside a tall, looming cloaked figure that I assume is my mother. But when they stop not far from us, the figure removes its hood, and I realize I'm looking at my mother's twin brother.

Sachar.

The eternal judge of the Beyond has the same pitch black hair and eyes as my mother, as well as the same colorless skin and symmetrical, hard features. The only difference is his much shorter hair, his square jaw, and the fact that he doesn't carry a scythe. His gaze falls on me, and there's something incredibly *penetrating* about it, as if he sees everything about me all at once.

He says nothing as Lillian runs forward and scoops up Annabel, both of them weeping with joy. It's a touching sight, and I'm genuinely happy for her.

But at the same time, my heart throbs strangely inside my chest.

I'm going to miss her so fucking much.

"Bye," I whisper as Annabel pulls on Lillian's hand, dragging her further into the whiteness.

Lillian looks back and waves one more time, a bright smile on her teary face.

I wave back.

Annabel beams over her shoulder, shouts a thank you, and just like that, they vanish into the white haze of the distance.

The bell stops tolling.

Several quiet moments later, tears are still trying to escape my eyes. I quickly take a deep breath before looking back at Sachar.

"Okay, Uncle Judge. Take me back."

He shakes his head silently.

I tense, my words coming out sharp. "What the fuck do you mean, no? Syntyche said I could only be here briefly. It's time for me to go."

Sachar shakes his head again, but says nothing. His expression tells me nothing.

Shit. If he's saying I can't go back, my quintet is going to be so fucking pissed at me for leaving.

Am I about to have to fight the judge of the Beyond? I didn't grab Cuttrina from the forest floor after killing Gideon, but Pierce is stashed in one of my boots. My hand is already itching toward it as I wonder if adamantine hurts divine beings.

But before I can attack my uncle and figure out a way back to the mortal realm by myself, someone clears his throat behind me.

"He can't speak, Sweet Pea."

Sweet Pea?

Irritation prickles over me as I turn, ready to give my best death glare to this stranger who's trying to give me yet *another* flower-based nickname.

"Who the fuck are you calling—"

My words cut off as I realize exactly who I'm looking at. My heart begins to pound as an unfamiliar emotion sinks in.

Aside from his warm olive-toned skin and messy black hair, I don't look much like Pietro Amato. He's nice looking but not striking, aside from his smile and sparkling hazel eyes. He's dressed in a simple white button up, slacks, and shoes.

But his presence is a palpable thing. Even as a spirit, it's like he has his own gravitational pull. Warm and kind and strong and...fatherly. Which is extremely fucking strange, but not bad.

At least, it's not bad until his eyes tear up.

"My little miracle," he whispers, half laughing and half on the brink of crying. "Dear gods, look at you. So grown up and beautiful. The spitting image of your mother. Seeing you finally, I'm just so..."

I wait, carefully keeping my expression blank so that if he admits he's ashamed to have a daughter as messed up as I am, I can pretend it doesn't hurt.

Pietro Amato finally shakes his head, wiping moisture from one of his cheeks. "I'm so proud of you, it hurts. Getting to watch you grow and fight and become *you* from my place in the Beyond has been the greatest reward I could have possibly asked for."

Oh.

The lump in my throat makes it impossible to form the words I can't even find, so I nod a little too aggressively. This is such unfamiliar territory that I'm completely out of my depth, so I blurt the one thing I think is relevant.

"I wish I knew you while you were alive."

So much for not getting sappy.

Amato beams, reaching out as if to brush my hair back from my face, but his hand passes through me. "We'll have so much time together in your afterlife someday, you'll get sick of me. But for now, I'll happily share in all your happiest moments from here. All right?"

I nod again. I can't help the feeling that's settled over me. I don't know this man, yet in a way, I do. He spent his life taking care of others. Although he's clearly a purer soul than I ever was, I like to think that I at least inherited a fraction of his altruistic side.

Sachar pulls a strange pocket watch from one of his cloak pockets and tucks it away, looking meaningfully at Amato. My father nods and smiles at me again.

"I love you, Sweet Pea. I always have and I always will. I just have a favor to ask."

A favor? I hesitate. "Okay."

"Stop thinking you're tainting our last name. You don't have to go by Amato if you don't want to, but…I would be extremely honored if you did."

Godsdamn it, now I'm seriously struggling to keep the moisture from escaping my eyes. I clear my throat, nodding.

"All right. I have a favor, too."

"What is it?"

"Whenever I end up here one day, don't call me Sweet Pea. I'm not a fucking flower."

He laughs. He doesn't bother making me that promise before Sachar makes a strange sign with one of his hands, and they both vanish, leaving me alone in the white nothingness. After I've stared at literal nothing for a few moments, letting the fact that I just met my real father sink in, Syntyche again appears.

I'm still not sure if she walks or floats under that cloak, but her movements are so graceful that it has the same effect either way. She stops in front of me.

"It's time to return."

I study her. "That was the favor you asked Sachar for. You just wanted me to meet Amato."

"Yes."

"So do you feel like…*that* about him?" I check, too curious for my own good.

"That is the first foolish question you have ever asked me," the goddess of death informs me before swinging her scythe to rip an entry back into the mortal realm.

I see where I inherited my dislike for handing out personal information.

I step out of the vestibule between the lowest planes of existence and find myself in the exact same spot I started. My quintet is still frozen in place in this dark, foreboding forest, but *gods,* I'm so fucking relieved to be back at their side.

As soon as I step toward them and the rip behind Syntyche and I seals itself, all four of my matches unfreeze. They blink in confusion to see me facing them. Silas rotates slightly to keep my mother out of his peripheral vision.

Changed your mind? Baelfire frowns, checking through the bond.

No. I just got back.

Holy shit, that was a fast goodbye.

Her mother is the goddess of time, you fucking dolt, Crypt points out.

I feel a million times more at peace than the last time I was standing in the dark thrall of Everbound Forest. My chest still aches, knowing Lillian is in the Beyond and I won't see her again in this lifetime. I'm not sure how soon that ache will go away, but closure makes a big fucking difference.

I turn back to Syntyche. "Thank you."

She dips her head slightly. "I anticipate more polite prayers from you in the future. Or from your mortal matches. Some of their prayers have amused me."

When her dark gaze moves to Everett, he turns redder than I've ever seen him and covers his face.

What is she talking about? I ask only him.

Nothing. But feel free to reap my soul to make this moment end sooner.

The goddess of death smirks at his reaction. It's the first real expression she's worn in the presence of my quintet, and I don't miss that they all flinch away from her again. With that, my mother pulls her hood up and dissolves into shadows.

47

SILAS

In the three days that have passed since the wraiths attacked the cultist temple, my quintet and I have done everything we can to comfort our keeper. The trouble is, Maven refuses to linger on her loss.

She was careful not to shed a tear at Lillian's simple burial service the morning after the attack. Everett crafted an elegant nevermelt headstone for Lillian, which now sits beside Maven's in Everbound's largest greenhouse. The snowdrop flowers in there bloomed contentedly under Asher Douglas's common magic spell as our quintet, the Baird quintet, Douglas, and a few other Reformists paid respect to the kind-hearted human who raised my keeper.

Maven left a colorful box of Crayons and a photograph of a young girl at Lillian's honorary grave. She hasn't teared up in front of us or anyone else. Even when our keeper told us about her experience in the vestibule to the Beyond, she kept it brief and then moved on with her careful planning of how we will take down Amadeus.

She's a force of nature—but all four of us know she's still in mourning.

I sit on the edge of the bed, watching my blood blossom as

she sleeps deeply in Baelfire's arms. Dawn is lacing its way into the dark sky outside our quintet apartment's primary bedroom. It's changed to summertime temperatures over the last few days, so I can see the starts of blooming plants far below. The natural world is finally returning to normal after Everett's perpetual cold snap.

Unfortunately, the improved weather has only encouraged the campers outside to remain here. Even despite the recent wraith attack in the forest, the refugees, Nether humans, cultists, and others are undeterred. They believe their presence shows support for "Maven Oakley."

She's been too busy plotting and giving instructions to the Reformist leaders to spare the lingerers any notice. To say that we've been busy is an understatement, but my blood blossom still hasn't shared the entirety of her plan with us.

I watch as Maven finally grows overheated in Baelfire's extra warm embrace. The big lug is passed out so hard that he doesn't even stir when our fucking *adorable* half-asleep keeper detangles herself from his arms and scoots closer to Everett. The ice elemental instinctively pulls her against his bare, scarred chest. Cooled off at once, she relaxes back into rest.

I sense Crypt nearby a moment before he materializes beside me. He wordlessly hands me an empty syringe—one of several I've spent the last couple of days tinkering with in an attempt to find a *reverium* concoction to allay his curse.

"Well?" I check, keeping my voice low so as not to wake Maven.

He answers by removing his leather jacket and holding out one of his arms. The swirling light and dark markings on it light up in an angry pattern. But then again, very few markings remain at all.

Godsdamn it.

Shelving that frustration for later, I glance back at our keeper and focus on the much bigger issue we've all been contemplating for the last few days.

"Within her subconscious, have you seen anything yet of the blood oath she made to Arati?"

He shakes his head, his violet gaze serious as he slips back into the ripped leather. "I've seen far too much of her bleeding golden ichor in Paradise, but nothing about that fucking oath."

Baelfire rolls over to squint at Crypt. I'm not surprised our lowered voices woke up the shifter with his keen hearing.

"Wait. Why the hell was she bleeding so much?" he asks, his voice quiet and groggy.

The Nightmare Prince is thoughtful. "The *why* is still a missing puzzle piece, much like her mysterious, soul-binding oath. Right, love?"

I thought she was still asleep, but Maven sits up and yawns. I don't bother trying to hide my sigh when she pulls the sheets up to cover her delicious nakedness—a reminder of the heated adoration we lavished her with most of the night. Instead of addressing the topic at hand, my ever-unexpected, beautiful keeper instead glances at the window.

"The demons will arrive this morning," she says as if she's announcing she likes cheese.

Everett is immediately awake, bolting upright to frown sleepily at her. The elemental is always testy, but especially first thing in the morning. "What?"

"I needed them to supply the final part of the plan."

Ah, yes. Her plan.

Much of yesterday was spent watching Maven go over attack strategies with the other Reformist leaders. Many troops not fully utilized elsewhere on the front lines have mobilized outside of Halfton as we prepare for the attack. Aside from the mass attack strategy, all I've gathered of Maven's plan so far is that she intends to use ghosts to boost our numbers.

I intend to do the same with Undead.

After all, as a necromancer, why shouldn't I take advantage of the dark arts for our benefit? For the last three days, I scouted out countless places of death around Everbound as I've prepared to raise a large number of reanimated beings. Others may object, but I know my blood blossom will understand the practicality of such measures, once I tell her.

Better to tell her now, since the attack is planned to take place in mere days.

"About this plan—" I begin.

"He's right, we absolutely can't rely on demons," Everett huffs, getting out of bed to search for those foolish silk pajamas on the floor.

I frown. "That's not what I was—"

"Hold up, what exactly are those demonic fuckers supplying?" Baelfire asks Maven, confused.

My blood blossom gets out of bed, too. I forget whatever I was about to say as she stretches slightly, showing off her beautifully strong, nude body. Crypt hums in approval beside me, and Baelfire sits up to see her better. Everett looks like he's forgotten that he was searching for clothes as he stares at her.

"Information and changelings," she answers.

When Maven brushes her dark hair out of her face, my attention drifts to her mouthwatering neck as I—

Wait.

"Changelings?" I repeat, certain I heard her incorrectly.

Maven nods and tells us the rest of her plan in brief, simplified terms. When she's finished, we all gawk at her, and not just because every move she makes is so enchanting as she begins searching through the discarded clothing that we practically ripped off of her last night.

It's a damn good plan.

"So that's why you opted to spare the changeling the cultists captured," I realize.

"Will that even work on changelings?" Baelfire asks, fascinated.

"We'll find out today," she says, searching in her discarded hoodie. "If not, I've thought of several ways to bribe them, if they choose to cooperate instead. That wouldn't be a surprise, since like most creatures in the Nether, they hate Amadeus so much that—"

She cuts off as she grips Cuttrina within her hoodie. As soon as Everett realizes she's in another memory trance, he scoops her up and sits on the edge of the bed to hold her. As we wait for her to come to, Crypt chuckles despite his glowing markings.

"An army of Mavens to confuse the Entity's visions of the battle. What a clever goddess we have."

"She's flawlessly vicious," I agree.

"As long as you don't fuck up making the heart and getting it into Amadeus's chest, I think this might actually work," Baelfire grins.

Everett studies Maven's face as she gazes out at nothing, recalling something from Paradise. "Her plan is great, except it separates some of us from her during the beginning of the battle."

"Amadeus would expect her to remain close to her quintet members," I point out. "She's right to pair us up with changelings until enough chaos has been sewn to further throw off his tactics."

"And only one of us is actually with her, because only one of us can fuck around in Limbo undetected," Baelfire grumbles, glaring at Crypt. "Lucky fucking bastard."

The incubus surprises us all by slumping to the bed and grimacing in pain as his markings light up more. "How lucky can a dying man be?"

We're all quiet at that.

Finally, Maven blinks and looks around, disoriented to find herself in Everett's arms.

"Anything about that blood oath you made?" Everett asks, voice tight with tension.

"No. That was just a memory of the time I showed up naked to ruin one of Arati's fancy formal dinners so she would be pissed off enough to kick me out of Paradise," she sighs, as frustrated as the rest of us about her unknown oath.

"You what?" Baelfire coughs.

"It's fine. She got over it eventually," our keeper mutters, getting out of Everett's arms to make her way toward the bathroom. She smirks at us over one bare shoulder. "Get dressed. I don't want Eisha drooling over what's mine any more than she has in the past."

Everett scowls at our keeper's use of the demon's name before the bathroom door closes behind her. The rest of us get ready quickly. Fifteen minutes later, our quintet makes its way through Everbound Castle toward the eastern exit. No matter how useful they are, there's no way in hell we're about to give the demons access inside the protective wards.

I almost walk right through the blue-haired ghost when she pops up from the ground. Stepping around the dead tribute, I notice even more ghosts have accumulated to haunt this castle as they await whatever my blood blossom has in mind for them.

Remember, Maven reminds us through the bond as we approach the arched doorway. *We want to try diplomacy with the changelings before resorting to anything extreme. They're unfeeling creatures that will swap loyalties in an instant if we offer something they really want. Mortal money, safety, shit like that.*

We nod, and Baelfire pushes open the big eastern door, leaving us all blinking at…a pile of dead changelings.

"There she is!" Eisha booms, gesturing happily at the pile of dead creatures as the demons around her applaud. "We come bearing gifts!"

"So much for diplomacy," Everett scoffs quietly, stepping slightly in front of Maven as if to keep her out of these infernal beings' sight.

As always, being in the presence of demons is unpleasant. There are almost a dozen here with Eisha and that simpering demon boyfriend of hers—the one Crypt is glowering at like he still wants to rip the demon's horns off. The other demons have apparently foregone the effort to blend in with humans since the Upheaval, and now their horns, tails, pointed teeth, and inky black eyes are on full display as they stare at Maven with fascination.

The one good thing about their presence is that it has driven back all of the other campers on this side of Everbound Castle. Only a few of them linger nearby, watching this interaction.

One of the male demons standing near Eisha lifts his chin. His nostrils flare before his eyes widen. "Oh, *fuck me.* Who knew a bloody demigoddess would smell so damned delicious? Wanna lick her all over and take a bite right outta that pretty, holy hide," he groans.

Maven's composure remains intact, but anger and disgust send magic surging to my blackened fingertips.

Before I can punish the demon for speaking that way about my keeper, Everett lifts his hand and impales the demon on a massive spike of ice jutting from the ground. The other demons shriek and leap away, looking far less worried about their writhing, dying comrade than they are about their own safety.

"Mind your forked tongues when speaking to or about my keeper, or you'll get worse," he warns, glaring at the infernal gathering.

Eisha's boyfriend—Melchom, I believe—takes a good look at the elemental and bursts into laughter. "Well, peg me with a pitchfork and call me a kebab! Looks like all those rumors about the scarred pretty boy are true. I heard you froze a bunch of deserters from the waist down on the front lines so your troops could hear what cowards sound like when they're getting devoured by shadow fiends. I bet the screaming was fucking fantastic—almost makes me wish I was there to see those cowardly fuckers humiliated before their upper halves were gobbled up."

Maven glances curiously at Everett, as do I and the rest of my quintet, because that punishment is surprisingly impressive. He continues to glower at the demons but responds to our stares through the bond.

They weren't just deserters. They were legacies who sat back and watched dozens of humans in their troop get slaughtered in a surge at the front lines. When I asked how they all survived when the humans didn't, they made jokes about how weak humans are in comparison to 'our kind.' I had enough shit to handle without adding politically prejudiced assholes to the mix, so I made an example out of them.

Good, Maven nods.

Eisha scoffs and looks at Melchom, unaware of my quintet's telepathic communication. "I kinda wish you were there, too—you could've joined the wimps and only the half of you I like would be preserved in ice."

"Loose-ass bitch," the demon scowls at her.

"Cuntfaced, microdicked manwhore," she shoots back before shoving him out of the way.

All this flirting is making me sick, Maven huffs through the bond.

Bael frowns. *Um...are we hearing the same things, Boo? They fucking hate each other's guts.*

Demons flirt through insults. It's a turn-on for them.

Baelfire does a double-take at the demons, obviously seeing their past interactions in a new light. I didn't know that about demons, either, but that does explain why Melchom is not so subtly adjusting himself as he checks out his girlfriend's ass.

The demoness focuses on Maven again, grinning with sharp teeth. "So! What d'you think of the haul? Took a couple of days to hunt down all these little fuckheads, but sure as sin, there should be a dozen or so here for you."

Maven glances at the pile of dead changelings. "I said to bring them alive."

"Did you? Damn! That communication spell you sent to us was fucking hard to hear through clearly," Eisha sighs. "Oh, well. I'll send these idiots to go round up some more."

"Don't," my keeper decides, glancing at me briefly to say we're moving on to her more extreme yet reliable version of the plan. "We'll make it work."

Eisha notices Maven's glance at me, and her black eyes widen before she bursts into laughter. "Fucking hell, I forgot how ballsy you are! I got the feeling you'd pop back into the mortal world, *telum*. It's not like that mother of yours would've really taken you to the Beyond, even if she is the crypt keeper."

Actually, I'm the Crypt keeper, Maven corrects smoothly through the bond, glancing back at the Nightmare Prince.

Crypt grins. *That you are, love. Well played.*

Baelfire laughs at her wordplay, drawing confused looks from some of the demons as Everett shakes his head, also smiling.

Maven looks back at Eisha. "Now for the information."

The demoness grimaces, stepping away from the other demons to lower her voice so this is a more private conversation. "Right, that. I managed to get Mel's twin cousins to squeal, but even they don't know much shit about that vamp."

"A vampire?" I frown, looking at Maven. "What vampire?"

Bertram, Everett realizes through the bond. *He's the one who killed Engela. My parents were using him to communicate with the Entity before he disappeared.*

Baelfire growls. "Then Bertram's the jackass we're going to burn to a fucking crisp."

"Cool your jets, dragon boy," Eisha chuckles, reaching up to scratch near one of her horns. "That vamp's a real sticky one. From what I've gathered, he's popped in and out of the mortal realm for centuries, doing the Entity's bidding or just stirring up shit. He's crazy good with hypnotism—almost undetectable. Rumor is, he even got inside Zuma's head a long time ago."

Maven considers that. "If he could hypnotize a member of the Immortal Quintet, he would have had no trouble hypnotizing someone in the Sanctuary to let himself and Engela out of it."

The idea of a vampire's abilities being strong enough to overcome the significant protective charms that most of my old mentor's acolytes wear is concerning.

"Where exactly is this vampire now?" Crypt demands,

vengeance written all over his features as his remaining markings light up.

Eisha shrugs. "Couldn't track him. My guess is somewhere back in that fucking citadel, but who knows? Anyway, your demigoddess said the changelings were the bigger priority." She kicks one of the corpses aside. "Hope these fuckheads help, but we're gonna bounce before any Reformists attack us. And you know, Mav—"

"Don't say my name," my keeper warns, her expression enough to make several demons move further away.

I adore how frightening she is when she chooses to be.

It's also wise of her to keep any of these infernal beings from saying her name in her presence. From my studies of banned demonology spellbooks within the Garnet Wizard's library long ago, I found that demonology relies heavily on namesaying. Quite a few of their spells begin with a name and end with soul scrying, claiming an eternal debt, striking an infernal deal, or worse.

Even if these demons support Maven, it's best not to trust them.

Eisha snorts. "Right, well—*Syntyche's daughter,* then. Maybe if you survive whatever shitshow comes next, you ought to consider putting an end to all the demon hunting that goes on in the mortal realm. We may not mix well with humans, and maybe we have different hobbies—"

"Morals don't exist to demons. You also enjoy cheating, stealing, and watching the innocent suffer," Maven clarifies.

"Like I said, different hobbies. Doesn't mean we need to be exterminated," the demoness shrugs before she looks at the other demons. "Hey. We did what we came here to do. Get a move on. You too, you pathetic little fucknugget," she adds, flipping off her demonic boyfriend.

Melchom says something back to her in the Nether tongue that I can't quite translate, but it's insulting enough that the demoness grins. The other demons amble away from the side of the castle. Eisha says farewell to Maven before following them, clearly enjoying the disgusted and disturbed looks they're earning from the other onlookers.

My keeper's attention moves to the dead changelings. "How disturbed do you think Asher Douglas will be if we ask him to move the bodies to the dungeon?"

"Extremely," I decide.

She smiles. "Excellent."

48

MAVEN

I BITE BACK a sound of pleasure when Silas grows rougher, pinning me to the wall of the dungeon as he moans and feeds from me. His stiff erection grinds hard against me as he pulls deeply from my neck again.

This is the least I can offer him, after he's spent hours resurrecting the changelings.

Not to mention, if blood loss didn't make me so lightheaded, I would ask him to feed from me all the time. The rush of his fangs sinking into my neck, the sting of pain and pleasure coursing through my veins—hearing his hungry groans as he becomes more desperate for my blood…

It's everything a girl could ask for.

"That's enough," Everett mutters from his chair.

We set up a makeshift study table in this section of the dungeons so the rest of my quintet could study the intricate red-crayon map I drew on the back of my list. Crypt is still studying it, but Everett is wearing his reading glasses as he glowers at how aggressive Silas has become while feeding from me.

Baelfire finishes locking yet another reanimated Maven look-alike inside one of the many cells. A few muttering ghosts mull around this dungeon, curiously watching our macabre process.

Silas swallows one last time before he releases my neck, shuddering as he licks away the remaining traces of blood.

"Godsdamn me, I can never get enough of your divine taste," he groans.

Grinning, I lace my fingers through his black curls to move his head so I can kiss him. I don't care that when his tongue sweeps against mine, it tastes coppery like my blood. He grinds against me again, his bloodied lips curling into a smile against mine.

"Feeling better?" I ask breathlessly.

"Than comper nas leathu," he murmurs, also trying to catch his breath. *"Tha galeath."*

Which is fae for, *I'm always better with you. I love you.*

I peer at him, growing serious. *"Tha galeath.* But I'm not sure how much help I'll be when crafting the heart."

"I can manage, *sangfluir,"* he promises, brushing my hair off my face with blackened fingertips.

His crimson gaze is so deep I could swim in it, but we're interrupted when Asher Douglas once again enters the dungeon. He glances at the table where Baelfire has now joined the others memorizing the map of the Nether, but when he sees Silas lick another streak of blood off my neck, he gags.

"Gross. Get a fucking room."

"I bought out the assets of the Legacy Council after they fled, so I own every room in this castle," Everett reminds him, making a mark on the map.

Douglas grunts unhappily before glancing at me again, his green eyes lighting up briefly as his unique ability must pick up on someone else's magic in the distance.

"Are there ghosts down here, too?" he checks.

"They follow me," I explain, grinning when the blue-haired ghost pantomimes smacking his ass.

The mercenary makes a face at all the Undead changeling Mavens in a cell before he turns to leave. "That lioness shifter wants to see you about where she'll be during the attack."

I had planned on the Baird quintet being in charge of this safe haven during the attack, but if Kenzie doesn't like being away from the action, I can think of a few places I could put her quintet. Nodding, I slip out of Silas's arms despite his sigh and move to leave the dungeons. As I do, I hear Baelfire mutter something to Crypt, who promptly drops into Limbo to follow me just in case.

At the top of the steep stone steps descending into the dungeon, I find Kenzie and Luka. She's pacing and looks frustrated while he folds his arms stubbornly. Unsure if they're annoyed with each other or me, I smile at Kenzie.

"There's the sexiest pregnant lady I know."

She lights up, preening. "Aww, shucks. Watch out, monk, or I'll try to add you to my quintet."

Luka grimaces. "Don't even joke about that."

Kenzie swats his arm before turning to me seriously. "I want to help with the attack. *Really* help. And I get that keeping an eye on this safe haven is really important and if anyone needs to retreat here, we're in charge of getting them healed and stuff—but I'm just so fucking worried about how this attack will go. We're outnumbered, May. *Really* outnumbered. We don't even know how many shadow fiends there are, but Reformist numbers have just been going down ever since the Upheaval started, so if even just one or two more people could help, I can—"

"She *can't* be in the battle," Luka cuts in, looking at me.

"Kenzie can handle herself," I point out coldly, disliking the idea of him underestimating her.

"No shit," the vampire huffs. "But she's not supposed to shift while she's pregnant. It's too fucking dangerous."

I've never even considered if shifting while pregnant was a thing, but Kenzie sighs. "It's highly discouraged, but I'm still not that far along. They say the second trimester is when it's a big no."

Luka shakes his head. "It's a big no already. I'm not risking you or the baby, Kenz. I'm just not."

When Kenzie looks torn and frustrated, I clear my throat. "Numbers won't be a problem. We have backup."

"From where?" Luka frowns.

I glance behind them at the hallway full of ghosts and think about all the corpses Silas is about to reanimate all around Everbound. With how many legacies have died while training at Everbound University, I'm more than willing to bet we'll have plenty of Undead soldiers to spare. Not to mention, ravens have been flocking to Everbound like they're aware I'm going to need them.

"The restless dead," I finally reply, looking at the other two living people in this hallway.

Kenzie's eyes get round. "Oh, shit. Are you about to pull some kind of demigoddess trick? Gods, that makes me feel so much better. I know people have rallied here for you, and I totally trust your plan—I was just getting worried. But if you think we've got it..."

"We do," I nod, more determined than ever.

With Kenzie's concerns eased, she reminds me to say goodbye to her before the actual attack, and then she and Luka leave. For a moment, I watch the ghosts wandering these halls in anticipation. With the ghosts and Undead, the Reformists and others who have gathered here to help, and the reanimated changelings…

It will be a brutal battle, but it all comes down to ending Amadeus.

Before, I would have settled for him merely falling from power. So long as he was no longer a risk to my quintet, I would have let him fade into obscurity peacefully.

But Amadeus sent me a warning through that first changeling. I didn't listen, so he took away Lillian.

Now, I don't just want him out of power. I want him gone. After taking away a light like Lillian's from this world, he deserves whatever will happen to him in the Beyond. And in order for us to kill him, he needs to be mortal again. Based on what I learned from Galene, Amadeus also has no heart. He has nothing but corrupted magic keeping him alive—but if I put a heart back inside his chest, I'll be giving him the very weakness I couldn't identify in him before.

And once Amadeus is dead…

Godsdamn it, I really fucking hope that whatever blood oath I made doesn't ruin the happily ever after I'm working so hard to have with my quintet.

Turning to walk back down the stairs to the dungeon, I absentmindedly check to make sure Pierce is in its place in one of my sleeves. Cuttrina is hidden near my waist—but the moment I touch my etherium blade, a new memory washes over me, dragging me back to my time in Paradise.

Arati and I are standing on a golden balcony high in the air overlooking stunning views. There is a beautiful white-and-gold city far below, filled with winged angels and nature spirits and countless other Paridisians going about their divine days. A multicolored mountain blooming with flowers and plants I can't identify rises far in the distance. Constellations still dance in the sky above. An idyllic forest rustles with a soft breeze far below to our right. Just beyond that, a lake shimmering like millions of liquefied stars sparkles in the sunlight.

I realize that I'm cupping my hand in this memory as more golden blood—no, *ichor*—drips from my palm.

"Here," Arati says, offering me a bandage she seems to have summoned from nowhere.

I wrap my hand and notice she's doing the same to one of hers. This must be right after our blood oath to one another. As much as I don't recall what I swore to do, I also don't remember what the queen of the gods swore to me in return.

My aunt sighs, looking out over Paradise once again. "Very

well. Now that the deed is done, I will tell you how a Paridisical being once gave up his divinity and descended to the mortal realm. I will warn you, he barely survived."

Ignoring her warning, I prompt, "He?"

Arati nods, looking lost in a memory from eons ago. "Yes. You see, after being driven from the Nether, the fae have worked to uphold their culture and remember their past, but there are things even they have forgotten…such as the story of their fifth queen. The world was still young when she came to be, but even I can recall how beautiful and fiercely protective of her people she was. All of us gods favored her—of course, at the time, our pantheon was different," she adds, shrugging. "A lot changes over the millennia. Only my sister and brother and I seem to stay the same."

The queen of the gods sighs and settles into a seat I previously didn't notice on this balcony. I sit in another chair, watching the constellations twirl and shift above us as I listen.

"So favored was she that we gods decided to give her gifts from Paradise to bless the fae people with. We sent an angel down to deliver the gifts. He fell for her at once, and before I knew it, he came to my palace to beg me to turn him mortal so he could live one lifetime at her side. I had never heard such a thing—giving up an eternity of perfection here for the never-ending difficulties down there," Arati adds, shaking her head in amusement. "But he was determined. I told him it was outside my power, but if fate itself agreed that he should become mortal, it would provide a way."

"And it did," Memory Me points out, impatient. "So what did he do?"

Arati looks at the mountain in the distance. "In Paradise, there is a flower called the corruinum that is so toxic, it is said to poison one's very soul. It grows at the foot of the mountain. The angel took one seed of that flower and watered it every day with his blood for months until it fully bloomed, and then he turned that poisonous bloom into tea. Drinking it weakened him enough that he could fall to mortality—and I do mean fall, for nothing mortal can remain in Paradise," she adds.

So he became mortal through…a blood blossom.

No wonder that term is still ingrained in the fae vocabulary. It almost makes Memory Me smile, remembering Silas calling me that—but at the same time, I ache. I've watched my matches through ravens in the mortal realm, so I know just how much he's suffering even as I'm sitting here talking to Arati.

"What happened to the angel?" I ask.

My aunt, the goddess of love, looks pleased as she explains that the angel barely survived his fall to the mortal realm and lost his wings in the process, but the fae queen found him and nursed him back to health. They quickly became obsessed with each other and had many, many children together. They were two of the most honored rulers to reign over the Nether, long before it fell to Amadeus's corruption.

When she's done with the tale, I stand.

"Where are you going, niece?" Arati asks, arching a brow.

"I have a seed to hunt down before I talk to your lover, because I don't have months," I tell her, turning to walk away.

"Koa's magic cannot speed up the process," she calls after me. "That bloom must be watered with your ichor until it matures. Magically growing the bloom will merely sprout another corruinum like the rest."

Memory Me swears vehemently in this recollection, but everything shifts and changes around me as I'm swept into a new memory. In this one, I once again sit at the edge of Paradise looking out over a sea of clouds. I'm holding my bleeding hand over a tiny green sprout that's barely visible above the dirt.

Each drop of ichor slowly soaks into the ground around the start of the flower, but Memory Me isn't focused on the flower. Her attention is on a winged silhouette far below Paradise, circling round and round beneath the very place I sit.

Oh, my gods.

It's Baelfire's dragon.

It was drawn to me even in Paradise, with no way to reach me.

A tall shadow appears next to me in this memory, and I glance up to see Syntyche hold out a scythe—Cuttrina.

"The memory-yielding scythe you requested. Consider this a reward for being far less annoying than most offspring I have witnessed," she says with no expression.

"Don't get sappy on me," I tease as I stand to take the wickedly sharp etherium weapon.

My mother's attention moves to the small sprout. "Falling from Paradise will be a pain unlike any you have experienced."

"How do you know?"

She looks out over the sea of clouds. "Years ago, I asked my brother to venture into the Beyond and ask the fallen angel about it. Even in his peaceful afterlife, the angel shuddered to recall that pain."

I stare at her, slowly putting it together. If she went far enough to find out from someone in the Beyond about this process…

"Oh my fucking gods. You were considering falling from Paradise to live a mortal life with Pietro Amato," I realize aloud, gawking at her.

Syntyche says nothing for a long time before she pulls her hood back up, preparing to go down and reap more souls. "In all possible attempts, Galene only foresaw my demise, for fate knows my path is one of immortal reaping. You carry more humanity within you, so perhaps your outcome will be more favorable."

"Darling?" Crypt's voice checks softly as I jolt back to the present.

As the memories fade, I realize I'm still standing on the stairs leading down into the dungeon. My incubus is standing on the step below me, pulling me close as he studies me as obsessively as ever. His scent, like sweet *reverium* and leather, is comforting.

"Remembering more of your attempts to piss off the gods?" the Nightmare Prince asks, grinning.

"Something like that," I manage.

Maybe later, I'll tell them that I essentially poisoned myself with my own ichor to fall from the heavens. But that's not important. The point is, I survived and now all I have to do is end Amadeus and figure out what the hell I swore to do—and then we have our entire future in front of us.

But as if the universe wants to mock me, Crypt tries not to grimace as his markings light up yet again. He's kept his leather jacket on all day to keep me from seeing more of his markings slowly vanishing.

I saw them last night, though. So many of them are gone.

My pounding heart aches. Maybe I don't have a future with him.

"Tell me why your markings are fading," I demand.

"My love, now is not the time to—"

"Tell me."

Crypt studies my eyes before looking away. "Historically speaking, only one incubus at a time can bear the markings of the gods. As their stewardship draws to a close, the steward is freed of their holy marks just before the next incubus is born into the curse."

That's a delicate way to put it very bluntly.

My Nightmare Prince is losing his marks because he's dying faster than I realized.

And the fucking curse doing this to him can't be broken.

My stomach churns so suddenly and angrily that I try to get out of Crypt's arms. He tightens them with a sigh. "Be angry at me, darling, but allow me to hold you. Or if my touch bothers you—"

"I'm going to be sick," I warn him, gagging.

He quickly releases me before I turn and vomit on the stairs.

It takes a moment before I can straighten again, wiping my mouth and swallowing down the remaining visceral reaction to the thought of one of my matches dying.

I refuse. I won't let it happen.

Somehow, there *has* to be a way to fix this. I'll find it.

Crypt pulls me back into his arms immediately, holding me so tightly I feel like it could almost put me back together as he murmurs against my ear. "I'm sorry for being such a gods-damned fool and speeding up this cursed process. You've no idea how sorry I am. How can I help you forgive me?"

"I won't," I finally manage, pulling away to glare up at his beautiful violet eyes. "I already lost Lillian. I can't do this. If I lose you, I'm never going to fucking forgive you for leaving me. Understand?"

They're angry words. I probably don't mean them all.

He nods anyway, gently cradling my face and looking more serious than I've ever seen him. "I understand."

"No, you—that's not—" I huff, so frustrated I can't even put it into words.

My incubus exhales, brushing a light kiss on my forehead. "I need this, darling. Every shade of your anger, your bliss, even your terror. Every fragment of you. I want everything I can get with you, so I ask that when I do give up the ghost—"

"Stop," I snap, wiping at my face because why the fuck is there moisture on my cheeks?

Crypt presses on anyway, his whisper bordering on desperate. "My darling, I only ask that you hold back from reaping whatever I have for a soul, when the time comes. Whatever I'll be after this, I'll belong to you just the same. Keep what's left of me in a bottle, if you like. Let my wretched soul haunt you and hate me if that's easier, but please just *keep me*."

If I could be sick again, I would. The idea of Crypt being one of the many ghosts that follow me everywhere is too much.

But at the same time, I already know I will never be able to let any of my quintet go. If anything happens to us in this battle, they're still *mine*. They'll have no choice except to haunt me until the day I pass on—and if my mother tries to reap them, so fucking help me, I will fight her myself.

Taking a deep breath, I nod. It's all I can seem to do.

Crypt smiles sadly, resting his forehead against mine. "What a brave muse I have."

I can't stand feeling all these feelings, so just like I used to do when I was young, I lock them in a box inside my chest.

There's a way for us all to survive this. I just have to find it.

49

CRYPT

"Boo, tell Professor Popsicle that I need a turn," Decimus huffs.

Ignoring the crippling pain in my joints and spine, I smoke *reverium* and watch Decimus and Frost say goodbye to Maven before dawn. The sky above is dark and starless above this courtyard where the greenhouse sits in peaceful silence.

Frost holds Maven even tighter, breathing out slowly as he tries to get a hold of himself. "Just another second. I just…I can't yet."

If it were Crane or myself hogging our keeper before this battle of all battles, I imagine Decimus would have already set us ablaze from sheer impatience. But Crane already said his goodbyes before he left with a group of Reformists to direct his Undead army—and the last time we were all in a battle together, Frost faced the brutal final moments with our dying keeper all on his own. We have a silent understanding that he gets a pass this time.

"We'll meet up in the citadel," Maven reminds the elemental, rubbing his back as his erratic breathing only worsens.

Our quintet will be separating at the beginning of the battle. I don't envy the others the fact that they'll set off with resurrected changelings that Crane ordered to imitate our keeper. Decimus is moving in at a northern angle with the Decimus family. Crane and his Undead army, along with all the ghosts Maven has summoned into this mortal realm, will move in from the south. All other Reformist troops have their orders to move in following the strategy Maven finalized with Brigid Decimus.

Maven and I will be passing through Limbo directly into the citadel. My obsession is dressed in simple black combat clothes, but the fact that they hug her delectable body has me constantly distracted.

I myself wear combat attire for once, but I also carry a simple, secured pouch. Within it is the jar that used to hold Maven's heart. Now, it contains a dark, humming shadow heart. Crane spent hours crafting it yesterday before passing out from pure exhaustion.

Our mission is to get it inside Amadeus before killing him. I've overheard my darling obsession and Crane discussing the logistics at length over the last few days enough to know that unlike Maven's shadow heart that constantly revived her, this one is a temporary spell. A mere tool to give the immortal Entity a weakness.

"Okay, we have to change the plan," Frost finally announces, still holding onto Maven as if he expects her to drift away any moment. "Crypt, you take a changeling. I can't do this."

Maven pulls away to look at him, and it's obvious they're having a telepathic exchange without the rest of us. I always dislike being on the outside of a conversation my muse is involved in, but finally, Frost takes a deep, grounding breath and releases her.

"Finally," Decimus mutters, sweeping her into a tight hug next. "Gods, I'm going to be so fucking distracted worrying about you, Boo."

"No distractions," Maven corrects, kissing his cheek. "Remember the plan. We'll check in with each other telepathically as much as we can."

As if to underline her point, Crane's voice echoes through the bond.

Your Undead army is officially on the move, ima thanafluir.

"That's our cue, love," I say, stepping on my cigarette to put it out as I reach for her.

"Wait," Decimus protests. He inhales against her neck and kisses the mating mark he left there. "Just another minute."

"Fucking hypocrite," Frost grumbles.

Finally, Maven pulls away from her dragon shifter and steps toward me, slipping her gloved hand into mine. "All right. Let's go kill the king of the Undead."

It hurts like fucking hell to slip into Limbo this time around, but I don't let it show. Maven doesn't bother closing her eyes this time as I guide her swiftly through the shattered, distorted realm of dreams. I suppose now it makes sense that my darling was never affected by Limbo—after all, her mother is the goddess of dreams, whom all incubi tend to worship the most.

Not me, obviously. But then, my mother-in-law clearly isn't keen on me, either.

Tell me you're still okay, Frost demands through the bond not twenty minutes into our travel, which is greatly expedited through Limbo.

Why, I'm right as rain, but thanks ever so much for your concern, my snow-white dove, I reply saccharinely.

I can hear Decimus laughing through the bond because he appreciates humor, and Maven is smirking, but Frost just swears at me.

Maven?

I'm fine, she promises him. *We're almost to the citadel.*

Decimus is surprised. *Damn, that was fast. Flying through Limbo must be so fucking convenient.*

You're a godsdamned dragon, Crane reminds him. *You can fly, too.*

Sure, as a twenty-five-ton gleaming golden monster. Not super convenient when it comes to landing, believe it or not. Are you still alive, Boo?

For now.

She probably means that to be funny, but the rest of my quintet doesn't like that reply at all. They remind her about context and "too soon" through the bond until we pass into the depths of the Nether. Here, Limbo is even more of a hazy mess that smells strongly of ozone as it seeps into this other, dimmer plane of existence. A few dim wisps float in the distance in every direction as my ragged dream world drifts more like a mist here.

Maven notices the difference and glances at me. "Limbo is different past the borders of the Nether."

I nod, admiring the subtle cacophony of colors in her dark gaze. My markings light up again, and I try to keep the pain out of my voice.

"The domain of dreams only started seeping into the Nether over the last few months, when I let it fragment. Limbo mostly overlaps the mortal realm, but in areas like this where it stretches past the Divide, it gets far weaker and more difficult to traverse," I explain.

Her brow furrows. "If it's hurting you—"

"Even if it were, I have you to kiss it all better," I remind her, kissing her temple.

Wrapping my arm more securely around the most important person in my existence, I kick off the ground so we float quickly through what I assume are misshapen, ancient trees. According to the map Maven made, this is the twisted forest surrounding the outskirts of Amadeus's arena and citadel. From her dreams, I know she grew up isolated in a small, austere hovel in a clearing near these woods. Only Lillian was permitted to visit the warded hovel so she could take care of Amadeus's favored mortal child.

I'm certain those very memories are on Maven's mind as she also studies the vague shapes of this forest through the foggy, deformed view of Limbo. The map she outlined mentioned all kinds of deadly things here. Bloodthirsty creatures. Poisonous bogs. Monster lairs.

Knowing she grew up in constant peril makes the aches in my dying bones even worse.

Maven? Crane's voice checks in.

Still fine.

You don't sound fine, Frost scowls. *What's wrong?*

I know Amadeus's kingdom the same way I know the exact weight and feel of Pierce in my hand, she muses through the bond, her arms circling around me more tightly. *It's just strange to be back.*

Are you at the citadel now? Decimus asks.

We break out of the murky woods. All at once, I find that we're gazing through the distortions of Limbo at an imposing wall and gates made of onyx. Several large adamantine spikes protrude from the ground surrounding the walls of the citadel, and hanging from them are disemboweled monsters rotting in the grayscale Nether. Beyond the gates, a massive temple-like structure rises over the inner ward of the Entity's lifeless kingdom.

Now we are, Maven confirms, before taking a deep breath. *Okay. After we get through this, I want ice cream.*

I'll buy you all the ice cream in the entire godsdamned world as long as you get back to me in one piece, Frost promises.

And I want more orgasms, she adds.

"It would be my pleasure," I grin.

Decimus groans through the bond. *Since I give you way more orgasms than the others combined, leave it to me, Mayflower.*

None of us fault your lizard brain for your inability to count, but I'm clearly in the lead when it comes to giving our keeper pleasure, Crane argues.

Smirking at their continued argument in the background of our bond, Maven glances at me and switches to speaking aloud. "Ready?"

"Lead the way, love."

She takes my hand and pulls me through the warped kaleidoscope of oddity that is Limbo until we reach a new section of the walls surrounding the citadel. It looks exactly the same to me as the rest of the outside, but my darling obsession spent most of her life in the Nether and knows the exact place to pass through the onyx.

We wind up inside a dark hallway beside ancient stone spiral steps. Maven grips my hand tightly as we take those steps, descending deep into abysmal darkness.

"Where are we?" I whisper, irritated that the darkness is prevalent enough to almost obscure my beautiful obsession from my incubus night vision. Having her out of my sight for even a moment is intolerable.

"This leads down and connects with the citadel's catacombs," Maven mutters. "Anytime they find a human who has manifested magic, or any other abnormality among the living that Amadeus wants to study or let his necromancers toy with, they're chained down here until they're either turned into a lich or tossed into the arena."

"Delightful. But why are we going there, darling?"

"There's an old, forgotten stairwell in one of the cells that connects to a hallway that will bring us close enough to Amadeus's chambers that we may be able to sneak in from there. If he's not in his chambers, we'll check the arena."

I hesitate. "And if he sees us coming?"

"Right now, Amadeus will be enduring a barrage of visions about an impending attack, including a dozen of my lookalikes to confuse him. He can prepare for some things he sees, but not everything. Predicting the future isn't truly possible until it's moments away," she adds. "By then, the attack will be here and I'll have this heart in his skeletal chest."

We finally reach the bottom of the spiral stone steps, and now I can just make out a system of surprisingly ornate tunnels, thanks to the flicker of a small green torch on one wall. As we pass it, I notice the runes etched into the stone walls.

"That's fae, isn't it?"

"This all used to belong to the fae thousands of years ago, before Amadeus drove them out and took over. Felix used to tell me about the knowledge all—"

Whatever she was about to say, she cuts off as Crane speaks telepathically.

The Undead have breached the Nether, and your ghosts are well ahead of them, sangfluir. *That blue-haired one appeared to be leading them, but I lost track.*

The Decimus clan is officially flying over the citadel, Decimus adds. *Please tell me you're somewhere safe so we can light this fucking place up.*

Do it, Maven agrees.

Deep in these catacombs and inside Limbo, I hear nothing of the outside world, but something must happen because a startled voice yelps from somewhere in these dark tunnels.

"W—what's going on up there?" a terrified man asks, his voice wavering as if he's about to burst into tears.

My markings light up again, and a shock of pain courses over my system so quickly that I nearly black out as I collapse. Agony pulses through me, my skin burning as more of my markings vanish from my body. I can hear Maven's worry and feel her cradling my head in her lap, but it takes a moment for my ears to function fully as the pain lessens once again.

It's then that I realize I dragged us out of Limbo.

"Crypt?" my darling whispers, her cool hand brushing against my forehead.

I realize she's so cool to the touch because I'm burning up. That can't be good.

Nevertheless, I smile up at her. "Is it a demigoddess trait to look mouthwatering at every angle, or is that just you?"

She huffs at my attempt to brush off the fact that I just collapsed, but someone else speaks in the tunnel.

"Who's there?" a raspy older woman's voice asks, every bit as frightened as the man.

Other voices mutter and whisper, terrified in this darkness.

Maven holds up a hand, whispers a word I've never heard, and holy light swirls around her hand, illuminating this space.

More gasps sound. Wide-eyed, gaunt faces of chained-up Nether humans stare back at us in abject terror—but my interest is piqued by a quiet whimper in one of the adjoining tunnels.

"Y—you're Maven Oakley," one of the chained-up tributes chokes nearby, his bloodshot eyes so big and wide on his gaunt face that they look chilling. "The *telum!* You're supposed to be dead—"

"If you value your life and freedom, you'll stop talking," I warn as we get to our feet. Stepping over an old skeleton, I guide my keeper to turn down into the tunnel where I heard the whimper.

The moment Maven's light falls upon the young woman curled in on herself in a cold stone corner, I halt.

"That's Frost's sister."

Maven inhales sharply, realizing I'm right. She darts forward to crouch beside the empath, using her magic to illuminate the girl better.

Frost's sister is wearing jeans and a jacket that are badly stained and ripped. Her butterscotch-colored hair is a mess. Like the other living people in these tunnels, her wrists and ankles are bound tightly together in rusty shackles. I can hear the poor girl quietly sobbing, but when Maven gently shakes her shoulder, she makes no reply.

"Heidi?" Maven whispers.

Something high above these catacombs explodes, and the ground around us trembles. When the people in the other hallway cry out in fear, Heidi sobs and curls in on herself more.

"Shit." My keeper glances at me. "Without the charm that keeps her from feeling what everyone around her is feeling all the time, she's going through an empathic overload. We have to…" She trails off with a slight frown. "You recognized her. Have you met her before?"

"Once, as children."

She lets her curiosity go in favor of the here and now. "Can you get her and the others out of their chains? We need to set them free and get them to safety before all hell breaks loose out there."

"Right away, darling," I reply as cheerfully as I can before dropping back into Limbo so she won't witness more of the searing agony.

50

MAVEN

Where are you? Everett demands telepathically, worry saturating his voice.

Now probably isn't the right moment to tell him I'm trying to get a response out of his unconscious sister, who he thought was dead, while a bunch of ghosts watch.

I'm in the catacombs, I reply.

Crypt and I won't stay here long. I doubt Amadeus is near his chambers now that the attack's begun. That's fine. It may even be easier to track him down in a fight.

The important thing is getting these living survivors out of here, especially Heidi.

Cautiously, I lift my glowing hand to see if my match's sister is hurt anywhere, but my attention is momentarily arrested by her face. She must have been wearing makeup in that picture of her I saw at Everbound, because now I can make out a pink port wine stain birthmark covering one of her cheekbones and ears, just under her right eye, all the way down to her upper lip.

So this is why her bitch of a mother made that comment about her children being disfigured.

What a fucking idiot. If anything, it makes Heidi's soft, pretty face far more interesting. She doesn't look much like Everett, aside from her nose. After another moment of examining her, I decide she's been incarcerated in hell for too long, but otherwise, she's unharmed.

Somewhere in the tunnels behind me, I hear chains clinking as Crypt frees the others. The ghosts drifting through these catacombs whisper and hiss unintelligibly.

"Heidi?" I whisper again.

No response.

Motherfucker, Baelfire swears through the bond about something I can't see.

I tense, all kinds of horrible possibilities for his alarm crossing my mind. *Bael?*

Aww. You almost never call me that. That's so fucking cute. I can't wait to hear you moan it next.

Never mind. If he can flirt, he's fine.

Your multifaceted plans to throw off the Entity's future sight appear to be working, sangfluir, Silas says next. *His forces are scrambling. We have the edge right now.*

It's a damn good thing we're bringing so many Undead on our side to this shitshow, Everett muses through the bond. *There are a* lot *of shadow fiends and old-world monsters here.*

A regular 'thank you for being the best of us' will suffice, Silas says smugly. Then he swears. *Baelfire, remind your draconic brother not to set our Undead army ablaze. Everett, let the other Reformists know we'll converge soon at the—gods above, is* that *the arena? It's fucking massive.*

Baelfire laughs. *That's what Maven said the first time she saw my—*

Shut up, lizard, Everett sighs.

I take their back-and-forth to mean that the Reformist attack is in full swing above us. Now is the time to target Amadeus early on, before the tide can turn toward either side in this battle and while we still have the advantage of his visions being skewed from all the possibilities.

Everett's sister is still unresponsive as she silently cries, too overwhelmed and paralyzed by the emotions of everyone nearby to move. Honestly, however long she's been here, I'm shocked she's still alive. Whatever Everett may think about his sister's ability to fight, she has to be strong in her own way to endure this.

"Ready, darling?" Crypt asks, slipping back into the catacomb tunnel behind me. His attention drops to the incapacitated empath. "I can carry her out with the others through Limbo. The dream realm is so thinned and damaged in the Nether, I doubt it will warp anyone's mind."

I trust his judgment. Since we need to get these people out of here as soon as fucking possible before I track down Amadeus in the chaos above, I nod. Crypt reaches down with a stolen key to unlock the shackles on Heidi's wrists. As he does, his fingers brush her arm.

"Fucking hell," Crypt hisses, yanking back immediately. His markings light up as his face contorts in pain. "Don't touch her, love. Whatever emotions and pain she's experiencing from this area of the Nether, she seems to be conducting, as well."

Another explosion up above sends dust sprinkling from the catacomb ceiling above. Swearing, I look back at Heidi. She's in pain, and she can't be left here.

The blue-haired young woman ghost appears in front of Crypt and me, popping out of one of the catacomb walls. She immediately crouches to check on Heidi, looking concerned as she peers up at me.

She gestures to herself, then to Heidi, and mouths, *Best friends.*

"Oh, shit," I realize aloud.

This girl was friends with Heidi before she died here. If she was Heidi's best friend, it's no wonder she was also particularly pissed off at Daphne Frost.

"I'm missing a ghostly interaction, aren't I?" Crypt guesses.

I glance at Heidi again as I debate how to get her out of here. Then it hits me, and I turn toward my incubus. "Put her to sleep.

She's stuck in an empathic meltdown right now, but she won't feel as much when she's unconscious."

He nods and reaches out to touch one of Heidi's shackled hands again, just briefly, before he jerks away like he's been burned. Still, that brief touch is enough that the empath's silent tears stop. All tension melts out of her curled-up body.

The next time Crypt touches her, he breathes out. "Still painful, but slightly more bearable. Where are we moving these survivors to, love?"

I consider our options. I didn't expect to find humans alive down here, but I guess I'm not surprised. Being immortal, Amadeus tends to view time differently. He's in no rush, whether it comes to conquering the world or toying with whatever humans he captured or received as tributes from the Frosts.

But now that we've found this handful of people and Heidi…

"Get them outside of the citadel," I decide. "To my old hovel on the outskirts of the woods. The wards should still be in place, so it will be the safest place for them until the battle is over."

Crypt's beautiful violet gaze narrows. "And leave you here, alone? I think not."

"I won't be alone. I have ghosts."

Nine of them, to be exact. They keep slowly gravitating to me through the walls of the catacombs.

"Darling—" he starts to protest, shaking his head.

"These catacombs connect below the arena and its surrounding area," I explain quickly. "I'll emerge where all the action is, and the others are already there. I'll be fine."

Okay, what are those ugly-ass giant scorpion things? Baelfire asks through the bond. *I've never seen that kind of shadow fiend before.*

I can't see the battle, but I know exactly what fiend he's talking about. *They're called namghirr, and their venom hurts like hell. It also kills in seconds unless you've recently ingested their blood, which helps slow the venom. But I don't recommend drinking their blood. It tastes like shit.*

I'm loath to realize how you must know all of that, Silas grits telepathically.

Just stay away from them. I'll be there soon, I add before looking at Crypt. "I need to get this heart into Amadeus and end this, but I also need you to get these innocent people to safety."

The Nightmare Prince glances down at Heidi, sighs, and straightens to pull me close, kissing the top of my head. "Fine, but if you're harmed while we're apart…"

I grin, tipping my head back. "Watch out. The green Jell-O threat was already utilized by Baelfire."

"Damn that big lizard for taking the best threat of them all," Crypt smiles back. He kisses me gently before growing serious. "If you're harmed while we're apart, you won't be the only one incapable of forgiving me. I'll be back as quickly as I can, my love."

"Good. I'll be in the arena waiting, covered in the blood of our enemies."

"Seduction at its finest," he sighs before grasping the edge of Heidi's ripped jacket and vanishing into Limbo. A second later, I hear the fearful whimpering of the other captive humans stop and know he's probably put them to sleep to move them through Limbo, too.

That leaves me and my fan club of specters to make our way swiftly through the cold, dim, colorless catacombs until I reach a small wooden door that separates the catacombs from underneath Amadeus's arena.

Taking a deep breath, I open the door to a huge portion of my childhood.

The scent of this dark place filled with onyx-barred cells assaults me. I practically choke on the memories that come with the overwhelming smell of stale sweat, blood, piss, rot, and death.

When I was a young teenager training to become the *telum,* the other competitors and I were left chained in here for hours at a time, waiting until we were brought out to show off our new skills in brutal combat. As we got older, they turned into bouts to the death.

I never lost.

I also never let anyone see me cry about what they were turning me into—not even Lillian. Over the course of months and years, I grew to love the combat and crave the adrenaline of a good fight. The buzz of death became a siren call. The blood and gore became nothing to me.

This arena made me who I am today. Being down here, knowing I'm about to step into the citadel to face Amadeus again…

My heart begins to pound with unfamiliar strength inside my chest. When I was very young, my so-called "father" terrorized me. He was cold, unfeeling, and inhuman. Brutal. Merciless.

Naturally, I admired him.

Before I ever learned about the humans being treated like animals in the Nether, I only knew that I wanted to survive—and to survive, I needed to impress Amadeus. So I trained and fought and killed and turned myself into a monster for him.

Out of all that bloodshed, the most unearthly father-daughter relationship was born. He was proud of me, in his own warped way, and I equally feared and even *respected* him.

And then he ripped out my heart.

I suppose it's about time I returned the favor.

Taking one more breath of putrid nostalgia, I stride past the cells where I used to hear other children and monsters snarling and weeping. I ascend the ancient stairs to the blood-soaked trap door and fling open the wooden door, emerging into the dim light of this world I once called home.

For one split second, all I can see is this colossal arena that I spent so much time in. Rows of concentric audience stands rise up on all sides to leer over the massive blood-stained dirt floor. Multiple tall columns made of bones and skulls rise up, lit at the top with green flames to illuminate this space despite the Nether's perpetual darkness. On one side of the arena,

Amadeus's ornate balcony looks out—and there, perched at the edge with the best possible view of the gory fights held here, is his throne made of bones.

He's not sitting in it right now.

In fact, I don't see the king of the Undead anywhere as I blink out of my reminiscing and finally register the chaos I just stepped into. Human and legacy Reformists, dozens of tangible ghosts, and hundreds of ravens are attacking ghouls, Undead, demons, Nether monsters, and other hellish creatures all around the arena. The sheer volume of the battle is staggering and tells me the fight extends outside this arena, probably all over the citadel. The air is thick with death and electric with the adrenaline of battle.

High in the dim, grayish sky of the Nether, three golden dragons soar past overhead. One of them lets loose a spine-tingling roar before breathing down blinding royal blue fire somewhere outside the arena. Instinctively, I know that one is mine. Seeing my dragon in action and not feral puts a smile on my face. I withdraw both Pierce and Cuttrina, my blood already pumping with the excitement of combat.

Barely ten seconds into this battle, I roll out of the way of a massive, lumbering ghoul and simultaneously slice across the tendons in the backs of its ankles. It falls with a garbled cry, crushing an enemy incubus on the way down.

Maven. Fucking gods, I can finally see you, Everett says, his voice pure relief.

I see a blast of ice streak through the raging battle somewhere near the top of the arena, freezing enemies in a wave. My gaze locks onto the white-haired elemental who is quickly making his way to me. A changeling that looks just like me is sticking to his side, defending every attack that comes their way as it holds a simple dagger.

She's on the battlefield? Fuck yes, Baelfire cheers through the bond. *My mate's about to take names and kick some Nether ass.*

As I dodge the magical attack of a lich several paces away, I still can't help smiling—because *gods,* I love hearing their voices in my head again.

As the lich calls another spell to its skeletal hands, one of the ghosts I made tangible passes through it. The lich shrieks and collapses as if it's choking, only to get stampeded over by a group of enemy Undead racing toward me.

Rolling my shoulders back, I let my instincts and training kick in as I take on the Undead. I dodge, dip, slash, and dismember until pieces of the living dead are all over. Just as I turn to face the last one, it gets frozen solid.

Everett is suddenly at my back, wielding a sword made of nevermelt, but he spares me a soft blue glance. "You took a while to get up here," he points out, having to raise his voice over the sounds of shrieks, thuds, wails, and shouts surrounding us.

"Something came up," I tell him, deciding that the news about Heidi can wait until we're not surrounded by so much death and violence.

The last thing I need is him getting distracted and injured. I am so fucking *not* going through that again.

Spotting a demon wielding an adamantine mace as it races toward us, I fling Pierce as hard as I can so it sinks deep into the monster's skull.

Still, just the sight of a mace makes me grin. I don't know when maces went out of style as weapons in the mortal realm, but I intend to bring them back.

The vampire drops dead just behind Everett, who hasn't even bothered looking over his shoulder as he scans our surroundings for threats to me. Meanwhile, the Fake Maven beside him has begun attacking a nearby banshee with a fervor I actually appreciate.

I catch a glimpse of another lookalike to me racing through the arena in the distance. There are twelve of them, scattered around this battle—and I'm sure wherever Amadeus is, it's irritating him.

I just need him to appear. Then I'll put an end to all of this.

Silas? I check in, realizing it's been too long since I've heard from my blood fae necromancer.

There's no response, which makes my already pounding heart grow painful.

I hear a dragon roar again before Baelfire lands on the edge of the massive arena, a changeling that looks like me riding on his back. Even despite the dim lighting, my dragon's golden scales gleam as he bites a ghoul in half. He swings his tail to knock over another lich before it can throw an attack at more Reformists who are pouring in through the massive entrance on the opposite side of the arena.

Si, Baelfire also says through the bond. *Earth to Silas. Hello?*

There's still no reply. Panic tries to creep into my veins, but I focus on fighting. Still, I'm relieved when Crypt joins the telepathic manhunt.

Wherever you are, Crane, answer our keeper or else I'll have no choice but to drag you by your pointed ears to her side. The survivors are safe, love, and I'll be there any moment, he adds.

"Survivors?" Everett asks, cutting down another banshee before he peers at me curiously.

"Later," I promise, yanking Pierce out of the dead demon and twirling it in my hand. We're surrounded by so many shadow fiends that all of my instincts are almost painfully heightened, like pinpricks dancing over my tensed nerves as I rejoin the fight.

This battle has turned into unmitigated, gruesome chaos. Aside from the growing concern over Silas's lack of response, I'm enjoying every minute of it as we continue to defend ourselves from countless fiends. It's nice that I'm no longer a fucking revenant, so no matter how into the battle I get, I don't have to worry about losing myself berserking.

I'm also keeping an eye out for Amadeus. I spot a necromancer or two, along with liches and wraiths, but there is still no sign of Galene's once-upon-a-time prophet.

Incoming, Baelfire warns. *But don't worry, these rotting corpses are friendly.*

On cue, dozens of Silas's Undead pour through the entryway into the arena at top speed. Instead of attacking the Reformists who are fighting for their lives, these corpse-like allies fling themselves at monsters, banshees, liches, demons, and other Nether creatures. I catch the barest glimpse of several ghosts clapping nearby before they pass through me, becoming tangible and joining the mounting battle once again.

A second later, I'm beyond relieved to see my blood fae appear, strolling through the midst of the living dead. His intense red gaze scans the slaughter until it lands on me. But just as I step in his direction, Silas lifts his blackened hands and sends a powerful blood magic spell careening toward me.

What the—

"Fuck!" Everett shouts, tackling me out of the way just before the blood magic decimates the changeling beside us.

What the hell just happened? Baelfire barks through the bond before arching his draconic neck to set a barreling wendigo on fire.

Rolling to my feet, I break into a run toward Silas. He's already preparing another attack, this time some kind of necromantic hex. But before I can pin him to keep him from being a danger to himself or anyone else, Crypt drops out of Limbo and twists the fae's arms back, taking him down.

Silas doesn't even struggle against the incubus as I reach them. A nearby demon takes advantage of our distracted struggle, and I hiss when a blade grazes my side. I kill off the annoyance quickly before crouching beside my fae.

He's gone insane again, Everett scowls, freezing several enemies on the way to us.

Overhead, I hear another one of the Decimuses roar before an explosion goes off somewhere outside the arena. I also hear the alarming song of a harbinger distantly and hope no ally tries to kill it off. I explicitly told Brigid Decimus and the other

Reformist leaders to instruct their troops not to kill harbingers to avoid their retroactively lethal swan songs.

When Silas slowly tries to aim a deadly magic spell at Crypt, I use one of the few holy magic spells I've mastered to block his attack before I grip his chin and squint, trying to make out his eyes. This isn't a changeling, which I'd already guessed thanks to how fucking powerful he is, but I see how widely blown his pupils are.

That combined with his slow movements and bizarre calm makes me swear. Those are all signs of being hypnotized by a vampire.

Bertram, I warn the others telepathically, wincing when my side that got nicked stings, warmth spreading under my black combat attire.

Godsdamn it, Crypt seethes, his remaining markings glowing. *Frost—*

"I'll snap him out of it. Go get that bastard's head for our keeper," Everett orders, taking over pinning Silas to the ground. Crypt vanishes, and my elemental looks at me. "I had to snap some Reformists out of a vampire's influence on the front lines, months ago. It won't be pretty, but—"

A chill rolls over my spine, and I move on instinct, whirling to jam Cuttrina into the center of a necromancer that was just trying to sneak up on us. I don't recognize this one, but he's screeching and writhing in pain as I kick him away.

Fuck. Maven, are you bleeding? Baelfire asks telepathically, panic in his voice.

A little.

"What? Where?" Everett demands even as he begins encapsulating Silas's chest in ice to keep his arms from moving.

I can smell it, Baelfire says quickly. *Your demigoddess blood is pretty damn fragrant, and I think the fiends are catching on to it. That's going to blow our whole changeling shtick out of the water.*

Shit. He's right.

But there's no point healing it now that my side is soaked in blood. The damage is done, so I focus on killing off any threat nearby as Everett tries to snap Silas out of it. I'm pretty sure my scarred elemental is freezing and unfreezing something inside Silas's body, but I can't focus on it because a scream goes up from the battle being waged at the edge of the arena.

That draws my attention to two namghirr as they scuttle into view. The giant, highly venomous namghirr move blindingly fast, impaling allies and throwing the writhing, poison-filled corpses aside. Their stingers are about as long as my arm—and I remember all too well what it feels like to be impaled by them repeatedly.

Baelfire is focused on taking down a group of particularly big ghouls, and I'm not about to let those namghirr get anywhere near Silas and Everett right now, so I wipe blood off my knives and take off toward the creatures, swerving around several fresh ghosts.

As I approach these creatures, I remember the last time I expired from their venomous stingers. I was nineteen at the time and woke up in my hovel later with Lillian crying nearby.

"Don't cry. I'm okay," I'd told her.

"Being okay isn't enough," she'd insisted. *"I watched how much pain you were in on that arena floor. Don't make me watch that ever again, little raven. Promise me that the next time you fight those things, you'll have a better strategy. You're far stronger and smarter than anything in this dead realm, so don't you dare let them hurt you like that again."*

And just like every other time I've fought namghirr since then, I've listened to her.

Falling into the same strategy I've used to kill dozens of these creatures, I ignore the worried shouts of Everett and Baelfire inside my head, and I drop to my knees. Sliding across the arena floor between the two front pincers of a namghirr, I raise my knives to score the underside of the deadly creature. Its blood gushes overhead, dousing me.

Rolling out from under it, I slash hard as its back stinger jabs where I just was. Its dismembered stinger falls uselessly to the arena floor. All it takes is leaping onto its back to stab through its screeching head, and I'm onto the next one to repeat my tried-and-true namghirr slaying method.

By the time I'm done, both of them are bleeding out, twitching on the arena floor as the fight continues to rage on throughout the citadel. I'm covered in namghirr blood, smiling and breathing hard from the thrill of taking down these deadly creatures, when Crypt appears out of Limbo in front of me.

He's also covered in fresh blood, but his gaze is pure obsession as he studies me, setting down a head on the arena floor beside us.

It's Bertram's head, complete with his bright red hair.

"Enjoying yourself, darling?"

"I'm having the time of my new life," I grin.

"My gods, you're so stunning in your element," he breathes before wrapping me up in a kiss.

I should probably tell him this may be one of the worst times in the world to be kissing, but his mouth is so desperate and perfect against mine. Even in battle, he smells like sweet *reverium* and leather, and soon I'm kissing him back as warfare rages around us.

I sense coolness behind me just before Crypt releases me, and suddenly my head is tipped back as Everett steals a kiss from me next. It's shorter but no less passionate before he wipes namghirr blood off my cheek.

"Silas is back," he tells me, his glacial gaze flicking around us to check for any threats.

Silas? I check, glancing over my shoulder to see that my fae is surrounded by loyal Undead as he braces himself on his knees, catching his breath. *Are you okay?*

I'm— His telepathic voice cuts off like he was just about to try lying. He straightens to meet my gaze through the battle, speaking in fae. *I'll be fine once I can apologize between your pretty thighs again for nearly harming the love of my life.*

Gods.

He doesn't owe me an apology, but I'm not about to point that out now that he's reminded me of how fucking fantastic he is at apologizing with his mouth.

A dragon roars overhead again, and blue fire bathes something far away in Amadeus's citadel. All of us are drawn back into battle for what feels like hours, but is more likely minutes. More shadow fiends are being drawn to me because of the scent of my demigoddess blood.

Not that I mind. I crave being surrounded by combat like this. Fighting beside my quintet is fulfilling, especially when we're all so much stronger thanks to our bond.

But when a petrifying chill reverberates through the air and down my spine, I go still.

Amadeus is here.

51

MAVEN

I SHOULD HAVE KNOWN he wouldn't emerge until he knew precisely where I was.

The Entity's presence is too corrupted and familiar to mistake. Instead of killing the basilisk in front of me, I let Crypt cut through it with his lighter sword as I turn. I don't even have to look for him—my gaze immediately finds the immortal being who called me his.

He just entered his arena from a side entrance. Towering over the grey-draped necromancers and liches that surround him, Amadeus is exactly how I remember. Wearing the attire of ancient kings, sapped of all color, he's an imposing skeletal figure with pitch black, whiteless eyes set in an emotionless face that would otherwise seem almost kind.

Like the rest of the necromancers in his court, his bald head is decorated with countless necromantic runes, but right now, he's wearing his intricate crown that is still missing the piece of etherium I stole years ago.

The sight of him brings back more memories. Things I've forgotten on purpose, like my so-called father ordering two of his necromancers to force-feed me meat once he learned I refused to eat it anymore. When I killed them, he locked me in the dungeons I was conditioned in and left me there for three days to fend off the Undead until I expired.

He had me fight in this arena every day for the last two years of my life in the Nether, threatening to feed Lillian to his court if I lost.

He molded me. Trained me. Called me daughter and gave me a purpose. He punished me severely when I wasn't measuring up to his expectations of his *telum,* and offered the barest of acknowledgment if I ever exceeded those expectations.

In a sick way, I do have Amadeus to thank for the way I turned out.

I also have him to thank for taking away Lillian.

That thought makes me turn to face Amadeus more fully as I grip the handles of my blades. Cuttrina extends into my scythe, the etherium curve gleaming in the faint light of the green fires burning around this arena. My heart pounds in a rhythm that tells me either something big is about to happen, or it really is malfunctioning this time.

Holy fucking shit, Baelfire says through the bond when his attention finally falls on the king of the Undead now entering the arena. *Fake Daddy's here and he's horrifying.*

That has each and every member of my quintet snapping to attention as they get their first glimpse of the being who has ruled and corrupted the Nether for thousands of years.

Silas scowls from his spot near my left as he wipes enemy blood off his face. *You'll have trouble getting to him through all those casters,* sangfluir. *I can take them out for you.*

Quit trying to be a hero. We'll all take those assholes out, Everett says, flinging another spike of ice that impales two demons together with ease. He moves to my other side.

I could just roast all these fuckers, Bael suggests, already swiveling his neck as a royal blue glow starts to rise up the scales on his neck.

Don't, I warn as the group of liches and necromancers draws closer through the battle, demolishing everything in their path. *I recognize some of those necromancers. They're marked with* vita lathantiem *charms.*

What the fuck is a feet alot than TM charm? my dragon shifter asks.

My gods, that was rough to listen to, Crypt cringes.

When an enemy swarm of half-rotted Undead see their cruel master in their midst, they panic and bolt towards my quintet in pure fear. Silas whispers a necromantic incantation, and dark magic consumes the Undead at once, eating away their rotting skin and insides until their bones clatter to the ground.

Silas's nose starts bleeding slightly. He pretends not to see my scowl of frustration at the sight of his strain as he wipes the blood away, replying through the bond. *The charm Maven mentioned is also called a life force link. Whichever necromancers carry the charm can revive each other—all it takes is one to survive for the rest to rise again.*

You're saying they all have to be killed at the same time, Everett summarizes. *Great.*

Lighting them on fire would work, then, Bael points out as his wings flare out, his throat glowing once again as he crushes a nearby ghoul under one big, clawed hand.

They wouldn't send all of the linked necromancers out at once, I explain as I finally start toward Amadeus's slowly moving group.

Right. I'll hunt down the missing link, Crypt says as he drops into Limbo.

Don't let it become a fight, or Amadeus will see it and know our plan, I warn.

Easy as pie, darling.

The rest of my quintet moves to flank my sides as I stride to meet Amadeus on the floor of his arena. I reap a few newly dead spirits as we walk, the hollow whistle of my scythe barely audible as the battle shifts. Allies and enemies alike are quick to move out of the Entity's way, but they don't want to be near my advance, so a clearing is starting to form.

With every step I take forward, all I can think about is the first time Lillian heard the mantras that were being drilled into me.

I had recited them to her. *"I feel nothing. I'm on my own. I need no one. I am but a weapon who is one with death. I am nothing but deadly calm."*

"What? None of that is true!" she'd snapped, so upset that she accidentally knocked over several chess pieces before swearing in fae. *"That* scútráche. *No, Maven. You are so much more than that."*

She was right all along.

I am more than I was made or trained to be. I'm alive. I *feel.* My heart pounds wildly as I stalk closer to the impending danger—but what a fucking gift, to be so alive that I can fear death again.

Feeling mortality so heavily is thrilling.

Perhaps that's why I'm smiling as I lift my hand, calling holy magic to protect myself and my quintet from the first round of attacks the necromancers and liches hurl at us. The cacophony of dark magic bounces harmlessly off the light swirling around us.

The second their attacks fade, my quintet is on the move. They work as a team so smoothly now that it almost takes my breath away. Ice flies and blasts of blood magic make my hair stand on end. Behind us, I sense a wave of heat as Baelfire's royal blue flames annihilate anyone trying to creep up on our quintet.

My matches are keeping Amadeus's casters busy enough that I only have to cut one of them out of my way with my scythe before I'm face-to-face with the Entity. His gleaming black eyes follow my advance, and when he speaks, his voice is the same deep, menacing rumble as always.

"And so my daughter returns to me."

I grip my scythe. "I am not your daughter."

His monotone response is almost drowned out by another dragon roar in the distance, but his cold, inhuman gaze remains on me. "Who but I could have turned you into this? The

Reaper's blood may run through you, but the fabric of your being was woven by me alone."

He's clearly caught wind of my true parentage, but I'm more interested in the fact that he still hasn't attacked. He's holding back.

Is the unfeeling king of the Undead hesitant to end me a second time, or am I missing something?

I found the spare, Crypt's voice echoes through the bond. *I can kill him now.*

I can take the rest of them at once, Everett says. *On my count.*

"Yield, my *telum,*" Amadeus rumbles as I keep my face perfectly blank to hide what my quintet is about to do. "This fray is but a passing moment to ones such as us. These mortals are subject to a fleeting existence, but your divinity may easily be traded for an eternity. I will show you—"

Everett starts counting down through the bond, so I tune out Amadeus and prepare myself.

As soon as he reaches zero, massive spikes of ice protrude from the ground, skewering every one of the necromancers and liches out here. When they shriek and wither away instead of reviving, I know Crypt has killed off the last of them.

Amadeus reacts quickly to his lack of protection. Whatever he was saying, he cuts off before a wave of crackling dark magic ripples out from around him. Summoning holy magic to my hands, I once again shield my quintet.

Everett, freeze his legs.

Before Everett can even register my words, Amadeus has already used magic to fling my elemental aside. He slams into one of the arena walls, swearing through the bond.

Shit. Since this has turned into a fight, Amadeus has a high chance of seeing our next move. His foresight isn't perfect, but I grimace when Silas's next powerful spell is countered perfectly with a wave of Amadeus's skeletal hand.

We need to jumble the future again. Don't communicate or strategize. Just attack.

My quintet understands immediately. Soon, each of us is throwing everything we can at Amadeus from all angles. Baelfire crawls closer to snap at Amadeus, who sees the attack coming and repels Baelfire with a spell just as Silas hurls more magical attacks. I swing my scythe, dodge a lethal spell Amadeus flings my way, and roll under one of Everett's spikes of ice as he rejoins the fight.

He's starting to struggle with keeping up. Our chaotic strategy is working—

And then Crypt launches out of the Nether, shoving the shadow heart directly into Amadeus's skeletal chest.

Amadeus's whiteless eyes widen as he grips Crypt by the neck. The Nightmare Prince drops back into Limbo to escape the Entity's clutches, but Amadeus is already reaching into his own chest, trying to get the heart back out.

We all launch forward, trying to stop him from pulling his new weakness back out. As if in slow motion, I see the moment Amadeus's attention snaps to Everett, instead. His skeletal, powerful hand plunges forward, and—

He rips Everett's heart out.

The elemental collapses immediately, twitching.

"No!" I scream, both aloud and through the bond.

Vaguely, I hear Silas shouting a spell, but it doesn't register as blind fury and unparalleled horror overwhelm me. Holy magic burns through me with this rush of rage, and suddenly I'm slamming into Amadeus, sweeping his legs out from under him with my scythe until we both crash to the ground. He's summoning dark magic to his hands, about to do something terrible to me.

But I move faster.

Withdrawing Pierce, I jam it deeply into Amadeus's now-occupied chest until my fingertips nearly sink into his crepe-paper-like, unnatural flesh.

The Entity's hoarse scream cuts through the air like the most beautiful hymn I've ever heard.

I want more. I want him to suffer the way he made me suffer.

Cuttrina has already morphed back into knife form in my other hand, and I stab that into his chest, too. Over and over. I'm so overwhelmed by fury and rage that it takes me a moment to realize that Amadeus is…crying.

The gleam of moisture is difficult to make out in the dim flicker of green light around us, but it trickles over his colorless temples as he wheezes.

"D—daughter….daughter…"

"I am not your motherfucking daughter," I snarl, my pulse pumping in my ears as my heart squeezes painfully.

Amadeus's breathing shudders as his ink-like blood pools on the arena floor below us. Somewhere nearby, I hear a fiend shriek at the sight of the dying Entity. Others in this battle begin to notice and react to his demise, but I pay it no attention as Silas quickly takes Everett's heart from Amadeus's limp hand and rushes to Everett's motionless side. My necromancer flips him over and begins chanting.

I can't breathe. Whatever Silas is doing, it has to work. *It has to work.*

Amadeus's black eyes roll to look at me. "I…I feel. I *feel,*" he gasps.

One of his skeletal hands grips my arm, and revulsion sweeps through me, but I'm arrested by something on his face.

It's wonder. Horror. Fear.

A dozen other emotions mixed together.

Amadeus is feeling the weight of mortality again for the first time in thousands of years, but unlike me, he can't stand it. All he can do is weep as he dies beside me.

"G—Galene chose this for me," he rasps. "This end. If—if it is by my daughter's hands that she wills me to go to the beyond…I—let it be mercifully. End me. *End me, daughter.*"

I used to fear this weeping creature, but now?

He's fucking pitiful. Just a withered, empty husk—a shadow of the prophet he once was.

Still…

With a small sigh, I remove one of my gloves and force one of my fingers to graze Amadeus's hand, still bloodied from Everett's heart. Whatever peace I instill in him, his eyes widen, and then they just stay open.

His chest stops rising and falling.

And a moment later, I sense it. New death, like a thick, heavy tide pulling away from this shore.

The moment Amadeus's spirit separates from his body, the Nether ripples around us. The darkness lifts, and clouds part. People shout and scream all over the citadel, shadow fiends shrieking as they run from the new light invading this twilight realm.

But I ignore it all as I rush to Everett's side, sitting beside Silas with my heart pounding in my throat. I haven't felt the bond snap. That means something, right?

You did it, Baelfire murmurs through the bond.

He's right. I did it.

Not that it matters if I lose Everett. I did all of this for a future with my quintet. Without him…

Crypt wraps me in a hug from behind, kneeling behind me as we ignore the chaos. Fiends flee all around. Reformists are driving them deeper into the Nether, shouting out orders and checking their motionless comrades for pulses.

I watch as Silas finally places Everett's heart back into the hole in his chest. Sweat beads on my necromancer's brow as he whispers more necromantic chants. His nose starts to bleed, but he perseveres.

Everett is still lying too still.

A moment later, Baelfire joins us. He's naked from shifting back and covered in soot, blood, and dirt. His brow is furrowed as he, too, watches Silas work.

A sob tries to escape, but I shove it down. Crypt still notices and squeezes me tighter as the few markings remaining on him glow in rapid succession.

I need you to do something for me, I tell only Everett telepathically, clinging to the fact that the bond hasn't broken for all I'm worth. *I need you to stay.*

Silas stumbles in his chant, swaying slightly. Baelfire quickly steadies him.

"Si?"

"I can do this," the fae grits, resuming his spell. "I cast a preservation spell on him the moment after Amadeus removed his heart. That means his life force is strong—I just need to make his heart realize that and beat again."

I don't even fucking know what spell he's using. Healing? Necromancy? All the words blur together as my heart tries to knock free from my chest.

And then finally—*fucking finally*—Everett gasps, his eyes flying open.

Thank you. Thank you. Thank you.

I'm not sure if I'm talking to the universe, the gods, or my quintet as I fling myself onto my elemental, careful not to bump the place where Silas is still healing up his injury. One of Everett's arms weakly wraps around me, but he's still wheezing.

"Fuck, that hurt like hell," he groans before glancing at the rest of my quintet and grimacing. "The lizard's naked again. Why am I not surprised? Worst sight ever to wake up to."

I'm so hysterical with everything that just happened that his barb at Baelfire actually earns a laugh from me.

Baelfire exhales in relief before smiling, gesturing at his naked self. "Sure, Professor Popsicle. We all know you only woke back up to get a good look at this."

Everett gags and then hisses in pain just as Silas finishes sealing up his chest. The scar remains, which doesn't surprise me—I'm sure my fae is barely hanging on, and scars can be healed later.

"What was that about not trying to be a hero?" Silas scoffs, but his voice is as relieved as I'm feeling.

"He just ripped my heart out like he was picking a fucking

apple. Nothing heroic about that," Everett mutters, slumping back to the bloodied ground in sheer exhaustion.

"At least it distracted that wanker so he didn't come after our girl again," Crypt says, patting Everett's head in a way that makes the elemental glower at him. "Way to take one for the team, Frost. Almost makes me like you."

Nearly delirious with relief that my quintet is all alive, I tune out of their ribbing to survey our surroundings. The Nether has continued to lighten until it's almost like the glow of midday in the mortal realm. Dead shadow fiends, monsters, liches, necromancers, Reformists, and ravens litter the ground of the arena as the alluring ambience of death hangs thickly in the air.

Two gleaming golden dragons soar overhead, and when they roar, it sounds triumphant. I can't put into words the way I know Amadeus's control is no longer holding this plane of existence captive—I just feel it. The Nether is brightening as the shadow of my would-be father melts away.

And finally, I look at Amadeus's spirit hovering over his body. It's distorted and torn, blurred and sad-looking. I can barely even make out the shape of a head, much less his face.

Before I can decide to reap him, I hear Everett choke like he's dying again. Whirling around in alarm, I quickly find that he's fine—he's just freaking out because my mother has appeared again.

The rest of my quintet flinches away as Syntyche's looming, dark, hooded figure appears as if from nowhere. I guess it's no surprise she's come to reap the many ghosts waiting in the Nether, where she couldn't reap before.

But it *is* a surprise when Galene also appears.

Galene is wearing the same garb she did when she disguised herself as Pia: dressed head to toe in white, concealing her beautiful face. The only difference is that she's glowing brightly as she moves toward us across the bloodied arena floor.

All around, Reformists gasp and drop to their knees, telling me these goddesses are visible to everyone.

"Daughter," Syntyche greets simply.

That one word elicits many more gasps from the Reformists, like not all of them completely believed that I'm this goddess's "crotch goblin," as Kenzie would put it.

"Hi." I gesture at Amadeus's decrepit, floating ghost. "That one is yours."

She dips her hooded head. A quiet whistling sound follows her scythe before, all at once, that final trace of Amadeus is gone. Without another word, she vanishes completely.

Maybe she's not reaping here, then?

My question is answered as Galene reads my mind in real time. I can hear the smile in her voice. "She has returned to await your visit to Paradise, my fearless one."

I tense, and so do my guys. Crypt pulls me away from Everett to hold me tightly, jaw clenched. Baelfire folds his arms to regard the goddess, not at all embarrassed to be naked as the day he was born.

Not that he needs to be embarrassed, with all those muscles and gorgeousness and a dick like that.

"She's not going," Baelfire growls.

"She's not," Everett agrees, trying to sound firm but failing because he's so weak. Silas also looks exhausted from all the magic he's used, but he looks relieved that Syntyche left.

Galene laughs. "Rest your fears, matches of Maven. She won't be coming to Paradise the way she did last time. This will be a mere projection of her soul to fulfill the blood oath she made to my queen, but I'm afraid swiftness is of the utmost importance."

Shit.

Shit.

My blood oath. My mouth runs dry as I stare at the white-cloaked goddess. The battle is still ending, and already I'm being summoned to speak with Arati? What the hell did I agree to pay for this to be the right timing?

My quintet looks sick to their stomachs. Baelfire's golden gaze moves to me, and he shakes his head.

"Don't. I don't like this."

"I'm with the lizard," Crypt rasps, burying his face in the side of my neck.

"Your fears are unnecessary," Galene says soothingly. "I give you my promise that Maven's soul shall return with the utmost haste. She cannot yet remember why this is so vital, but she will know soon. Come along, my fearless one. Your sworn fate awaits."

She waves her hand, and just like that, my vision goes white.

52

MAVEN

THIS TIME, when I wake in Paradise, I recognize it right away.

I'm sitting in Arati's grand dining room. I remember it from the time I showed up here naked, back when I was still trying to piss off my aunt. It's an ornate, massive dining room connected to the balcony that overlooks Paradise.

I'm in one of the dining room chairs beside a long, golden table etched with patterns like fire. Figures made of blue flames arrange gleaming plates and bowls full of strange, beautiful foods and pour a glowing purple liquid into golden goblets. A few of them wave at me before disappearing into smoke.

It looks like they're setting up for a celebration, but I'm the only guest. Confused, I reach for one of the goblets to get a better look at it, but my hand passes through the gold.

"Projections are not corporeal," Syntyche says behind me.

She moves into my view before sitting in one of the chairs beside me. Her hand wraps around the goblet in front of her, but she doesn't drink the liquid in it. She just sits in thoughtful silence.

"What oath did I make?" I finally ask.

"That was between you and my sister. But even with only your soul here in Paradise, you should have free access to the missing pieces within your mind," Syntyche muses, finally taking a sip from the goblet.

I have my memories?

Oh, my gods.

She's right.

I can remember everything about that blood oath now. I made it right here, in this very room. I can still remember Arati, smirking at me.

"If you really want to return to your fate-given matches so desperately, it will come at a price you already well know. You must first exchange a blood oath with me."

"I accept."

"I knew you would. As much a menace as you've been, my dear niece, your passion and depth of love have earned my respect. There's fire in you where fear should be. Let's hope you don't regret that later."

And I recall my golden ichor swirling into a bowl alongside Arati's as we exchanged unbreakable oaths.

My words echo in my mind first. *"I swear this oath in my own blood, that should I survive my fall to mortality, I shall claim the Nether from the one who has corrupted it. I will tie mine and my quintet's souls to that plane of existence to cleanse and reign over it until the end of our days. This I swear, and seal in blood."*

Oh, shit.

I agreed to rule the Nether? I even sealed my quintet's souls to it, along with mine? That's insane.

What the hell could I have asked from Arati that would make this permanent exchange worth it?

Arati's powerful voice booms next, her gleaming ichor dripping into the bowl. *"I swear this oath in my own blood, on behalf of all gods and goddesses and with the approval of fate itself, that should you uphold your oath sealed this day in blood, I shall lift the entirety of the Legacy Curse from the face of the mortal realm to free all living and future legacies from this antiquated burden. This I swear, and seal in blood."*

"Holy fucking gods," I exhale aloud, blinking back to myself in utter shock.

I asked Arati to break the Legacy Curse.

She agreed.

And I just fulfilled my end of the bargain. Which means…

"Blaspheming in our presence! Why, I never," someone laughs on the opposite side of the table.

I realize that while I was lost in my Paradisical memories, the rest of the pantheon walked into this room. It's disorienting to look at someone and feel like they're both a stranger and familiar at once, but that's what it feels like as I take in Arati, Koa, Galene, Raan, and Pheli.

Pheli is the one sitting across from me, smiling cheerfully. He's the god of the skies, change, happiness, hope, and many other things. His skin is sky blue, and he's shorter than the other gods with a robust build, sky-blue eyes, and a curly blond beard to match his hair.

His smile is blinding as he raises his goblet like a toast. "Well done down there, my dear!"

My attention drifts to the god beside him. This one is taller and beautifully graceful. His dark midnight blue skin is striking against his solemn moonlight-colored irises. The white robe he wears drifts slightly as if he's underwater, as does his long, dark hair. Everything about him is slender and delicate as he offers me a kind, soft smile.

I remember him. Raan, god of the oceans, moonlight, serenity, and a bunch of other shit. With his dominion over water, he was the one who hand-blessed Everett as a baby with his ice abilities. I even remember Raan telling me months ago that he favored Everett because of his gentle spirit and bestowed on my elemental a more mild curse than his powerful capabilities would otherwise demand.

Koa lifts a goblet, as well. "To Maven."

"To Maven," the rest of the gods echo before downing their goblets.

"Fate divine, that's good ambrosia!" Pheli hiccups, going to pour more from one of the goblets. Raan waves his hand, and no matter how Pheli tries to pour it, the liquid won't go into his goblet. The sun god huffs, looking at the moon god. "Just another sip. We're celebrating!"

Raan shakes his head with a small, affectionate smile.

"Well, my niece, you've done it. You defeated Amadeus and freed the Nether," Arati announces, popping some kind of Paradisical fruit into her mouth at the head of the table as she, too, raises her goblet.

The others are chiming in to congratulate me more, but I'm distracted as more important memories re-emerge.

I remember the day I finally found that the golden corruinum flower had bloomed. I hadn't hesitated to turn it into a poisonous potion to drink so I could give up my divine status and return to my quintet.

I remember downing the golden liquid and feeling pain unlike I've ever known as I fell careening from the heavens, unsure if I would live or die.

Shaking off those memories, I tune back in and look at Arati. "So?"

"*So* is not a full sentence," she says, sipping her ambrosia again.

"*So* then use your brain and read between the fucking lines," I shoot back.

Whoa. That response came like a knee-jerk reaction, and now I feel bitchy. Did I really argue with my aunt so much in my time here in Paradise that it's become like second nature?

Koa does a spit-take with his ambrosia, clearing his throat and shooting me a chastising look. "You may not recall fully, but we've been over this many times, Maven. You cannot insult the queen of the gods. Have some decorum, if only for your mother's sake."

"As if I mind," Syntyche says without missing a beat, setting down her goblet.

Arati rolls her eyes at her triplet before she stands at the head of the table, towering and beautiful and fierce all at once. She smiles down at me.

"Pheli is right. You did a good job. It's time for us to finalize the second part of your oath to me, and then I shall fulfill my oath to you."

"You're really going to remove all curses from the earth?" I gawk.

"Yes."

A realization strikes me, and I tense, staring her down. "Even the steward of Limbo's?"

Arati flaps her hand at me like I'm bothering her. "We've been over this, even before we swore the oaths. You made it beyond crystal clear that you would agree to nothing unless that mortal incubus's curse was alleviated with the others. Or don't you recall the arguments you made in favor of ending the Legacy Curse and shifting the maintenance of Limbo onto all living incubi?"

Her words sound kind of familiar. I still struggle for a moment to pick the right memory from my head before I realize she's right. We'd argued about it in this very room.

"The Legacy Curse was made to unite the monsters of old to stop their warfare. That's what all legacies in the world believe—but that's manticore shit," I had pointed out. *"Galene herself told me fate picks matches. The Legacy Curse was a way to tame the more violent legacies long ago. It gave them a selfish reason to accept their matches and work together, but now it's time for you to trust in the humanity of legacies. I can tell you from firsthand experience that the urge to find one's quintet is now so ingrained in legacies, down to the fiber of their beings, that having a curse on top of it is fucking ridiculous. It's antiquated."*

"Fine," Arati had snapped at me. *"I'll lift the Legacy Curse."*

"From everyone?"

"Yes. All legacies living and yet unborn. Let's just get on with it, then."

I'd stopped her from cutting her hand to make the blood oath. *"The steward of Limbo needs to be freed, too."*

"What? No. The Limbo must be tended to."

"I agree," I'd shrugged. *"But there are thousands of incubi in the world. They can all go into Limbo. Why can't they all maintain it? Why make only one suffer? If all curses are gone, that burden needs to be shared. My incubus will be freed with every other legacy, or I'll drop this blood oath right now and good fucking luck finding someone else stupid enough to tie their soul to the Nether."*

It took more arguing, but Arati had agreed.

Relief hits me hard and fast as I refocus on the six gods around this table. They're all watching me expectantly, but I keep my face carefully unreadable as powerful emotions well inside me.

I told Crypt I would find a way to fix it, not realizing I already had.

I may have sealed my quintet's fates to the Nether along with mine without asking for their permission, but…I have no regrets.

Galene was right. Coming here was vital.

"All right," I nod. "Seal my soul to the Nether."

"I will," Arati shrugs before impaling something on one of her plates with a golden fork and savoring the taste of it. She smiles, half smug and half amused. "But first, you'll have dinner with us. *Clothed,* this time."

I stare at her. "I can't eat. Or drink. Or touch anything."

Koa glances at me. "We've enjoyed watching you in the mortal realm, but despite the rather awful wringer you put us through when you first arrived in Paradise, we've…well, we've missed you."

"You will visit us in projections like this in the future, but not often," Galene adds. "Therefore, allow us to enjoy this small celebration with you before we make such great changes to the world. Syntyche, especially, is pleased to have you here."

Could've fooled me. She looks as expressionless as always as she scoots something across her plate as if she's bored.

Whatever. If the gods want a one-sided dinner with me before I get my happily ever after with my quintet, I suppose I can suffer through it.

Several angels slip into the grandiose golden room while the gods eat. They start setting up instruments. One of them clears their throat before they begin playing music and dancing.

"Dinner comes with a show," Arati adds, smirking at me

"And dessert!" Pheli grins, guzzling another goblet of wine. "You'll be here a while, my dear, and we couldn't be happier."

Oh, my gods. This isn't just dinner and a show. It's payback for all the shit I put them through when I first came here. There's no other explanation for these holy sadists wanting to watch such a boring dance routine while I sit here and watch them enjoy dinner together.

Gag me with a fucking knife.

53

BAELFIRE

Almost a full day has passed since the battle officially ended, and color is beginning to saturate the world once again.

So are the idiots.

"But what is she doing now?" one of the reporters demands. "Everyone wants to see her!"

"Is your quintet the new Immortal Quintet?"

"Tell us what happened to the Entity!"

"What will happen to the Nether now? Is it still spreading?" another shouts. "Is it gone? What about Limbo?"

"The world needs to know what happens next!"

They're all speaking over each other. Cameras flash as I stand beside Silas, glowering at the massive crowd of humans, legacies, and Nether humans gathered outside of Everbound Castle.

This is where we brought Maven's body yesterday, after Galene put her into some kind of trance. My mate is inside the heavily guarded castle, in our apartment with Crypt guarding her closely.

After the Entity took his final breaths and Maven's mom reaped his soul, everything happened so quickly. What was left of Silas's Undead army came back to their graves in this area. Fiends and monsters ran to hide deeper inside the Nether, which is no longer growing further into the mortal realm. The Reformists and all our allies have been recovering, burying the dead, and mourning—but they've also been celebrating.

In fact, most people have started celebrating, even if they're a little confused about what the hell went down in the Nether yesterday. As the leader of the Reformists, my mom's been dealing with a shit ton of cameras in her face, just like this.

Everyone has questions, and they keep coming to us. It's annoying as hell that they can't read the room and leave us alone when we just went through so fucking much. Especially when I can barely think about anything except Maven's current condition.

She's still unconscious as she talks with the gods. Which means my quintet's extremely on edge, which means Everett keeps freezing anyone who looks at him wrong, Silas is a breath away from losing his mind again, Crypt is a nightmare as usual, and I'm *so fucking done* with being apart from Maven.

I need my mate. I'm so desperate to hold her and covet her after all the chaos that it fucking hurts.

Finally, Silas steps forward, drawing everyone's attention. He adjusts his gloves. Probably a good thing that he's wearing them —a lot of people already know he's a necromancer, but with so many Nether beings being killed off and driven back into the Nether right now, it's smart of him not to remind the humans what he's capable of now.

"As with any great change in history, much will remain unclear until everything has had time to settle. All you must know is that the Entity is dead," he announces.

Gasps ring out through the crowd, and a microphone is quickly shoved at his face. My temper sparks. Gods, these people are so fucking entitled. Would it really be that bad if I set them all on fire?

Temper, Silas reminds me telepathically when he sees the blue flames flickering under my skin.

Let's just get this over with and get back to her, I grumble back.

It's a good thing he and I agreed to deal with this shit together, because if an annoying but innocent human shoved anything in Crypt's or Everett's faces right now, they'd be dead.

Not that my patience is much better when a frantic human demands, "How do we know you're telling the truth?"

Silas's expression almost makes me laugh. He looks at this guy like he's a moron and enunciates slowly, gesturing at his pointed ears. "I'm *fae*. We are literally incapable of lying."

"And do you have concrete proof that fae can't lie?" the human asks like he's onto something big.

I thought brainlessness was reserved for the Undead, he grits through the bond. When he sees that I'm trying not to laugh out loud, he huffs. *Prick. Your turn.*

Fine. Sighing, I shove the microphone out of our faces and look out at everyone here. "Look, the Entity's dead as a fucking doornail. Anyone with half a brain has started rebuilding the things we lost during the Upheaval. We don't know what the hell is going on with the Nether yet, but when we do, the Reformist Council will issue an official statement or something. Until then, I'd better not see my keeper's precious name in any of your motherfucking headlines."

"But what about—" another one starts to whine, shoving another mic in my face.

My inner dragon growls at the same time I do, beyond pissed that they're not getting it.

I'm back, Everett informs us all through the bond.

Thank all six gods. That's our cue.

Ignoring the heated pain it takes, I breathe fire and set the fucking mic ablaze. The reporter yelps and drops it as I turn to glare at everyone else.

"That's it. Sharing time is over, so get the fuck off Everbound property before you become dragon chow."

The flashing lights go wild for a moment before the reporters scramble away, eager to get out of here alive with what little update they just got.

"Way to keep your cool," Silas snorts as we stalk back into the castle.

How is she? I demand telepathically while the big double doors shut behind us and we hurry through the halls.

Still communing with the gods, Crypt manages to rasp.

He sounds like shit. Like…really weak shit. After Galene did whatever the hell she did to Maven, the incubus collapsed and I had to carry his ass back here.

When we step into our old quintet apartment and slip into Maven's room, the Nightmare Prince looks just as feverish and exhausted as he did earlier. He's lying beside Maven, gazing at her with sweat beaded on his brow. I'm not sure if he has any markings left, but he's clearly in pain.

Everett is already in the room, too, sitting beside the bed and fidgeting nonstop with the reading glasses he holds in his hand. His attention sweeps to us and back to our keeper. "About time."

My mate looks like she's resting peacefully, but it's bothering the hell out of me that her soul projection has been in Paradise for so long. If we didn't still feel the bond thriving between the five of us, the world would be on fire right now.

"How did it go?" Silas asks Everett, but his red gaze stays on Maven.

"The town's officially unfrozen," Everett yawns.

None of us has slept since our little goddess went into this trance.

"What about your creepy-ass ice sculptures in the courtyards? You gonna unfreeze those, too?" I ask.

He shrugs, indifferent as he rubs his scarred face. "Maybe later. I can't leave her again. It's taking too damned long."

I glance at Crypt, noting how ragged his breathing is. "Hey. Stalker Boy. You see anything in her subconscious?"

He reaches up to toy with a piece of her black hair. "She's not asleep, so I cannot enter her subconscious. I can't sense—"

He breaks off and jerks away from Maven as a fit of coughing takes over. I wince when I see all the blood he's coughing up, and then he struggles to catch his breath, his chest rattling.

Fuck. He's in bad shape. I don't even know how long he has left.

"Want another injection?" Silas finally asks, solemn.

"Piss off, Crane," Crypt groans, wiping his face and grimacing.

For a second, we're all quiet, but then I tip my head when I hear the barest sound from outside the front door of our apartment. No one else in here notices it, but I swear my shifter hearing has only gotten stronger just like everything else since I was rebonded to Maven's heart.

"Incoming," I warn the others.

They each swear, irritated.

None of us is surprised to hear that someone else is approaching our apartment. The last almost twenty-four hours have been filled with nonstop visits from various members of the newly-formed Reformist Council—including Kenzie and her quintet, Harlow Carter, Asher Douglas, my mom and her quintet, and almost a dozen others.

I leave the bedroom and stride to the front door, ready to fling it open and tell whoever it is to fuck off. But when I open the door, I pause at the sight of a young woman with warm caramel colored hair, big brown eyes, and a pink splotchy birthmark that covers half of her face. She looks nervous as hell as she clutches some kind of amulet and clears her throat, glancing behind me.

"Oh. I didn't realize this was such a bad time. Sorry. I can come back and talk to Everett later."

I frown. It *is* a bad time, but I didn't say that, so how did she—

Everett appears at my side in the doorway, and it looks like the world just dropped out from under him. He exhales sharply in shock.

"Heidi?"

Whoa. Hold up. This is his sister?

I look between them, confused. Where Everett is tall and cold-looking, his sister is petite, curvy, and warm as she smiles with relief at her brother. They look absolutely nothing alike.

He steps out of the apartment like he's about to wrap her in a hug, but Heidi scrambles back, holding up the amulet like it will ward him away.

"Don't! Sorry, it's not you. I—it's a long story, but…" She trails off before looking curious, gesturing at the left side of her face to indicate his. "Did…did that hurt?"

Everett almost goes to cover his scar before putting his hand back down. "At the time. It's fine now."

"Oh—I'm so sorry. I didn't mean to bring up a memory that painful. And dear gods, you're already *so* stressed out about your keeper right now, and so tired and frustrated and your quintet is struggling so much and—"

"You're alive," Everett breathes, studying her with the intensity of an overprotective older brother. "How?"

"It's a long story. My best friend made sure I survived for as long as I did," she adds, her face falling for a second before she fidgets with the hem of her shirt. "And…well, I came here for two reasons. The first was to thank your keeper and Crypt DeLune for getting me out of the citadel."

"What? The citadel?"

Uh oh. Looks like Frosty is about to have a fucking aneurysm.

Heidi flinches hard, taking a big step back like his freakout is physically assaulting her. Everett notices and swears, taking a deep, calming breath and glaring at the amulet she's holding.

"You lost your dampening charm."

"T—the liches took it away," she says faintly.

Everett pinches his nose, taking two more deep breaths like he's trying not to lose his shit. "*Liches.* You were around liches. Okay."

Heidi puts on a smile, but it's strained. "I'm fine now. Really.

I'll find other things to help with it. And I can tell this is a really bad time, so I'll come back later about the other thing I wanted to talk to you about, because it's kind of big. I just..." She trails off again, her brow furrowing as she glances behind us through the doorway. "Wow. She's *really* exasperated. Is everything okay?"

Wait. She can sense Maven's emotions right now?

"You're an empath," I realize, feeling stupid for not catching on earlier.

Heidi nods, fidgeting again.

"Tell me what else she's feeling," I press, desperate for any scrap of information about my mate.

Everett's sister hesitates, clutching the amulet close to her chest. "This is blocking a lot, so I can't pick up on minor emotions, but…it seems like she's getting impatient. She's also really happy, I think—but in a hopeful way. Like she has something good to look forward to."

That's enough for me to breathe fully again, optimism flooding my system. I thank Heidi and leave the front door, returning to Maven's room. Everett quickly finishes his conversation with her before rejoining us and pacing in the bedroom.

Silas glances at us from the chair beside the bed. "Who was it?"

"Everett's sister," I explain.

"Heidi," Crypt supplies, still exhausted as he breathes raspily beside Maven. "So she survived after all. Good."

"At some point, you're going to tell me how the fuck you know my sister," Everett warns, glaring at Crypt.

"If she hasn't shared that tidbit of her life with you, it's not my business to share," Crypt drawls before breaking into a fit of wheezing coughs again. He hisses in pain, wipes more blood from his mouth, and lays his head on Maven's chest to listen to her heartbeat. "I'm going to sleep."

"What do you mean?" I frown. "I thought you couldn't sleep."

The incubus doesn't bother answering my confusion as he shuts his eyes and murmurs, "If I don't last until our goddess opens her pretty eyes again, tell her it's still the best rest I've ever had."

The silence in the room grows heavier with every second that ticks by. Everett paces while Silas and I watch Maven and Crypt lay motionless on the bed. I really fucking hope the Nightmare Prince is just sleeping. I think I still see him breathing, but I can't be sure. He just looks feverish and pale and…

"Fuck," I mutter. "He really is dying, isn't he?"

Silas examines his blackened-fingertip hands. "Yes."

"And there's nothing we can do?"

He shakes his head.

Godsdamn it, this is going to hurt Maven so fucking much. Seeing her break over Lillian was pure torture—but now this? Not to mention, the idea of Crypt just not being around to pop out of Limbo and annoy us all the time is just bleak as hell.

After everything we've been through, is our quintet seriously about to never be complete again?

"That damn incubus," Everett mutters, stopping his pacing to rub his face.

The tip of the new scar on the center of his chest peeks out from under his shirt, leftover from Amadeus ripping his heart out. He still hasn't asked Silas to heal the scar, and based on his face, I'm going to take a wild guess and say he doesn't really give a shit about how he looks anymore.

More time passes. Finally, I can't take it anymore and blurt, "What if Maven comes back with bad news? Or what if—fuck, what if the gods refuse to let her return to the mortal realm again?"

"She can't stay in Paradise," Silas argues. "She made herself mortal to fall from that plane of existence, and mortals aren't permitted there. Galene said her soul would return."

"She also said *with the utmost of haste,* and that was clearly a fucking lie," I growl.

Everett adjusts one of his sleeves six times in a row. "I don't like that it's taking so long for her to fulfill the blood oath, whatever it is."

That fun little reminder that she swore something none of us has a clue about makes me want to throw up. I start pacing the room alongside Everett, ignoring the heat under my skin and the restlessness urging me to shift and fly to burn off this suffocating impatience.

It feels like hours pass, but it's probably only a few more minutes before the strangest thing happens. The air pressure changes around us as the morning light sneaking in through the drapes brightens. My entire body tingles with the same feeling I get when casters are wielding powerful magic anywhere near me.

"That's holy magic," Silas realizes, getting to his feet. "It's so fucking potent. This is gods-level magic at work outside."

Alarmed, I throw open the drapes so we can see what the fuck is happening.

At the height of our quintet apartment, we have a view over the nevermelt walls Everett built far outside of Everbound. The world in the distance is gray and colorless, proof that the Nether's reach spread there—but as we watch, lights begin to rain down from the heavens. It's like a meteor shower in the middle of the day, with thousands of tendrils of holy magic falling to the earth.

One beam of light veers sharply, passing through the window before any of us can react and absorbing into Crypt's motionless body.

Crypt gasps and bolts upright before scrambling to get his clothes off like they're on fire.

"What the fuck just happened?" I demand, my heart pounding.

The incubus throws his shirt to the ground, and we all watch as swirling markings reappear on his skin like surfacing ink.

Instead of both light and dark markings, these ones are only dark as they cover his body once again.

Crypt lifts his hands, sees the curling markings all over his arms and palms, and looks at us with wide purple eyes.

"I'm…something just changed," he breathes, looking down at Maven with awed disbelief. His lips curl into a smile. "Our girl is making some hefty demands of the gods."

"What do you mean? Is your curse back?" Everett asks, as confused as the rest of us.

The Nightmare Prince studies his new marks. "No. I sense I'm no longer the steward of Limbo."

Silas blinks. "But how? I thought your curse was unbreakable. It was killing you."

"It was," Crypt murmurs, slipping off the bed to join us in looking out the window. He's thoughtful as lights continue to rain from heaven. "Which is why I suspect our little goddess is doing some significant cosmic meddling."

The heavenly light show comes to an end just before a ripple of energy pulses across everything in our sight. Trees in Everbound Forest bend slightly in a wave from the force of whatever just happened, the castle trembles, and something inside my chest burns slightly for half a moment.

I swear all colors get fractionally brighter before all at once, everything goes really fucking still.

Whatever the fuck just happened, there's something different that I can't put my finger on.

"I highly recommend waking up to the sight of four sexy asses," Maven yawns behind us.

Oh, *thank gods.*

I'm on her at once, straddling her with my arms braced over her shoulders so I can kiss my mate deep and hard. The tense worry that's been eating at me finally goes away as she kisses me back, her lips curling up into the best fucking smile in the world.

There's my Boo, I sigh telepathically, soaking up her scent and presence.

Silas moves beside us, shoving me off of her to kiss her next —and then Crypt materializes between them, pushing Silas back to wrap Maven tightly in his arms.

"Stop mauling her," Everett huffs, pulling a laughing Maven out of what was quickly becoming a dogpile and steadying her on her feet.

He kisses her gently before examining her face. It's easy to tell from their expressions that he's checking on her telepathically, and I'm pretty sure my mate is reassuring him with a bit of morbid dry humor thrown in to tease him.

Not ready to be anywhere but wrapped around my keeper, I hop off the bed to hug her from behind, beaming down at her. "All right, Boo. For the next fifteen minutes, you're going to tell us what the fuck just happened and why you were just in Paradise for an entire day—"

She blinks. "That was an entire day?"

"Yep. And that's way too damn long, so once we get the gist, we're bathing you and feeding you and spoiling your gorgeous ass before we fuck you for hours," I declare.

"I second this plan," Crypt grins.

"Third it," Everett and Silas say at the same time.

Maven is smiling, but she also seems disoriented as she looks around in confusion. "Where's Cuttrina?"

Eager to get her everything and anything she needs from now on, I dart from the bedroom and return a second later, handing my mate her wickedly sharp etherium knife. The moment she touches it, she inhales sharply as the blade lights up. Her eyes go out of focus, and then she blinks several times.

"Oh, fuck."

"Well?" Silas checks in a strained voice, pulling her back to the bed to hold her close. "What was your blood oath, *sangfluir?* Tell us what we missed."

Maven brushes black hair out of her face and looks between us, hesitant. "Shit. I sort of fucked up your fates. You might all be pissed."

"We'll only be pissed if it put you in danger," Everett says firmly.

We all nod in agreement, waiting for her explanation.

Maven's beautiful, haunting eyes settle on me for a second, and she sighs. "The blood oath I made to Arati was to cleanse, restore, and…rule the Nether. My soul is kind of tied to it until the end of my life."

I rock back on my heels as those words sink in. "Holy fuck."

"I also kind of tied your souls to the Nether alongside mine," she adds, clearing her throat. "My bad."

"Oh, thank the fucking gods," Everett breathes, sitting on the bed near her and Silas like he's beyond relieved. "I was worried you agreed to do that alone. Good."

"Very good," I grin. "As long as I'm tied to you, Raincloud, I'm really fucking happy that's all the blood oath was."

A beautifully mischievous smile blooms on her face. "That wasn't all."

"Oh, gods above," Silas grimaces. "Please tell me you didn't swear to more."

"I didn't. But Arati swore to permanently remove the Legacy Curse, which she just did."

Wait.

Wait, wait, wait.

"What?" I gawk.

Our shocked faces must be priceless, because Maven actually laughs. That sound is so fucking heavenly, but all I can think about is what this means. If the Legacy Curse is lifted...fuck, it means the existence of our kind is about to change. It's like a fresh slate—a chance to finally belong in the mortal realm without having to lay down our lives at the Divide.

Maven just rewrote all the fucking rules.

"Snowdrop," Everett breathes, shaking his head. "That's…"

"A lot," she agrees. "Arati didn't like it at first, and it meant the gods had to make some changes. For example, they won't be putting the Divide back up. Instead, they're making a singular

Gateway into the Nether. Since Amadeus won't be corrupting and terrorizing the Nether anymore, far fewer shadow fiends will try to flee into the mortal realm. We'll be in charge of the Nether, and we'll guard the Gateway to keep anything from escaping." Maven pauses, and her attention moves to Crypt before she smiles softly. "It also meant changing some things about Limbo. No more stewards."

He swallows. I've never seen the Nightmare Prince so fucking shaken.

"Darling…"

"All incubi will share the burden of taking care of Limbo equally," she explains, moving to kiss his cheek. She lifts her hand to trace his new markings, admiring them. "Syntyche said she would mark all incubi so they would understand the call, whatever that means."

"Those were the other lights we saw raining down," Silas realizes, blown away.

We're *all* blown away.

Maven nods, looking at Crypt again. "Your markings are different, though. Yours are tied to the Gateway. You don't have to take care of Limbo anymore, and you're not cursed. You're not —" Her voice breaks before she takes a deep breath, looking at him with that fierce determination that's all her. "You're not dying. I didn't come this far to lose any of you, and now, all that's left is a lifetime with the men I…love."

I fucking melt.

All of this extreme change, all for the better. All because of my mate. I wonder if she even knows how much she just did for gods know how many legacies—and she did it with us in mind.

Silas is fighting a smile, too. "Gods above, I adore you. You may drive me mad until the end of our fate, but I'll crave every moment of it just as acutely as I crave your precious blood."

Maven smiles at the fae's morbid confession of love before she fixes each of us with a serious look. "I'm chained to the

Nether now, but it wasn't fair of me to weave your existences into mine without asking. Sorry for bartering with your souls."

I laugh. "No, you're not."

"You're right. I'm not. I'd do it again because you're all fucking *mine*."

We're all grinning like idiots. I'm so fucking happy that I scoop our keeper away from Crypt's side and stand with her in my arms to peck her on the lips.

"Yeah, I'm pretty sure we're all good with your sexy, eternally possessive side, Boo."

"For the last time, that nickname is dead."

"Nah," I grin, kissing the tip of her nose.

Everett's smile turns into thoughtfulness as he stands, running a hand through his white hair. "To clean and protect the Nether, we'll need to fight shadow fiends, right?"

"I will. You four can do whatever you want. Including photography," she adds, giving me a meaningful look.

Oh, my gods.

My mate read me like a fucking book, back when I mentioned my past passion to her in my room in the Decimus territory. My heart feels like it's going to explode.

"I really fucking love you," I manage.

"Not as much as I do," Crypt grins at her. "And when our lifetime bettering the Nether ends, I'll remain at your side until our corpses decompose hand in hand."

Maven smiles like that creepy sentiment is the most romantic thought ever. She kisses me. I'm getting pretty damn wrapped up in her kiss until Everett nudges me toward the bed.

I get the hint.

Setting our keeper down on the bed, I continue kissing her as Crypt begins to remove her clothing gently. Silas is already stripping as Everett groans at the sight of her naked body. Maven is breathless when I pull back, her beautiful, dark gaze consuming my face with a loving possessiveness that feels like an oath. A promise. A blessing.

You're all mine.

Hell yes, we are, I agree, kissing my keeper again.

EPILOGUE
MAVEN

I NEVER GET tired of the way Crypt loses control when he wakes up to the realization that I've already gotten us started.

For someone with a raging somnophilia kink, he can't get enough of being on the receiving end. Being his muse only makes it better, because each of our subconsciouses melt together as an intimate melting pot of desire, obsession, and violent need.

"Fuck," I bite out, gasping when Crypt thrusts even harder into me.

We've been at this for an hour, and he still hasn't calmed down after waking up to me nearly finishing him off with my mouth. Now his pace is rough and punishing, knocking the breath from my lungs with every stroke as those fucking *amazing* piercings rub me in all the right places.

His hand cradles my head as he groans brokenly into my neck. My feet are somewhere near my ears because he's folding me like a fucking pretzel and fucking me like he'll die if he doesn't.

Feeling another orgasm building and clenching low in my stomach, I firmly guide my incubus' face back to mine so I can kiss him as my subconscious melts into his, clouding this dream space within our own home. The intimate muse bond between us quivers as I sense Crypt's intense pleasure building hot and fast alongside mine.

Just as I feel his control slipping, my Nightmare Prince reaches between us to pinch my clit in such a brutally delicious way that my release takes my breath away. I shake and swear, clutching him tightly as his own sharp pleasure follows mine, leaving us panting and delirious.

Gods, I love this. This obsession. This suffocating need.

I constantly have it for all of my quintet.

Speaking of…

"How much longer do you need to stall me?" I check once I can finally use words again, interrupting Crypt as he scatters satisfied kisses along my neck and jaw.

His lips curl up against my skin before he pulls away, silver-flecked violet eyes sparkling wickedly. "Am I really so obvious?"

"You're all obvious. Especially Baelfire."

I'm pretty sure my dragon shifter is the one spearheading this surprise, since he's been practically jumping out of his skin anytime I've walked into the room while he was on his phone. Not to mention, Baelfire not-so-subtly had me sample over seventeen different cake flavors over the last few weeks.

But he wasn't the only one who tipped me off. Everett has also been evasive as hell, and Silas has been avoiding the topic of my birthday like the plague. Anytime I've brought it up, he's immediately turned the topic to the approaching Starfall Eve—something he won't have to fail at lying about.

My poor fae. I've been having far too much fun watching him squirm while I played innocent.

Now that the day is here, I'm not surprised that the others encouraged me to sleep in and left Crypt here to distract me for good measure. In their defense, my incubus makes for the perfect distraction to nearly anything.

Including a surprise party.

Crypt hums and kisses me again. "Truth be told, the others

have been telepathically crucifying me for the last fifteen minutes, since everyone's waiting on us now. It's really their fault for assuming I could possibly give up enjoying my muse at my leisure like this."

I smile, tracing the dark swirling markings on his neck and bare shoulders. His markings are now attuned to the much smaller Gateway into the Nether, which is located off a beach in Maine. As my head of security, Crypt is the first to know if anyone or anything with hostile intentions tries to enter or leave the Nether because his markings will light up to tell him.

It happens often enough to keep us on our toes, but it's calming down. Few people outside our quintet ever see shadow fiends these days. There are no legacies being sent to the front lines of the nonexistent Divide, and Everbound University is no longer a place to train for combat and possible death just for being born a legacy or manifesting as an atypical caster.

Instead, the world is gradually adjusting as legacies and humans find a new, equal kind of harmony. Legacies study whatever the fuck they want to prepare them for a life and career in the mortal realm, just like any other university. It will take time for things to really fall into place—but I've already found mine.

Here in the Nether, with my matches. Spending every second with them whenever I'm not hunting fiends to my beating heart's content.

It's my own version of Paradise.

Hey, Boo? Baelfire checks in telepathically, clearly trying to hide exasperation from whatever conversation he's been having with Crypt. *How much would it bug you if I beat Crypt to a pulp for hogging you?*

You hogged me last night, I point out.

Doesn't count since all three of your voyeurs enjoyed the show. Not that I minded you enjoying them enjoying you, but this is different.

I sit up on the quintet-sized bed in the massive room they named mine inside our house. Everett pulled strings and greased hands to get this place built in record time, and I have to say, his high-end tastes really come in handy.

We now live in luxury in this house that is heavily warded by the etherium shields that used to protect the safe havens. Everyone has their own space here. My own room off the main suite is mercifully minimalistic, Baelfire's has a studio filled with his photography of landscapes in the Nether, Silas has a small laboratory for all the spells and potions he's constantly trying, and Everett has a fencing room he pretty much never uses anymore. He spends most of his time going back and forth between here and the mortal realm for business and for the nonprofit he started to help Nether humans.

But despite all the space and extra rooms, we all sleep in here.

And fuck in here.

Needless to say, it's my favorite room. Even though it's still weird to have an actual home, I kind of love it. Especially because it's just my quintet here. We're hardly left in peace, but this is our own bubble.

Glancing out one of the floor to ceiling glass windows, I gaze out over the plane of existence that I tied my soul to. The Nether is starting to heal itself slowly, color returning as less twisted, less gnarly plants begin to grow.

Especially in the greenhouse that Everett had carefully relocated here, along with my fake headstone and Lillian's resting place, which I visit almost every day.

Angel of Death, Baelfire prompts through the bond. *I might pick you up myself.*

I can't resist teasing my dragon. *Earlier, you were all for Crypt keeping me in bed. Why the change? Is there something I'm missing?*

Me, he insists quickly. *You're missing me. Tell Stalker Boy to quit all the canoodling and come find us.*

Canoodling is still a banned word, I remind him.

Punish me for using it later and get your sweet ass over here.

Crypt sighs like this is the biggest inconvenience in the world before he helps me stand, running his hands everywhere he gets the chance as he returns to kissing my jaw.

I pull away from Crypt to sigh. "I should probably wear clothes if it's not just our quintet."

"Or put on a show," he grins and then tips his head. "Although Frost might destroy the Baird quintet for seeing you naked. The Decimus family, too."

Grinning, I kiss him one more time before I clean up and get dressed. Several minutes later, as I'm lacing up one of my combat boots, Baelfire strides into the room and punches Crypt hard in the arm as payback, which just makes the incubus laugh. My tall dragon shifter stops in front of me with a bright smile on his handsome face.

"Come on, my queen. I've got a little something for you."

"She's already seen your *little something,* Decimus—you've disappointed her with it plenty of times," Crypt drawls, shrugging into another ripped leather jacket.

He keeps ripping those, which is why I hope he'll like what I have stashed in my pocket void. It took me several tries to get the spell right a couple of months ago, but at least I'm starting to really get the hang of holy magic.

Baelfire snorts. "Yeah, we all know how not little I am, and I'm way ahead of the rest of you in that bet."

"In your dreams," Crypt scoffs.

I fight a smile. I know all about their bet to see who can get me to orgasm the most. While their last bet was really fucking annoying, I have to say I don't mind reaping the rewards of this one.

Baelfire and Crypt walk with me out of our home and into the Nether. The Gateway is about a quarter of a mile from the wards surrounding our property, so it doesn't take us long until we approach the massive, arched, mist-like wall of white. Its sides are ringed with etherium that glows with holy magic, drawing me closer.

"Ready?" Baelfire grins, taking my hand.

I nod, ready for a surprise party.

The thing is, I've never been to a surprise party. I can't even picture what one would look like, since most of my birthdays were quietly celebrated between Lillian and me in the past.

Which is why I genuinely startle and nearly draw Cuttrina from my side when the second I step through the Gateway, a shit ton of people scream, *"Surprise!"*

My heart pounds from residual shock as I see that Crypt was right and my quintet, the Baird quintet, the Decimus clan, and Everett's sister, Heidi, are all here as they clap and cheer to greet me.

Everyone is dressed warmly, since it's December in fucking Maine, but someone—probably Silas—put up warming spells to make this a cozy area. There are several tables set up on the beach with the stormy gray seas in the distance, and presents are clustered on one of the tables. Several ravens flutter to land nearby, croaking happily when they see me. No ghosts are here yet, but I know it's just a matter of time because anywhere I go in the Nether or the mortal realm, they find me.

Everett is immediately at my side, kissing my temple and wrapping his trench coat around me for good measure. "Happy birthday, Snowdrop."

Silas moves to join the rest of us, too, his crimson irises captivating as he smirks at me. "This year, I believe twenty-four orgasms are in order."

"Twenty-one," Crypt corrects. "I already got our goddess started on her birthday orgasms."

Baelfire snorts. "If I'd been the one who stayed behind with her, she wouldn't need any more. I mean, we'd still give you more," he adds, grinning at me.

I roll my eyes. "You four are ridiculous."

"Ridiculously *in love,*" Bael flirts, bouncing his eyebrows at me.

"May!" Kenzie squeals happily, the first guest to approach.

"Whoa," I blurt on accident when I see her belly.

It's been about a month since I saw her last, and I swear that thing has fucking doubled in size. I guess that makes sense, since two babies would take up more space. Kenzie sees me staring at it and bursts into laughter as the rest of her quintet waves and smiles at me from their table.

"Hey, now. Remember, you once said I'm the sexiest pregnant lady that you know. You have to stick to that because after six fucking months of this, I'm already beyond ready to get these little crotch goblins out. I want to see my feet again and not have to pee every sixteen seconds. Hey, do you think they'll start letting legacies join professional sports teams anytime in the next few decades? If not, we should start our own league or something because I swear these kids think my ribs are a soccer ball and I'm ready to—"

"There's my favorite sister-in-law!" Cace Decimus cheers, approaching with a smile. "How's the hunt for fiends these days?"

"She slaughters them with ease and waters the ground of the Nether with their blood," Crypt smiles, squeezing my hand.

Cace doesn't seem to know what to say to that, but Brigid Decimus and her quintet are right behind him, greeting me and once again gushing about the fact that Declan's quintet is having a baby. It's definitely Declan's, which means that the scales Baelfire gave to Silas to work on the dragon shifter fertility problem worked. For the first time in over two decades, another dragon shifter is finally on the way.

Brigid Decimus is also thriving in her new position as the headmaster of Everbound University. She and her quintet took up residence there and are changing a lot of the old tradition and beliefs about needing to weed out weak legacies.

When the Decimuses and Kenzie return to their tables to eat pizza and chatter happily, the next person to greet me with a shy smile and big brown eyes is Heidi—no, Elise.

I keep forgetting she prefers to go by Elise, her middle name.

My ice elemental's sister is unbelievably sweet and happy,

despite the things she's been through. She's also been incredibly useful. After the final battle of the Nether, the type four empath let Everett know that while she was incarcerated in the Nether, she sensed people asleep far beneath the citadel. I'd never heard of anything below it, but word spread to Felix. Ever since, we've begun excavations to discover what or who could be down there.

Whatever it is, it's been thousands of years since they were put to sleep. Felix, Silas, and several others have been heading the excavations, and they're excited to finally be getting close to whatever Heidi was sensing.

Everett's sister beams at me and hands me a small gift wrapped in sparkly pink wrapping paper.

"Happy birthday," she chirps. "Go ahead, unwrap it!"

I do. It's a pair of gloves. Really soft, black gloves that are just my style.

I thank her and she returns to the rest of the party as Baelfire leads me over to one of the tables that has two dome-looking things on it.

"Maven's going to cut the cake," my shifter announces loudly. He removes the first dome-looking thing to reveal—

A cake with a picture of green Jell-O on it.

I look at him. "Cruel."

He bursts into laughter along with the rest of my quintet and everyone else at my birthday party.

"That one is an ice cream cake," Baelfire tells me through his laughter.

They make ice cream into *cake,* too?

Genius.

"This one is the cake you'll be cutting," Everett adds, removing the other dome from the table.

I study the black heart-shaped cake, appreciating its simplicity. Crypt hands me the cake-cutting knife and murmurs, "Stab it, love," in my ear.

Stab it? I don't have to be asked twice.

When I jam the knife into the cake, sweet-smelling liquid spurts out of it, and the guests at my party react with surprise and laughter. It's a morbid dessert that has me grinning up at Baelfire, who looks smug as fuck.

You made me a bleeding cake, I tell only him through the bond.

I knew you'd like it.

I love it. My mate is the best fucking mate in the world, I add, knowing the praise will go straight to his cock.

His gaze grows molten. *Watch your pretty mouth, hellion. I'm not above snatching you away and fucking you on the beach, but we have gifts for you first.*

The cakes are dished and served up to everyone except for my food-indifferent incubus. We dig in, but it doesn't take long for my quintet to get their gifts for me from the big table full of presents, leaving me alone for a second. Taking another bite of cake, I study the gathering with a sense of contentment unlike anything I've experienced until the last six months.

Thanks to the legacy and human governments merging and reforming, many positive changes are being made. All Four Houses have representation now, as do atypical casters and Nether humans who are still getting settled in this colorful plane of existence. Humans and legacies are no longer in constant danger of fiends slipping into this world, and the temples of the gods are being cleaned up and rebuilt.

Lillian would be happy about that.

I'm sure she's happy, anyway, enjoying her afterlife with her daughter. That thought makes me smile as I watch another raven perch nearby, tipping its head at me.

"Ready for your gifts, *ima sangfluir?*" Silas asks, smiling at me as he reapproaches with the rest of my quintet to pull me out of my thoughts.

He sits beside me at the table and sets down a carefully-wrapped gift before kissing my cheek. With the rest of my matches watching, I quickly unwrap Silas's gift.

It's a knife with a clear handle. Swirled around in the handle are four flowers—a purple orchid, a dead snapdragon, a white snowdrop, and a blood red rose.

It's obviously supposed to represent each member of my quintet.

I examine the blade. "I fucking *love* this. Thank you."

"My turn," Baelfire insists, sliding an envelope toward me.

When I open it, I'm not sure what I'm looking at. It's a photograph of...something. I squint.

"Is it a...saddle?"

He nods, beaming at me.

"Thanks for the picture of a saddle."

My other quintet members laugh, but Baelfire hurries to explain. "No—it's not just a picture, it's just that the actual thing is kinda big and still being built by Declan. But it's a dragon saddle. For you," he adds. "That way, you can finally ride on me and I won't be scared out of my mind of you just falling off."

Oh.

I grin at him. "I do like riding you. I can't wait to ride you as a dragon, too."

"There's more," he says, motioning at the envelope.

Moving aside more pictures of the saddle, I realize there's also several pages of some kind of list in here. It takes reading the first few lines and feeling my face warm before I realize what this is.

"Is this...your list of ways to fuck me?" I gawk.

"The one I wrote right after I met you at Everbound, and you were still pretending to hate my guts," he confirms, preening. "I'm glad to say we've already checked off some of the things I wrote down, but we're still a long way from done with it, Cutie Pie."

Oh, my gods. I can't believe he hung on to this.

I'm going to fuck the hell out of him later for this, right along with the rest of my quintet.

I'm still smiling like an idiot when Everett clears his throat and scoots another envelope toward me on the table, along with a small box. He's surprisingly nervous, adjusting one of his sleeves and straightening the gifts in front of me several times before he mutters, "Okay, I can't take it anymore. Just open the damn things."

In the envelope are a bunch of legal documents. I browse through them, again not sure what I'm looking at—until my gaze snags on a name at the top.

Everett Amato.

"You actually changed your name," I realize, looking at him with wide eyes.

Silas, Crypt, and Baelfire all look at Everett quickly in surprise, apparently not being in on this gift. Everett's cheeks pinken as he scratches near his scar.

"Yeah. I meant what I said. I just wanted to show you."

Baelfire looks at the documents over my shoulder. "Holy shit. You're Everett Amato now. This is about to get really damn confusing, because Crypt only calls us by our last names," he adds, laughing.

"He'll just have to finally call me by my first name," Everett shrugs.

Crypt stares at him for a long moment. "Okay…Everett."

All four of my matches shudder at the same time, with Baelfire doing a full-body roll for added drama. I burst into laughter at their antics. Crypt looks like he has a bad taste in his mouth, and Everett is shaking his head.

"Hell no. I take it all back. That was weird as fuck."

"So weird," Silas agrees, shuddering again.

"Don't ever do that again. Just keep calling me Frost," Everett grumbles.

Still laughing, I open the small box to find a set of stunning black diamond earrings. I got my ears pierced four months ago, on one of my first visits to Kenzie in Halfton, where she and her quintet now live. She'd been debating the best time to get her kids' ears pierced, talking about how painful it is, and I was curious, so I had it done.

I'd felt nothing, but she had assured me it was because of my "freakish pain tolerance."

"They're beautiful," I say, already putting them in.

Everett checks them in my ears before he kisses my cheek. "*You're* beautiful."

Crypt is next and promptly pulls out a bouquet of orchids and a set of keys. He hands me both with a wink. "I know how much you liked those demons' bikes, love."

Wait. "You got me a motorcycle?" I blink, looking around for it.

"You got her a *fucking motorcycle?*" Everett repeats. My elemental is already a hair away from panicking, looking like he's envisioning my brains smeared on a back road. "She doesn't even have a license yet."

"Which is why the bike is still in our garage in the Nether," Crypt shrugs, looking back at me to grin. "It's got a skull on it."

"I love it already," I grin back.

Everett holds up a hand. "You have to get a license before touching it. And take a motorcycle safety course. And always wear a helmet and protective gear and—"

"I'm a demigoddess. I think I can handle a motorcycle."

"Hopefully better than you handle driving a car," Crypt teases, earning a swat on the arm from me.

I love all the presents they gave me, but if they're done, it's my turn. Reaching into the pocket void, I rummage around and pull out the first gift, setting it in front of Baelfire. It's badly wrapped, since I apparently have no fucking idea how to use wrapping paper, but he blinks at it in surprise.

"What is this?"

"For you. I missed getting you guys presents last Starfall, so I decided to get twice the amount this year," I shrug, setting the next poorly-wrapped gift in front of Crypt.

"You don't owe us gifts," Silas protests, prodding the box I set in front of him. "That was a year ago, *sangfluir*."

"So?"

Crypt isn't putting up a fight as his curiosity wins out, and soon he's unwrapped the black leather jacket I carefully picked out for him. He grins at me. "You know my wardrobe well, I see."

"It's enchanted to repair itself," I clarify. "Now you won't have to keep buying new ones every other week."

He slips out of his old one and into the new. "Right. Because I was *buying* them," he winks. "I love it, darling."

Baelfire quickly unwraps his gift and lights up when he sees the camera. I asked Kenzie for help picking out a good one, and he's already turning it on. "Fuck, this is nice."

"I took a few pictures on it already," I add innocently.

"Really?" he asks, holding it up to see past photos. "I'd love to see what you—oh, fuck. *Fuck me,* that's so damn hot."

"Wait, are they nudes?" Crypt demands, trying to grab the camera from Baelfire. "Let me see."

"Fuck off, these are mine," Baelfire grins, shoving the incubus away before switching to the next one and groaning. "I knew you'd look good in leather."

"Okay, we're all going to see those photos at some point. Right?" Everett checks, looking at me hopefully.

I laugh and tell Silas to unwrap his next. He does, and pulls out several thick-ass tomes written in the ancient fae. He skims the covers and looks at me in surprise. "These are…?"

"Grimoires that are thousands of years old. Felix found a few of them and happened to tell me about it first. You'll have to translate them to new fae from ancient fae, but I figured you wouldn't mind."

"I truly don't," he smiles, already browsing the first dusty grimoire like an excited child on Starfall morning.

"Nerd," Baelfire snorts.

Finally, I turn to Everett and pull his gift out of my pocket void, handing him the papers carefully.

He realizes what he's looking at and goes still. "You…it's fully translated."

"I know holy tongue now, so you'll know the truth about the prophecy you were given as a kid."

Everett swallows hard as he squints at the page to read it without his glasses.

I already have the lines memorized.

Favored of Raan, ye walk alone,
Divine blood binds thine fate unknown,
Ye telum-bound, cursed, long misled,
Vice of ice and thine keeper dead,
Yet death's child returns, ichor crowned,
Lost heart to bind, five fates bound.

My beautiful, scarred ice elemental looks at me, relief on his face. I think he's surprised how harmless the prophecy was all along—just a statement of what would happen, and of course as obnoxiously rhymey as anything else written in the holy tongue.

Everett kisses me, pocketing the prophecy with a raspy voice. "Thank you."

The party goes on as Quinn announces it's time for me to unwrap the rest of the gifts they brought. With my quintet at my side and people I care about all around me, I remind myself once again of my new mantras.

I'm alive. I deserve to be happy. I choose my own fate, and it will always be them.

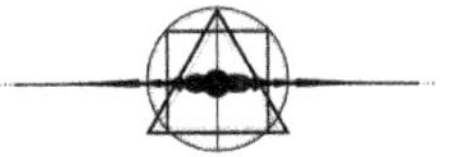

The End

A NOTE FROM MORGAN

This series has been my love letter to the paranormal academy romance genre.

It's also been life-changing.

Without getting into the woeful nitty-gritty of it, I began writing the Cursed Legacies series during a really difficult time in my personal life. Spinning this story, meeting these characters, and crafting this world started as a simple escape and grew into a rekindling of my first love and forever obsession: storytelling.

I figured, why not share? It couldn't hurt.

Fast forward to now, and holy *wow*. The amount of excitement, support, love, and absolutely hilarious messages offering everything from firstborn children to taking up the dark arts in order to read what comes next has honestly brought me unadulterated joy.

I cannot thank you enough for joining me in this world and enjoying it just as much as I have.

I love you freaky little fiends, and I hope you'll join me in more love letters to more genres to come.

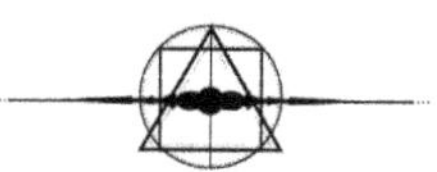

ABOUT THE AUTHOR

Morgan is a certified nerd who loves long bubble baths and big, bad, OTT possessive sexy cinnamon roll book boyfriends. When she's not busy reading spice or lint-rolling cat hair off of her yoga pants, she writes to her little black heart's content while daydreaming about the before-mentioned cinnamon roll book boyfriends.

www.ingramcontent.com/pod-product-compliance
Lightning Source LLC
Chambersburg PA
CBHW070611310726
48982CB00001B/45
9798993632438